The
ELOQUENT
SHORT STORY

Other Persea Anthologies

THE ELOQUENT ESSAY
An Anthology of Classic and Creative Nonfiction
Edited by John Loughery

IMAGINING AMERICA
Stories from the Promised Land
Edited by Wesley Brown and Amy Ling

VISIONS OF AMERICA
Personal Narratives from the Promised Land
Edited by Wesley Brown and Amy Ling

FIRST SIGHTINGS
Contemporary Stories About American Youth
Edited by John Loughery

INTO THE WIDENING WORLD
International Coming-of-Age Stories
Edited by John Loughery

STARTING WITH "I"
Personal Essays by Teenagers
by Youth Communication
Edited by Andrea Estepa and Philip Kay

AMERICA STREET
An Anthology of Multicultural Short Stories
Edited by Anne Mazer

PAPER DANCE: 55 LATINO POETS
Edited by Victor Hernández Cruz,
Leroy V. Quintana, and Virgil Suarez

The ELOQUENT SHORT STORY

VARIETIES OF NARRATION

AN ANTHOLOGY

Edited, with an Introduction by

LUCY ROSENTHAL

A KAREN AND MICHAEL BRAZILLER BOOK

PERSEA BOOKS / NEW YORK

For permission to reprint or for any other information, write to the publisher:

Persea Books, Inc.
853 Broadway
New York, New York 10003

Library of Congress Cataloging-in-Publication Data

The eloquent short story : varieties of narration an anthology / edited, with an introduction by Lucy Rosenthal.— 1st ed.
p. cm.
Includes bibliographical references.
ISBN 0-89255-292-1 (original trade pbk. : alk. paper)
1. Short stories, American. 2. Short stories, English.
3. Narration (Rhetoric) I. Rosenthal, Lucy.
PS648.S5E46 2003
813'.0108—dc22   2003019973

Designed by Rita Lascaro

Manufactured in the United States of America

First Edition

Contents

THIS COLLECTION BRINGS TOGETHER short stories that are contemporary, of exceptional merit, and, not least, enjoyable to read. Rich and diverse, it covers an astonishing variety of narrative approaches. The short story, always supple—invested with the original magic of oral storytelling—can take the form of memoir, compressed novel, prose poem, essay or commentary, character study, reportage, letters, or fable. It can borrow from—even replicate—all of these. The embrace is wide. Rick Moody's story, "Demonology," for example, takes the form of memoir in its expression of loss. Jhumpa Lahiri's "Mrs. Sen's" offers a character study of a woman struggling to preserve herself in an unfamiliar culture. Junot Díaz's "Nilda," through his characters' crossed paths, offers a commentary on efforts to escape the crushing deprivations of the ghetto.

To the sheer pleasure of taking in a good story, the reader here can add the enjoyment of sleuthing—that is, of looking more closely at *how* the story has managed to capture us. What keeps us turning pages? How did these stories, each fashioned very differently, achieve their powerful effects? What is this story's secret? Each of these authors has planted clues within the stories, many of them inadvertently, which if identified and tracked can shed light on answers to these questions. The aim of the categories under which these stories are grouped is to furnish this illumination.

Two questions determine the stories' placement in their categories: What category, for purposes of discussion, would best illuminate the story? What story would most precisely illustrate the category? In cases of overlapping, the decision was based on selecting the element that seemed to have the most weight in the story taken as a whole. For example, in Tim O'Brien's "On the Rainy River," the addition of an eloquent anti-war argument to searing personal recollection tipped the balance in favor of essay or commentary rather than memoir or confession. In Ward Just's "About Boston," revelation of the narrator's character becomes more important than his reporting of experience; the recounting is in the service of the character study.

These twenty-three stories are by writers of the English-speaking world, the bulk of them post-dating the Second World War. Earlier stories by such writers as Katherine Anne Porter, James Thurber, and Truman Capote are included as classic examples of flawless execution. Kathrine Kressmann Taylor's "Address Unknown," published on the eve of the Second World War, is important for its historical prescience as well as its artistry. All of the writers are American, with the exception of A. A. Milne. The author of *Winnie the Pooh* transcends borders, and his story, the epistolary "The Rise and Fall of Mortimer Scrivens," offers irresistible delights.

The collection demonstrates that although there may be only a limited number of stories to tell, there are now in our literature countless ways to tell them.

THE STORY AS MEMOIR OR CONFESSION

The category is represented by four stories. Toni Cade Bambara's "Sweet Town" offers an adolescent's original and vivid account of romantic hope and disappointment. The narrator in Gish Jen's "The Water Faucet Vision," Callie, tries to reconcile contradictory needs: belief in the power of miracles to erase loss and undo pain versus the need to comprehend and endure life's real hurts. In Rick Moody's unflinching "Demonology," the narrator's outpouring of grief combines with a tribute to a dead sister that is as tender as it is wrenching. Lizzie, the child in Joy Williams' "Escapes," seeks to come to terms with the skewed and unsteady version of reality transmitted to her by a mother who loves her and alcohol equally.

Each of these stories features a narrator who entrusts the reader with an account of intimate personal experience. The story is confided not to make a point or judgment primarily, but to make an experience that may be indecipherable as lived, legible and lasting on the page. In each of these stories, the power lies in the word to give form to events that make no sense.

In "Sweet Town," for example, when Kit's vocabulary is not grounded by the grit and disillusionment of everyday life, she resorts to a language that counteracts it, wild, fanciful, and careless all at once. Similarly, in "The Water Faucet Vision," Gish Jen's Callie converts the violence and hurt in her surroundings into a language capable of accommodating miracles. Simple beads, "slightly humped toward the center, like a jellyfish" become, for her, talismanic. She reports that her Chinese parents pronounce "pains" as "pens," in a play on words that may not be unintentional. In Rick Moody's "Demonology," the abundance of delicately traced detail mitigates, as much as it can, the blank finality of death. Lizzie, in Joy Williams' "Escapes," longs for the ability to read. "Written words," she confides, "were something between me and a place I could not go." Written words hold open the possibility of rescue. In all of these commemorative stories, there is the suggestion that storytelling itself can be redemptive.

THE STORY AS COMPRESSED NOVEL

Two very different stories comprise this category: John Updike's "Playing with Dynamite" and Lex Williford's "Pendergast's Daughter." Each of these stories—the Updike in the span of a few pages and the Williford, astonishingly, in just one—manages to encompass whole lives. Though the stories vary radically in length and technique, we see life-cycles in each. By witnessing a moment in the life of a family, "Pendergast's Daughter," even in the form of "flash fiction," or short short, allows us to infer its patterns over two Pendergast generations. "Playing with Dynamite" offers us a virtually complete biography of Geoffrey Fanshawe, in its tracing of his life's trajectory and examination of its layers.

The economy of John Updike's narrative is facilitated by a brilliantly fashioned serpentine structure, weaving in and out of time, and by the gorgeous density of the writer's prose. The story's scope is established at the outset: "One aspect of childhood Fanshawe had not expected to return in old age was the mutability of things . . . " The juxtaposition of youth and age in Updike's opening sentence is key. It is a kind of traffic sign, the first of many in this story, guiding us along a twisting—and remarkably inviting—path, illuminating both the story's method and its meaning.

By contrast, Lex Williford's story employs a linear narrative that is deceptively straightforward and simple. In the course of a story composed of eight short paragraphs, a relationship breaks up shockingly and a family's violent history is exposed. At the outset, the narrator's fiancée, Leann, is taking him home to meet her folks. Right away she assures him that things will be just fine, that there's nothing to be nervous about. ("Relax . . . Lighten up, she kept saying.") But in the next paragraph, the leisurely pace changes abruptly, propelling the narrative forward. A rapid succession of details—Leann's agitated kid brother, a bulldozer ramming a tree—forewarns us that a family fistfight is in progress. When Leann urges the narrator to intervene, he freezes, then blames himself for the relationship's end. The story probably has more than enough blame to go around. But if, as seems likely, this slugfest is not a first, it is worth noting that the immediate agent of the precipitating incident has been Leann, the Pendergasts' daughter, whose reassurances to the narrator at the story's start have misled him.

THE STORY AS PROSE POEM

The two stories in this category, Ann Beattie's "Snow" and Katherine Anne Porter's "The Grave," both marvelously condensed, are models of their form. In them, a carefully fashioned succession of images conveys the stories' action and meanings. The images that, in prose fiction, can include a story's props, its artifacts, and objects, encapsulate narrative. Ann Beattie, for example, in her rueful and piercing "Snow," brings the pain and regret of a past love affair home to us in this way: "It was as hopeless as giving a child a matched cup and saucer." A description of a wallpaper pattern featuring "purple grapes as big and round as Ping-Pong balls" gives us a sense of the relationship's troubling incongruities as well. The images travel through the story, with new meanings attaching to them en route. With each recurrence, the narrative is advanced.

As Porter's story begins, the graves are real. A young brother and his sister, Miranda, taking time off from hunting, are playing among them, trespassing. Both are heedless of the labor—the exhuming of bodies—taking place around them. Miranda especially has an indifferent relation to cause and effect. This undergoes profound alteration when the brother shoots and kills a rabbit. "'Look,' he said in a low amazed voice. 'It was going to have young ones.'" Miranda, gazing at "their little blind faces," says, "'Oh, I want to *see*.'" What Miranda sees, in this moment that is the center of the story, is the sudden, shocking joining of birth and death. The incident, set aside for twenty years, is re-evoked in the story's brief flash-forward to Miranda as an adult when "... that far-off day leaped from its burial place before her mind's eye." The grave has been a repository for the now-surfacing memory.

THE STORY AS ESSAY OR COMMENTARY

Four stories, markedly dissimilar in narrative method, subject matter, and language, represent this category. What unites them is that each serves to illustrate—or demonstrate—a point. In contrast to the model of memoir or confession, here, the narrative, while telling a story, unfolds or builds an argument. It is not a didactic argument; it is filtered through the characters' individual voices, distinctive deeds, or crucial decisions.

Junot Díaz's "Nilda" is a tale of a Dominican American girl's losing fight to escape the cruelty and deprivation of the ghetto and the intersecting story of the narrator's bitter victory over the same conditions.

Ian Frazier's "Laws concerning food and drink; household principles; lamentations of the father," a tongue-in-cheek manual on parenting, takes the form of an instructional essay. It consists of a series of witty, secretly warm-hearted parental exhortations to a child, borrowing from the language and cadences of Deuteronomy. On table manners: "When you have drunk, let the empty cup then remain upon the table and do not bite upon its edge and by your teeth hold it to your face in order to make noises in it sounding like a duck; for you will be sent away."

The narrator of Tim O'Brien's "On the Rainy River" looks back unsparingly at his younger self as a soldier in the Vietnam War. The notice from his draft board arrives at the story's outset in June of 1968. Opposition to the war instantly has ceased to be theoretical. He can go to Canada to avoid a war in which he does not believe, opting for exile from home, country, and family. He can risk that embarrassment—or he can go to the war. As he retraces the steps he took, between Minnesota and Canada, to the path he chose, the story tracks a journey of conscience. The story becomes a moral statement in the narrator's contemplation of war and the issues it raises: "It was my view then, and still is, that you don't make war without knowing why."

Lorrie Moore's "How to Become a Writer," like Frazier's "Laws," unfolds as a series of tongue-in-cheek, primer-like instructions. It is an address to writers, in which wry humor and wonderful wordplay combine with pitch-perfect notes of melancholy. Moore advises: "First try to be something, anything, else . . . Fail miserably." The story can be read as a deliciously funny meditation on writing as well as a cautionary tale of the writer's life. Not least, it offers sound advice.

THE STORY AS CHARACTER STUDY

Each of the three stories in this category revolves around a central character whose life is unveiled, and its meaning illuminated, as the story unfolds.

The narrator of Ward Just's "About Boston" may be as unrevealing as he is voluble. A successful divorce lawyer, he seems steady and forthcoming in voice and manner as he details his life as a longstanding outsider in Boston. But his account contains artful omissions. About a broken engagement, he says cryptically, "the usual reasons." Without elaborating, he alludes to a social life spent on weekends in New York. Reading the invisible ink between the lines is the challenge, as well as the pleasure, of this complex and finely crafted story.

In Jhumpa Lahiri's "Mrs. Sen's," the main character, like Ward Just's, contends with an unwelcoming culture. In both stories, culture and place are presences, helping to define each protagonist. Mrs. Sen is the baby-sitter for Eliot, an observant, caring eleven-year-old, in his own way as isolated as she but with more escape routes. Homesick for India, Mrs. Sen experiences her life in America almost as a sensory deprivation chamber. Adding to her sense of exclusion is the remoteness of her husband and her inability to drive. Eliot's unquestioning and generous entry into her life carries the reader with it. Their tenuous bond becomes the world of the story.

In James Thurber's wonderfully humorous "The Secret Life of Walter Mitty," the sequence of the character's daydreams provides a key to the truth of his life. The progression is clear. In "the remote, intimate airways of his mind," Mitty becomes, in the following order, a dashing and heroic naval commander; renowned surgeon; defendant in a murder trial; volunteer pilot for a suicide mission; and a figure, lone but defiant, facing a firing squad. ("To hell with the handkerchief," said Walter Mitty scornfully.)

THE STORY AS REPORTED EXPERIENCE

Denis Johnson's "Car Crash While Hitchhiking" and ZZ Packer's "Brownies" both recount their main character's experience of a pivotal event. Johnson's story is blunt, spare—the bare-bone facts of a car-crash recorded without comment. Comment is provided by the story's numbed telling and fractured point-of-view, both results of the drugs the hitchhiker has taken from an extensive menu offered en route. The story's beat is one of fits and starts, sometimes abrupt and sharp, sometimes meandering and dazed; and the narrative proceeds in the same way. The event's impact and shock are transmitted to the reader with realistic immediacy; the low-key and drug-disoriented telling makes the account all the more convincing and stunning.

The pivotal event of Packer's story is a camping excursion of a troop of Brownies, all of them, like the narrator, nine years old and black. The narrator looks back at her observant nine-year-old self in this setting and childhood society, where a life-lesson is learned. The girls giggle, whisper, gossip, gang up on one another, and bond against adults. An enticing target for the girls' mischief presents itself in the form of a Brownie troop of white girls using the campgrounds too. What sets the narrator apart from her peers is her need and natural ability to interpret events while experiencing them. In this way too, the story's events, as they unfold, are invested movingly with meaning.

THE STORY AS LETTERS

The two stories representing this category demonstrate the surprising range and versatility of the story as letters. A. A. Milne's "The Rise and Fall of Mortimer Scrivens" is a smart, entertaining, and mischievous comedy of manners. Kathrine Kressmann Taylor's "Address Unknown," published first in

1938, is at once a powerful anti-Nazi statement that warns against the rise of Hitler and a drama of revenge.

In these vastly different tales, the epistolary form provides immediacy as well as suspense. Each story, like a film or stage play, unfolds in the present tense. The form permits viewpoints to be presented, if not quite simultaneously, in such rapid succession that they almost seem so, giving the page the occasional effect of a split screen. In the Milne, this dexterous orchestration of viewpoints enriches the comedy. In the Kressmann Taylor, it contributes to the story's dark and grim irony.

The lead correspondents of "The Rise and Fall of Mortimer Scrivens" are booklovers, neighbors in the English countryside, given to book-borrowing and backbiting in equal measure. Henry Winters writes asking Brian and Sally Haverhill to return a rare book he lent them. The book, by one Mortimer Scrivens, is titled *Country Tilth*. (Sally Haverhill initially remembers it as *Country Filth*.) The letters the parties exchange are delicious examples of hypocritical politeness, with a nice seasoning of literary and social snobbery and accumulating little lies.

"Address Unknown" is considered a classic of the epistolary form. It is a spellbinding story, told through letters exchanged between 1932 and 1934 by two men, Germans both, once business partners and close friends. Max is Jewish, Martin not. Max remains in America while Martin returns to Germany. It is at this point that their correspondence begins. "Address Unknown" is a stark and suspenseful exposé of human indecency.

THE STORY AS FANTASY OR FABLE

Each of the four stories in this final category departs from realism to usher us into the realms of fantasy or fable. The tales are Robert Olen Butler's witty and touching "Jealous Husband Returns in Form of Parrot," Truman Capote's masterly "Miriam," Louise Erdrich's wise and profound "The Shawl," and Zora Neale Hurston's eerie, tough-minded "Spunk." Seemingly realistic storytelling and rounded characters draw us into these stories' singular worlds. From them all, some larger truth emerges about the human situation.

In Butler's story, the narrator, formerly a jealous husband, is now a jealous parrot. His transformation occurred when he fell to his death from a tree he had climbed to spy on his wife. Relocated to a pet shop, he has been purchased by his wife and taken home to witness, once again, this time from a cage, his wife cavorting with her lovers. The straightforward, authoritative, and, above all, *felt* storytelling, coupled with a specificity of detail that can be known only to parrots, supports the story's premise.

Capote's "Miriam" introduces Mrs. Miller as an elderly widow set in her ways. Her unvarying daily routines and her life's fixed furnishings are increasingly disrupted in the course of the story. She meets by chance an odd little girl, Miriam, who more and more intrudes into Mrs. Miller's life, tracking her even to her home. What Miriam wants, she takes as if it were her due. As if compelled, Mrs. Miller offers her hospitality. In this unwanted intimacy, Miriam thrives, and Mrs. Miller weakens; one by one, the supports of her life give way. The language provides clues to Miriam's identity.

Louise Erdrich's "The Shawl" unfolds initially as legend or fable. A woman in the grip of a "wrong-hearted love" is likened to a cloud, becomes "a gray sky." The characters are driven by forces other and more powerful than psychology. The horrific events flowing from the woman's action appear inevitable, having as much to do with nature's design as with human choice or will. Here, the telling, though first person, seems omniscient. Subsequently, the same narrator recounts, now more realistically, the ripple effect of the earlier happenings on the next generation. An ending, whose breadth and depth of insight astonish, illuminates the story as a whole.

Zora Neale Hurston's "Spunk" tells a tale of retribution. Spunk, frightening and larger than life, "a giant of a brown-skinned man," has commandeered another man's wife, then shot and killed the wronged husband. A prowling black bobcat appears, stalking Spunk's house. The circle saw at the sawmill where Spunk works is described as "singing, snarling, biting." The characters attribute the ensuing events to the supernatural, which becomes a powerful presence for the reader too.

Taken together, these stories illustrate that the way the author tells the story is as important as what the story is about. It is the narrative approach, among other choices, that reveals how the storyteller views the world. For example, "Jealous Husband Returns in Form of Parrot," if written realistically, exclusively from a human point of view, would be a very different story from the one told from the perspective of Butler's bird. The unfiltered voices of the letter-writers in "Address Unknown" underscore the story's urgency and desperation. Here, as elsewhere, content dictates form. The form conveys the author's unique vision, which is what invites us into the story. This vision illuminates the reader's experience and has the power to cast new light on, even to reshape, our own values. Above all, it is a key source of our delight.

I.

The Story

AS MEMOIR OR CONFESSION

In each of these stories, the narrator entrusts us with an account of intimate personal experience. Not intended to make a point or judgment primarily, the story takes an experience that may be hard to understand as lived and makes it legible and lasting on the page—suggesting that the storytelling itself can be redemptive.

SWEET TOWN

I T IS HARD TO BELIEVE that there was only one spring and one summer apiece that year, my fifteenth year. It is hard to believe that I so quickly squandered my youth in the sweet town playground of the sunny city, that wild monkeybardom of my fourth-grade youthhood. However, it was so.

"Dear Mother"—I wrote one day on her bathroom mirror with a candle sliver—"please forgive my absence and my decay and overlook the freckled dignity and pockmarked integrity plaguing me this season."

I used to come on even wilder sometimes and write her mad cryptic notes on the kitchen sink with charred matches. Anything for a bit, we so seldom saw each other. I even sometimes wrote her a note on paper. And then one day, having romped my soul through the spectrum of sunny colors, I dashed up to her apartment to escape the heat and found a letter from her which eternally elated my heart to the point of bursture and generally endeared her to me forever. Written on the kitchen table in cake frosting was the message, "My dear, mad, perverse young girl, kindly take care and paint the fire escape in your leisure . . ." All the *i*'s were dotted with marmalade, the *t*'s were crossed with orange rind. Here was a sight to carry with one forever in the back of the screaming eyeballs somewhere. I howled for at least five minutes out of sheer madity and vowed to love her completely. Leisure. As if bare-armed spring ever let up from its invitation to perpetuate the race. And as if we ever owned a fire escape. "Zweep," I yelled, not giving a damn for intelligibility, and decided that if ever

I was to run away from home, I'd take her with me. And with that in mind, and with Penelope splintering through the landscape and the pores secreting animal champagne, I bent my youth to the season's tempo and proceeded to lose my mind.

There is a certain glandular disturbance all beautiful, wizardy, great people have second sight to, that trumpets through the clothes, sets the nerves up for the kill, and torments the senses to orange explosure. It has something to do with the cosmic interrelationship between the cellular atunement of certain designated organs and the firmental correlation with the axis shifts of the globe. My mother calls it sex and my brother says it's groin-fever time. But then, they were always ones for brevity. Anyway, that's the way it was. And in this spring race, the glands always win and the muses and the brain core must step aside to ride in the trunk with the spare tire. It was during this sweet and drugged madness time that I met B. J., wearing his handsomeness like an article of clothing, for an effect, and wearing his friend Eddie like a necessary pimple of adolescence. It was on the beach that we met, me looking great in a pair of cut-off dungarees and them with beards. Never mind the snows of yesteryear, I told myself, I'll take the sand and sun blizzard any day.

"Listen, Kit," said B. J. to me one night after we had experienced such we-encounters with the phenomenal world at large as two-strawed mocha, duo-jaywalking summons, twosome whistling scenes, and other such like we-experiences, "the thing for us to do is hitch to the Coast and get into films."

"Righto," said Ed. "And soon."

"Sure thing, honeychile," I said, and jumped over an unknown garbage can. "We were made for celluloid—beautifully chiseled are we, not to mention well-buffed." I ran up and down somebody's stoop, whistling "Columbia the Gem of the Ocean" through my nose. And Eddie made siren sounds and walked a fence. B. J. grasped a parking-sign pole and extended himself parallel to the ground. I applauded, not only the gymnastics but also the offer. We liked to make bold directionless overtures to action like those crazy teenagers you're always running into on the printed page or MGM movies.

"We could buy a sleeping bag," said B. J., and challenged a store cat to duel.

"We could buy a sleeping bag," echoed Eddie, who never had any real contribution to make in the way of statements.

"Three in a bag," I said while B. J. grasped me by the belt and we went flying down a side street. "Hrumph," I coughed, and perched on a fire hydrant. "Only one bag?"

"Of course," said B. J.

"Of course," said Ed. "And hrumph."

We came on like this the whole summer, even crazier. All of our friends abandoned us, they couldn't keep the pace. My mother threatened me with disinheritance. And my old roommate from camp actually turned the hose on me one afternoon in a fit of Florence Nightingale therapy. But hand in hand, me and Pan, and Eddie too, whizzed through the cement kaleidoscope making our own crazy patterns, singing our own song. And then one night a crazy thing happened. I dreamt that B. J. was running down the street howling, tearing his hair out and making love to the garbage cans on the boulevard. I was there laughing my head off and Eddie was spinning a beer bottle with a faceless person I didn't even know. I woke up and screamed for no reason I know of and my roommate, who was living with us, threw a Saltine cracker at me in way of saying something about silence, peace, consideration, and sleepdom. And then on top of that another crazy thing happened. Pebbles were flying into my opened window. The whole thing struck me funny. It wasn't a casement window and there was no garden underneath. I naturally laughed my head off and my roommate got really angry and cursed me out viciously. I explained to her that pebbles were coming in, but she wasn't one for imagination and turned over into sleepdom. I went to the window to see who I was going to share my balcony scene with, and there below, standing on the milkbox, was B. J. I climbed out and joined him on the stoop.

"What's up?" I asked, ready to take the world by storm in my mixed-match baby-doll pajamas. B. J. motioned me into the foyer and I could see by the distraught mask that he was wearing that serious discussion was afoot.

"Listen, Kit," he began, looking both ways with unnecessary caution. "We're leaving, tonight, now. Me and Eddie. He stole me some money from his grandmother, so we're cutting out."

"Where're ya going?" I asked. He shrugged. And just then I saw Eddie dash across the stoop and into the shadows. B. J. shrugged and he made some kind of desperate sound with his voice like a stifled cry. "It's been real great. The summer and you . . . but . . . "

"Look here," I said with anger. "I don't know why the hell you want to hang around with that nothing." I was really angry but sorry too. It wasn't at all what I wanted to say. I would have liked to have said, "Apollo, we are the only beautiful people in the world. And because our genes are so great, our kid can't help but burst through the human skin into cosmic significance." I wanted to say, "You will bear in mind that I am great, brilliant, talented, good-looking, and am going to college at fifteen. I have the most interesting complexes ever, and despite Freud and Darwin I have made a healthy adjustment as an earthworm." But I didn't tell him this. Instead, I revealed that petty, small, mean side of me by saying, "Eddie is a shithead."

B. J. scratched his head, swung his foot in an arc, groaned and took off. "Maybe next summer . . . " he started to say but his voice cracked and he and Eddie went dashing down the night street, arm in arm. I stood there with my thighs bare and my soul shook. Maybe we will meet next summer, I told the mailboxes. Or maybe I'll quit school and bum around the country. And in every town I'll ask for them as the hotel keeper feeds the dusty, weary traveler that I'll be. "Have you

seen two guys, one great, the other acned? If you see 'em, tell
'em Kit's looking for them." And I'd bandage up my cactus-
torn feet and sling the knapsack into place and be off. And in
the next town, having endured the dust storms, tornadoes,
earthquakes, and coyotes, I'll stop at the saloon and inquire.
"Yeh, they travel together," I'd say in a voice somewhere
between W. C. Fields and Gladys Cooper. "Great buddies.
Inseparable. Tell 'em for me that Kit's still a great kid."

And legends'll pop up about me and my quest. Great long
twelve-bar blues ballads with eighty-nine stanzas. And a
strolling minstrel will happen into the feedstore where B. J.'ll
be and hear and shove the farmer's daughter off his lap and
mount up to find me. Or maybe we won't meet ever, or we
will but I won't recognize him cause he'll be an enchanted frog
or a bald-headed fat man and I'll be God knows what. No matter. Days other than the here and now, I told myself, will be
dry and sane and sticky with the rotten apricots oozing slowly
in the sweet time of my betrayed youth.

THE WATER FAUCET VISION

To protect my sister, Mona, and me from the pains—or, as they pronounce it, the pens—of life, my parents did their fighting in Shanghai dialect, which we didn't understand; and when my father one day pitched a brass vase through the kitchen window, my mother told us he had done it by accident.

"By accident?" said Mona.

My mother chopped the foot off a mushroom.

"By accident?" said Mona. "By *accident?*"

Later, I tried to explain to her that she shouldn't have persisted like that, but it was hopeless.

"What's the matter with throwing things?" she shrugged. "He was *mad.*"

That was the difference between Mona and me: fighting was just fighting to her. If she worried about anything, it was only that she might turn out too short to become a ballerina, in which case she was going to be a piano player.

I, on the other hand, was going to be a martyr. I was in fifth grade then, and the hyperimaginative sort—the kind of girl who grows morbid in Catholic school, who longs to be chopped or frozen to death and then has nightmares about it from which she wakes up screaming and clutching a stuffed bear. It was not a bear that I clutched, though, but a string of three malachite beads that I had found in the marsh by the old aqueduct one day. Apparently once part of a necklace, they were each wonderfully striated and swirled, and slightly humped toward the center, like a jellyfish; so that if I squeezed one, it would slip smoothly away, with a grace that altogether enthralled and—on those dream-harrowed nights—soothed me, soothed me as nothing had before or has since. Not that I've lacked occasion for soothing: Though it's been four months since my mother died, there are still nights when sleep stands away from me, stiff as a well-paid sentry. But that is another story. Back then, I had my malachite beads, and if I worried them long and patiently enough, I was sure to start feeling better, more awake, even a little special—imagining, as I liked to, that my nightmares were communications from the Almighty Himself, preparation for my painful destiny. Discussing them with Patty Creamer, who had also promised her life to God, I called them "almost visions"; and Patty, her mouth wadded with the three or four sticks of Doublemint she always seemed to have going at once, said, "I bet you'll be doin' miracleth by seventh grade."

Miracles. Today Patty laughs to think she ever spent good time stewing on such matters, her attention having long turned to rugs, and artwork, and antique Japanese bureaus— things she believes in.

"A good bureau's more than just a bureau," she explained last time we had lunch. "It's a hedge against life. I tell you, if there's one thing I believe, it's that cheap stuff's just money out the window. Nice stuff, on the other hand—now *that* you can always cash out, if life gets rough. *That* you can count on."

In fifth grade, though, she counted on different things.

"You'll be doing miracles, too," I told her, but she shook her shaggy head and looked doleful.

"Na' me," she chomped. "Buzzit's okay. The kin' things I like, prayers work okay on."

"Like?"

"Like you 'member that dreth I liked?"

She meant the yellow one, with the crisscross straps.

"Well gueth what."

"Your mom got it for you."

She smiled. "And I only jutht prayed for it for a week," she said.

As for myself, though, I definitely wanted to be able to perform a wonder or two. Miracle working! It was the carrot of carrots. It kept me doing my homework, taking the sacraments; it kept me mournfully on key in music hour, while my classmates hiccuped and squealed their carefree hearts away. Yet I couldn't have said what I wanted such powers for, exactly. That is, I thought of them the way one might think of, say, an ornamental sword—as a kind of collectible, which also happened to be a means of defense.

But then Patty's father walked out on her mother, and for the first time, there was a miracle I wanted to do. I wanted it so much, I could see it: Mr. Creamer made into a spitball. Mr. Creamer shot through a straw into the sky. Mr. Creamer unrolled and replumped, plop back on Patty's doorstep. I would've cleaned out his mind and given him a shave en route. I would've given him a box of peanut fudge, tied up with a ribbon, to present to Patty with a kiss.

But instead, all I could do was try to tell her he'd come back.

"He will not, he will not!" she sobbed. "He went on a boat to Rio Deniro. To Rio Deniro!"

I tried to offer her a stick of gum, but she wouldn't take it.

"He said he would rather look at water than at my mom's fat face. He said he would rather look at water than at me." Now she was really wailing, and holding her ribs so tightly that she almost seemed to be hurting herself—so tightly that just looking at her arms wound around her like snakes made my heart feel squeezed.

I patted her on the arm. A one-winged pigeon waddled by.

"He said I wasn't even his kid, he said I came from Uncle Johnny. He said I was garbage, just like my mom and Uncle Johnny. He said I wasn't even his kid, he said I wasn't his Patty, he said I came from Uncle Johnny!"

"From your Uncle Johnny?" I said stupidly.

"From Uncle Johnny," she cried. "From Uncle Johnny!"

"He said that?"

She kept crying.

I tried again. "Oh Patty, don't cry," I said. Then I said, "Your dad was a jerk anyway."

The pigeon produced a large runny dropping.

It was a good twenty minutes before Patty was calm enough for me to run to the girls' room to get her some toilet paper; and by the time I came back she was sobbing again, saying "to Rio Deniro, to Rio Deniro" over and over, as though the words had stuck in her and couldn't be gotten out. Seeing as how we had missed the regular bus home and the late bus, too, I had to leave her a second time to go call my mother, who was only mad until she heard what had happened. Then she came and picked us up, and bought us each a Fudgsicle.

Some days later, Patty and I started a program to work on getting her father home. It was a serious business. We said extra prayers, and lit votive candles. I tied my malachite beads to my uniform belt, fondling them as though they were a rosary, and I a nun. We even took to walking about the school halls with our hands folded—a sight so ludicrous that our wheeze of a principal personally took us aside one day.

"I must tell you," she said, using her nose as a speaking tube, "that there is really no need for such peee-ity."

But we persisted, promising to marry God and praying to every saint we could think of. We gave up gum, then gum and Slim Jims both, then gum and Slim Jims and ice cream; and when even that didn't work, we started on more innovative things. The first was looking at flowers. We held our hands beside our eyes like blinders as we hurried past the violets by the flagpole. Next it was looking at boys: Patty gave up angel-eyed Jamie Halloran, and I, gymnastic Anthony Rossi. It was hard, but in the end our efforts paid off. Mr. Creamer came back a month later, and though he brought

with him nothing but dysentery, he was at least too sick to
have all that much to say.

Then, in the course of a fight with my father, my mother
somehow fell out of their bedroom window.

Recently—thinking a mountain vacation might cheer me—I
sublet my apartment to a handsome but somber newlywed
couple, who turned out to be every bit as responsible as I'd
hoped. They cleaned out even the eggshell chips I'd sprinkled
around the base of my plants as fertilizer, leaving behind only
a shiny silver-plate cake server and a list of their hopes and
goals for the summer. The list, tacked precariously to the back
of the kitchen door, began with a fervent appeal to God to help
them get their wedding thank-yous written in three weeks or
less. (You could see they had originally written "two weeks"
but scratched it out—no miracles being demanded here.) It
went on:

> *Please help us, Almighty Father in Heaven Above, to get Ann
> a teaching job within a half-hour drive of here in a nice neigh-
> borhood.*
>
> *Please help us, Almighty Father in Heaven Above, to get
> John a job doing anything where he won't strain his back and
> that is within a half-hour drive of here.*
>
> *Please help us, Almighty Father in Heaven Above, to get us
> a car.*
>
> *Please help us, A. F. in H. A., to learn French.*
>
> *Please help us, A. F. in H. A., to find seven dinner recipes
> that cost less than 60 cents a serving and can be made in a half
> hour. And that don't have tomatoes, since You in Your Heavenly
> Wisdom made John allergic.*
>
> *Please help us, A. F. in H. A., to avoid books in this
> apartment such as You in Your Heavenly Wisdom allowed
> John, for Your Heavenly Reasons, to find three nights ago
> (June 2nd).*

Et cetera. In the left-hand margin they had kept score of how they had fared with their requests, and it was heartening to see that nearly all of them were marked "Yes! Praise the Lord" (sometimes shortened to "PTL"), with the sole exception of learning French, which was mysteriously marked "No! PTL to the Highest."

That note touched me. Strange and familiar both, it seemed as though it had been written by some cousin of mine—some cousin who had stayed home to grow up, say, while I went abroad and learned painful things. This, of course, is just a manner of speaking. In fact, I did my growing up at home, like anybody else.

But the learning was painful. I never knew exactly how it happened that my mother went hurtling through the air that night years ago, only that the wind had been chopping at the house, and that the argument had started about the state of the roof. Someone had been up to fix it the year before, but it wasn't a roofer, only a man my father had insisted could do just as good a job for a quarter of the price. And maybe he could have, had he not somehow managed to step through a knot in the wood under the shingles and break his uninsured ankle. Now the shingles were coming loose again, and the attic insulation was mildewing besides, and my father was wanting to sell the house altogether, which he said my mother had wanted to buy so she could send pictures of it home to her family in China.

"The Americans have a saying," he said. "They saying, 'You have to keep up with Jones family.' I'm saying if Jones family in Shanghai, you can send any picture you want, *an-y* picture. Go take picture of those rich guys' house. You want to act like rich guys, right? Go take picture of those rich guys' house."

At that point, my mother sent Mona and me to wash up, and started speaking Shanghainese. They argued for some time in the kitchen, while we listened from the top of the stairs, our faces wedged between the bumpy Spanish scrolls of the wrought-iron railing. First my mother ranted, then my father, and then they both ranted at once, until finally there was a thump, followed by a long quiet.

"Do you think they're kissing now?" said Mona. "I bet they're kissing, like this." She pursed her lips like a fish, and was about to put them to the railing when we heard my mother locking the back door. We hightailed it into bed; my parents creaked up the stairs. Everything at that point seemed fine. Once in their bedroom though, they started up again, first softly, then more and more loudly, until my mother turned on a radio to try to disguise the noise. A door slammed; they began shouting at each other; another door slammed; a shoe or something banged the wall behind Mona's bed.

"How're we supposed to *sleep?*" said Mona, sitting up.

There was another thud; more yelling in Shanghainese; and then my mother's voice pierced the wall, in English. "So what you want I should do? Go to work like Theresa Lee?"

My father rumbled something back.

"You think you are big shot, but you never get promotion, you never get raise. All I do is spend money, right? So what do you do, you tell me. So what do you do!"

Something hit the floor so hard, our room shook.

"So kill me," screamed my mother. "You know what you are? You are failure. Failure! You are failure!"

Then there was a sudden, terrific, bursting crash—and after it, as if on a bungled cue, the serene blare of an a capella soprano picking her way down a scale.

By the time Mona and I knew to look out the window, a neighbor's pet beagle was already on the scene, sniffing and barking at my mother's body, his tail crazy with excitement. Then he was barking at my stunned and trembling father, at the shrieking ambulance, at the police, at crying Mona in her bunny-footed pajamas, and at me, barefoot in the cold grass, squeezing my sister's shoulder with one hand and clutching my malachite beads with the other.

My mother wasn't dead, only unconscious—the paramedics

figured that out right away—but there was blood everywhere, and though they were reassuring about her head wounds as they strapped her to the stretcher—commenting on how small she was, how delicate, how light—my father kept saying, *I killed her, I killed her* as the ambulance screeched and screeched headlong, forever, to the hospital. I was afraid to touch her, and glad of the metal rail between us, even though its sturdiness made her seem even frailer than she was. I wished she were bigger, somehow, and noticed, with a pang, that the new red slippers we had given her for Mother's Day had been lost somewhere along the way. How much she seemed to be leaving behind, as we careened along—still not there, still not there—Mona and Dad and the medic and I taking up the whole ambulance, all the room, so that there was no room for anything else, no room even for my mother's real self, the one who should have been pinching the color back to my father's gray face, the one who should have been calming Mona's cowlick—the one who should have been bending over us, to help us be strong, to help us get through, even as we bent over her.

Then suddenly we were there, the glowing square of the emergency room entrance opening like the gates of heaven; and immediately the talk of miracles began. Alive, a miracle. No bones broken, a miracle. A miracle that the hemlocks had cushioned her fall, a miracle that they hadn't been trimmed in a year and a half. It was a miracle that all that blood, the blood that had seemed that night to be everywhere, was from one shard of glass, a single shard, can you imagine, and as for the gash in her head, the scar would be covered by hair. The next day, my mother cheerfully described just how she would part it so that nothing would show at all.

"You're a lucky duck-duck," agreed Mona, helping herself, with a little pirouette, to the cherry atop my mother's chocolate pudding.

That wasn't enough for me, though. I was relieved, yes, but what I wanted by then was a real miracle. Not for my mother simply to have survived, but for the whole thing never to have happened—for my mother's head never to have been shaved and bandaged like that, for her high, proud forehead never to have been swollen down over her eyes, for her face and neck and hands never to have been painted so many shades of blue-black, and violet, and chartreuse. I still want those things— for my parents not to have had to live with this affair like a prickle bush between them, for my father to have been able to look my mother in her swollen eyes and curse the madman, the monster who had dared do this to the woman he loved. I wanted to be able to touch my mother without shuddering, to be able to console my father, to be able to get that crash out of my head, the sound of that soprano—so many things that I didn't know how to pray for them, that I wouldn't have known where to start even if I had had the power to work miracles, right there, right then.

A week later, when my mother's head was beginning to bristle with new hairs, I lost my malachite beads. I had been carrying them in a white cloth pouch that Patty had given me, and was swinging the pouch on my pinkie on my way home from school, when I swung just a bit too hard; the pouch went sailing in a long arc through the air, *whooshing* like a perfectly thrown basketball through one of the holes of a nearby sewer. There was no chance of fishing it out. I looked and looked, crouching on the sticky pavement until the asphalt had crazed the skin of my hands and knees, but all I could discern was an evil-smelling murk, glassy and smug and impenetrable.

My loss didn't quite hit me until I was home, but then it produced an agony all out of proportion to my string of pretty beads. I hadn't cried at all during my mother's accident, but now I was crying all afternoon, all through dinner, and then after dinner, too—crying past the point where I knew what I was crying for, wishing dimly that I had my beads to hold, wishing dimly that I could pray, but refusing, refusing, I didn't know why, until I finally fell into an exhausted sleep on the couch. There my parents left me for the night—glad, no doubt, that one of the more tedious of my childhood crises seemed to be winding off the reel of life, onto the reel of memory. They covered me, and somehow grew a pillow under my head, and, with uncharacteristic disregard for the living room rug, left some milk and Pecan Sandies on the coffee table, in case I woke up hungry. Their thoughtfulness was prescient. I did wake up in the early part of the night; and it was then, amid the unfamiliar sounds and shadows of the living room, that I had what I was sure was a true vision.

Even now, what I saw remains an odd clarity: the requisite strange light flooding the room, first orange, and then a bright yellow-green. A crackling bright burst like a Roman candle going off near the piano. There was a distinct smell of coffee, and a long silence. The room seemed to be getting colder. Nothing. A creak; the light starting to wane, then waxing again, brilliant pink now. Still nothing. Then, as the pink started to go a little purple, a perfectly normal, middle-aged man's voice, speaking something very like pig latin, told me not to despair, not to despair, my beads would be returned to me.

That was all. I sat a moment in the dark, then turned on the light, gobbled down the cookies—and in a happy flash understood that I was so good, really, so near to being a saint that my malachite beads would come back through the town water system. All I had to do was turn on all the faucets in the house. This I did, stealing quietly into the bathroom and kitchen and basement. The old spigot by the washing machine was too gunked up to be coaxed very far open, but that didn't matter. The water didn't have to be full blast, I understood that. Then I gathered together my pillow and blanket and trundled up to my bed to sleep.

By the time I woke in the morning, I knew that my beads hadn't shown up; but when I knew it for certain, I was still disappointed. And as if that weren't enough, I had to face my parents and sister, who were all abuzz with the mystery of the faucets. Not knowing what else to do, I, like a puddlebrain, told them the truth. The results were predictably painful.

"Callie had a *vision*," Mona told everyone at the bus stop. "A vision with lights, and sinks in it!"

Sinks, visions. I got it all day, from my parents, from my classmates, even from some sixth and seventh graders. Someone drew a cartoon of me with a halo over my head in one of the girls' room stalls; Anthony Rossi made gurgling noises as he walked on his hands at recess. Only Patty tried not to laugh, though even she was something less than unalloyed understanding.

"I don' think miracles are thupposed to happen in *thewers*," she said.

Such was the end of my saintly ambitions. It wasn't the end of all holiness. The ideas of purity and goodness still tippled my brain, and over the years I came slowly to grasp of what grit true faith is made. Last night, though, when my father called to say that he couldn't go on living in our old house, that he was going to move to a smaller place, another place, maybe a condo—he didn't know how, or where—I found myself still wistful for the time religion seemed all I wanted it to be. Back then, the world was a place that could be set right. One had only to direct the hand of the Almighty and say, Just here, Lord, we hurt here—and here, and here, and here.

Rick Moody

DEMONOLOGY

THEY CAME IN TWOS AND THREES, dressed in the fashionable Disney costumes of the year, Lion King, Pocahontas, Beauty and the Beast or in the costumes of televised superheroes, Protean, shape-shifting, thus arrayed, in twos and threes, complaining it was too hot with the mask on, *Hey, I'm really hot!,* lugging those orange plastic buckets, bartering, haggling with one another, *Gimme your Smarties, please?* as their parents tarried behind, grownups following after, grownups bantering about the schools, or about movies, about local sports, about their marriages, about the difficulties of long marriages, kids sprinting up the next driveway, kids decked out as demons or superheroes or dinosaurs or as advertisements for our multinational entertainment-providers, beating back the restless souls of the dead, in search of sweets.

They came in bursts of fertility, my sister's kids, when the bar drinking, or home-grown dope-smoking, or bed-hopping had lost its luster; they came with shrill cries and demands—little gavels, she said, instead of fists—*Feed me! Change me! Pay attention to me!* Now it was Halloween and the mothers in town, my sister among them, trailed after their kids, warned them away from items not fully wrapped, *Just give me that, you don't even like apples,* laughing at the kids hobbling in their bulky costumes—my nephew dressed as a shark, dragging a mildewed gray tail behind him. But what kind of shark? A great white? A blue? A tiger shark? A hammerhead? A nurse shark?

/   /   /   /

She took pictures of costumed urchins, my sister, as she always took pictures, e.g., my nephew on his first birthday (six years prior), blackfaced with cake and ice cream, a dozen relatives attempting in turn to read to him—about a tugboat—from a brand new rubberized book. *Toot toot!* His desperate, needy expression, in the photo, all out of phase with our excitement. The first nephew! The first grandchild! He was trying to get the cake in his mouth. Or: a later photo of my niece (his younger sister) attempting to push my nephew out of the shot—against a backdrop of autumn foliage; or a photo of my brother wearing my dad's yellow double-knit paisley trousers (with a bit of flair in the cuffs), twenty-five years after the heyday of such stylings; or my father and stepmother on their powerboat, peaceful and happy, the riotous wake behind them; or my sister's virtuosic photos of *dogs*—Mom's irrepressible golden retriever chasing a tennis ball across an overgrown lawn, or my dad's setter on the beach with a perspiring Löwenbräu leaning against his snout. Fifteen or twenty photo photo albums on the shelves in my sister's living room, a whole range of leathers and faux-leathers, no particular order, and just as many more photos loose, floating around the basement, castoffs, and files of negatives in their plastic wrappers.

She drank *the demon rum,* and she taught me how to do it, too, when we were kids; she taught me how to drink. We stole drinks, or we got people to steal them for us; we got reprobates of age to venture into the pristine suburban liquor stores. Later, I drank bourbon. My brother drank beer. My father drank single malt scotches. My grandmother drank half-gallons and then fell ill. My grandfather drank the finest collectibles. My sister's ex-husband drank more reasonably priced facsimiles. My brother drank until a woman lured him out of my mother's house. I drank until I was afraid to go outside. My uncle drank until the last year of his life. And I car-

ried my sister in a blackout from a bar once—she was mum-
bling to herself, humming melodies, mostly unconscious. I
took her arms; Peter Hunter took her legs. She slept the whole
next day. On Halloween, my sister had a single gin and tonic
before going out with the kids, before ambling around the
condos of Kensington Court, circling from multifamily unit
to multifamily unit, until my nephew's shark tail was grass-
stained from the freshly mown lawns of the common areas.
Then she drove her children across town to her ex-husband's
house, released them into his supervision and there they
walked along empty lots, beside a brook, under the stars.

When they arrived home, these monsters, disgorged from
their dad's Jeep, there was a fracas between girl and boy about
which was superior (in the Aristotelian hierarchies), Milky
Way, Whoppers, Slim Jim, Mike 'n Ikes, Sweet Tarts or Pez—
this bounty counted, weighed and inventoried (on my niece's
bed). Which was the Pez dispenser of greatest value? A
Hanna-Barbera Pez dispenser? Or, say, a demonic *totem pole Pez
dispenser?* And after this fracas, which my sister refereed
wearily *(Look, if he wants to save the Smarties, you can't make him
trade!),* they all slept, and this part is routine, my sister was
tired as hell; she slept the sleep of the besieged, of the over-
worked, she fell precipitously into whorls of unconsciousness,
of which no snapshot can be taken.

In one photograph, my sister is wearing a Superman outfit. This
from a prior Halloween. I think it was a *Supermom* outfit, actually, because she always liked these bad jokes, degraded jokes,
things other people would find ridiculous. (She'd take a joke
and repeat it until it was leaden, until it was funny only in its
awfulness.) Jokes with the fillip of sentimentality. Anyway, in
this picture her blond hair—brightened a couple of shades with
the current technologies—cascades around her shoulders, disor-
dered and impulsive. *Supermom.* And her expression is skeptical,

as if she assumes the mantle of Supermom—raising the kids, accepting wage-slavery, growing old and contented—and thinks it's dopey at the same time.

Never any good without coffee. Never any good in the morning. Never any good until the second cup. Never any good without freshly ground Joe, because of my dad's insistence, despite advantages of class and style, on *instant coffee*. No way. Not for my sister. At my dad's house, where she stayed in summer, she used to grumble derisively, while staring out the kitchen windows, out the expanse of windows that gave onto the meadow there, *Instant coffee!* There would be horses in the meadow and the ocean just over the trees, the sound of the surf and *instant coffee!* Thus the morning after Halloween, with my nephew the shark (who took this opportunity to remind her, in fact, that last year he saved his Halloween candy *all the way till Easter, Mommy)* and my niece, the Little Mermaid, orbiting around her like a fine dream. My sister was making this coffee with the automatic grinder and the automatic drip device, and the dishes were piled in the sink behind her, and the wall calendar was staring her in the face, with its hundred urgent appointments, e.g., *jury duty* (the following Monday) and *R & A to pediatrician;* the kids whirled around the kitchen, demanding to know who got the last of the Lucky Charms, who had to settle for the Kix. My sister's eyes barely open.

Now this portrait of her cat, Pointdexter, twelve years old— he slept on my face when I stayed at her place in 1984— Pointdexter with the brain tumor, Pointdexter with the Phenobarbital habit. That morning—All Saints' Day—he stood entirely motionless before his empty dish. His need was clear. His dignity was immense. Well, except for the seizures. Pointdexter had these seizures. He was possessed. He was a demon. He would bounce off the walls, he would get up *a head of steam,* mouth frothing, and run straight at the wall, smack into it, shake off the ghosts and start again. His screeches were unearthly. Phenobarbital was prescribed. My sister medicated him preemptively, before any other chore, before diplomatic initiatives on matters of cereal allocation. *Hold on, you guys, I'll be with you in a second.* Drugging the cat, slipping him the Mickey Finn in the Science Diet, feeding the kids, then getting out the door, pecking her boyfriend on the cheek (he was stumbling sleepily down the stairs),

She printed snapshots. At this photo lab. She'd sold cameras (mnemonic devices) for years, and then she'd been kicked upstairs to the lab. Once she sold a camera to Pete Townshend, the musician. She told him—in her way both casual and rebellious—that she didn't really like The Who. Later, from her job at the lab, she used to bring home *other people's pictures,* e.g., an envelope of photographs of the Pope. Had she been out to Giants Stadium to use her telephoto lens to photograph John Paul II? No, she'd just printed up an extra batch of, say, Agnes Venditi's or Joey Mueller's photos. *Caveat emptor.* Who knew what else she'd swiped? Those Jerry Garcia pix from the show right before he died? Garcia's eyes squeezed tightly shut, as he sang in that heartbroken, exhausted voice of his? Or: somebody's trip to the Caribbean or to the Liberty Bell in Philly? Or: her neighbor's private documentations of love? Who knew? She'd get on the phone at work and gab, call up her friends, call up family, printing pictures while gabbing, sheet after sheet of negatives, memories. Oh, and circa Halloween, she was working in the lab with some new, exotic chemicals. She had a wicked headache.

My sister didn't pay much attention to the church calendar. Too busy. Too busy to concentrate on theologies, too busy to go to the doctor, too busy to deal with her finances, her credit-card debt, etc. Too busy. (And maybe afraid, too.) She was unclear on this day set aside for God's awesome tabernacle, unclear on the feast for the departed faithful, didn't know about the church of the Middle Ages, didn't know about the particulars of the Druidic ritual of Halloween—it was a Hallmark thing, a marketing event—or how All Saints' Day emerged as an alternative to Halloween. She was not much preoccupied with, nor attendant to articulations of loss nor interested in how this feast in the church calendar was hewn into separate holy days, one for the saints, *that great cloud of witnesses,* one for the dearly departed, the regular old believers. She didn't know of any attachments that bound together these constituencies, didn't know, e.g., that God would *wipe away all tears from our eyes and there would be no more death,* according to the evening's reading from the book of Revelation. All this academic stuff was lost on her, though she sang in the church choir, and though on All Saints' Day, a guy from the church choir happened to come into the camera store, just to say hi, a sort of an angel (let's say), and she said, *Hey Bob, you know, I never asked you what you do.*

To which Bob replied, *I'm a designer.*

My sister: *What do you design?*

Bob: *Steel wool.*

She believed him.

She was really small. She barely held down her clothes. Five feet tall. Tiny hands and feet. Here's a photo from my brother's wedding (two weeks before Halloween); we were dancing on the dance floor, she and I. She liked *to pogo* sometimes. It was the dance we preferred when dancing together. We created mayhem on the dance floor. Scared people off. We were demons for dance, for noise and excitement. So at my brother's wedding reception I hoisted her up onto my shoulder, and she was so light, just as I remembered from years before, twenty years of dances, still tiny, and I wanted to crowd-surf her across the reception, pass her across upraised hands, I wanted to impose her on older couples, gentlemen in their cummerbunds, old guys with tennis elbow or arthritis, with red faces and gin-blossoms; they would smile, passing my sister hither, to the microphone, where the wedding band was playing, where she would suddenly burst

into song, into some sort of reconciliatory song, backed by the
wedding band, and there would be stills of this moment, flash
bulbs popping, a spotlight on her face, a tiny bit of reverb on
her microphone, she would smile and concentrate and sing.
Unfortunately, the situation around us, on the dance floor, was
more complicated than this. Her boyfriend was about to have
back surgery. He wasn't going to do any heavy lifting. And my
nephew was too little to hold her up. And my brother was preoccupied with his duties as groom. So instead I twirled her once
and put her down. We were laughing, out of breath.

On All Saints' Day she had lunch with Bob the angelic designer
of steel wool (maybe he had a crush on her) or with younger guys
from the lab (because she was a middle-aged free spirit), and then
she printed more photos of Columbus Day parades across Jersey,
or photos of other people's kids dressed as Pocahontas or as the
Lion King, and then at 5:30 she started home, a commute of
forty-five minutes, Morristown to Hackettstown, on two-laners.
She knew every turn. Here's the local news photo that never was:
my sister slumped over the wheel of her Plymouth Saturn after
having run smack into a local deer. All along these roads the deer
were up-ended, disemboweled, set upon by crows and hawks,
and my sister on the way back from work, or on the way home
from a bar, must have grazed an entire herd of them at one time
or another, missed them narrowly, frozen in the headlights of her
car, on the shoulders of the meandering back roads, pulverized.

Her boy lives on air. Disdains food. My niece, meanwhile, will
eat only candy. By dinnertime, they had probably made a dent
in the orange plastic bucket with the Three Musketeers, the
Cadbury's, Hot Tamales, Kit Kats, Jujyfruits, Baby Ruths,
Bubble Yum—at least my niece had. They had insisted on
bringing a sampling of this booty to school and from there to
their afterschool play group. Neither of them wanted to eat
anything; they complained about the whole idea of supper,

and thus my sister offered, instead, to take them to the *McDonaldLand play area* on the main drag in Hackettstown, where she would buy them a Happy Meal, or equivalent, a hamburger topped with *American processed cheese food,* and, as an afterthought, she would insist on their each trying a little bit of a salad from the brand new McDonald's salad bar. She had to make a deal to get the kids to accept the salad. She suggested six mouthfuls of lettuce each and drew a hard line there, but then she allowed herself to be talked down to two mouthfuls each. They ate indoors at first, the three of them, and then went out to the playground, where there were slides and jungle gyms in the reds and yellows of Ray Kroc's empire. My sister made the usual conversation, *How did the other kids make out on Halloween? What happened at school?* and she thought of her boyfriend, fresh from spinal surgery, who had limped downstairs in the morning to give her a kiss, and then she thought about *bills, bills, bills,* as she caught my niece at the foot of a slide. It was time to go sing. Home by nine.

My sister as she played the guitar in the late sixties with her hair in braids; she played it before anyone else in my family, wandering around the chords, "House of the Rising Sun" or "Blackbird," on classical guitar, sticking to the open chords of guitar tablature. It never occurred to me to wonder about which instruments were used on those AM songs of the period (the Beatles with their sitars and cornets, Brian Wilson with his theremin), not until my sister started to play the guitar. (All of us sang—we used to sing and dance in the living room when my parents were married, especially to *Abbey Road* and *Bridge Over Troubled Water.*) And when she got divorced she started hanging around this bar where they had live music, this Jersey bar, and then she started hanging around at a local record label, an indy operation, and then she started *managing a band* (on top of everything else), and then she started to sing again. She joined the choir at St. James Church of

Hackettstown and she started to sing, and after singing she started to pray—prayer and song being, I guess, styles of the same beseechment.

I don't know what songs they rehearsed at choir rehearsal, but Bob was there, as were others, Donna, Frank, Eileen and Tim (I'm making the names up), and I know that the choir was warm and friendly, though perhaps a little bit out of tune. It was one of those Charles Ives small-town choruses that slips in and out of pitch, that misses exits and entrances. But they had a good time rehearsing, with the kids monkeying around in the pews, the kids climbing sacrilegiously over the furniture, dashing up the aisle to the altar and back, as somebody kept half an eye on them (five of the whelps in all) and after the last notes ricocheted around the choir loft, my sister offered her summation of the proceedings, *Totally cool! Totally cool!,* and now the intolerable part of this story begins—with joy and excitement and a church interior. My sister and her kids drove from St. James to her house, her condo, this picturesque drive home, Hackettstown as if lifted from picture postcards of autumn, the park with its streams and ponds and lighted walkways, leaves in the streetlamps, in the headlights, leaves three or four days past their peak, the sound of leaves in the breeze, the construction crane by her place (they were digging up the road), the crane swaying above a fork in the road, a left turn after the fast-food depots, and then into her parking spot in front of the condo. The porch by the front door with the Halloween pumpkins: a cat's face complete with whiskers, a clown, a jack-o'-lantern. My sister closed the front door of her house behind her. Bolted it. Her daughter reminded her to light the pumpkins. Just inside the front door, Pointdexter, on the top step, waiting.

Her keys on the kitchen table. Her coat in the closet. She sent the kids upstairs to get into their pajamas. She called up to her boyfriend, who was in bed reading a textbook, *What are you doing in bed, you total slug!* and then, after checking the messages on the answering machine, looking at the mail, she trudged up to my niece's room to kiss her good night. Endearments passed between them. My sister loved her kids, above all, and in spite of all the work and the hardships, in spite of my niece's reputation as a firecracker, in spite of my nephew's sometimes diabolical smarts. She loved them. There were endearments, therefore, lengthy and repetitive, as there would have been with my nephew, too. And my sister kissed her daughter multiply, because my niece is a little impish redhead, and it's hard *not* to kiss her. *Look, it's late, so I can't read to you tonight, okay?* My niece protested temporarily, and then my sister arranged the stuffed animals around her daughter (for the sake of arranging), and plumped a feather pillow, and switched off the bedside lamp on the bedside table, and she made sure the night light underneath the table (a plug-in shaped like a ghost) was illumined, and then on the way out the door she stopped for a second. And looked back. The tableau of domesticity was what she last contemplated. Or maybe she was composing endearments for my nephew. Or maybe she wasn't looking back at my niece at all. Maybe she was lost in this next tempest.

Out of nowhere. All of a sudden. All at once. In an instant. Without warning. In no time. Helter-skelter. *In the twinkling of an eye.* Figurative language isn't up to the task. My sister's legs gave out, and she fell over toward my niece's desk, by the door, dislodging a pile of toys and dolls (a Barbie in evening wear, a poseable Tinkerbell doll), colliding with the desk, sweeping its contents off with her, toppling onto the floor, falling heavily, her head by the door. My niece, startled, rose up from under covers.

More photos: my sister, my brother and I, *back in our single digits,* dressed in matching, or nearly matching outfits (there was a

naval flavor to our look), playing with my aunt's basset hound—
my sister grinning mischievously; or: my sister, my father, my
brother and I, in my dad's Karmann-Ghia, just before she totaled
it on the straightaway on Fishers Island (she skidded, she said, *on*
antifreeze or something slippery); or: my sister, with her newborn
daughter in her lap, sitting on the floor of her living room—
mother and daughter with the same bemused impatience.

My sister started to seize.

The report of her fall was, of course, loud enough to stir her
boyfriend from the next room. He was out of bed fast. (Despite
physical pain associated with his recent surgery.) I imagine
there was a second in which other possibilities occurred to
him—hoax, argument, accident, anything—but quickly the
worst of these seemed most likely. You know these things
somewhere. You know immediately the content of all middle-
of-the-night telephone calls. He was out of bed. And my niece
called out to her brother, to my nephew, next door. She called
my nephew's name, plaintively, like it was a question.

My sister's hands balled up. Her heels drumming on the car-
peting. Her muscles all like nautical lines, pulling tight
against cleats. Her jaw clenched. Her heart rattling desperately. Fibrillating. If it was a conventional seizure, she was
unconscious for this part—maybe even unconscious through-
out—because of reduced blood flow to the brain, because of
the fibrillation, because of her heart condition; which is to say
that my sister's *mitral valve prolapse*—technical feature of her
broken heart—was here engendering an arrhythmia, and now,
if not already, she began to hemorrhage internally. Her son
stood in the doorway, in his pajamas, shifting from one foot to
the other (there was a draft in the hall). Her daughter knelt at
the foot of the bed, staring, and my sister's boyfriend watched,
as my poor sister shook, and he held her hand, and then
changed his mind and bolted for the phone.

/   /   /   /

After the seizure, she went slack. (Meredith's heart stopped. And her breathing. She was still.) For a second, she was alone in the room with her children, silent. After he dialed 911, Jimmy appeared again, to try to restart her breathing. Here's how: he pressed his lips against hers. He didn't think to say, *Come on, breathe dammit,* or to make similar imprecations, although he did manage to shout at the kids, *Get the hell out of here, please! Go downstairs!* (It was advice they followed only for a minute.) At last, my sister took a breath. Took a deep breath, a sigh, and there were two more of these. Deep resigned sighs. Five or ten seconds between each. For a few moments more, instants, she looked at Jimmy, as he pounded on her chest with his fists, thoughtless about anything but results, stopping occasionally to press his ear between her breasts. Her eyes were sad and frightened, even in the company of the people she most loved. So it seemed. More likely she was unconscious. The kids sat cross-legged on the floor in the hall, by the top of the stairs, watching. Lots of stuff was left to be accomplished in these last seconds, even if it wasn't anything unusual, people and relationships and small kindnesses, the best way to fry pumpkin seeds, what to pack for Thanksgiving, whether to make turnips or not, snapshots to be culled and arranged, photos to be taken—these possibilities spun out of my sister's grasp, torrential futures, my beloved sister, solitary with pictures taken and untaken, gone.

EMS technicians arrived and carried her body down to the living room where they tried to start her pulse with expensive engines and devices. Her body jumped while they shocked her—she was a revenant in some corridor of simultaneities—but her heart wouldn't start. Then they put her body on the stretcher. To carry her away. Now the moment arrives when they bear her out the front door of her house and she leaves it to us, leaves to us the house and her things and her friends and her memories and the involuntary assemblage of these into language. Grief. The sound of the ambulance. The road is mostly clear on the way to the hospital; my sister's route is clear.

I should fictionalize it more, I should conceal myself. I should consider the responsibilities of characterization, I should conflate her two children into one, or reverse their genders, or otherwise alter them, I should make her boyfriend a husband, I should explicate all the tributaries of my extended family (its remarriages, its internecine politics), I should novelize the whole thing, I should make it multigenerational, I should work in my forefathers (stonemasons and newspapermen), I should let artifice create an elegant surface, I should make events orderly, I should wait and write about it later, I should wait until I'm not angry, I shouldn't clutter a narrative with fragments, with mere recollections of good times, or with regrets, I should make Meredith's death shapely and persuasive, not blunt and disjunctive, I shouldn't have to think the unthinkable, I shouldn't have to suffer, I should address her here directly (these are the ways I miss you), I should write only of affection, I should make our travels in this earthly landscape safe and secure, I should have a better ending, I shouldn't say her life was short and often sad, I shouldn't say she had her demons, as I do too.

ESCAPES

WHEN I WAS VERY SMALL, my father said, "Lizzie, I want to tell you something about your grandfather. Just before he died, he was alive. Fifteen minutes before."

I had never known my grandfather. This was the most extraordinary thing I had ever heard about him.

Still, I said, No.

"No!" my father said. "What do you mean, 'No.'" He laughed.

I shook my head.

"All right," my father said, "it was one minute before. I thought you were too little to know such things, but I see you're not. It was even less than a minute. It was one *moment* before."

"Oh stop teasing her," my mother said to my father.

"He's just teasing you, Lizzie," my mother said.

In warm weather once we drove up into the mountains, my mother, my father and I, and stayed for several days at a resort lodge on a lake. In the afternoons, horse races took place in the lodge. The horses were blocks of wood with numbers painted on them, moved from one end of the room to the other by ladies in ball gowns. There was a long pier that led out into the lake and at the end of the pier was a nightclub that had a twenty-foot-tall champagne glass on the roof. At night, someone would pull a switch and neon bubbles would spring out from the lit glass onto the black air. I very much wanted such a glass on the roof of our own house and I wanted to be the one who, every night, would turn on the switch. My mother always said about this, "We'll see."

I saw an odd thing once, there in the mountains. I saw my father, pretending to be lame. This was in the midst of strangers in the gift shop of the lodge. The shop sold hand-carved canes, among many other things, and when I came in to buy bubble gum in the shape of cigarettes, to which I was devoted, I saw my father, hobbling painfully down the aisle, leaning heavily on a dully gleaming, yellow cane, his shoulders hunched, one leg turned out at a curious angle. My handsome, healthy father, his face drawn in dreams. He looked at me. And then he looked away as though he did not know me.

My mother was a drinker. Because my father left us, I assumed he was not a drinker, but this may not have been the case. My mother loved me and was always kind to me We spent a great deal of time together, my mother and I. This was before I knew how to read. I suspected there was a trick to reading, but I did not know the trick. Written words were something between me and a place I could not go. My mother went back and forth to that place all the time, but couldn't explain to me exactly what it was like there. I imagined it to be a different place.

As a very young child, my mother had seen the magician Houdini. Houdini had made an elephant disappear. He had also made an orange tree grow from a seed right on the stage. Bright oranges hung from the tree and he had picked them and thrown them out into the audience. People could eat the oranges or take them home, whatever they wanted.

How did he make the elephant disappear, I asked.

"He disappeared in a puff of smoke," my mother said. "Houdini said that even the elephant didn't know how it was done."

Was it a baby elephant, I asked.

My mother sipped her drink. She said that Houdini was more than a magician, he was an escape artist. She said that he could escape from handcuffs and chains and ropes.

"They put him in straitjackets and locked him in trunks and threw him in swimming pools and rivers and oceans and he escaped," my mother said. "He escaped from water-filled vaults. He escaped from coffins."

I said that I wanted to see Houdini.

"Oh, Houdini's dead, Lizzie," my mother said. "He died a long time ago. A man punched him in the stomach three times and he died."

Dead. I asked if he couldn't get out of being dead.

"He met his match there," my mother said.

She said that he turned a bowl of flowers into a pony who cantered around the stage.

"He sawed a lady in half too, Lizzie." Oh, how I wanted to be that lady, sawed in half and then made whole again!

My mother spoke happily, laughing. We sat at the kitchen table and my mother was drinking from a small glass which rested snugly in her hand. It was my favorite glass too but she never let me drink from it. There were all kinds of glasses in our cupboard but this was the one we both liked. This was in Maine. Outside, in the yard, was our car which was an old blue convertible.

Was there blood, I asked.

"No, Lizzie, no. He was a magician!"

Did she cry that lady, I wanted to know.

"I don't think so," my mother said. "Maybe he hypnotized her first."

It was winter. My father had never ridden in the blue convertible which my mother had bought after he had gone. The car was old then, and was rusted here and there. Beneath the rubber mat on my side, the passenger side, part of the floor had rusted through completely. When we went anywhere in the car, I would sometimes lift up the mat so I could see the road rushing past beneath us and feel the cold round air as it came up through the hole. I would pretend that the coldness was trying to speak to me, in the same way that words written down tried to speak. The air wanted to tell me something, but I didn't care about it, that's what I thought. Outside, the car stood in snow.

I had a dream about the car. My mother and I were alone together as we always were, linked in our hopeless and incomprehending love of one another, and we were driving to a house. It seemed to be our destination but we only arrived to move on. We drove again, always returning to the house which we would circle and leave, only to arrive at it again. As we drove, the inside of the car grew hair. The hair was gray and it grew and grew. I never told my mother about this dream just as I had never told her about my father leaning on the cane. I was a secretive person. In that way, I was like my mother.

I wanted to know more about Houdini. Was Houdini in love, did Houdini love someone, I asked.

"Rosabelle," my mother said. "He loved his wife, Rosabelle."

I went and got a glass and poured some ginger ale in it and I sipped my ginger ale slowly in the way that I had seen my mother sip her drink many, many times. Even then, I had the gestures down. I sat opposite her, very still and quiet, pretending.

But then I wanted to know was there magic in the way he loved her. Could he make her disappear. Could he make both of them disappear was the way I put my question.

"Rosabelle," my mother said. "No one knew anything about Rosabelle except that Houdini loved her. He never turned their love into loneliness which would have been beneath him of course."

We ate our supper and after supper my mother would have another little bit to drink. Then she would read articles from the newspaper aloud to me.

"My goodness," she said, "what a strange story. A hunter shot a bear who was carrying a woman's pocketbook in its mouth."

Oh, oh, I cried. I looked at the newspaper and struck it with my fingers. My mother read on, a little oblivious to me. The woman had lost her purse years before on a camping trip.

Everything was still inside it, her wallet and her compact and her keys.

Oh, I cried. I thought this was terrible. I was frightened, thinking of my mother's pocketbook, the way she carried it always, and the poor bear too.

Why did the bear want to carry a pocketbook, I asked.

My mother looked up from the words in the newspaper. It was as though she had come back into the room I was in.

"Why, Lizzie," she said.

The poor bear, I said.

"Oh, the bear is all right," my mother said. "The bear got away."

I did not believe this was the case. She herself said the bear had been shot.

"The bear escaped," my mother said. "It says so right here," and she ran her finger along a line of words. "It ran back into the woods to its home." She stood up and came around the table and kissed me. She smelled then like the glass that was always in the sink in the morning, and the smell reminds me still of daring and deception, hopes and little lies.

I shut my eyes and in that way I felt I could not hear my mother. I saw the bear holding the pocketbook, walking through the woods with it, feeling fine in a different way and pretty too, then stopping to find something in it, wanting something, moving its big paw through the pocketbook's small things.

"Lizzie," my mother called to me. My mother did not know where I was which alarmed me. I opened my eyes.

"Don't cry, Lizzie," my mother said. She looked as though she were about to cry too. This was the way it often was at night, late in the kitchen with my mother.

My mother returned to the newspaper and began to turn the pages. She called my attention to the drawing of a man holding a hat with stars sprinkling out of it. It was an advertisement for a magician who would be performing not far away. We decided we would see him. My mother knew just the seats she wanted for us, good seats, on the aisle close to the stage. We might be called up on the stage, she said, to be part of the performance. Magicians often used people from the audience, particularly children. I might even be given a rabbit.

I wanted a rabbit.

I put my hands on the table and I could see the rabbit between them. He was solid white in the front and solid black in the back as though he were made up of two rabbits. There are rabbits like that. I saw him there, before me on the table, a nice rabbit.

My mother went to the phone and ordered two tickets, and not many days after that, we were in our car driving to Portland for the matinee performance. I very much liked the word matinee. Matinee, matinee, I said. There was a broad hump on the floor between our seats and it was here where my mother put her little glass, the glass often full, never, it seemed, more than half empty. We chatted together and I thought we must have appeared interesting to others as we passed by in our convertible in winter. My mother spoke about happiness. She told me that happiness that comes out of nowhere, out of nothing, is the very best kind. We paid no attention to the coldness which was speaking in the way that it had, but enjoyed the sun which beat through the windshield upon our pale hands.

My mother said that Houdini had black eyes and that white doves flew from his fingertips. She said that he escaped from a block of ice.

Did he look like my father, Houdini, I asked. Did he have a moustache.

"Your father didn't have a moustache," my mother said, laughing. "Oh, I wish I could be more like you."

Later, she said, "Maybe he didn't escape from a block of ice, I'm not sure about that. Maybe he wanted to, but he never did."

We stopped for lunch somewhere, a dark little restaurant along the road. My mother had cocktails and I myself drank something cold and sweet. The restaurant was not very nice. It smelled of smoke and dampness as though once it had burned down, and it was so noisy that I could not hear my mother very well. My mother looked like a woman in a bar, pretty and disturbed, hunched forward saying, who do you think I look like, will you remember me? She was saying all matter of things. We lingered there, and then my mother asked the time of someone and seemed surprised. My mother was always surprised by time. Outside, there were woods of green fir trees whose lowest branches swept the ground, and as we were getting back into the car, I believed I saw something moving far back in the darkness of the woods beyond the slick, snowy square of the parking lot. It was the bear, I thought. Hurry, hurry, I thought. The hunter is playing with his children. He is making them something to play in as my father had once made a small playhouse for me. He is not the hunter yet. But in my heart I knew the bear was gone and the shape was just the shadow of something else in the afternoon.

My mother drove very fast but the performance had already begun when we arrived. My mother's face was damp and her good blouse had a spot on it. She went into the ladies' room and when she returned the spot was larger, but it was water now and not what it had been before. The usher assured us that we had not missed much. The usher said that the magician was not very good, that he talked and talked, he told a lot of jokes and then when you were bored and distracted, something would happen, something would have changed. The usher smiled at my mother. He seemed to like her, even know her in some way. He was a small man, like an old boy, balding. I did not care for him. He led us to our seats, but there were people sitting in them and there was a small disturbance as the strangers rearranged themselves. We were both expectant, my mother and I, and we watched the magician intently.

My mother's lips were parted, and her eyes were bright. On the stage were a group of children about my age, each with a hand on a small cage the magician was holding. In the cage was a tiny bird. The magician would ask the children to jostle the cage occasionally and the bird would flutter against the bars so that everyone would see it was the real thing with bones and breath and feelings too. Each child announced that they had a firm grip on the bars. Then the magician put a cloth over the cage, gave a quick tug and cage and bird vanished. I was not surprised. It seemed just the kind of thing that was going to happen. I decided to withhold my applause when I saw that my mother's hands too were in her lap. There were several more tricks of the magician's invention, certainly nothing I would have asked him to do. Large constructions of many parts and colors were wheeled onto the stage. There were doors everywhere which the magician opened and slammed shut. Things came and went, all to the accompaniment of loud music. I was confused and grew hot. My mother too moved restlessly in the next seat. Then there was an intermission and we returned to the lobby.

"This man is a far, far cry from the great Houdini," my mother said.

What were his intentions exactly, I asked.

He had taken a watch from a man in the audience and smashed it for all to see with a hammer. Then the watch, unharmed, had reappeared behind the man's ear.

"A happy memory can be a very misleading thing," my mother said. "Would you like to go home?"

I did not want to leave really. I wanted to see it through. I held the glossy program in my hand and turned the pages. I stared hard at the print beneath the pictures and imagined all sorts of promises being made.

"Yes, we want to see how it's done, don't we, you and I," my mother said. "We want to get to the bottom of it."

I guessed we did.

"All right, Lizzie," my mother said, "but I have to get something out of the car. I'll be right back."

I waited for her in a corner of the lobby. Some children looked at me and I looked back. I had a package of gum cigarettes in my pocket and I extracted one carefully and placed the end in my mouth. I held the elbow of my right arm with my left hand and smoked the cigarette for a long time and then I folded it up in my mouth and I chewed it for a while. My mother had not yet returned when the performance began again. She was having a little drink, I knew, and she was where she went when she drank without me, somewhere in herself. It was not the place where words could take you but another place even. I stood alone in the lobby for a while, looking out into the street. On the sidewalk outside the theater, sand had been scattered and the sand ate through the ice in ugly holes. I saw no one like my mother who passed by. She was wearing a red coat. Once she had said to me, You've fallen out of love with me, haven't you, and I knew she was thinking I was someone else, but this had happened only once.

I heard the music from the stage and I finally returned to our seats. There were not as many people in the audience as before. On stage with the magician was a woman in a bathing suit and high-heeled shoes holding a chain saw. The magician demonstrated that the saw was real by cutting up several pieces of wood with it. There was the smell of torn wood for everyone to smell and sawdust on the floor for all to see. Then a table was wheeled out and the lady lay down on it in her bathing suit which was in two pieces. Her stomach was very white. The magician talked and waved the saw around. I suspected he was planning to cut the woman in half and I was eager to see this. I hadn't the slightest fear about this at all. I did wonder if he would be able to put her together again or if he would cut her in half only. The magician said that what was about to happen was too dreadful to be seen directly, that he did not want anyone to faint from the sight, so he brought out a small screen and placed it in front of the lady so that we could no longer see her white stomach, although everyone could still see her face and her shoes. The screen seemed unnecessary to me and I would have preferred to have been seated on the other side of it. Several people in the audience screamed. The lady who was about to be sawed in half began to chew on her lip and her face looked worried.

It was then that my mother appeared on the stage. She was crouched over a little, for she didn't have her balance back from having climbed up there. She looked large and strange in her red coat. The coat, which I knew very well, seemed the strangest thing. Someone screamed again, but more uncertainly. My mother moved toward the magician, smiling and speaking and gesturing with her hands, and the magician said, No, I can't of course, you should know better than this, this is a performance, you can't just appear like this, please sit down. . . .

My mother said, But you don't understand I'm willing, though I know the hazards and it's not that I believe you, no one would believe you for a moment but you can trust me, that's right, your faith in me would be perfectly placed because I'm not a part of this, that's why I can be trusted because I don't know how it's done. . . .

Someone near me said, Is she kidding, that woman, what's her plan, she comes out of nowhere and wants to be cut in half. . . .

Lady . . . the magician said, and I thought a dog might appear for I knew a dog named Lady who had a collection of colored balls.

My mother said, Most of us don't understand I know and it's just as well because the things we understand that's it for them, that's just the way we are. . . .

She probably thought she was still in that place herself, but everything she said were the words coming from her mouth. Her lipstick was gone. Did she think she was in disguise, I wondered.

But why not, my mother said, to go and come back, that's what we want, that's why we're here and why can't we expect something to be done you can't expect us every day we get tired of showing up every day you can't get away with this forever then it was different but you should be thinking about the children. . . . She moved a little in a crooked fashion, speaking.

My God, said a voice, that woman's drunk. Sit down, please! someone said loudly.

My mother started to cry then and she stumbled and pushed her arms out before her as though she were pushing away someone who was trying to hold her, but no one was trying to hold her. The orchestra began to play and people began to clap. The usher ran out onto the stage and took my mother's hand. All this happened in an instant. He said something to her, he held her hand and she did not resist his holding it, then slowly the two of them moved down the few steps that led to the stage and up the aisle until they stopped beside me for the usher knew I was my mother's child. I followed them, of course, although in my mind I continued to sit in my seat. Everyone watched us leave. They did not notice that I remained there among them, watching too.

We went directly out of the theater and into the streets, my mother weeping on the little usher's arm. The shoulders of his jacket were of cardboard and there was gold braid looped around it. We were being taken away to be murdered which seemed reasonable to me. The usher's ears were large and he had a bump on his neck above the collar of his shirt. As we walked he said little soft things to my mother which gradually seemed to be comforting her. I hated him. It was not easy to walk together along the frozen sidewalks of the city. There was a belt on my mother's coat and I hung onto that as we moved unevenly along.

Look, I've pulled myself through, he said. You can pull yourself through. He was speaking to my mother.

We went into a coffee shop and sat down in a booth. You can collect yourself in here, he said. You can sit here as long as you want and drink coffee and no one will make you leave. He asked me if I wanted a donut. I would not speak to him. If he addressed me again, I thought, I would bite him. On the wall over the counter were pictures of sandwiches and pies. I did not want to be there and I did not take off either my mittens or my coat. The little usher went up to the counter and brought back coffee for my mother and a donut on a plate for me. Oh, my mother said, what have I done, and she swung her head from side to side.

I could tell right away about you, the usher said. You've got to pull yourself together. It took jumping off a bridge for me and breaking both legs before I got turned around. You don't want to let it go that far.

My mother looked at him. I can't imagine, my mother said.

Outside, a child passed by, walking with her sled. She looked behind her often and you could tell she was admiring the way the sled followed her so quickly on its runners.

You're a mother, the usher said to my mother, you've got to pull yourself through.

His kindness made me feel he had tied us up with rope. At last he left us and my mother lay her head down upon the table and fell asleep. I had never seen my mother sleeping and I watched her as she must once have watched me, the same way everyone watches a sleeping thing, not knowing how it would turn out or when. Then slowly I began to eat the donut with my mittened hands. The sour hair of the wool mingled with the tasteless crumbs and this utterly absorbed my attention. I pretended someone was feeding me.

As it happened, my mother was not able to pull herself through, but this was later. At the time, it was not so near to the end and when my mother woke we found the car and left Portland, my mother saying my name. Lizzie, she said. Lizzie. I felt as though I must be with her somewhere and that she knew that too, but not in that old blue convertible traveling home in the dark, the soft, stained roof ballooning up in the way I knew it looked from the outside. I got out of it, but it took me years.

II.

The Story

AS COMPRESSED NOVEL

Whole lives are encompassed in stories that take the form of a compressed novel. Though they may vary radically in length and technique, we see life cycles in each.

John Updike

PLAYING WITH DYNAMITE

ONE ASPECT OF CHILDHOOD Fanshawe had not expected to return in old age was the mutability of things—the willingness of a chair, say, to become a leggy animal in the corner of his vision, or the sensation that the solid darkness of an unlit room is teeming with inimical presences. Headlights floated on the skin of Fanshawe's windshield like cherry blossoms on black water, whether signifying four motorcycles or two trucks he had no idea, and he drove braced, every second, to crash into an invisible obstacle.

It had taken him over fifty years to internalize the physical laws that overruled a ten-year-old's sense of nightmare possibilities—to overcome irrational fear and to make himself at home in the linear starkness of a universe without a supernatural. As he felt the ineluctable logic of decay tightening its grip on his body, these laws seemed dispensable; he had used them, and now was bored with them. Perhaps an object *could* travel faster than the speed of light, and we each have an immortal soul. It didn't, terribly, matter. The headlines in the paper, with their campaigns and pestilences, seemed directed at somebody else, like the new movies and television specials and pennant races and beer commercials—somebody younger and more easily excited, somebody for whom the world still had weight. Living now in death's immediate neighborhood, he was developing a soldier's jaunty indifference; if the bathtub in the corner of his eye as he shaved were to take on the form of a polar bear and start mauling him, it wouldn't be the end of the world. Even the end of the world, strange to say, wouldn't be the end of the world.

His wife was younger than he, and spryer. Frequently, she impatiently passed him on the stairs. One Sunday afternoon, when they were going downstairs to greet some guests, he felt her at his side like a little gust of wind, and then he saw her, amazingly reduced in size, kneeling on the stairs, which were thickly carpeted, several steps below him. He called her name, and thought of reaching down to restrain her, but she, having groped for a baluster and missed, rapidly continued on her way, sledding on her shins all the way to the bottom, where she reclined at the feet of their astonished visitors, who had knocked and entered. "She's all right," Fanshawe assured them, descending at his more stately pace, for he knew, watching her surprising descent, that she had met no bone-breaking snag in her progress.

And, indeed, she did rise up as resiliently as a cartoon cat, brimming with girlish embarrassment, though secretly pleased, he could tell, with having so spontaneously provided their little party a lively initial topic of discussion. Their guests, who included a young doctor, set her up on the sofa, with a bag of ice on the more bruised and abraded of her shins, and conducted a conversational investigation that concluded she had caught her heel in the hem of her dress, unusually long, in the new fashion. A little rip in the stitching of the hem seemed to confirm the analysis and to remove all mystery from the event.

Yet later, after she had limped into bed beside her husband, she asked, "Wasn't I good, not to tell everybody how you pushed me?"

"I never touched you," Fanshawe protested, but without much passion, because he was not entirely sure. He remembered only her appearance, oddly shrunk by perspective on the stairs in their downward linear recession, and the flash of his synapses that pictured his reaching out and restraining her, and his dreamlike inability to do so. She blamed him, he knew, for not having caught her, for not having done the impossible, and this was as good as his pushing her. She was, in their old age, a late-blooming feminist, and he accepted his role in her mind as the murderous man with whom she happened to be stuck, in a world of murderous men. The forces that had once driven them together now seemed to her all the product of male conspiracy. If he had not literally pushed her on the stairs, he had compelled her to live in a house with a grandiose stairway and had dictated, in collusion with male fashion designers, the dangerous length of her skirt and height of her heels; and this was as good as a push. He tried to recall his emotions as he watched her body cascade out of his reach, and came up with a cool pang of what might be called polite astonishment, underneath a high hum of constant grief, like the cosmic background radiation. He recalled a view of a town's rooftops covered in snow, beneath a dome of utterly emptied blue sky.

His wife relented, seeing him so docilely ready to internalize her proposition. "Sweetie, you didn't push me," she said. "But I did think you might have caught me."

"It was all too quick," he said, unconvinced by his own self-defense. With the reality of natural law had receded any conviction of his own virtue. Their guests that afternoon had included his wife's daughter, by an old and almost mythical marriage. He could scarcely distinguish his stepchildren from his children by his own former marriage, or tell kin from spouses. He was polite to all these tan, bouncy, smooth-skinned, sure-footed, well-dressed young adults—darlings of the advertisers, the now generation—who claimed to be related to him, and he was flattered by their mannerly attentions, but he secretly doubted the reality of the connection. His own mother, some years ago, had lain dead for two days at the bottom of the cellar stairs of a house where he had allowed her to live alone, feeble and senile. He was an unnatural son and father both, why not a murderous husband? He knew that the incident would live in his wife's head as if he had in fact pushed her, and thus he might as well remember it also, for the sake of marital harmony.

/   /   /   /

At the Central Park Zoo, the yellow-white polar bears eerily float in the cold water behind the plate glass, water the blue-green color on a pack of Kool cigarettes (the last cigarettes Fanshawe had smoked, thinking the menthol possibly medicinal), and if a polar bear, dripping wet, were to surface up through his bathtub tomorrow morning while he shaved, the fatal swat of the big clawed paw would feel like a cloud of pollen.

Things used to be more substantial. In those middle years, as Fanshawe gropingly recalled them, you are hammering out your destiny on bodies still molten and glowing. One day, he had taken his children ice-skating on a frozen river—its winding course miraculously become a road, hard as steel, hissing beneath their steel edges. As he stood talking to the mother of some other young children, his six-year-old son had fallen at his feet, without a cry or thump, simply melting out of the lower edge of Fanshawe's vision, which was fastened on the reddened cheeks and shining eyes, the perfect teeth and flirtatiously curved lips of Lorna Kramer, his fellow-parent. A noise softly bubbled up through the cracks in their conversation; the little body on the ice was whimpering, and when Fanshawe impatiently directed his son to shut up and to get up, the muffled words "I can't" rose as if from beneath the ice.

It developed that the boy's leg was broken. Just standing there complaining about the cold, he had lost his balance with his skate caught in a crack, and twisted his shinbone to the point of fracture. How soft and slender our growing skeletons are! Fanshawe, once his wife and the other woman and their clustering children had made the problem clear to him, carried the boy in his arms up the steep and snowy riverbank. He felt magnificent, doing so. This was real life, he remembered feeling—the idyllic Sunday afternoon suddenly crossed by disaster's shadow, the gentle and strenuous rescue, the ride to the hospital, the emergency-room formalities, the arrival of the jolly orthopedic surgeon in his parka and Ski-Doo boots, the laying on of the cast in warm plaster strips, the drying tears, the imminent healing. Children offer access to the tragic, to the great dark that stands outside our windows, and in the urgency of their needs bestow significance; their fragile lives veer toward the dangerous margins and measure the breadth beyond the narrow path we have learned to tread.

"It wouldn't have happened, of course," his first wife said, "if you had been paying attention to him instead of to Lorna."

"What does Lorna have to do with it? She was the first one to realize that the poor kid wasn't kidding."

"Lorna has everything to do with it, as you perfectly well know."

"This is paranoid talk," he said. "This is Nixon-era paranoid talk."

"I've gotten used to your hurting me, but I'm not going to have you hurting our children, Geoff."

"Now we're getting really crazy."

"Don't you think I know why you decided to take us all ice-skating, when poor Timmy and Rose don't even have skates that fit? It was so unlike you—you usually just want to laze around reading the *Times* and complaining about your hangover and watching 'Wide World of Golf.' It was to see her. Her or somebody else. That whole party crowd, you don't get enough of them Saturday nights anymore. Why don't you go live with them? Live with somebody else, anybody except me! Go. Go!"

She didn't mean it, but it was thrilling to see her so energized, such a fury, her eyes flashing, her hair crackling, her slicing gestures carving large doomed territories out of the air. At that age, Fanshawe saw now, we are creating selves, potent and plastic, making and unmaking homes, the world in our hands. We are playing with dynamite. All around them, as he and his wife stood hip-deep in children, marriages blew up. Marriage counselors, child psychiatrists, lawyers, real-estate agents prospered in the ruins. Now, in old age, it remained only to generate a little business for the mortician, and an hour's pleasant work for the local clergymen. Just as insurance salesmen had at last stopped approaching him, and the moviemakers had written him out of audience demographics, so the armies of natural law, needed all over the globe to detonate dynamite where it counted, left him to wander in a twilight of inconsequence.

In early August, a pair of birds decided they had to build a nest on the Fanshawes' porch. They were warblers too far north, if he could trust his eyes and the battered old bird book. Something must have gone wrong with their biological clocks. It was too late in the season for nesting, but, even more willful than children, they persisted, while warbling back and forth furiously, in piling up twigs and wands of hay on the small shelves created by the capitals of his porch pillars. The twiggy accumulations blew off, or Mrs. Fanshawe briskly knocked them off with a broom. She had always been less sentimental than he. It was her clean white porch and her porch boards that would be splattered with bird shit. But the warblers kept coming back, as children keep demanding to go to an amusement park or to buy a certain kind of heavily advertised candy, until finally, the adult world wearying, they have their way. A pillar next to the house afforded shelter enough from the wind; the twigs and grass accumulated, and from its precarious pile the stone-colored head of the female bird haughtily stared down one afternoon when the Fanshawes returned from a day in town shopping. The warbling ceased. The male had vanished. Then, after two weeks, the female, it dawned on the Fanshawes, had vanished. Vanished without a warble of goodbye. All the time she had been in the nest, her profile had radiated anger.

Getting out the stepladder, Fanshawe fetched down an empty, eggless nest, its rim tidily circled round with guano, its rough materials worked in the center to a perfect expectant cavity. A nest in vain. What ever had those birds been thinking of? His impulse was to save the nest—his mother had always been saving bird's nests, setting them in bookshelves, or on top of the piano—but his wife held out an open garbage bag, as though the innocent wild artifact were teeming with germs. Bird's nests shouldn't go in garbage bags, he thought, but dropped it in. We're in this together, he aimlessly thought, as in the shade of the porch his wife stared up at him, with shining dark eyes, trying to control her impatience as he wrestled with his sentimental scruple.

At his fifth (at a guess) birthday party, a piece of cake mysteriously vanished from the plate in front of him and reappeared a few seconds later in his lap. He had never touched it, so it must have been a miracle, there in the candlelight and childish babble. He could still see it lying on his corduroy lap, the cake peeping out from its inverted dish—a chocolate cake with caramel icing of a type only his mother had ever made for him, its sugary stiffness most delicious where the icing between the layers met the outside layer in a thick, sweet T. A few years later, lying in bed with a fever, he had seen a black stick, at a slight angle, hop along beyond the edge of the bed, like one of the abstract sections of *Fantasia*. In those years, the knit of the physical world was stretched thin, and held a number of holes. When he was in the fourth grade, his new glasses vanished from his pocket, in their round-ended case with its murderous metallic *snap,* and a week later, cutting across a weedy vacant lot thinking of them and of how hard his father would have to work to buy him another pair, he looked down, and there the case was, like a long egg in the tangled damp grass. Inside it, the glasses had become steamy, as if worn by an overexcited, myopic ghost. Perhaps this was less a miracle than the transposed birthday cake, but the fact that he had been thinking of them *at that very moment* made it the strangest of all. Could it be that our mind does, secretly, control the atoms? On that possibility, Fanshawe had never quite broken his childish habit of prayer. Yet, staring at a model airplane that had unaccountably disintegrated during the night, or confronting the bulging shadows at the head of the stairs, it was hard to think of God and Jesus; one seemed to be down among frivolous demons, in a supernatural no more elevated in its aims than a Disney animated feature.

That curious cartoon lightness and jumpiness had returned. Fanshawe would find himself in a room with no knowledge of how he got there—as if the film had been broken and spliced. As he lay in bed, the house throbbed with footsteps, heard through the pillow, that fell silent when he lifted his head. Perhaps it had been his heartbeat.

In the sedate neighborhood where he now lived, everyone was old, more or less. For years he had watched the neighbor to his right, a widower, slowly deteriorate, his stride becoming a shuffle, his house and yard gradually growing shabbier and shaggier, inch by inch, season by season, in increments so small that only a speeded-up film would show the process. The two men would converse across the fence from time to time; Fanshawe once or twice offered to do some pruning for his neighbor. "No, thanks," would be the answer. "I'll get to it, when I'm feeling a little more lively." We look ahead and see random rises and falls; the linear diminishment so plain to others is invisible to us.

One Saturday morning, a fire engine appeared along his neighbor's curb, though there was no sign of smoke. The fireman, who had moved up the front walk with some haste, stayed inside so long that Fanshawe grew tired of spying. An hour later, with the fire engine still parked there, its great throbbing motor wastefully running, a small foreign convertible appeared, and a fashionably dressed young woman—all things are relative, perhaps she was forty—uncoiled rapidly out of the low-slung interior, flashing her long smooth shins, and clicked up the flagstone walk. This was his neighbor's daughter, who explained to Fanshawe later, at the party after the funeral, that her father had been found by the cleaning lady, sitting up in his favorite chair, shaved and dressed in a coat and tie as if expecting a caller. So that was death, Fanshawe realized—a jerky comedy of unusual comings and goings on a Saturday morning, followed in a few days by a funeral and a "For Sale" sign on the house.

"Thank you for being such a good neighbor to my father," the daughter said. "He often mentioned it."

"But I wasn't," Fanshawe protested. "I never did a thing for him."

Why had the dead man benignly lied? Why had the cleaning lady called the fire department and not the police? And why had the fireman never shut off his engine, discharging carbon monoxide and consuming fossil fuel at taxpayer expense? Fanshawe didn't ask.

He often felt now, going through the motions of living— shaving, dressing, responding to questions, measuring up to small emergencies—that he was enacting a part in a play at the end of its run, while mentally rehearsing his lines in the next play to be put on. It was repertory theater, evidently. When he remembered how death had once loomed at him, so vivid and large that it had a distinct smell, like the scent of chalk up close to the schoolroom blackboard, he marveled, rather patronizingly. When had he ceased to fear death—or, so to say, to grasp it? The moment was as clear in his mind as a black-and-white-striped gate at a border crossing: the moment when he first slept with Lorna Kramer.

How inky her black eyes seemed, amid the snowy whiteness of the sheets! There was snow outside, too, hushing the world in sunstruck brilliance. Melt-water tapped in the aluminum gutters. There had been a feeling of coolness, of freshly laundered sheets, of contacts never before achieved, by fingertips icy with nervousness. He had peeled off her black lace bra— her back arched up from the mattress to give him access to the catches—almost reluctantly, knowing there would be a white flash that would obliterate everything that had existed of his life before. She had smiled encouragingly, timorously. They were in it together. Her teeth were, after all, less than perfect, with protuberant canines that made the bicuspids next to them seem shadowy. Her pupils were contracted to the size of pencil leads by the relentless light; he had never seen anything so clearly as he saw her now, the fine mechanism of her, the specialized flesh of her lips, the trip wires of her hair; he got out of bed to lower the shade, the sight of her was such a blinding assault.

A dull reddish bird, a female cardinal, was hopping about on the delicately tracked-up snow beneath the bird feeder a story below, pecking at scattered seed. A whole blameless town of roofs and smoking chimneys and snow-drenched trees stretched beyond, under an overturned bowl of blue light that made Fanshawe's vision wince. He drew the curtain on it and in merciful twilight returned to where Lorna lay still as a stick. He heard his blood striding in his skull, he felt so full of life. Sex or death, you pick your poison. That had been forever ago. She was still younger and spryer than he, but all things were relative. He did not envy those forever-ago people, for whom the world had such a weight of consequence. Like the Titans, they seemed beautiful but sad in their brief heyday, transition figures between chaos and an airier pantheon.

Lex Williford

⌒⌒

PENDERGAST'S DAUGHTER

L EANN AND I WERE DRIVING to her father's new A-frame on Lake Nacogdoches, and I was nervous about meeting her folks for the first time.

Relax, Leann said. Drink a few Old Mils with Dad, maybe catch a large mouth or two off the dock Saturday. When I got the nerve Sunday, she said, I could spring the news on the old man about wanting to marry his little girl. Then the two of us could get the hell out, head on back to Dallas. Lighten up, she kept saying.

When we got there her kid brother ran to my car, flinging his arms all around. An acre lot across a little inlet was being cleared, flat red clay and loblollies tied with red ribbons. A bulldozer was ramming one of the pines without much luck. Hurry, Leann's brother said.

The lake house was all glass in front so from the gravel drive we could see Mrs. Pendergast inside, slapping the old man's face. Once, twice, then again. She shouted something about him not having any goddamn imagination, about some girl, twenty-six years old, young enough to be his goddamn daughter. He took her flat palms rigid-faced, just stood there blinking at her. Then his face fell all apart, and he hit her in the sternum with his fist. She staggered back through the open door and up to the balcony rail as he hit her over and over again.

Do something, Leann shouted at me. But I just stood there. I just watched till the old man pushed his wife over the rail.

At the hospital in Lufkin I told Leann, I don't know what the hell happened to me. But then an intern came into the waiting room and said her mom would be all right, just some stitches, some bruised ribs.

Next week I must have left a hundred messages on Leann's answering machine. I'm sorry, they said, you got to believe me.

I remember we used to shower together every morning I stayed at her garage apartment in University Park. I'd slick her taut brown shoulders with Zest and I'd think, Jesus, this is good.

III.

The Story

AS PROSE POEM

Marvelously condensed, these stories employ a careful succession of images that convey the story's action and meaning. These images travel through the story, with new meanings attaching to them en route. With each recurrence, the narrative is advanced.

SNOW

I REMEMBER THE COLD NIGHT you brought in a pile of logs and a chipmunk jumped off as you lowered your arms. "What do you think *you're* doing in here?" you said, as it ran through the living room. It went through the library and stopped at the front door as though it knew the house well. This would be difficult for anyone to believe, except perhaps as the subject of a poem. Our first week in the house was spent scraping, finding some of the house's secrets, like wallpaper underneath wallpaper. In the kitchen, a pattern of white-gold trellises supported purple grapes as big and round as Ping-Pong balls. When we painted the walls yellow, I thought of the bits of grape that remained underneath and imagined the vine popping through, the way some plants can tenaciously push through anything. The day of the big snow, when you had to shovel the walk and couldn't find your cap and asked me how to wind a towel so that it would stay on your head— you, in the white towel turban, like a crazy king of snow. People liked the idea of our being together, leaving the city for the country. So many people visited, and the fireplace made all of them want to tell amazing stories: the child who happened to be standing on the right corner when the door of the ice-cream truck came open and hundreds of Popsicles crashed out; the man standing on the beach, sand sparkling in the sun, one bit glinting more than the rest, stooping to find a diamond ring. Did they talk about amazing things because they thought we'd turn into one of them? Now I think they probably guessed it wouldn't work. It was as hopeless as giving a child a matched cup and saucer. Remember the night, out on the lawn, knee-deep in snow, chins pointed at the sky as the wind whirled down all that whiteness? It seemed that the world had been turned upside down, and we were looking into an enormous field of Queen Anne's lace. Later, headlights off, our car was the first to ride through the newly fallen snow. The world outside the car looked solarized.

You remember it differently. You remember that the cold settled in stages, that a small curve of light was shaved from the moon night after night, until you were no longer surprised the sky was black, that the chipmunk ran to hide in the dark, not simply to a door that led to its escape. Our visitors told the same stories people always tell. One night, giving me a lesson in storytelling, you said, "Any life will seem dramatic if you omit mention of most of it."

This, then, for drama: I drove back to that house not long ago. It was April, and Allen had died. In spite of all the visitors, Allen, next door, had been the good friend in bad times. I sat with his wife in their living room, looking out the glass doors to the backyard, and there was Allen's pool, still covered with black plastic that had been stretched across it for winter. It had rained, and as the rain fell, the cover collected more and more water until it finally spilled onto the concrete. When I left that day, I drove past what had been our house. Three or four crocuses were blooming in the front—just a few dots of white, no field of snow. I felt embarrassed for them. They couldn't compete.

This is a story, told the way you say stories should be told: Somebody grew up, fell in love, and spent a winter with her lover in the country. This, of course, is the barest outline, and futile to discuss. It's as pointless as throwing birdseed on the ground while snow still falls fast. Who expects small things to survive when even the largest get lost? People forget years and remember moments. Seconds and symbols are left to sum things up: the black shroud over the pool. Love, in its shortest form, becomes a word. What I remember about all that time is one winter. The snow. Even now, saying "snow," my lips move so that they kiss the air.

No mention has been made of the snowplow that seemed always to be there, scraping snow off our narrow road—an artery cleared, though neither of us could have said where the heart was.

THE GRAVE

THE GRANDFATHER, DEAD for more than thirty years, had been twice disturbed in his long repose by the constancy and possessiveness of his widow. She removed his bones first to Louisiana and then to Texas as if she had set out to find her own burial place, knowing well she would never return to the places she had left. In Texas she set up a small cemetery in a corner of her first farm, and as the family connection grew, and oddments of relations came over from Kentucky to settle, it contained at last about twenty graves. After the grandmother's death, part of her land was to be sold for the benefit of certain of her children, and the cemetery happened to lie in the part set aside for sale. It was necessary to take up the bodies and bury them again in the family plot in the big new public cemetery, where the grandmother had been buried. At last her husband was to lie beside her for eternity, as she had planned.

The family cemetery had been a pleasant small neglected garden of tangled rose bushes and ragged cedar trees and cypress, the simple flat stones rising out of uncropped sweet-smelling wild grass. The graves were lying open and empty one burning day when Miranda and her brother Paul, who often went together to hunt rabbits and doves, propped their twenty-two Winchester rifles carefully against the rail fence, climbed over and explored among the graves. She was nine years old and he was twelve.

They peered into the pits all shaped alike with such purposeful accuracy, and looking at each other with pleased adventurous eyes, they said in solemn tones: "These were graves!" trying by words to shape a special, suitable emotion in their minds, but they felt nothing except an agreeable thrill of wonder: they were seeing a new sight, doing something they had not done before. In them both was also a small disappointment at the entire commonplaceness of the actual spectacle. Even if it had once contained a coffin for years upon years, when the coffin was gone a grave was just a hole in the ground. Miranda leaped into the pit that had held her grandfather's bones. Scratching around aimlessly and pleasurably as any young animal, she scooped up a lump of earth and weighed it in her palm. It had a pleasantly sweet, corrupt smell, being mixed with cedar needles and small leaves, and as the crumbs fell apart, she saw a silver dove no larger than a hazel nut, with spread wings and a neat fan-shaped tail. The breast had a deep round hollow in it. Turning it up to the fierce sunlight, she saw that the inside of the hollow was cut in little whorls. She scrambled out, over the pile of loose earth that had fallen back into one end of the grave, calling to Paul that she had found something, he must guess what . . . His head appeared smiling over the rim of another grave. He waved a closed hand at her. "I've got something too!" They ran to compare treasures, making a game of it, so many guesses each, all wrong, and a final showdown with opened palms. Paul had found a thin wide gold ring carved with intricate flowers and leaves. Miranda was smitten at the sight of the ring and wished to have it. Paul seemed more impressed by the dove. They made a trade, with some little bickering. After he had got the dove in his hand, Paul said, "Don't you know what this is? This is a screw head for a *coffin!* . . . I'll bet nobody else in the world has one like this!"

Miranda glanced at it without covetousness. She had the gold ring on her thumb; it fitted perfectly. "Maybe we ought to go now," she said, "maybe one of the niggers'll see us and tell somebody." They knew the land had been sold, the cemetery was no longer theirs, and they felt like trespassers. They climbed back over the fence, slung their rifles loosely under their arms—they had been shooting at targets with various kinds of firearms since they were seven years old—and set out to look for the rabbits and doves or whatever small game might happen along. On these expeditions Miranda always followed at Paul's heels along the path, obeying instructions about handling her gun when going through fences; learning how to stand it up properly so it would not slip and fire unexpectedly; how to wait her time for a shot and not just bang away in the air without looking, spoiling shots for Paul, who really could hit things if given a chance. Now and then, in her excitement at seeing birds whizz up suddenly before her face, or a rabbit leap across her very toes, she lost her head, and almost without sighting she flung her rifle up and pulled the trigger. She hardly ever hit any sort of mark. She had no proper sense of hunting at all. Her brother would be often completely disgusted with her. "You don't care whether you get your bird or not," he said. "That's no way to hunt." Miranda could not understand his indignation. She had seen him smash his hat and yell with fury when he had missed his aim. "What I like about shooting," said Miranda, with exasperating inconsequence, "is pulling the trigger and hearing the noise."

"Then, by golly," said Paul, "whyn't you go back to the range and shoot at bulls-eyes?"

"I'd just as soon," said Miranda, "only like this, we walk around more."

"Well, you just stay behind and stop spoiling my shots," said Paul, who, when he made a kill, wanted to be certain he had made it. Miranda, who alone brought down a bird once in twenty rounds, always claimed as her own any game they got when they fired at the same moment. It was tiresome and unfair and her brother was sick of it.

"Now, the first dove we see, or the first rabbit, is mine," he told her. "And the next will be yours. Remember that and don't get smarty."

"What about snakes?" asked Miranda idly. "Can I have the first snake?"

Waving her thumb gently and watching her gold ring glitter, Miranda lost interest in shooting. She was wearing her summer roughing outfit: dark blue overalls, a light blue shirt, a hired-man's straw hat, and thick brown sandals. Her brother had the same outfit except his was a sober hickory-nut color. Ordinarily Miranda preferred her overalls to any other dress, though it was making rather a scandal in the countryside, for the year was 1903, and in the back country the law of female decorum had teeth in it. Her father had been criticized for letting his girls dress like boys and go careering around astride barebacked horses. Big sister Maria, the really independent and fearless one, in spite of her rather affected ways, rode at a dead run with only a rope knotted around her horse's nose. It was said the motherless family was running down, with the Grandmother no longer there to hold it together. It was known that she had discriminated against her son Harry in her will, and that he was in straits about money. Some of his old neighbors reflected with vicious satisfaction that now he would probably not be so stiffnecked, nor have any more high-stepping horses either. Miranda knew this, though she could not say how. She had met along the road old women of the kind who smoked corn-cob pipes, who had treated her grandmother with most sincere respect. They slanted their gummy old eyes side-ways at the granddaughter and said, "Ain't you ashamed of yoself, Missy? It's aginst the Scriptures to dress like that. Whut yo Pappy thinkin about?" Miranda, with her powerful social sense, which was like a fine set of antennae radiating from every pore of her skin, would feel ashamed because she knew well it was rude and ill-bred to shock anybody, even bad-tempered old crones, though she had faith in her father's judgment and was perfectly comfortable in the clothes. Her father had said, "They're just what you need, and they'll save your dresses for school . . . " This sounded quite simple and natural to her. She had been brought up in rigorous economy. Wastefulness was vulgar. It was also a sin. These were truths; she had heard them repeated many times and never once disputed.

Now the ring, shining with the serene purity of fine gold on her rather grubby thumb, turned her feelings against her overalls and sockless feet, toes sticking through the thick brown leather straps. She wanted to go back to the farmhouse, take a good cold bath, dust herself with plenty of Maria's violet talcum powder—provided Maria was not present to object, of course—put on the thinnest, most becoming dress she owned, with a big sash, and sit in a wicker chair under the trees . . . These things were not all she wanted, of course; she had vague stirrings of desire for luxury and a grand way of living which could not take precise form in her imagination but were founded on family legend of past wealth and leisure. These immediate comforts were what she could have, and she wanted them at once. She lagged rather far behind Paul, and once she thought of just turning back without a word and going home. She stopped, thinking that Paul would never do that to her, and so she would have to tell him. When a rabbit leaped, she let Paul have it without dispute. He killed it with one shot.

When she came up with him, he was already kneeling, examining the wound, the rabbit trailing from his hands. "Right through the head," he said complacently, as if he had aimed for it. He took out his sharp, competent bowie knife and started to skin the body. He did it very cleanly and quickly. Uncle Jimbilly knew how to prepare the skins so that Miranda always had fur coats for her dolls, for though she never cared much for her dolls she liked seeing them in fur coats. The children knelt facing each other over the dead animal. Miranda watched admiringly while her brother stripped the skin away as if he were taking off a glove. The flayed flesh emerged dark scarlet, sleek, firm; Miranda with thumb and finger felt the long fine muscles with the silvery flat strips binding them to the joints. Brother lifted the oddly bloated belly. "Look," he said, in a low amazed voice. "It was going to have young ones."

Very carefully he slit the thin flesh from the center ribs to the flanks, and a scarlet bag appeared. He slit again and pulled the bag open and there lay a bundle of tiny rabbits, each wrapped in a thin scarlet veil. The brother pulled these off and there they were, dark gray, their sleek wet down lying in minute even ripples, like a baby's head just washed, their unbelievably small delicate ears folded close, their little blind faces almost featureless.

Miranda said, "Oh, I want to *see,*" under her breath. She looked and looked—excited but not frightened, for she was accustomed to the sight of animals killed in hunting—filled with pity and astonishment and a kind of shocked delight in the wonderful little creatures for their own sakes, they were so pretty. She touched one of them ever so carefully, "Ah, there's blood running over them," she said and began to tremble without knowing why. Yet she wanted most deeply to see and to know. Having seen, she felt at once as if she had known all along. The very memory of her former ignorance faded, she had always known just this. No one had ever told her anything outright, she had been rather unobservant of the animal life around her because she was so accustomed to animals. They seemed simply disorderly and unaccountably rude in their habits, but altogether natural and not very interesting. Her brother had spoken as if he had known about everything all along. He may have seen this all before. He had never said a word to her, but she knew now a part at least of what he knew. She understood a little of the secret, formless intuitions in her own mind and body, which had been clearing up, taking form, so gradually and so steadily she had not realized that she was learning what she had to know. Paul said cautiously, as if he were talking about something forbidden: "They were just about ready to be born." His voice dropped on the last word.

"I know," said Miranda, "like kittens. I know, like babies." She was quietly and terribly agitated, standing again with her rifle under her arm, looking down at the bloody heap. "I don't want the skin," she said, "I won't have it." Paul buried the young rabbits again in their mother's body, wrapped the skin around her, carried her to a clump of sage bushes, and hid her away. He came out again at once and said to Miranda, with an eager friendliness, a confidential tone quite unusual in him, as if he were taking her into an important secret on equal terms: "Listen now. Now you listen to me, and don't ever forget. Don't you ever tell a living soul that you saw this. Don't tell a soul. Don't tell Dad because I'll get into trouble. He'll say I'm leading you into things you ought not to do. He's always saying that. So now don't you go and forget and blab out sometime the way you're always doing . . . Now, that's a secret. Don't you tell."

Miranda never told, she did not even wish to tell anybody. She thought about the whole worrisome affair with confused unhappiness for a few days. Then it sank quietly into her mind and was heaped over by accumulated thousands of impressions, for nearly twenty years. One day she was picking her path among the puddles and crushed refuse of a market street in a strange city of a strange country, when without warning, plain and clear in its true colors as if she looked through a frame upon a scene that had not stirred nor changed since the moment it happened, the episode of that far-off day leaped from its burial place before her mind's eye. She was so reasonlessly horrified she halted suddenly staring, the scene before her eyes dimmed by the vision back of them. An Indian vendor had held up before her a tray of dyed sugar sweets, in the shapes of all kinds of small creatures: birds, baby chicks, baby rabbits, lambs, baby pigs. They were in gay colors and smelled of vanilla, maybe . . . It was a very hot day and the smell in the market, with its piles of raw flesh and wilting flowers, was like the mingled sweetness and corruption she had smelled that other day in the empty cemetery at home: the day she had remembered always until now vaguely as the time she and her brother had found treasure in the opened graves. Instantly upon this thought the dreadful vision faded, and she saw clearly her brother, whose childhood face she had forgotten, standing again in the blazing sunshine, again twelve years old, a pleased sober smile in his eyes, turning the silver dove over and over in his hands.

IV.

The Story

AS ESSAY OR COMMENTARY

Stories that take the form of an essay or commentary serve to illustrate—or to demonstrate—a point. In contrast to the model of memoir or confession, here the narrative builds or unfolds an argument filtered through the characters' individual voices, distinctive deeds, or crucial decisions.

NILDA

Nilda was my brother's girlfriend.
This is how all these stories begin.

She was Dominican from here and had super-long hair, like those Pentecostal girls, and a chest you wouldn't believe—I'm talking world-class. Rafa would sneak her down into our basement bedroom after our mother went to bed and do her to whatever was on the radio right then. The two of them had to let me stay, because if my mother heard me upstairs on the couch everybody's ass would have been fried. And since I wasn't about to spend my night out in the bushes this is how it was.

Rafa didn't make no noise, just a low something that resembled breathing. Nilda was the one. She seemed to be trying to hold back from crying the whole time. It was crazy hearing her like that. The Nilda I'd grown up with was one of the quietest girls you'd ever meet. She let her hair wall away her face and read *The New Mutants,* and the only time she looked straight at anything was when she looked out a window.

But that was before she'd gotten that chest, before that slash of black hair had gone from something to pull on the bus to something to stroke in the dark. The new Nilda wore stretch pants and Iron Maiden shirts; she had already run away from her mother's and ended up at a group home; she'd already slept with Toño and Nestor and Little Anthony from Parkwood, older guys. She crashed over at our apartment a lot because she hated her moms, who was the neighborhood borracha. In the morning she slipped out before my mother woke up and found her. Waited for heads at the bus stop, fronted

like she'd come from her own place, same clothes as the day
before and greasy hair so everybody thought her a skank.
Waited for my brother and didn't talk to anybody and nobody
talked to her, because she'd always been one of those quiet,
semi-retarded girls who you couldn't talk to without being
dragged into a whirlpool of dumb stories. If Rafa decided that
he wasn't going to school then she'd wait near our apartment
until my mother left for work. Sometimes Rafa let her in right
away. Sometimes he slept late and she'd wait across the street,
building letters out of pebbles until she saw him crossing the
living room.

She had big stupid lips and a sad moonface and the driest
skin. Always rubbing lotion on it and cursing the moreno
father who'd given it to her.

It seemed like she was always waiting for my brother. Nights
she'd knock and I'd let her in and we'd sit on the couch while
Rafa was off at his job at the carpet factory or working out at the
gym. I'd show her my newest comics and she'd read them real
close, but as soon as Rafa showed up she'd throw them in my lap
and jump into his arms. I missed you, she'd say in a little-girl
voice, and Rafa would laugh. You should have seen him in those
days: he had the face bones of a saint. Then Mami's door would
open and Rafa would detach himself and cowboy-saunter over
to Mami and say, You got something for me to eat, vieja? Claro
que sí, Mami'd say, trying to put her glasses on.

He had us all, the way only a pretty nigger can.

Once when Rafa was late from the job and we were alone in
the apartment a long time, I asked her about the group home.
It was three weeks before the end of the school year and everybody had entered the Do-Nothing Stage. I was fourteen and
reading *Dhalgren* for the second time; I had an I.Q. that would
have broken you in two but I would have traded it in for a
halfway decent face in a second.

It was pretty cool up there, she said. She was pulling on the
front of her halter top, trying to air her chest out. The food was

bad but there were a lot of cute guys in the house with me. They *all* wanted me.

She started chewing on a nail. Even the guys who worked there were calling me after I left, she said.

The only reason Rafa went after her was because his last full-time girlfriend had gone back to Guyana—she was this dougla girl with a single eyebrow and skin to die for—and because Nilda had pushed up to him. She'd only been back from the group home a couple of months, but by then she'd already gotten a rep as a cuero. A lot of the Dominican girls in town were on some serious lockdown—we saw them on the bus and at school and maybe at the Pathmark, but since most families knew exactly what kind of tígueres were roaming the neighborhood these girls weren't allowed to hang out. Nilda was different. She was brown trash. Her moms was a mean-ass drunk and always running around South Amboy with her white boyfriends—which is a long way of saying Nilda could hang and, man, did she ever. Always out in the world, always cars stopping where she was smoking cigarettes. Before I even knew she was back from the group home she got scooped up by this older nigger from the back apartments. He kept her on his dick for almost four months, and I used to see them driving around in his fucked-up rust-eaten Sunbird while I delivered my papers. Motherfucker was like three hundred years old, but because he had a car and a record collection and foto albums from his Vietnam days and because he bought her clothes to replace the old shit she was wearing, Nilda was all lost on him.

I hated this nigger with a passion, but when it came to guys there was no talking to Nilda. I used to ask her, What's up with Wrinkle Dick? And she would get so mad she wouldn't speak to me for days, and then I'd get this note, *I want you to respect my man. Whatever*, I'd write back. Then the old cat bounced, no one knew where, the usual scenario in my neighborhood, and for a couple of months she got tossed by those cats from Parkwood. On Thursdays, which was comic-book day, she'd drop in to see what I'd picked up and she'd talk to me about how unhappy she was. We'd sit together until it got dark and then her beeper would fire up and she'd peer into its display and say, I have to go. Sometimes I could grab her and pull her back on the couch, and we'd stay there a long time, me waiting for her to fall in love with me, her waiting for whatever, but other times she'd be serious. I have to go see my man, she'd say.

One of those comic-book days she saw my brother coming back from his five-mile run. Rafa was still boxing then and he was cut up like crazy, the muscles on his chest and abdomen so striated they looked like something out of a Frazetta drawing. He noticed her because she was wearing these ridiculous shorts and this tank that couldn't have blocked a sneeze and a thin roll of stomach was poking from between the fabrics and he smiled at her and she got real serious and uncomfortable and he told her to fix him some iced tea and she told him to fix it himself. You a guest here, he said. You should be earning your fucking keep. He went into the shower and as soon as he did she was in the kitchen stirring, and I told her to leave it, but she said, I might as well. We drank all of it.

I wanted to warn her, tell her he was a monster, but she was already headed for him at the speed of light.

The next day Rafa's car turned up broken—what a coincidence—so he took the bus to school and when he was walking past our seat he took her hand and pulled her to her feet and she said, Get off me. Her eyes were pointed straight at the floor. I just want to show you something, he said. She was pulling with her arm but the rest of her was ready to go. Come on, Rafa said, and finally she went. Save my seat, she said over her shoulder, and I was like, Don't worry about it. Before we even swung onto 516 Nilda was in my brother's lap and he had his hand so far up her skirt it looked like he was performing a surgical procedure. When we were getting off the bus Rafa pulled me aside and held his hand in front of my nose. Smell this, he said. This, he said, is what's wrong with women.

You couldn't get anywhere near Nilda for the rest of the day. She had her hair pulled back and was glorious with victory. Even the white girls knew about my overmuscled about-to-be-a-senior brother and were impressed. And while Nilda sat at the end of our lunch table and whispered to some girls me and my boys ate our crap sandwiches and talked about the X-Men—this was back when the X-Men still made some kind of sense—and even if we didn't want to admit it the truth was now patent and awful: all the real dope girls were headed up to the high school, like moths to a light, and there was nothing any of us younger cats could do about it. My man José Negrón—a.k.a. Joe Black—took Nilda's defection the hardest, since he'd actually imagined he had a chance with her. Right after she got back from the group home he'd held her hand on the bus, and even though she'd gone off with other guys, he'd never forgotten it.

I was in the basement three nights later when they did it. That first time neither of them made a sound.

They went out that whole summer. I don't remember anyone doing anything big. Me and my pathetic little crew hiked over to Morgan Creek and swam around in water stinking of leachate from the landfill; we were just getting serious about the licks that year and Joe Black was stealing bottles out of his father's stash and we were drinking them down to the corners on the swings behind the apartments. Because of the heat and because of what I felt inside my chest a lot, I often just sat in the crib with my brother and Nilda. Rafa was tired all the time and pale: this had happened in a matter of days. I used to say, Look at you, white boy, and he used to say, Look at you, you black ugly nigger. He didn't feel like doing much, and besides his car had finally broken down for real, so we would all sit in the air-conditioned apartment and watch TV. Rafa had decided he wasn't going back to school for his senior year, and even though my moms was heartbroken and trying to guilt him into it five times a day, this was all he talked about. School had never been his gig, and after my pops left us for his twenty-five-year-old he didn't feel he needed to pretend any longer. I'd like to take a long fucking trip, he told us. See California before it slides into the ocean. California, I said. California, he said. A nigger could make a showing out there. I'd like to go there, too, Nilda said, but Rafa didn't answer her. He had closed his eyes and you could see he was in pain.

We never talked about our father. I'd asked Rafa once, right at the beginning of the Last Great Absence, where he thought he was, and Rafa said, Like I fucking care.

End of conversation. World without end.

On days niggers were really out of their minds with boredom we trooped down to the pool and got in for free because Rafa was boys with one of the lifeguards. I swam, Nilda went on missions around the pool just so she could show off how tight she looked in her bikini, and Rafa sprawled under the awning and took it all in. Sometimes he called me over and we'd sit together and for a while he'd close his eyes and I'd watch the water dry on my ashy legs and then he'd tell me to go back to the pool. When Nilda finished promenading and came back to where Rafa was chilling she kneeled at his side and he would kiss her real long, his hands playing up and down the length of her back. Ain't nothing like a fifteen-year-old with a banging body, those hands seemed to be saying, at least to me.

Joe Black was always watching them. Man, he muttered, she's so fine I'd lick her asshole *and* tell you niggers about it.

Maybe I would have thought they were cute if I hadn't known Rafa. He might have seemed enamora'o with Nilda but he also had mad girls in orbit. Like this one piece of white trash from Sayreville, and this morena from Amsterdam

Village who also slept over and sounded like a freight train when they did it. I don't remember her name, but I do remember how her perm shone in the glow of our night-light.

In August Rafa quit his job at the carpet factory—I'm too fucking tired, he complained, and some mornings his leg bones hurt so much he couldn't get out of bed right away. The Romans used to shatter these with iron clubs, I told him while I massaged his shins. The pain would kill you instantly. Great, he said. Cheer me up some more, you fucking bastard. One day Mami took him to the hospital for a checkup and afterward I found them sitting on the couch, both of them dressed up, watching TV like nothing had happened. They were holding hands and Mami appeared tiny next to him.

Well?

Rafa shrugged. The doc thinks I'm anemic.

Anemic ain't bad.

Yeah, Rafa said, laughing bitterly. God bless Medicaid.

In the light of the TV, he looked terrible.

That was the summer when everything we would become was hovering just over our heads. Girls were starting to take notice of me; I wasn't good-looking but I listened and was sincere and had boxing muscles in my arms. In another universe I probably came out O.K., ended up with mad novias and jobs and a sea of love in which to swim, but in this world I had a brother who was dying of cancer and a long dark patch of life like a mile of black ice waiting for me up ahead.

One night, a couple of weeks before school started—they must have thought I was asleep—Nilda started telling Rafa about her plans for the future. I think even she knew what was about to happen. Listening to her imagining herself was about the saddest thing you ever heard. How she wanted to get away from her moms and open up a group home for runaway kids. But this one would be real cool, she said. It would be for normal kids who just got problems. She must have loved him because she went on and on. Plenty of people talk about having a flow, but that night I really heard one, something that was unbroken, that fought itself and worked together all at once. Rafa didn't say nothing. Maybe he had his hands in her hair or maybe he was just like, Fuck you. When she finished he didn't even say wow. I wanted to kill myself with embarrassment. About a half hour later she got up and dressed. She couldn't see me or she would have known that I thought she was beautiful. She stepped into her pants and pulled them up in one motion, sucked in her stomach while she buttoned them. I'll see you later, she said.

Yeah, he said.

After she walked out he put on the radio and started on the speed bag. I stopped pretending I was asleep; I sat up and watched him.

Did you guys have a fight or something?

No, he said.

Why'd she leave?

He sat down on my bed. His chest was sweating. She had to go.

But where's she gonna stay?

I don't know. He put his hand on my face, gently. Why ain't you minding your business?

A week later he was seeing some other girl. She was from Trinidad, a coco pañyol, and she had this phony-as-hell English accent. It was the way we all were back then. None of us wanted to be niggers. Not for nothing.

I guess two years passed. My brother was gone by then, and I was on my way to becoming a nut. I was out of school most of the time and had no friends and I sat inside and watched Univisión or walked down to the dump and smoked the mota I should have been selling until I couldn't see. Nilda didn't fare so well either. A lot of the things that happened to her, though, had nothing to do with me or my brother. She fell in love a couple more times, really bad with this one moreno truck driver who took her to Manalapan and then abandoned her at the end of the summer. I had to drive over to get her, and the house was one of those tiny box jobs with a fifty-cent lawn and no kind of charm; she was acting like she was some Italian chick and offered me a joint in the car, but I put my hand on hers and told her to stop it. Back home she fell in with more stupid niggers, relocated kids from the City, and they came at her with drama and some of their girls beat her up, a Brick City beat-down, and she lost her bottom front teeth. She was in and out of school and for a while they put her on home instruction, and that was when she finally dropped.

My junior year she started delivering papers so she could make money, and since I was spending a lot of time outside I saw her every now and then. Broke my heart. She wasn't at her lowest yet but she was aiming there and when we passed each other she always smiled and said hi. She was starting to put on weight and she'd cut her hair down to nothing and her moon-face was heavy and alone. I always said Wassup and when I had cigarettes I gave them to her. She'd gone to the funeral, along with a couple of his other girls, and what a skirt she'd worn, like maybe she could still convince him of something, and she'd kissed my mother but the vieja hadn't known who she was. I had to tell Mami on the ride home and all she could remember about her was that she was the one who smelled good. It wasn't until Mami said it that I realized it was true.

It was only one summer and she was nobody special, so what's the point of all this? He's gone, he's gone, he's gone. I'm twenty-three and I'm washing my clothes up at the minimall on Ernston Road. She's here with me—she's folding her shit and smiling and showing me her missing teeth and saying, It's been a long time, hasn't it, Yunior?

Years, I say, loading my whites. Outside the sky is clear of gulls, and down at the apartment my moms is waiting for me with dinner. Six months earlier we were sitting in front of the TV and my mother said, Well, I think I'm finally over this place.

Nilda asks, Did you move or something?

I shake my head. Just been working.

God, it's been a long, long time. She's on her clothes like magic, making everything neat, making everything fit. There are four other people at the counters, broke-ass-looking niggers with knee socks and croupier's hats and scars snaking up their arms, and they all seem like sleepwalkers compared with her. She shakes her head, grinning. Your brother, she says.

Rafa.

She points her finger at me like my brother always did.

I miss him sometimes.

She nods. Me, too. He was a good guy to me.

I must have disbelief on my face because she finishes shaking out her towels and then stares straight through me. He treated me the best.

Nilda.

He used to sleep with my hair over his face. He used to say it made him feel safe.

What else can we say? She finished her stacking, I hold the door open for her. The locals watch us leave. We walk back through the old neighborhood, slowed down by the bulk of our clothes. London Terrace has changed now that the landfill has shut down. Kicked-up rents and mad South Asian people and white folks living in the apartments, but it's our kids you see in the streets and hanging from the porches.

Nilda is watching the ground as though she's afraid she might fall. My heart is beating and I think, We could do anything. We could marry. We could drive off to the West Coast. We could start over. It's all possible but neither of us speaks for a long time and the moment closes and we're back in the world we've always known.

Remember the day we met? she asks.

I nod.

You wanted to play baseball.

It was summer, I say. You were wearing a tank top.

You made me put on a shirt before you'd let me be on your team. Do you remember?

I remember, I say.

We never spoke again. A couple of years later I went away to college and I don't know where the fuck she went.

Ian Frazier

LAWS CONCERNING FOOD AND DRINK; HOUSEHOLD PRINCIPLES; LAMENTATIONS OF THE FATHER

OF THE BEASTS OF THE FIELD, and of the fishes of the sea, and of all foods that are acceptable in my sight you may eat, but not in the living room. Of the hoofed animals, broiled or ground into burgers, you may eat, but not in the living room. Of the cloven-hoofed animal, plain or with cheese, you may eat, but not in the living room. Of the cereal grains, of the corn and of the wheat and of the oats, and of all the cereals that are of bright color and unknown provenance you may eat, but not in the living room. Of the quiescently frozen dessert and of all frozen after-meal treats you may eat, but absolutely not in the living room. Of the juices and other beverages, yes, even of those in sippy-cups, you may drink, but not in the living room, neither may you carry such therein. Indeed, when you reach the place where the living room carpet begins, of any food or beverage there you may not eat, neither may you drink.

But if you are sick, and are lying down and watching something, then may you eat in the living room.

LAWS WHEN AT TABLE

And if you are seated in your high chair, or in a chair such as a greater person might use, keep your legs and feet below you as they were. Neither raise up your knees, nor place your feet upon the table, for that is an abomination to me. Yes, even when you have an interesting bandage to show, your feet upon the table are an abomination, and worthy of rebuke. Drink your milk as it is given you, neither use on it any utensils, nor fork, nor knife, nor spoon, for that is not what they are for; if you will dip your blocks in the milk, and lick it off, you will be sent away. When you have drunk, let the empty cup then remain upon the table, and do not bite it upon its edge and by your teeth hold it to your face in order to make noises in it sounding like a duck; for you will be sent away.

When you chew your food, keep your mouth closed until you have swallowed, and do not open it to show your brother or your sister what is within; I say to you, do not so, even if your brother or your sister has done the same to you. Eat your food only; do not eat that which is not food; neither seize the table between your jaws, nor use the raiment of the table to wipe your lips. I say again to you, do not touch it, but leave it as it is. And though your stick of carrot does indeed resemble a marker, draw not with it upon the table, even in pretend, for we do not do that, that is why. And though the pieces of broccoli are very like small trees, do not stand them upright to make a forest, because we do not do that, that is why. Sit just as I have told you, and do not lean to one side or the other, nor slide down until you are nearly slid away. Heed me; for if you sit like that, your hair will go into the syrup. And now behold, even as I have said, it has come to pass.

LAWS PERTAINING TO DESSERT

For we judge between the plate that is unclean and the plate that is clean, saying first, if the plate is clean, then you shall have dessert. But of the unclean plate, the laws are these: If you have eaten most of your meat, and two bites of your peas, with each bite consisting of not less than three peas each, or in total six peas, eaten where I can see, and you have also eaten enough of your potatoes to fill two forks, both forkfuls eaten where I can see, then you shall have dessert. But if you eat a lesser number of peas, and yet you eat the potatoes, still you shall not have dessert; and if you eat the peas, yet leave the potatoes uneaten, you shall not have dessert, no, not even a small portion thereof. And if you try to deceive by moving the potatoes or peas around with a fork, that it may appear you have eaten what you have not, you will fall into iniquity. And I will know, and you shall have no dessert.

ON SCREAMING

Do not scream; for it is as if you scream all the time. If you are given a plate on which two foods you do not wish to touch each other are touching each other, your voice rises up even to the ceiling, while you point to the offense with the finger of your right hand; but I say to you, scream not, only remonstrate gently with the server, that the server may correct the fault. Likewise if you receive a portion of fish from which every piece of herbal seasoning has not been scraped off, and the herbal seasoning is loathsome to you, and steeped in vileness, again I say, refrain from screaming. Though the vileness overwhelm you, and cause you a faint unto death, make not that sound from within your throat, neither cover your face, nor press your fingers to your nose. For even now I have made the fish as it should be; behold, I eat of it myself, yet do not die.

CONCERNING FACE AND HANDS

Cast your countenance upward to the light, and lift your eyes to the hills, that I may more easily wash you off. For the stains are upon you; even to the very back of your head, there is rice thereon. And in the breast pocket of your garment, and upon the tie of your shoe, rice and other fragments are distributed in a manner wonderful to see. Only hold yourself still; hold still, I say. Give each finger in its turn for my examination thereof, and also each thumb. Lo, how iniquitous they appear.

What I do is as it must be; and you shall not go hence until I have done.

VARIOUS OTHER LAWS, STATUTES, AND ORDINANCES

Bite not, lest you be cast into quiet time. Neither drink of your own bath water, nor of bath water of any kind; nor rub your feet on bread, even if it be in the package; nor rub yourself against cars, nor against any building; nor eat sand.

Leave the cat alone, for what has the cat done, that you should so afflict it with tape? And hum not that humming in your nose as I read, nor stand between the light and the book. Indeed, you will drive me to madness. Nor forget what I said about the tape.

COMPLAINTS AND LAMENTATIONS

O my children, you are disobedient. For when I tell you what you must do, you argue and dispute hotly even to the littlest detail; and when I do not accede, you cry out, and hit and kick. Yes, and even sometimes do you spit, and shout "stupid-head" and other blasphemies, and hit and kick the wall and the molding thereof when you are sent to the corner. And though the law teaches that no one shall be sent to the corner for more minutes than he has years of age, yet I would leave you there all day, so mighty am I in anger. But upon being sent to the corner you ask straightaway, "Can I come out?" and I reply, "No, you may not come out." And again you ask, and again I give the same reply. But when you ask again a third time, then you may come out.

Hear me, O my children, for the bills they kill me. I pay and pay again, even to the twelfth time in a year, and yet again they mount higher than before. For our health, that we may be covered, I give six hundred and twenty talents twelve times in a year; but even this covers not the fifteen hundred deductible for each member of the family within a calendar year. And yet for ordinary visits we still are not covered, nor for many medicines, nor for the teeth within our mouths. Guess not at what rage is in my mind, for surely you cannot know.

For I will come to you at the first of the month and the fifteenth of the month with the bills and a great whining and moan. And when the month of taxes comes, I will decry the wrong and unfairness of it, and mourn with wine and ashtrays, and rend my receipts. And you shall remember that I am that I am: before, after, and until you are twenty-one. Hear me then, and avoid me in my wrath, O children of me.

ON THE RAINY RIVER

THIS IS ONE STORY I've never told before. Not to anyone. Not to my parents, not to my brother or sister, not even to my wife. To go into it, I've always thought, would only cause embarrassment for all of us, a sudden need to be elsewhere, which is the natural response to a confession. Even now, I'll admit, the story makes me squirm. For more than twenty years I've had to live with it, feeling the shame, trying to push it away, and so by this act of remembrance, by putting the facts down on paper, I'm hoping to relieve at least some of the pressure on my dreams. Still, it's a hard story to tell. All of us, I suppose, like to believe that in a moral emergency we will behave like the heroes of our youth, bravely and forthrightly, without thought of personal loss or discredit. Certainly that was my conviction back in the summer of 1968. Tim O'Brien: a secret hero. The Lone Ranger. If the stakes ever became high enough—if the evil were evil enough, if the good were good enough—I would simply tap a secret reservoir of courage that had been accumulating inside me over the years. Courage, I seemed to think, comes to us in finite quantities, like an inheritance, and by being frugal and stashing it away and letting it earn interest, we steadily increase our moral capital in preparation for that day when the account must be drawn down. It was a comforting theory. It dispensed with all those bothersome little acts of daily courage; it offered hope and grace to the repetitive coward; it justified the past while amortizing the future.

In June of 1968, a month after graduating from Macalester College, I was drafted to fight a war I hated. I was twenty-one years old. Young, yes, and politically naive, but even so the American war in Vietnam seemed to me wrong. Certain blood was being shed for uncertain reasons. I saw no unity of purpose, no consensus on matters of philosophy or history or law. The very facts were shrouded in uncertainty: Was it a civil war? A war of national liberation or simple aggression? Who started it, and when, and why? What really happened to the USS *Maddox* on that dark night in the Gulf of Tonkin? Was Ho Chi Minh a Communist stooge, or a nationalist savior, or both, or neither? What about the Geneva Accords? What about SEATO and the Cold War? What about dominoes? America was divided on these and a thousand other issues, and the debate had spilled out across the floor of the United States Senate and into the streets, and smart men in pinstripes could not agree on even the most fundamental matters of public policy. The only certainty that summer was moral confusion. It was my view then, and still is, that you don't make war without knowing why. Knowledge, of course, is always imperfect, but it seemed to me that when a nation goes to war it must have reasonable confidence in the justice and imperative of its cause. You can't fix your mistakes. Once people are dead, you can't make them undead.

In any case those were my convictions, and back in college I had taken a modest stand against the war. Nothing radical, no hothead stuff, just ringing a few doorbells for Gene McCarthy, composing a few tedious, uninspired editorials for the campus newspaper. Oddly, though, it was almost entirely an intellectual activity. I brought some energy to it, of course, but it was the energy that accompanies almost any abstract endeavor; I felt no personal danger; I felt no sense of an impending crisis in my life. Stupidly, with a kind of smug removal that I can't begin to fathom, I assumed that the problems of killing and dying did not fall within my special province.

The draft notice arrived on June 17, 1968. It was a humid afternoon, I remember, cloudy and very quiet, and I'd just come in from a round of golf. My mother and father were having lunch out in the kitchen. I remember opening up the letter, scanning the first few lines, feeling the blood go thick behind my eyes. I remember a sound in my head. It wasn't thinking, it was just a silent howl. A million things all at once—I was too *good* for this war. Too smart, too compassionate, too everything. It couldn't happen. I was above it. I had the world dicked—Phi Beta Kappa and summa cum laude and president of the student body and a full-ride scholarship for grad studies at Harvard. A mistake, maybe—a foul-up in the paperwork. I was no soldier. I hated Boy Scouts. I hated camping out. I hated dirt and tents and mosquitoes. The sight of blood made me queasy, and I couldn't tolerate authority, and I didn't know a rifle from a slingshot. I was a *liberal,* for Christ sake: If they needed fresh bodies, why not draft some back-to-the-stone-age hawk? Or some dumb jingo in his hard hat and Bomb Hanoi button? Or one of LBJ's pretty daughters? Or Westmoreland's whole family—nephews and nieces and baby grandson? There should be a law, I thought. If you support a war, if you think it's worth the price, that's fine, but you have to put your own life on the line. You have to head for the front and hook up with an infantry unit and help spill the blood. And you have to bring along your wife, or your kids, or your lover. A *law,* I thought.

I remember the rage in my stomach. Later it burned down to a smoldering self-pity, then to numbness. At dinner that night my father asked what my plans were.

"Nothing," I said. "Wait."

I spent the summer of 1968 working in an Armour meat-packing plant in my hometown of Worthington, Minnesota. The plant specialized in pork products, and for eight hours a day I stood on a quarter-mile assembly line—more properly, a disassembly line—removing blood clots from the necks of dead pigs. My job title, I believe, was Declotter. After slaughter, the hogs were decapitated, split down the length of the belly, pried open, eviscerated, and strung up by the hind hocks on a high conveyer belt. Then gravity took over. By the time a carcass reached my spot on the line, the fluids had mostly drained out, everything except for thick clots of blood in the neck and upper chest cavity. To remove the stuff, I used a kind of water gun. The machine was heavy, maybe eighty pounds, and was suspended from the ceiling by a heavy rubber cord. There was some bounce to it, an elastic up-and-down give, and the trick was to maneuver the gun with your whole body, not lifting with the arms, just letting the rubber cord do the work for you. At one end was a trigger; at the muzzle end was a small nozzle and a steel roller brush. As a carcass passed by, you'd lean forward and swing the gun up against the clots and squeeze the trigger, all in one motion, and the brush would whirl and water would come shooting out and you'd hear a quick splattering sound as the clots dissolved into a fine red mist. It was not pleasant work. Goggles were a necessity, and a rubber apron, but even so it was like standing for eight hours a day under a lukewarm blood-shower. At night I'd go home smelling of pig. I couldn't wash it out. Even after a hot bath, scrubbing hard, the stink was always there—like old bacon, or sausage, a dense greasy pig-stink that soaked deep into my skin and hair. Among other things, I remember, it was tough getting dates that summer. I felt isolated; I spent a lot of time alone. And there was also that draft notice tucked away in my wallet.

In the evenings I'd sometimes borrow my father's car and drive aimlessly around town, feeling sorry for myself, thinking about the war and the pig factory and how my life seemed to be collapsing toward slaughter. I felt paralyzed. All around me the options seemed to be narrowing, as if I were hurtling down a huge black funnel, the whole world squeezing in tight. There was no happy way out. The government had ended most graduate school deferments; the waiting lists for the National Guard and Reserves were impossibly long; my health was solid; I didn't qualify for CO status—no religious grounds, no history as a pacifist. Moreover, I could not claim to be opposed to war as a matter of general principle. There were occasions, I believed, when a nation was justified in using military force to achieve its ends, to stop a Hitler or some comparable evil, and I told myself that in such circumstances I would've willingly marched off to the battle. The problem, though, was that a draft board did not let you choose your war.

Beyond all this, or at the very center, was the raw fact of terror. I did not want to die. Not ever. But certainly not then, not there, not in a wrong war. Driving up Main Street, past the courthouse and the Ben Franklin store, I sometimes felt the fear spreading inside me like weeds. I imagined myself dead. I imagined myself doing things I could not do—charging an enemy position, taking aim at another human being.

At some point in mid-July I began thinking seriously about Canada. The border lay a few hundred miles north, an eight-hour drive. Both my conscience and my instincts were telling me to make a break for it, just take off and run like hell and never stop. In the beginning the idea seemed purely abstract, the word Canada printing itself out in my head; but after a time I could see particular shapes and images, the sorry details of my own future—a hotel room in Winnipeg, a battered old suitcase, my father's eyes as I tried to explain myself over the telephone. I could almost hear his voice, and my mother's. Run, I'd think. Then I'd think, Impossible. Then a second later I'd think, *Run.*

It was a kind of schizophrenia. A moral split. I couldn't make up my mind. I feared the war, yes, but I also feared exile. I was afraid of walking away from my own life, my friends and my family, my whole history, everything that mattered to me. I feared losing the respect of my parents. I feared the law. I feared ridicule and censure. My hometown was a conservative little spot on the prairie, a place where tradition counted, and it was easy to imagine people sitting around a table down at the old Gobbler Café on Main Street, coffee cups poised, the conversation slowly zeroing in on the young O'Brien kid, how the damned sissy had taken off for Canada. At night, when I couldn't sleep, I'd sometimes carry on fierce arguments with those people. I'd be screaming at them, telling them how much I detested their blind, thoughtless, automatic acquiescence to it all, their simpleminded patriotism, their prideful ignorance, their love-it-or-leave-it platitudes, how they were sending me off to fight a war they didn't understand and didn't want to understand. I held them responsible. By God, yes, I *did.* All of them—I held them personally and individually responsible—the polyestered Kiwanis boys, the merchants and farmers, the pious churchgoers, the chatty housewives, the PTA and the Lions club and the Veterans of Foreign Wars and the fine upstanding gentry out at the country club. They didn't know Bao Dai from the man in the moon. They didn't know history. They didn't know the first thing about Diem's tyranny, or the nature of Vietnamese nationalism, or the long colonialism of the French—this was all too damned complicated, it required some reading—but no matter, it was a war to stop the Communists, plain and simple, which was how they liked things, and you were a treasonous pussy if you had second thoughts about killing or dying for plain and simple reasons.

I was bitter, sure. But it was so much more than that. The emotions went from outrage to terror to bewilderment to guilt to sorrow and then back again to outrage. I felt a sickness inside me. Real disease.

Most of this I've told before, or at least hinted at, but what I have never told is the full truth. How I cracked. How at work one morning, standing on the pig line, I felt something break open in my chest. I don't know what it was. I'll never know. But it was real, I know that much, it was a physical rupture—a cracking-leaking-popping feeling. I remember dropping my water gun. Quickly, almost without thought, I took off my apron and walked out of the plant and drove home. It was midmorning, I remember, and the house was empty.

Down in my chest there was still that leaking sensation, something very warm and precious spilling out, and I was covered with blood and hog-stink, and for a long while I just concentrated on holding myself together. I remember taking a hot shower. I remember packing a suitcase and carrying it out to the kitchen, standing very still for a few minutes, looking carefully at the familiar objects all around me. The old chrome toaster, the telephone, the pink and white Formica on the kitchen counters. The room was full of bright sunshine. Everything sparkled. My house, I thought. My life. I'm not sure how long I stood there, but later I scribbled out a short note to my parents.

What it said, exactly, I don't recall now. Something vague. Taking off, will call, love Tim.

I drove north.

It's a blur now, as it was then, and all I remember is a sense of high velocity and the feel of the steering wheel in my hands. I was riding on adrenaline. A giddy feeling, in a way, except there was the dreamy edge of impossibility to it—like running a dead-end maze—no way out—it couldn't come to a happy conclusion and yet I was doing it anyway because it was all I could think of to do. It was pure flight, fast and mindless. I had no plan. Just hit the border at high speed and crash through and keep on running. Near dusk I passed through Bemidji, then turned northeast toward International Falls. I spent the night in the car behind a closed-down gas station a half mile from the border. In the morning, after gassing up, I headed straight west along the Rainy River, which separates Minnesota from Canada, and which for me separated one life from another. The land was mostly wilderness. Here and there I passed a motel or bait shop, but otherwise the country unfolded in great sweeps of pine and birch and sumac. Though it was still August, the air already had the smell of October, football season, piles of yellow-red leaves, everything crisp and clean. I remember a huge blue sky. Off to my right was the Rainy River, wide as a lake in places, and beyond the Rainy River was Canada.

For a while I just drove, not aiming at anything, then in the late morning I began looking for a place to lie low for a day or two. I was exhausted, and scared sick, and around noon I pulled into an old fishing resort called the Tip Top Lodge. Actually it was not a lodge at all, just eight or nine tiny yellow cabins clustered on a peninsula that jutted northward into the Rainy River. The place was in sorry shape. There was a dangerous wooden dock, an old minnow tank, a flimsy tar paper boathouse along the shore. The main building, which stood in a cluster of pines on high ground, seemed to lean heavily to one side, like a cripple, the roof sagging toward Canada. Briefly, I thought about turning around, just giving up, but then I got out of the car and walked up to the front porch.

The man who opened the door that day is the hero of my life. How do I say this without sounding sappy? Blurt it out— the man saved me. He offered exactly what I needed, without questions, without any words at all. He took me in. He was there at the critical time—a silent, watchful presence. Six days later, when it ended, I was unable to find a proper way to thank him, and I never have, and so, if nothing else, this story represents a small gesture of gratitude twenty years overdue.

Even after two decades I can close my eyes and return to that porch in the Tip Top Lodge. I can see the old guy staring at me. Elroy Berdahl: eighty-one years old, skinny and shrunken and mostly bald. He wore a flannel shirt and brown work pants. In one hand, I remember, he carried a green apple, a small paring knife in the other. His eyes had the bluish gray color of a razor blade, the same polished shine, and as he peered up at me I felt a strange sharpness, almost painful, a cutting sensation, as if his gaze were somehow slicing me open. In part, no doubt, it was my own sense of guilt, but even so I'm absolutely certain that the old man took one look and went right to the heart of things—a kid in trouble. When I asked for a room, Elroy made a little clicking sound with his tongue. He nodded, led me out to one of the cabins, and dropped a key in my hand. I remember smiling at him. I also remember wishing I hadn't. The old man shook his head as if to tell me it wasn't worth the bother.

"Dinner at five-thirty," he said. "You eat fish?"

"Anything," I said.

Elroy grunted and said, "I'll bet."

We spent six days together at the Tip Top Lodge. Just the two of us. Tourist season was over, and there were no boats on the river, and the wilderness seemed to withdraw into a great permanent stillness. Over those six days Elroy Berdahl and I took most of our meals together. In the mornings we sometimes went out on long hikes into the woods, and at night we played Scrabble or listened to records or sat reading in front of his big stone fireplace. At times I felt the awkwardness of an intruder, but Elroy accepted me into his quiet routine without fuss or ceremony. He took my presence for granted, the same way he might've sheltered a stray cat—no wasted sighs or pity—and there was never any talk about it. Just the opposite. What I remember more than anything is the man's willful, almost ferocious silence. In all that time together, all those hours, he never asked the obvious questions: Why was I there? Why alone? Why so preoccupied? If Elroy was curious about any of this, he was careful never to put it into words.

My hunch, though, is that he already knew. At least the basics. After all, it was 1968, and guys were burning draft cards, and Canada was just a boat ride away. Elroy Berdahl was no hick. His bedroom, I remember, was cluttered with books and newspapers. He killed me at the Scrabble board, barely concentrating, and on those occasions when speech was necessary he had a way of compressing large thoughts into small, cryptic packets of language. One evening, just at sunset, he pointed up at an owl circling over the violet-lighted forest to the west.

"Hey, O'Brien," he said. "There's Jesus."

The man was sharp—he didn't miss much. Those razor eyes. Now and then he'd catch me staring out at the river, at the far shore, and I could almost hear the tumblers clicking in his head. Maybe I'm wrong, but I doubt it.

One thing for certain, he knew I was in desperate trouble. And he knew I couldn't talk about it. The wrong word—or even the right word—and I would've disappeared. I was wired and jittery. My skin felt too tight. After supper one evening I vomited and went back to my cabin and lay down for a few moments and then vomited again; another time, in the middle of the afternoon, I began sweating and couldn't shut it off. I went through whole days feeling dizzy with sorrow. I couldn't sleep; I couldn't lie still. At night I'd toss around in bed, half awake, half dreaming, imagining how I'd sneak down to the beach and quietly push one of the old man's boats out into the river and start paddling my way toward Canada. There were times when I thought I'd gone off the psychic edge. I couldn't tell up from down, I was just falling, and late in the night I'd lie there watching weird pictures spin through my head. Getting chased by the Border Patrol—helicopters and search-lights and barking dogs—I'd be crashing through the woods, I'd be down on my hands and knees—people shouting out my name—the law closing in on all sides—my hometown draft board and the FBI and the Royal Canadian Mounted Police. It all seemed crazy and impossible. Twenty-one years old, an ordinary kid with all the ordinary dreams and ambitions, and all I wanted was to live the life I was born to—a mainstream life—I loved baseball and hamburgers and cherry Cokes—and now I was off on the margins of exile, leaving my country forever, and it seemed so impossible and terrible and sad.

I'm not sure how I made it through those six days. Most of it I can't remember. On two or three afternoons, to pass some time, I helped Elroy get the place ready for winter, sweeping down the cabins and hauling in the boats, little chores that kept my body moving. The days were cool and bright. The nights were very dark. One morning the old man showed me how to split and stack firewood, and for several hours we just worked in silence out behind his house. At one point, I remember, Elroy put down his maul and looked at me for a long time, his lips drawn as if framing a difficult question, but then he shook his head and went back to work. The man's self-control was amazing. He never pried. He never put me in a position that required lies or denials. To an extent, I suppose, his reticence was typical of that part of Minnesota, where privacy still held value, and even if I'd been walking around with some horrible deformity—four arms and three heads—I'm sure the old man would've talked about everything except those extra arms and heads. Simple politeness was part of it. But even more than that, I think, the man understood that words were insufficient. The problem had gone beyond discussion. During that long summer I'd been over and over the various arguments, all the pros and cons, and it was no longer a question that could be decided by an act of pure reason. Intellect had come up against emotion. My conscience told me to run, but some irrational and powerful force was resisting, like a weight pushing me toward the war. What it came down to, stupidly, was a sense of shame. Hot, stupid shame. I did not want people to think badly of me. Not my parents, not my brother and sister, not even the folks down at the Gobbler Café. I was ashamed to be there at the Tip Top Lodge. I was ashamed of my conscience, ashamed to be doing the right thing.

Some of this Elroy must've understood. Not the details, of course, but the plain fact of crisis.

Although the old man never confronted me about it, there was one occasion when he came close to forcing the whole thing out into the open. It was early evening, and we'd just finished supper, and over coffee and dessert I asked him about my bill, how much I owed so far. For a long while the old man squinted down at the tablecloth.

"Well, the basic rate," he said, "is fifty bucks a night. Not counting meals. This makes four nights, right?"

I nodded. I had three hundred and twelve dollars in my wallet.

Elroy kept his eyes on the tablecloth. "Now that's an on-season price. To be fair, I suppose we should knock it down a peg or two." He leaned back in his chair. "What's a reasonable number, you figure?"

"I don't know," I said. "Forty?"

"Forty's good. Forty a night. Then we tack on food—say another hundred? Two hundred sixty total?"

"I guess."

He raised his eyebrows. "Too much?"

"No, that's fair. It's fine. Tomorrow, though . . . I think I'd better take off tomorrow."

Elroy shrugged and began clearing the table. For a time he fussed with the dishes, whistling to himself as if the subject had been settled. After a second he slapped his hands together.

"You know what we forgot?" he said. "We forgot wages. Those odd jobs you done. What we have to do, we have to figure out what your time's worth. Your last job—how much did you pull in an hour?"

"Not enough," I said.

"A bad one?"

"Yes. Pretty bad."

Slowly then, without intending any long sermon, I told him about my days at the pig plant. It began as a straight recitation of the facts, but before I could stop myself I was talking about the blood clots and the water gun and how the smell had soaked into my skin and how I couldn't wash it away. I went on for a long time. I told him about wild hogs squealing in my dreams, the sounds of butchery, slaughterhouse sounds, and how I'd sometimes wake up with that greasy pig-stink in my throat.

When I was finished, Elroy nodded at me.

"Well, to be honest," he said, "when you first showed up her, I wondered about all that. The aroma, I mean. Smelled like you was awful damned fond of pork chops." The old man almost smiled. He made a snuffling sound, then sat down with a pencil and a piece of paper. "So what'd this crud job pay? Ten bucks an hour? Fifteen?"

"Less."

Elroy shook his head. "Let's make it fifteen. You put in twenty-five hours here, easy. That's three hundred seventy-five bucks total wages. We subtract the two hundred sixty for food and lodging, I still owe you a hundred and fifteen."

He took four fifties out of his shirt pocket and laid them on the table.

"Call it even," he said.

"No."

"Pick it up. Get yourself a haircut."

The money lay on the table for the rest of the evening. It was still there when I went back to my cabin. In the morning, though, I found an envelope tacked to my door. Inside were the four fifties and a two-word note that said EMERGENCY FUND.

The man knew.

Looking back after twenty years, I sometimes wonder if the events of that summer didn't happen in some other dimension, a place where your life exists before you've lived it, and where it goes afterward. None of it ever seemed real. During my time at the Tip Top Lodge I had the feeling that I'd slipped out of my own skin, hovering a few feet away while some poor yo-yo with my name and face tried to make his way toward a future he didn't understand and didn't want. Even now I can see myself as I was then. It's like watching an old home movie:

I'm young and tan and fit. I've got hair—lots of it. I don't smoke or drink. I'm wearing faded blue jeans and a white polo shirt. I can see myself sitting on Elroy Berdahl's dock near dusk one evening, the sky a bright shimmering pink, and I'm finishing up a letter to my parents that tells what I'm about to do and why I'm doing it and how sorry I am that I'd never found the courage to talk to them about it. I ask them not to be angry. I try to explain some of my feelings, but there aren't enough words, and so I just say that it's a thing that has to be done. At the end of the letter I talk about the vacations we used to take up in this north country, at a place called Whitefish Lake, and how the scenery here reminds me of those good times. I tell them I'm fine. I tell them I'll write again from Winnipeg or Montreal or wherever I end up.

On my last full day, the sixth day, the old man took me out fishing on the Rainy River. The afternoon was sunny and cold. A stiff breeze came in from the north, and I remember how the little fourteen-foot boat made sharp rocking motions as we pushed off from the dock. The current was fast. All around us, I remember, there was a vastness to the world, an unpeopled rawness, just the trees and the sky and the water reaching out toward nowhere. The air had the brittle scent of October.

For ten or fifteen minutes Elroy held a course upstream, the river choppy and silver-gray, then he turned straight north and put the engine on full throttle. I felt the bow lift beneath me. I remember the wind in my ears, the sound of the old outboard Evinrude. For a time I didn't pay attention to anything, just feeling the cold spray against my face, but then it occurred to me that at some point we must've passed into Canadian waters, across that dotted line between two different worlds, and I remember a sudden tightness in my chest as I looked up and watched the far shore come at me. This wasn't a daydream. It was tangible and real. As we came in toward land, Elroy cut the engine, letting the boat fishtail lightly about twenty yards off shore. The old man didn't look at me or speak. Bending down, he opened up his tackle box and busied himself with a bobber and a piece of wire leader, humming to himself, his eyes down.

It struck me then that he must've planned it. I'll never be certain, of course, but I think he meant to bring me up against the realities, to guide me across the river and to take me to the edge and to stand a kind of vigil as I chose a life for myself.

I remember staring at the old man, then at my hands, then at Canada. The shoreline was dense with brush and timber. I could see tiny red berries on the bushes. I could see a squirrel up in one of the birch trees, a big crow looking at me from a boulder along the river. That close—twenty yards—and I could see the delicate latticework of the leaves, the texture of the soil, the browned needles beneath the pines, the configurations of geology and human history. Twenty yards. I could've done it. I could've jumped and started swimming for my life. Inside me, in my chest, I felt a terrible squeezing pressure. Even now, as I write this, I can still feel that tightness. And I want you to feel it—the wind coming off the river, the waves, the silence, the wooded frontier. You're at the bow of a boat on the Rainy River. You're twenty-one years old, you're scared, and there's a hard squeezing pressure in your chest.

What would you do?

Would you jump? Would you feel pity for yourself? Would you think about your family and your childhood and your dreams and all you're leaving behind? Would it hurt? Would it feel like dying? Would you cry, as I did?

I tried to swallow it back. I tried to smile, except I was crying.

Now, perhaps, you can understand why I've never told this story before. It's not just the embarrassment of tears. That's part of it, no doubt, but what embarrasses me much more, and always will, is the paralysis that took my heart. A moral freeze: I couldn't decide, I couldn't act, I couldn't comport myself with even a pretense of modest human dignity.

All I could do was cry. Quietly, not bawling, just the chest-chokes.

At the rear of the boat Elroy Berdahl pretended not to notice. He held a fishing rod in his hands, his head bowed to hide his eyes. He kept humming a soft, monotonous little tune. Everywhere, it seemed, in the trees and water and sky, a great worldwide sadness came pressing down on me, a crushing sorrow, sorrow like I had never known it before. And what was so sad, I realized, was that Canada had become a pitiful fantasy. Silly and hopeless. It was no longer a possibility. Right then, with the shore so close, I understood that I would not do what I should do. I would not swim away from my hometown and my country and my life. I would not be brave. That old image of myself as a hero, as a man of conscience and courage, all that was just a threadbare pipe dream. Bobbing there on the Rainy River, looking back at the Minnesota shore, I felt a sudden swell of helplessness come over me, a drowning sensation, as if I had toppled overboard and was being swept away by the silver waves. Chunks of my own history flashed by. I saw a seven-year-old boy in a white cowboy hat and a Lone Ranger mask and a pair of holstered six-shooters; I saw a twelve-year-old Little League shortstop pivoting to turn a double play; I saw a sixteen-year-old kid decked out for his first prom, looking spiffy in a white tux and a black bow tie, his hair cut short and flat, his shoes freshly polished. My whole life seemed to spill out into the river, swirling away from me, everything I had ever been or ever wanted to be. I couldn't get my breath; I couldn't stay afloat; I couldn't tell which way to swim. A hallucination, I suppose, but it was as real as anything I would ever feel. I saw my parents calling to me from the far shoreline. I saw my brother and sister, all the townsfolk, the mayor and the entire Chamber of Commerce and all my old teachers and girlfriends and high school buddies. Like some weird sporting event: everybody screaming from the sidelines, rooting me on—a loud stadium roar. Hotdogs and popcorn—stadium smells, stadium heat. A squad of cheerleaders did cartwheels along the banks of the Rainy River; they had megaphones and pompoms and smooth brown thighs. The crowd swayed left and right. A marching band played fight songs. All my aunts and uncles were there, and Abraham Lincoln, and Saint George, and a nine-year-old girl named Linda who had died of a brain tumor back in fifth grade, and several members of the United States Senate, and a blind poet scribbling notes, and LBJ, and Huck Finn, and Abbie Hoffman, and all the dead soldiers back from the grave, and the many thousands who were later to die—villagers with terrible burns, little kids without arms or legs—yes, and the Joint Chiefs of Staff were there, and a couple of popes, and a first lieutenant named Jimmy Cross, and the last surviving veteran of the American Civil War, and Jane Fonda dressed up as Barbarella, and an old man sprawled beside a pigpen, and my grandfather, and Gary Cooper, and a kind-faced woman carrying an umbrella and a copy of Plato's *Republic,* and a million ferocious citizens waving flags of all shapes and colors—people in hard hats, people in headbands—they were all whooping and chanting and urging me toward one shore or the other. I saw faces from my distant past and distant future. My wife was there. My unborn daughter waved at me, and my two sons hopped up and down, and a drill sergeant named Blyton sneered and shot up a finger and shook his head. There was a choir in bright purple robes. There was a cabbie from the Bronx. There was a slim young man I would one day kill with a hand grenade along a red clay trail outside the village of My Khe.

The little aluminum boat rocked softly beneath me. There was the wind and the sky.

I tried to will myself overboard.

I gripped the edge of the boat and leaned forward and thought, *Now.*

I did try. It just wasn't possible.

All those eyes on me—the town, the whole universe—and I couldn't risk the embarrassment. It was as if there were an audience to my life, that swirl of faces along the river, and in my head I could hear people screaming at me. Traitor! they yelled. Turncoat! Pussy! I felt myself blush. I couldn't tolerate it. I couldn't endure the mockery, or the disgrace, or the patriotic ridicule. Even in my imagination, the shore just twenty yards away, I couldn't make myself be brave. It had nothing to do with morality. Embarrassment, that's all it was.

And right then I submitted.

I would go to the war—I would kill and maybe die— because I was embarrassed not to.

That was the sad thing, And so I sat in the bow of the boat and cried.

It was loud now. Loud, hard crying.

Elroy Berdahl remained quiet. He kept fishing. He worked his line with the tips of his fingers, patiently, squinting out at his red and white bobber on the Rainy River. His eyes were flat and impassive. He didn't speak. He was simply there, like the river and the late-summer sun. And yet by his presence, his mute watchfulness, he made it real. He was the true audience. He was a witness, like God, or like the gods, who look on in absolute silence as we live our lives, as we make our choices or fail to make them.

"Ain't biting," he said.

Then after a time the old man pulled in his line and turned the boat back toward Minnesota.

I don't remember saying goodbye. That last night we had dinner together, and I went to bed early, and in the morning Elroy fixed breakfast for me. When I told him I'd be leaving, the old man nodded as if he already knew. He looked down at the table and smiled.

At some point later in the morning it's possible that we shook hands—I just don't remember—but I do know that by the time I'd finished packing the old man had disappeared. Around noon, when I took my suitcase out to the car, I noticed that his old black pickup truck was no longer parked in front of the house. I went inside and waited for a while, but I felt a bone certainty that he wouldn't be back. In a way, I thought, it was appropriate. I washed up the breakfast dishes, left his two hundred dollars on the kitchen counter, got into the car, and drove south toward home.

The day was cloudy. I passed through towns with familiar names, through the pine forests and down to the prairie, and then to Vietnam, where I was a soldier, and then home again. I survived, but it's not a happy ending. I was a coward. I went to the war.

Lorrie Moore

HOW TO BECOME A WRITER

FIRST, TRY TO BE SOMETHING, anything, else. A movie star/astronaut. A movie star/missionary. A movie star/kindergarten teacher. President of the World. Fail miserably. It is best if you fail at an early age—say, fourteen. Early, critical disillusionment is necessary so that at fifteen you can write long haiku sequences about thwarted desire. It is a pond, a cherry blossom, a wind brushing against sparrow wing leaving for mountain. Count the syllables. Show it to your mom. She is tough and practical. She has a son in Vietnam and a husband who may be having an affair. She believes in wearing brown because it hides spots. She'll look briefly at your writing, then back up at you with a face blank as a donut. She'll say: "How about emptying the dishwasher?" Look away. Shove the forks in the fork drawer. Accidentally break one of the freebie gas station glasses. This is the required pain and suffering. This is only for starters.

In your high school English class look at Mr. Killian's face. Decide faces are important. Write a villanelle about pores. Struggle. Write a sonnet. Count the syllables: nine, ten, eleven, thirteen. Decide to experiment with fiction. Here you don't have to count syllables. Write a short story about an elderly man and woman who accidentally shoot each other in the head, the result of an inexplicable malfunction of a shotgun which appears mysteriously in their living room one night. Give it to Mr. Killian as your final project. When you get it back, he has written on it: "Some of your images are quite nice, but you have no sense of plot." When you are home, in the privacy of your own room, faintly scrawl in pencil beneath his black-inked comments: "Plots are for dead people, pore-face."

Take all the babysitting jobs you can get. You are great with kids. They love you. You tell them stories about old people who die idiot deaths. You sing them songs like "Blue Bells of Scotland," which is their favorite. And when they are in their pajamas and have finally stopped pinching each other, when they are fast asleep, you read every sex manual in the house, and wonder how on earth anyone could ever do those things with someone they truly loved. Fall asleep in a chair reading Mr. McMurphy's *Playboy*. When the McMurphys come home, they will tap you on the shoulder, look at the magazine in your lap, and grin. You will want to die. They will ask you if Tracey took her medicine all right. Explain, yes, she did, that you promised her a story if she would take it like a big girl and that seemed to work out just fine. "Oh, marvelous," they will exclaim.

Try to smile proudly.

Apply to college as a child psychology major.

As a child psychology major, you have some electives. You've always liked birds. Sign up for something called "The Ornithological Field Trip." It meets Tuesdays and Thursdays at two. When you arrive at Room 134 on the first day of class, everyone is sitting around a seminar table talking about metaphors. You've heard of these. After a short, excruciating while, raise your hand and say diffidently, "Excuse me, isn't this Birdwatching One-oh-one?" The class stops and turns to look at you. They seem to all have one face—giant and blank as a vandalized clock. Someone with a beard booms out, "No, this is Creative Writing." Say: "Oh—right," as if perhaps you knew all along. Look down at your schedule. Wonder how the hell you ended up here. The computer, apparently, has made an error. You start to get up to leave and then don't. The lines at the registrar this week are huge. Perhaps you should stick with this mistake. Perhaps your creative writing isn't all that bad. Perhaps it is fate. Perhaps this is what your dad meant when he said, "It's the age of computers, Francie, it's the age of computers."

Decide that you like college life. In your dorm you meet many nice people. Some are smarter than you. And some, you notice, are dumber than you. You will continue, unfortunately, to view the world in exactly these terms for the rest of your life.

The assignment this week in creative writing is to narrate a violent happening. Turn in a story about driving with your Uncle Gordon and another one about two old people who are accidentally electrocuted when they go to turn on a badly wired desk lamp. The teacher will hand them back to you with comments: "Much of your writing is smooth and energetic. You have, however, a ludicrous notion of plot." Write another story about a man and a woman who, in the very first paragraph, have their lower torsos accidentally blitzed away by dynamite. In the second paragraph, with the insurance money, they buy a frozen yogurt stand together. There are six more paragraphs. You read the whole thing out loud in class. No one likes it. They say your sense of plot is outrageous and incompetent. After class someone asks you if you are crazy.

Decide that perhaps you should stick to comedies. Start dating someone who is funny, someone who has what in high school you called a "really great sense of humor" and what now your creative writing class calls "self-contempt giving rise to comic form." Write down all of his jokes, but don't tell him you are doing this. Make up anagrams of his old girlfriend's name and name all of your socially handicapped characters with them. Tell him his old girlfriend is in all of your stories and then watch how funny he can be, see what a really great sense of humor he can have.

/ / / /

Your child psychology advisor tells you you are neglecting courses in your major. What you spend the most time on should be what you're majoring in. Say yes, you understand.

In creative writing seminars over the next two years, everyone continues to smoke cigarettes and ask the same things: "But does it work?" "Why should we care about this character?" "Have you earned this cliché?" These seem like important questions.

On days when it is your turn, you look at the class hopefully as they scour your mimeographs for a plot. They look back up at you, drag deeply, and then smile in a sweet sort of way.

You spend too much time slouched and demoralized. Your boyfriend suggests bicycling. Your roommate suggests a new boyfriend. You are said to be self-mutilating and losing weight, but you continue writing. The only happiness you have is writing something new, in the middle of the night, armpits damp, heart pounding, something no one has yet seen. You have only those brief, fragile, untested moments of exhilaration when you know: you are a genius. Understand what you must do. Switch majors. The kids in your nursery project will be disappointed, but you have a calling, an urge, a delusion, an unfortunate habit. You have, as your mother would say, fallen in with a bad crowd.

Why write? Where does writing come from? These are questions to ask yourself. They are like: Where does dust come from? Or: Why is there war? Or: If there's a God, then why is my brother now a cripple?

These are questions that you keep in your wallet, like calling cards. These are questions, your creative writing teacher says, that are good to address in your journals but rarely in your fiction.

The writing professor this fall is stressing the Power of the Imagination. Which means he doesn't want long descriptive stories about your camping trip last July. He wants you to start in a realistic context but then to alter it. Like recombinant DNA. He wants you to let your imagination sail, to let it grow big-bellied in the wind. This is a quote from Shakespeare.

Tell your roommate your great idea, your great exercise of imaginative power: a transformation of Melville to contemporary life. It will be about monomania and the fish-eat-fish world of life insurance in Rochester, New York. The first line will be "Call me Fishmeal," and it will feature a menopausal suburban husband named Richard, who because he is so depressed all the time is called "Mopey Dick" by his witty wife Elaine. Say to your roommate: "Mopey Dick, get it?" Your roommate looks at you, her face blank as a large Kleenex. She comes up to you, like a buddy, and puts an arm around your burdened shoulders. "Listen, Francie," she says, slow as speech therapy. "Let's go out and get a big beer."

The seminar doesn't like this one either. You suspect they are beginning to feel sorry for you. They say: "You have to think about what is happening. Where is the story here?"

The next semester the writing professor is obsessed with writing from personal experience. You must write from what you know, from what has happened to you. He wants deaths, he wants camping trips. Think about what has happened to you. In three years there have been three things: you lost your virginity; your parents got divorced; and your brother came home from a forest ten miles from the Cambodian border with only half a thigh, a permanent smirk nestled into one corner of his mouth.

About the first you write: "It created a new space, which hurt and cried in a voice that wasn't mine, 'I'm not the same anymore, but I'll be okay.'"

About the second you write an elaborate story of an old married couple who stumble upon an unknown land mine in their kitchen and accidentally blow themselves up. You call it: "For Better or for Liverwurst."

About the last you write nothing. There are no words for this. Your typewriter hums. You can find no words.

At undergraduate cocktail parties, people say, "Oh, you write? What do you write about?" Your roommate, who has consumed too much wine, too little cheese, and no crackers at all, blurts: "Oh, my god, she always writes about her dumb boyfriend."

Later on in life you will learn that writers are merely open, helpless texts with no real understanding of what they have written and therefore must half-believe anything and everything that is said of them. You, however, have not yet reached this stage of literary criticism. You stiffen and say, "I do not," the same way you said it when someone in the fourth grade accused you of really liking oboe lessons and your parents really weren't just making you take them.

Insist you are not very interested in any one subject at all, that you are interested in the music of language, that you are interested in—in—syllables, because they are the atoms of poetry, the cells of the mind, the breath of the soul. Begin to feel woozy. Stare into your plastic wine cup.

"Syllables?" you will hear someone ask, voice trailing off, as they glide slowly toward the reassuring white of the dip.

Begin to wonder what you do write about. Or if you have anything to say. Or if there even is such a thing as a thing to say. Limit these thoughts to no more than ten minutes a day; like sit-ups, they can make you thin.

You will read somewhere that all writing has to do with one's genitals. Don't dwell on this. It will make you nervous.

Your mother will come visit you. She will look at the circles under your eyes and hand you a brown book with a brown briefcase on the cover. It is entitled: *How to Become a Business Executive*. She has also brought the *Names for Baby* encyclopedia you asked for; one of your characters, the aging clown-school teacher, needs a new name. Your mother will shake her head and say: "Francie, Francie, remember when you were going to be a child psychology major?"

Say: "Mom, I like to write."

She'll say: "Sure you like to write. Of course. Sure you like to write."

Write a story about a confused music student and title it: "Schubert Was the One with the Glasses, Right?" It's not a big hit, although your roommate likes the part where the two violinists accidentally blow themselves up in a recital room. "I went out with a violinist once," she says, snapping her gum.

Thank god you are taking other courses. You can find sanctuary in nineteenth-century ontological snags and invertebrate courting rituals. Certain globular mollusks have what is called "Sex by the Arm." The male octopus, for instance, loses the end of one arm when placing it inside the female body during intercourse. Marine biologists call it "Seven Heaven." Be glad you know these things. Be glad you are not just a writer. Apply to law school.

From here on in, many things can happen. But the main one will be this: you decide not to go to law school after all, and, instead, you spend a good, big chunk of your adult life telling people how you decided not to go to law school after all. Somehow you end up writing again. Perhaps you go to graduate school. Perhaps you work odd jobs and take writing courses at night. Perhaps you are working on a novel and writing down all the clever remarks and intimate personal confessions you hear during the day. Perhaps you are losing your pals, your acquaintances, your balance.

You have broken up with your boyfriend. You now go out with men who, instead of whispering "I love you," shout: "Do it to me, baby." This is good for your writing.

Sooner or later you have a finished manuscript more or less. People look at it in a vaguely troubled sort of way and say, "I'll bet becoming a writer was always a fantasy of yours, wasn't it?" Your lips dry to salt. Say that of all the fantasies possible in the world, you can't imagine being a writer even making the top twenty. Tell them you were going to be a child psychology major. "I bet," they always sigh, "you'd be great with kids." Scowl fiercely. Tell them you're a walking blade.

Quit classes. Quit jobs. Cash in old savings bonds. Now you have time like warts on your hands. Slowly copy all of your friends' addresses into a new address book.

Vacuum. Chew cough drops. Keep a folder full of fragments.

> *An eyelid darkening sideways.*
> *World as conspiracy.*
> *Possible plot? A woman gets on a bus.*
> *Suppose you threw a love affair and nobody came.*

At home drink a lot of coffee. At Howard Johnson's order the cole slaw. Consider how it looks like the soggy confetti of a map: where you've been, where you're going—"You Are Here," says the red star on the back of the menu.

Occasionally a date with a face blank as a sheet of paper asks you whether writers often become discouraged. Say that sometimes they do and sometimes they do. Say it's a lot like having polio.

"Interesting," smiles your date, and then he looks down at his arm hairs and starts to smooth them, all, always, in the same direction.

V.

The Story

AS CHARACTER STUDY

These stories revolve around a protagonist whose life is unveiled and illuminated as the story unfolds. The revealing of character becomes more important than the recounting of events.

ABOUT BOSTON

BETH WAS TALKING and I was listening. She said, "This was years ago. I was having a little tryst. On a Thursday, in New York, in the afternoon. He telephoned: 'Is it this Thursday or next?' I told him it was never, if he couldn't remember the *week*. Well." She laughed. "It makes your point about letters. Never would've happened if we'd written letters because you write something and you remember it. Don't you?"

"Usually," I said.

"There isn't a record of anything anymore, it's just telephone calls and bad memory."

"I've got a filing cabinet full of letters," I said, "and most of them are from ten years ago and more. People wrote a lot in the sixties, maybe they wanted a record of what they thought. There was a lot to think about, and it seemed a natural thing to do, write a letter to a friend, what with everything that was going on."

"I wonder if they're afraid," she said.

"No written record? No," I said. "They don't have the time. They won't make the time and there aren't so many surprises now, thanks to the sixties. We're surprised-out. They don't write and they don't read either."

"That one read," she said, referring to the man in the tryst. "He read all the time—history, biography. Sports books, linebackers' memoirs, the strategy of the full-court press." She lowered her voice. "And politics."

"Well," I said. I knew who it was now.

"But he didn't know the week." She lit a cigarette, staring

at the match a moment before depositing it, just so, in the ashtray. "You always wrote letters."

I smiled. "A few close friends."

She smiled back. "Where do you think we should begin?"

"Not at the beginning."

"No, you know that as well as I do."

I said, "Probably better."

"Not better," she said.

"I don't know if I'm the man—"

"No," she said firmly. She stared at me across the room, then turned to look out the window. It was dusk, and the dying sun caught the middle windows of the Hancock tower, turning them a brilliant, wavy orange. In profile, with her sharp features and her short black hair, she looked like a schoolgirl. She said, "You're the man, all right. I want you to do it. I'd feel a lot more comfortable, we've known each other so long. Even now, after all this time, we don't have to finish sentences. It'd be hard for me, talking about it to a stranger."

"Sometimes that's easiest," I said.

"Not for me it isn't."

"All right," I said at last. "But if at any time it gets awkward for you—" I was half hoping she'd reconsider. But she waved her hand in a gesture of dismissal, subject closed. She was sitting on the couch in the corner of my office, and now she rose to stand at the window and watch the last of the sun reflected on the windows of the Hancock. A Mondrian among Turners, she had called it, its blue mirrors a new physics in the Back Bay. And who cared if in the beginning its windows popped out like so many ill-fitting contact lenses. The Hancock governed everything around it, Boston's past reflected in Boston's future. And it was miraculous that in the cascade of falling glass the casualties were so few.

I watched her: at that angle and in the last of the light her features softened and she was no longer a schoolgirl. I checked my watch, then rang my assistant and said she could lock up;

we were through for the day. I fetched a yellow legal pad and a pen and sat in the leather chair, facing Beth. She was at the window, fussing with the cord of the venetian blind. She turned suddenly, with a movement so abrupt that I dropped my pad; the blind dropped with a crash. There had always been something violent and unpredictable in her behavior. But now she only smiled winningly, nodded at the sideboard, and asked for a drink before we got down to business.

I have practiced law in the Back Bay for almost twenty-five years. After Yale I came to Boston with the naïve idea of entering politics. The city had a rowdy quality I liked; it reminded me of Chicago, a city of neighborhoods, which wasn't ready for reform. But since I am a lapsed Catholic, neither Irish nor Italian, neither Yankee nor Democrat nor rich, I quickly understood that for me there were no politics in Boston. Chicago is astronomically remote from New England, and it was of no interest to anyone that I had been around politicians most of my life and knew the code. My grandfather had been, briefly, a congressman from the suburbs of Cook Country, and I knew how to pull strings. But in Boston my antecedents precluded everything but good-government committees and the United Way.

Beth and I were engaged then, and Boston seemed less daunting than New York, perhaps because she knew it so intimately; it was her town as Chicago was mine. I rented an apartment in the North End and for the first few months we were happy enough, I with my new job and she with her volunteer work at the Mass. General. We broke off the engagement after six months—the usual reasons—and I looked up to find myself behind the lines in enemy territory. I had misjudged Boston's formality and its network of tribal loyalties and had joined Hamlin & White, one of the old State Street firms. I assumed that H, W—as it had been known for a hundred years—was politically connected. An easy error to make, for the firm was counsel to Boston's largest bank and handled the wills and trusts of a number of prominent Brahmin Republicans, and old Hamlin had once been lieutenant governor of Massachusetts. In Chicago that would have spelled political, but in Boston it only spelled probate. There were thirty men in the firm, large for Boston in those days. The six senior men were Hamlin and Hamlin Junior and White III, and Chelm, Warner, and Diuguid. Among the associates were three or four recognizable Mayflower names. The six senior men were all physically large, well over six feet tall and in conspicuous good health, by which I mean ruddy complexions and a propensity to roughhouse. They all had full heads of hair, even old Hamlin, who was then eighty. Their talk was full of the jargon of sailing and golf, and in their company I felt the worst sort of provincial rube.

Of course I was an experiment—a balding, unathletic Yale man from Chicago, of middling height, of no particular provenance, and book-smart. I was no one's cousin and no one's ex-roommate. But I was engaged to a Boston girl and I had been first in my class at Yale and the interview with Hamlin Junior had gone well. All of them in the firm spoke in that hard, open-mouthed bray peculiar to Massachusetts males of the upper classes. The exception was Hamlin Junior, who mumbled. When it was clear, after two years, that their experiment had failed—or had not, at any event, succeeded brilliantly, it was Hamlin Junior who informed me. He called me into his dark-brown office late one afternoon, poured me a sherry, and rambled for half an hour before he got to the point, which was that I was an excellent lawyer mumble mumble damned able litigator mumble mumble but the firm has its own personality, New England salt sort of thing ha-ha mumble sometimes strange to an outsider but it's the way we've always done things mumble question of style and suitability, sometimes tedious but can't be helped wish you the best you're a damned able trial man, and of course you've a place here so long's you want though in fairness I wanted mumble make it known that you wouldn't be in the first foursome as it were mumble mumble. Just one question, I've always wondered: 'S really true that you wanted to go into politics here?

It was my first professional failure, and in my anger and frustration I put it down to simple snobbery. I did not fit into their clubs and I hated the North Shore and was not adept at games. I was never seen "around" during the winter or on the Cape or the Islands or in Maine in the summer. I spent my vacations in Europe, and most weekends I went to New York, exactly as I did when I was at law school in New Haven. New York remains the center of my social life. Also, I was a bachelor. Since the breakup of my engagement, I had become an aggressive bachelor. Beth was bitter and I suspected her of spreading unflattering stories. Of course this was not true, but in my humiliation I believed that it was and that as a consequence the six senior men had me down as homosexual. In addition, I was a hard drinker in a firm of hard drinkers though unlike them I never had whiskey on my breath in the morning and I never called in sick with Monday grippe. I could never join in the hilarious retelling of locker-room misadventures. They drank and joked. I drank and didn't joke.

When I left H, W, I opened an office with another disgruntled provincial—he was from Buffalo, even farther down the scale of things than Chicago—half expecting to fail but determined not to and wondering what on earth I would do and where I would go, now that I'd been drummed out of my chosen city: blackballed. Young litigators are not as a rule peripatetic: you begin in a certain city and remain there; you are a member of the bar, you know the system, you build friendships and a clientele and a reputation. Looking back on it, Deshais and I took a terrible risk. But we worked hard and prospered, and now there are twenty lawyers in our firm, which we have perversely designed to resemble a squad of infantry in a World War II propaganda movie: Irish, Italians, Jews, three blacks in the past ten years, one Brahmin, Deshais, and me. Of course we are always quarreling; ours is not a friendly, clubby firm. In 1974, we bought a private house, a handsome brownstone, in the Back Bay, only two blocks from my apartment on Commonwealth Avenue. This is so convenient, such an agreeable way to live—it is my standard explanation to my New York friends who ask why I remain here—that we decided not to expand the firm because it would require a larger building and all of us love the brownstone, even the younger associates who must commute from Wayland or Milton. Sometimes I think it is the brownstone and the brownstone alone that holds the firm together.

I suppose it is obvious that I have no affection for this spoiled city and its noisy inhabitants. It is an indolent city. It is racist to the bone and in obvious political decline and like any declining city is by turns peevish and arrogant. It is a city without civility or civic spirit, or Jews. The Jews, with their prodigious energies, have tucked themselves away in Brookline, as the old aristocrats, with their memories and trust funds, are on the lam on the North Shore. Remaining are the resentful Irish and the furious blacks. Meanwhile, the tenured theory class issues its pronouncements from the safety of Cambridge, confident that no authority will take serious notice. So the city of Boston closes in on itself, conceited, petulant, idle, and broke.

I observe this from a particular vantage point. To my surprise, I have become a divorce lawyer. The first cases I tried after joining forces with Deshais were complicated divorce actions. They were women referred to me by Hamlin Junior, cases considered—I think he used the word "fraught"—too mumble "fraught" for H, W. In Chicago we used the word "messy," though all this was a long time ago; now they are tidy and without fault. However, then as now there was pulling and hauling over the money. Hamlin Junior admired my trial work and believed me discreet and respectable enough to represent in the first instance his cousin and in the second a dear friend of his wife's. He said that he hoped the matter of the cousin would be handled quietly, meaning without a lengthy trial and without publicity, but that if the case went to trial he wanted her represented by a lawyer ahem who was long off the tee. You know what it is you must do? he asked. I nodded. At that time divorces were purchased; you bought a judge for the afternoon. Happily, the cousin was disposed of in conference, quietly and very expensively for her husband. The success of that case caused Hamlin Junior to send me the second woman, whose disposition was not quite so quiet. Fraught it certainly was, and even more expensive.

I was suddenly inside the bedroom, hearing stories the obverse of those I had heard after hours at H, W. The view from the bedroom was different from the view from the locker room. It was as if a light-bulb joke had been turned around and told from the point of view of the bulb. Hundred-watt Mazda shocks WASP couple! I discovered that I had a way with women in trouble. That is precisely because I do not pretend to understand them, as a number of my colleagues insist that they "understand women." But I do listen. I listen very carefully, and then I ask questions and listen again. They ask me questions and I am still listening hard, and when I offer my answers they are brief and as precise as I can make them. And I never, never compromise. No woman has ever rebuked me with "But you *said,* and now you've broken your word."

The cousin and the wife's friend were satisfied and told Hamlin Junior, who said nothing to his colleagues. He seemed to regard me as the new chic restaurant in town, undiscovered and therefore underpriced; it would become popular soon enough, but meanwhile the food would continue excellent and the service attentive and the bill modest. For years he referred clients and friends to me, and I always accepted them even when they were routine cases and I had to trim my fees. And when Hamlin Junior died, I went to his funeral, and was not at all startled to see so many familiar female faces crowding the pews.

My divorce business was the beginning and there was a col-
lateral benefit—no, bonanza. I learned how money flows in
Boston, and where; which were the rivers and which were the
tributaries and which were the underground streams. Over the
years, I have examined hundreds of trusts and discovered a mul-
tiformity of hidden assets, liquid and solid, floating and stationary, lettered and numbered, aboveground and below. The
trusts are of breathtaking ingenuity, the product of the flintiest
minds in Massachusetts, and of course facilitated over the years
by a willing legislature. And what has fascinated me from the
beginning is this: The trust that was originally devised to avoid
taxes or to punish a recalcitrant child or to siphon income or to
"protect" an unworldly widow or to reach beyond the grave to
control the direction of a business or a fortune or a marriage can
fall apart when faced with the circumstances of the present, an
aggrieved client, and a determined attorney.

This is not the sort of legal practice I planned, but it is
what I have. Much of what I have discovered in divorce proceedings I have replicated in my trust work, adding a twist
here and there to avoid unraveling by someone like me,
sometime in the future. Wills and trusts are now a substantial part of my business, since I have access to the flintiest
minds in Massachusetts. Turn, and turn about. However, it
is a risible anomaly of the upper classes of Boston that the
estates have grown smaller and the trusts absurdly complex—Alcatraz to hold juvenile delinquents.

So one way and another I am in the business of guarantee-
ing the future. A trust, like a marriage, is a way of getting a
purchase on the future. That is what I tell my clients, especially the women; women have a faith in the future that men,
as a rule, do not. I am careful to tell my clients that although
that is the objective, it almost never works; or it does not work
in the way they intend it to work. It is all too difficult reading the past, without trying to read the future as well. It is my

view that men, at least, understand this, having, as a rule, a sense of irony and proportion. At any event, this is my seat at the Boston opera. It is lucrative and fascinating work. There was no compelling reason, therefore, not to listen to the complaint of Beth Earle Doran Greer, my former fiancée.

She said quietly, "It's finished."

I said nothing.

She described their last year together, the two vacations and the month at Edgartown, happy for the most part. They had one child, a boy, now at boarding school. It had been a durable marriage, fifteen years; the first one had lasted less than a year, and she had assumed that despite various troubles this one would endure. Then last Wednesday he said he was leaving her and his lawyer would be in touch.

"Has he?"

"No," she said.

"Who is he?"

She named a State Street lawyer whom I knew by reputation. He was an excellent lawyer. I was silent again, waiting for her to continue.

"Frank didn't say anything more than that."

"Do you know where he is?"

"I think he's at the farm." I waited again, letting the expression on my face do the work. There were two questions. Is he alone? Do you want him back? She said again, "It's finished." Then, the answer to the other question: "There is no one else." I looked at her, my face in neutral. She said, "Hard as that may be to understand."

Not believe, *understand*; a pointed distinction. I nodded, taking her at her word. It was hard, her husband was a great bon vivant.

"That's what he says, and I believe him. His sister called me to say that there isn't anybody else, but I didn't need her to tell me. Believe me, I know the signs. There isn't a sign I don't know and can't see a mile away, and he doesn't show any of them. Five years ago—that was something else. But she's married and not around anymore, and that's over and done with. And besides, if there was someone else he'd tell me. It'd be like him."

I nodded again and made a show of writing on my pad.

"And there isn't anyone else with me either."

"Well," I said, and smiled.

"Is it a first?"

I laughed quietly. "Not a first," I said. "Maybe a second."

She laughed, and lit a cigarette. "You were afraid it would be another cliché, she would be twenty and just out of Radcliffe. Meanwhile, I would've taken up with the garage mechanic or the gamekeeper. Or Frank's best friend; they tell me that's chic now." She looked at me sideways and clucked. "You know me better than that. Clichés aren't my style."

I said, "I never knew you at all."

"Yes, you did," she said quickly. I said nothing. "You always listened, in those days you were a very good listener. And you're a good listener now."

"The secret of my success," I said. But I knew my smile was getting thinner.

"The mouthpiece who listens," she said. "That's what Nora told me, when she was singing your praises. Really, she did go on. Do they fall in love with you, like you're supposed to do with a psychiatrist?"

Nora was a client I'd represented in an action several years before, a referral from Hamlin Junior. She was a great friend of Beth's but a difficult woman and an impossible client. I said, "No."

"It was a pretty good marriage," she said after a moment's pause. "You'd think, fifteen years . . . " I leaned forward, listening. Presently, in order to focus the conversation, I would ask the first important question: What is it that you want me to do now? For the moment, though, I wanted to hear more. I have never regarded myself as a marriage counselor, but it is always wise to know the emotional state of your client. So far, Beth seemed admirably rational and composed, almost cold-blooded. I wondered if she had ever consulted a psychiatrist, then decided she probably hadn't. There was something impersonal about her locution "like you're supposed to." She said abruptly, "How did you get into this work? It's so unlike you. Remember the stories you told me about your grandfather and his friend? The relationship they had, and how that was the kind of lawyer you wanted to be?"

I remembered all right, but I was surprised that she did. My grandfather and I were very close, and when I was a youngster we lunched together every Saturday. My father drove me to the old man's office, in an unincorporated area of Cook County, near Blue Island. I'd take the elevator to the fourth floor, the building dark and silent on Saturday morning. My grandfather was always courteous and formal, treating me as he would treat an important adult. On Saturday mornings my grandfather met with Tom. Tom was his lawyer. I was too young to know exactly what they were talking about, though as I look back on it, their conversation was in a private language. There was a "matter" that needed "handling," or "a man"—perhaps "sound," perhaps "a screwball"—who had to be "turned." Often there was a sum of money involved—three, four, fi' thousand dollars. These questions would be discussed sparely, long pauses between sentences. Then, as a signal that the conversation was near its end, my grandfather would say, "Now this is what I want to do," and his voice would fall. Tom would lean close to the old man, listening hard; I never saw him make a note. Then, "Now you figure out how I can do it." And Tom would nod, thinking, his face disappearing into the collar of his enormous camel's-hair coat. He never removed the coat, and he sat with his gray fedora in both hands, between his knees, turning it like the steering wheel of a car. When he finished thinking, he would rise and approach me and gravely shake hands. Then he would offer me a piece of licorice from the strand he kept in his coat, the candy furry with camel's hair. He pressed it on me until I accepted. I can remember him saying good-bye to my grandfather and, halting at the door, smiling slightly and winking. Tom would exit whistling, and more often than not my grandfather would make a telephone call, perhaps two, speaking inaudibly into the receiver. Finally, rumbling in his basso profundo, he would make the ritual call to the Chicago Athletic Club to reserve his usual table for two, "myself and my young associate."

In those days children were not allowed in the men's bar, so we ate in the main dining room, a huge chamber with high ceilings and a spectacular view of the lakefront. We sat at a table by the window, and on a clear day we could see Gary and Michigan City to the southeast. Long-hulled ore boats were smudges on the horizon. Once, during the war, we saw a pocket aircraft carrier, a training vessel for Navy pilots stationed at Great Lakes. The old man would wave his hand in the direction of the lake and speak of the Midwest as an ancient must have spoken of the Fertile Crescent: the center of the world, a homogeneous, God-fearing, hardworking *region,* its interior position protecting it from its numerous enemies. With a sweep of his hand he signified the noble lake and the curtain of smoke that hung over Gary's furnaces, thundering even on Saturdays. Industry, he'd say, *heavy* industry working at one hundred percent of capacity. Chicagoland, foundry to the world. His business was politics, he said; and his politics was business. "We can't let them take it away from us, all this . . ."

When the old man died, Tom was his principal pallbearer. It was a large funeral; the governor was present with his suite, along with a score of more or lesser politicians. Tom was dry-eyed, but I knew he was grieving. At the end of it he came over to me and shook my hand, solemnly as always, and said, "Your grandfather was one of the finest men who ever lived, a great friend, a great Republican, a great American, and a great client." I thought that an extraordinary inventory and was about to say so when he gripped my arm and exclaimed, "You ever need help of any kind, you come to me. That man and

I . . ." He pointed at my grandfather's casket, still above-ground under its green canopy, then tucked his chin into the camel's hair. "We've been through the mill, fought every day of our lives. I don't know what will happen without him." He waved dispiritedly at the gravestones around us, stones as far as the eye could see, and lowered his voice so that I had to bend close to hear. "The world won't be the same without him," Tom said. "The Midwest's going to hell."

Tom died a few years later, without my having had a chance to take him up on his offer. But from my earliest days in that fourth-floor office I knew I would be a lawyer. I wanted to be Tom to someone great, and prevent the world from going to hell. Tom was a man who listened carefully to a complex prob-lem, sifting and weighing possibilities. Then, settled and secure in his own mind, he figured a way to get from here to there. It was only an idiosyncrasy of our legal system that the route was never a straight line.

"I mean," she said brightly, leaning forward on the couch, "listening to a bunch of hysterical women with their busted marriages, that wasn't what I expected at all."

"They are not always hysterical," I said, "and some of them are men."

"And you never married," she said.

That was not true, but I let it pass.

"No," she said, rapping her knuckles on the coffee table. "You *were* married. I heard that, a long time ago. I heard that you were married, a whirlwind romance in Europe, but then it broke up right away."

"That's right," I said.

"She was French."

"English," I said.

"And there were no children."

"No," I said. We were silent while I walked to the side-board, made a drink for myself, and refilled hers.

"Do you remember how we used to talk, that place on

Hanover Street we used to go to, all that pasta and grappa? I practiced my Italian on them. Always the last one out the door, running down Hanover Street to that awful place you had on—where was it?"

"North Street," I said.

"North Street. We'd get dinner and then we'd go to your place and you'd take me back to Newton in your red Chevrolet. Three, four o'clock in the morning. I don't know how you got any work done, the hours we kept."

I nodded, remembering.

"And of course, when I heard you'd been sacked at H, W, I didn't know what to think, except that it was for the best." She paused. "Which I could've told you if you'd asked." I handed her the highball and sat down, resuming my lawyerly posture, legs crossed, the pad in my lap. "Do you ever think about your grandfather? Or what would've happened if you'd gone back to Chicago instead of following me here? Whether you'd've gone into politics, like him?"

"I don't follow you," I said. "We came together. It was where we intended to live, together."

"Whatever." She took a long swallow of her drink. "Chicago's such a different place from Boston, all that prairie. Boston's close and settled and old, so charming." I listened, tapping the pencil on my legal pad. It was dark now. At night the city seemed less close and settled. The cars in the street outside were bumper to bumper, honking. There was a snarl at the intersection, one car double-parked and another stalled. A car door slammed and there were angry shouts. She looked at me, smiling. "I don't want anything particular from him."

I made a note on my pad.

"I have plenty of money; so does he. Isn't that the modern way? No punitive damages?" She hesitated. "So there won't be any great opportunity to delve into the assets. And Frank's trust. Or mine."

I ignored that. "Of course there's little Frank."

She looked at me with the hint of a malicious grin. "How did you know his name?"

"Because I follow your every movement," I said, with as much sarcasm as I could muster. "For Christ's sake, Beth. I don't know how I know his name. People like Frank Greer always name their children after themselves."

"Don't get belligerent," she said. "A more devoted father—" she began and then broke off.

"Yes," I said.

"—he's devoted to little Frank." She hesitated, staring out the window for a long moment. She was holding her glass with both hands, in her lap. She said, "What was the name of that man, your grandfather's lawyer?"

"Tom," I said.

"God, yes," she said, laughing lightly. "Tom, one of those sturdy midwestern names."

"I think," I said evenly, "I think Tom is a fairly common name. I think it is common even in Boston.

She laughed again, hugely amused. "God, yes, it's common."

I glared at her, not at all surprised that she remembered which buttons worked and which didn't. Beth had an elephant's memory for any man's soft spots. Why Tom was one of mine was not so easily explained; Beth would have one explanation, I another. But of course she remembered. My background was always a source of tension between us, no doubt because my own attitude was ambiguous. She found my grandfather and Tom . . . quaint. They were colorful provincials, far from her Boston milieu, and she condescended to them exactly as certain English condescend to Australians.

"It's a riot," she said.

"So," I said quietly, glancing at my watch. "What is it that you want me to do now?"

"A quick, clean divorce," she said. "Joint custody for little Frank, though it's understood he lives with me. Nothing changes hands, we leave with what we brought, *status quo ante.*

I take my pictures, he takes his shotguns. Except, naturally, the house in Beverly. It's mine anyway, though for convenience it's in both our names. He understands that."

"What about the farm?"

"We split that, fifty-fifty."

"Uh-huh," I said.

"Is it always this easy?"

"We don't know how easy it'll be," I said carefully. "Until I talk to his lawyer. Maybe it won't be easy at all. It depends on what he thinks his grievances are."

"He hasn't got any."

"Well," I said.

"So it'll be easy," she said, beginning to cry.

We had agreed to go to dinner after meeting in my office. I proposed the Ritz; she countered with a French restaurant I had never heard of. She insisted, Boylston Street nouvelle cuisine, and I acceded, not without complaint. I told her about a client, a newspaperman who came to me every six years for his divorce. The newspaperman said that the nouvelle cuisine reminded him of the nouveau journalisme—a colorful plate, agreeably subtle, wonderfully presented with inspired combinations, and underdone. The portions were small, every dish had a separate sauce, and you were hungry when you finished. A triumph of style over substance.

She listened patiently, distracted.

I was trying to make her laugh. "But I can get a New York strip here, which they'll call an entrecôte, and there isn't a lot you can do to ruin a steak. Though they will try."

"You haven't changed," she said bleakly.

"Yes, I have," I said. "In the old days I would've been as excited about this place as you are. I'd know the names of the specialties of the house and of the chef. In the old days I was as al dente as the veggies. But not anymore." I glanced sourly around the room. The colors were pastel, various tints of yellow, even to a limp jonquil in the center of each table, all of it illuminated by candles thin as pencils and a dozen wee chandeliers overhead. It was very feminine and not crowded; expensive restaurants rarely were in Boston now; the money was running out.

"I'm sorry about the tears," she said.

I said, "Don't be."

"I knew I was going to bawl when I made that remark about Tom and you reacted."

"Yes," I said. I'd known it too.

"It made me sad. It reminded me of when we were breaking up and the arguments we had."

I smiled gamely. "I was al dente then, and I broke easily." I knew what she was leading up to, and I didn't want it. When the waiter arrived I ordered a whiskey for us both, waiting for the little superior sneer and feeling vaguely disappointed when he smiled pleasantly and flounced off. I started to tell her a story but she cut me off, as I knew she would.

"It reminded me of that ghastly dinner and how awful everything was afterward."

I muttered something noncommittal, but the expression on her face told me she wanted more, so I said it was over and forgotten, part of the past, etcetera. Like hell. We had argued about the restaurant that night, as we had tonight, except I won and we went to the Union Oyster House. My parents were in town, my father ostensibly on business; in fact they were in Boston to meet Beth. The dinner did not go well from the beginning; the restaurant was crowded and the service indifferent. My parents didn't seem to care, but Beth was irritated—"The Union Oyster Tourist Trap"—and that in turn put me on edge, or perhaps it was the other way around. Halfway through dinner, I suspect in an effort to salvage things, my father shyly handed Beth a wrapped package. It was a bracelet he had selected himself; even my mother didn't know about it. It was so unlike him, and such a sweet gesture, tears jumped into my eyes. Even before she opened it, I knew it would not be right. Beth had a particular taste in jewelry and as a consequence rarely wore any. I hoped she could disguise her feelings, but as it happened she giggled. And did not put the bracelet on, but hurried it into her purse, after leaning over the table and kissing my father. He did not fail to notice the bracelet rushed out of sight. Probably he didn't miss the giggle, either. In the manner of families, after a suitable silent interval my father and I commenced to quarrel. On the surface it was a quarrel about businessmen and professional men, but actually it had to do with the merits of the East and the merits of the Midwest and my father's knowledge that I had rejected the values of his region. The Midwest asserted its claims early, and if you had a restless nature you left. It forced you to leave; there were no halfway measures in the heartland, at that time a province as surely as Franche-Comté or Castile, an interior region pressed by the culture of the coasts, defensive, suspicious and claustrophobic. When I left I tried to explain to him that a New Yorker's restlessness or ambition could take him to Washington as a Bostonian's could take him to New York, the one city representing power and the other money. No midwesterner, making the momentous decision to leave home, would go from Chicago to Cleveland or from Minneapolis to Kansas City. These places are around the corner from one another. The Midwest is the same wherever you go, the towns larger or smaller but the culture identical. Leaving the Midwest, one perforce rejects the Midwest and its values; its sense of inferiority—so I felt then—prevented any return. In some way it had failed. What sound reason could there be for leaving God's country, the very soul of the nation, to live and work on the cluttered margins? It had failed you and you had failed it, whoring after glitter. My father's chivalry did not allow him to blame "that girl" publicly, but I knew that privately he did. Too much—too much Boston, too much money, too determined, too self-possessed. He hated to

think that his son—flesh of my flesh, blood of my blood!—
could be led out of Chicagoland by a woman. The image I
imagine it brought to his mind was of an ox dumbly plodding
down a road, supervised by a young woman lightly flicking its
withers with a stick. That ghastly dinner!

"The thing is." She smiled wanly, back in the present now:
that is, her own life, and what she had made of it. "It's so—*tiresome.* I know the marriage is over, it's probably been finished for
years. But starting over again. I don't want to start over again.
I haven't the energy." She sighed. "He's said for years that he's
got to find himself. He's forty-eight years old and he's lost and
now he wants to be found. And I'm sure he will be."

"Usually it's the other way around," I said. "These days, it's
the women who want to find themselves. Or get lost, one or
the other."

"Frank has a feminine side." I nodded, thinking of Frank
Greer as a pastel. Frank in lime-green and white, cool and
pretty as a gin and tonic. "But the point isn't Frank," Beth
said. "It's me. I don't want to start over again. I started over
again once and that didn't work and then I started over again
and it was fun for a while and then it was a routine, like everything else. I like the routine. And I was younger then."

I did not quite follow that, so I said, "I know."

"Liar," she said. "How could you? You've never been married."

"Beth," I said.

She looked at me irritably. "That doesn't count. You've got
to be married for at least five years before it's a marriage. And
there have to be children, or at least a child. Otherwise it's just
shacking up and you can get out of it as easily and painlessly
as you got into it, which from the sound of yours was pretty
easy and painless."

I looked away while the waiter set down our drinks and,
with a flourish, the menus.

"How long ago was it?"

"Almost twenty years ago," I said.

"Where is she now?"

I shrugged. I had no idea. When she left me she went back to London. I heard she had a job there; then, a few years ago, I heard she was living in France, married, with children. Then I heard she was no longer in France but somewhere else on the Continent, unmarried now.

"That's what I mean," she said. "You don't even know where she *is*."

"Well," I said. "She knows where I am."

"What was her name?"

"Rachel," I said.

Beth thought a moment. "Was she Jewish?"

"Yes," I said.

Beth made a little sound, but did not comment. The amused look on her face said that my father must have found Rachel even more unsuitable than Beth. As it happppened, she was right, but it had nothing to do with Rachel's Jewishness. She was a foreigner with pronounced political opinions. "And you like living alone," Beth said.

"At first I hated it," I said. "But I like it now and I can't imagine living any other way. It's what I do, live alone. You get married, I don't. Everyone I know gets married and almost everyone I know gets divorced."

"Well, you see it from the outside."

"It's close enough," I said.

"Yes, but it's not *real*." She glanced left into Boylston Street. It was snowing, and only a few pedestrians were about, bending into the wind. She shivered when she looked at the stiff-legged pedestrians, their movements so spiritless and numb against the concrete of the sidewalk, the sight bleaker still by contrast with the pale monochrome and the fragrance of the restaurant. Outside was a dark, malicious, European winter, Prague perhaps, or Moscow. "We might've made it," she said tentatively, still looking out the window.

I said nothing. She was dead wrong about that.

She sat with her chin in her hand, staring into the blowing snow. "But we were so different, and you were so bad."

The waiter was hovering and I turned to ask him the specialties of the day. They were a tiny bird en croûte, a fish soufflé, and a vegetable ensemble. Beth was silent, inspecting the menu; she had slipped on a pair of half-glasses for this chore. I ordered a dozen oysters and an entrecôte, medium well. I knew that if I ordered it medium well I had a fair chance of getting it medium rare. Then I ordered a baked potato and a Caesar salad and another drink. The waiter caught something in my tone and courteously suggested that medium well was excessive. I said all right, if he would promise a true medium rare. Beth ordered a fish I never heard of and called for the wine list. The waiter seemed much happier dealing with Beth than with me. They conferred over the wine list for a few moments, and then he left.

She said, "You're always so defensive."

"I don't like these places, I told you that." I heard the Boston whine in my voice and retreated a step. "The waiter's okay."

"You never did like them," she said. "But at least *before . . .*" She shook her head, exasperated.

"Before, what?" I asked.

"At least you were a provincial, there was an excuse."

I pulled at my drink, irritated. But when I saw her smiling slyly I had to laugh. Nothing had changed, though we had not seen each other in fifteen years and had not spoken in twenty. The occasion fifteen years ago was a wedding reception. I saw her standing in a corner talking to Frank Greer. She was recently divorced from Doran. I was about to approach to say hello; then I saw the expression on her face and withdrew. She and Greer were in another world, oblivious of the uproar around them, and I recognized the expression: it was the one I thought was reserved for me. Now, looking at her across the restaurant table, it was as if we had never been apart, as if our attitudes were frozen in aspic. We were still like a divided legislature, forever arguing over the economy, social policy, the defense budget, and the cuisine in the Senate dining room. The same arguments, conducted in the same terms; the same old struggle for control of our future. Her prejudice, my pride.

"You have to tell me one thing." She turned to inspect the bottle the waiter presented, raising her head so she could see through the half-glasses. She touched the label of the wine with her fingernails and said yes, it was fine, excellent really, and then, turning, her head still raised, she assured me that I would find it drinkable, since it came from a splendid little chateau vineyard near the Wisconsin Dells. The waiter looked at her dubiously and asked whether he should open it now and put it on ice, and she said yes, of course, she wanted it so cold she'd need her mittens to pour it. I was laughing and thinking how attractive she was, a woman whose humor improved with age, if she would just let up a little on the other. Also, I was waiting for the "one thing" I would have to tell her.

I said, "You're a damn funny woman."

"I have good material," she said.

"Not always," I replied.

"The one thing," she said, "that I can't figure out. Never could figure out. Why did you stay here? This isn't your kind of town at all, never was. It's so circumspect, and sure of itself. I'm surprised you didn't go back to Chicago after you were canned by H, W."

"I like collapsing civilizations," I said. "I'm a connoisseur of collapse and systems breakdown and bankruptcy—moral, ethical, and financial. So Boston is perfect." I thought of the town where I grew up, so secure and prosperous then, so down-at-heel now, the foundry old, exhausted, incidental, and off the subject. We lived in Chicago's muscular shadow and were thankful for it, before the world went to hell. "And I wasn't about to be run out of town by people like that," I added truculently.

"So it was spite," she said.

"Not spite," I said equably. "Inertia."

"And you're still spending weekends in New York?"

I nodded. Not as often now as in the past, though.

"Weird life you lead," she said.

I said, "What's so weird about it?"

"Weekdays here, weekends in New York. And you still have your flat near the brownstone, the same one?"

I looked at her with feigned surprise. "How did you know about my flat?"

"For God's sake," she said. "Nora's a friend of mine."

It was never easy to score a point on Beth Earle. I said, "I've had it for almost twenty years. And I'll have it for twenty more. It's my Panama Canal. I bought it, I paid for it, it's mine, and I intend to keep it."

She shook her head, smiling ruefully. She said that she had lived in half a dozen houses over the years and remembered each one down to the smallest detail: the color of the tile in the bathroom and the shape of the clothes closet in the bedroom. She and Doran had lived in Provincetown for a year, and then had moved to Gloucester. That was when Doran was trying to paint. Then, after Doran, she lived alone in Marblehead. When she was married to Frank Greer they went to New York, then returned to Boston; he owned an apartment on Beacon Hill. They lived alone there for two years, and then moved to Beverly—her idea; she was tired of the city. She counted these places on her fingers. "Six," she said. "And all this time, you've been in the same place in the Back Bay." She was leaning across the table, and now she looked up. The waiter placed a small salad in front of her and the oysters in front of me. The oysters were Cotuits. She signaled for the wine and said that "Monsieur" would taste. She told the waiter I was a distinguished gourmet, much sought after as a taster, and that my wine cellar in Michigan City was the envy of the region. She gave the impression that the restaurant was lucky to have me as a patron. The waiter shot me a sharp look and poured the wine into my glance. I pronounced it fine.

Actually, I said it was "swell," and then, gargling heartily, "dandy." I gave Beth one of the oysters and insisted that she eat it the way it was meant to be eaten, naked out of the shell, without catsup or horseradish. She sucked it up, and then leaned across the table once again. "Don't you miss them, the arguments? The struggle, always rubbing off something else? The fights, the friction—?"

I laughed loudly. "Miss them to death," I said.

We finished the bottle of white, and ordered a bottle of red; she said she preferred red with fish. I suspected that that was a concession to my entrecôte, which at any event was rare and bloody. She continued to press, gently at first, then with vehemence. She was trying to work out her life and thought that somehow I was a clue to it. At last she demanded that I describe my days in Boston. She wanted to know how I lived, the details, "the quotidian." I was reluctant to do this, having lived privately for so many years. Also, there was very little to describe. I had fallen into the bachelor habit of total predictability. Except to travel to the airport and the courts, I seldom left Back Bay. My terrain was bordered by the Public Garden and the Ritz, Storrow Drive, Newbury Street, the brownstone where I worked and Commonwealth Avenue where I lived. I walked to work, lunched at the Ritz, took a stroll in the Garden, returned to the brownstone, and at seven or so went home. People I knew tended to live in the Back Bay or on the Hill, so if I went out in the evening I walked. Each year it became easier not to leave the apartment; I needed an exceptional reason to do so. I liked my work and worked hard at it.

She listened avidly, but did not comment. The waiter came to clear the table and offer dessert. We declined, ordering coffee and cognac.

"What kind of car do you have?" she asked suddenly.

I said I didn't own one.

"What kind of car does she own?"

I looked at her: Who?

"Your secretary," she said. "I hear you have a relationship with your secretary."

"She's been my assistant for a very long time," I said.

"Her car," Beth said.

I said, "A Mercedes."

"Well," she said.

"Well, what?"

"Well, nothing," she said. "Except so do I."

"Two cheers for the Krauts," I said.

"Is she a nice woman?"

I laughed. "Yes," I said. "Very. And very able."

"She approves of the arrangement."

"Beth," I said.

Beth said, "I wonder what she gets out of it?"

"She won't ever have to get divorced," I said. "That's one thing she gets out of it."

"Was she the woman in the outer office?"

"Probably," I said.

Beth was silent a moment, toying with her coffee cup. There was only one other couple left in the restaurant, and they were preparing to leave. "You were always secretive," she said.

"You were not exactly an open book."

She ignored that. "It's not an attractive trait, being secretive. It leaves you wide open."

For what? I wondered. I looked at her closely, uncertain whether it was she talking or the wine. We were both tight, but her voice had an edge that had not been there before. I poured more coffee, wondering whether I should ask the question that had been in my mind for the past hour. I knew I would not like the answer, whatever it was, but I was curious. Being with her again, I began to remember things I had not thought of in years; it was as if the two decades were no greater distance than the width of the table, and I had only to lean across the space and take her hand to be twenty-five again. The evening had already been very unsettling and strange; no reason, I thought, not to make it stranger still.

I said quietly, "How was I so bad?"

"You never let go," she said. "You just hung on for dear life."

"Right," I said. I had no idea what she was talking about.

"Our plans," she began.

"Depended on me letting go?"

She shrugged. "You tried to fit in and you never did."

"In Boston," I said.

She moved her head, yes and no; apparently the point was a subtle one. "I didn't want to come back here and you insisted. I was depending on you to take me away, or at least make an independent life. You never understood that I had always been on the outs with my family."

I stifled an urge to object. I had never wanted to come to Boston. It was where she lived. It was her town, not mine. Glorious Boston, cradle of the Revolution. I had no intrinsic interest in Boston, I only wanted to leave the Midwest. Boston was as good a city as any, and she lived there—

"You were such a damn good *listener.*" She bit the word off, as if it were an obscenity. "Better than you are now, and you're pretty good now. Not so good at talking, though. You listened so well a woman forgot that you never talked yourself, never let on what it was *that was on your mind.* Not one of your strong points, talking."

"Beth," I said evenly. She waited, but I said nothing more; there was nothing more to say anyhow, and I knew the silence would irritate her.

"And it was obvious that it would never work; we never got grounded here. And it was obvious you never would, you could never let go or your damned prairie *complexe d'infériorité.* And as a result you were"—she sought the correct word—*"louche."*

"I am not André Malraux," I said. "What the hell does that mean?"

"It means secretive," she said. "And something more. Furtive."

"Thanks," I said.

"It's a mystery to me why I'm still here. Not so great a mystery as you, but mystery enough. You had to lead the way, though, and you didn't. And I knew H, W was a mistake."

"It was your uncle who suggested it," I said.

"After you asked him," she said.

"At your urging," I said.

"When it looked like you wouldn't land anything and I was tired of the griping."

"You were the one who was nervous," I said.

"I didn't care where we lived," she said. "That was the point you never got." Her voice rose, and I saw the waiter turn and say something to the maître d'. The other couple had left and we were alone in the restaurant. Outside, a police car sped by, its lights blazing, but without sirens. The officer in the passenger seat was white-haired and fat, and he was smoking a cigar. It had stopped snowing but the wind was fierce, blowing debris and rattling windows. The police car had disappeared. I motioned to the waiter for the check. But Beth was far from finished.

"So I married Doran."

"And I didn't marry anybody."

"You married Rachel."

"According to you, Rachel doesn't count."

"Neither did Doran."

The waiter brought the check and I automatically reached for my wallet. She said loudly, "No," and I looked at her, momentarily confused. I had forgotten it was her treat. I had become so absorbed in the past; always when we had been together, I had paid, and it seemed cheap of me to let her pay now. But that was what she wanted and I had agreed to it. She had the check in her hand and was inspecting it for errors. Then, satisfied, she pushed it aside along with a credit card. She exhaled softly and turned to look out the window.

She said quietly, talking to the window, "Do you think it will be easy?"

"I don't know," I said.

"Please," she said. She said it hesitantly, as if the word were unfamiliar. "Just tell me what you think. I won't hold you to it, if you're wrong."

"His lawyer," I began.

"Please," she said again, more forcefully.

"You're asking me for assurances that I can't give. I don't know."

"Just a guess," she said. "In your line of work you must make guesses all the time. Make one now, between us. Between friends."

"Well, then," I said. "No."

"The first one was easy."

"Maybe this one will be too," I said.

"But you don't think so."

"No," I said. I knew Frank Greer.

She said, "You're a peach." She put on her glasses.

I did not reply to that.

"I mean it," she said.

Apparently she did, for she looked at me and smiled warmly.

"I have disrupted your life."

I shook my head, No.

"Yes, I have. That's what I do sometimes, disrupt the lives of men."

There was so much to say to that, and so little to be gained. I lit a cigarette, listening.

With a quick movement she pushed the half-glasses over her forehead and into her hair, all business. "Get in touch with me tomorrow. Can you do that?"

"Sure," I said.

"And let me know what he says, right away."

"Yes," I said.

"I don't think it's going to be so tough."

"I hope you're right," I said.

"But I've always been an optimist where men are concerned."

I smiled and touched her hand. I looked at her closely, remembering her as a young woman; I knew her now and I knew her then, but there was nothing in between. That was undiscovered territory. I saw the difficulties ahead. They were big as mountains, Annapurna-sized difficulties, a long slog at high altitudes, defending Beth. I took my hand away and said, "You can bail out any time you want, if this gets difficult or awkward. I know it isn't easy. I can put you in touch with any one of half a dozen—" She stared at me for a long moment. In the candlelight her face seemed to flush. Suddenly I knew she was murderously angry.

"I think you're right," she said.

"Look," I began.

"Reluctant lawyers are worse than useless." She took off her glasses and put them in her purse. When she snapped the purse shut it sounded like a pistol shot.

"I'll call you tomorrow," I said. I knew that I had handled it badly, but there was no retreat now.

She stood up and the waiter swung into position, helping her with her chair and bowing prettily from the waist.

Outside on Boylston Street the wind was still blowing, and the street was empty except for two cabs at the curb. We stood a moment on the sidewalk, not speaking. She stood with her head turned away, and I thought for a moment she was crying. But when she turned her head I saw the set of her jaw. She was too angry to cry. She began to walk up the street, and I followed. The wind off the Atlantic was vicious. I thought of it as originating in Scotland or Scandinavia, but of course that was wrong. Didn't the wind blow from west to east? This one probably originated in the Upper Midwest or Canada. It had a prairie feel to it. We both walked unsteadily with our heads tucked into our coat collars. I thought of Tom and his camel's-hair coat. At Arlington Street she stopped and fumbled for her keys, and then resumed the march. A beggar was at our heels, asking for money. I turned, apprehensive, but he was a sweet-faced drunk. I gave him a dollar and he ambled off. Her car was parked across the street from the Ritz, a green Mercedes convertible with her initials in gold on the door. The car gleamed in the harsh white light of the streetlamps. She stooped to unlock the door, and when she opened it the smell of leather, warm and inviting, spilled into the frigid street. I held the door for her, but she did not get in. She stood looking at me, her face expressionless. She started to say something, but changed her mind. She threw her purse into the back seat and the next thing I knew I was reeling backward, then slipping on an icy patch and falling. Her fist had come out of nowhere and caught me under the right eye. Sprawled on the sidewalk, speechless, I watched her get into the car and drive away. The smell of leather remained in my vicinity.

The doorman at the Ritz had seen all of it, and now he hurried across Arlington Street. He helped me up, muttering and fussing, but despite his best intentions he could not help smiling. He kept his face half turned away so I would not see. Of course he knew me, I was a regular in the bar and the café.

Damn woman, I said. She could go ten with Marvin Hagler.

He thought it was all right then to laugh.

Not like the old days, I said.

Packed quite a punch, did she, sir? Ha-ha.

I leaned against the iron fence and collected my wits.

Anything broken? he asked.

I didn't think so. I moved my legs and arms, touched my eye. It was tender but there was no blood. I knew I would have a shiner and wondered how I would explain that at the office.

Let's get you into the bar, he said. A brandy—

No. I shook my had painfully and reached for my wallet. The doorman waited, his face slightly averted as before. I

found a five, then thought better of it and gave him twenty.
He didn't have to be told that twenty dollars bought silence.
He tucked the money away in his vest and tipped his hat,
frowning solicitously.

You wait here one minute, he said. I'll fetch a cab.

No need, I replied. Prefer to walk. I live nearby.

I know, he said, looking at me doubtfully. Then, noticing
he had customers under the hotel canopy, he hurried back
across the street. I watched him go, assuring the people with
a casual wave of his hand that the disturbance was a private
matter, minor and entirely under control.

I moved away too, conscious of being watched and realizing
that I was very tight. I was breathing hard and could smell my
cognac breath. I felt my eye beginning to puff and I knew that
I would have bruises on my backside. I decided to take a long
way home and walked through the iron gate into the Garden.
There was no one about, but the place was filthy, papers blowing everywhere and ash cans stuffed to overflowing. The flur-
ries had left a residue of gray snow. I passed a potato-faced
George Washington on horseback on my way along the path
to the statue facing Marlborough Street. This was my favorite.
Atop the column a physician cradled an unconscious patient,
"to commemorate the discovery that the inhaling of ether
causes insensibility to pain. First proved to the world at the
Mass. General Hospital." It was a pretty little Victorian sculp-
ture. On the plinth someone had scrawled *Up the I.R.A.* in red
paint.

I exited at the Beacon Street side. A cab paused, but I waved
him on. I labored painfully down Beacon to Clarendon and
over to Commonwealth, my shoes scuffing little shards of blue
glass, hard and bright as diamonds; this was window glass
from the automobiles vandalized nightly. While I waited at
the light a large American sedan pulled up next to me, its
fender grazing my leg, two men and women staring menac-
ingly out the side windows. I took a step backward, and the

sedan sped through the red light, trailing rock music and laughter. Tires squealed as the car accelerated, wheeling right on Newbury.

My flat was only a few blocks away. I walked down the deserted mall, my eyes up and watchful. Leafless trees leaned over the walkway, their twisted branches grotesque against the night sky. I walked carefully, for there was ice and dog shit everywhere. The old-fashioned streetlights, truly handsome in daytime, were useless now. It was all so familiar; I had walked down this mall every day for twenty years. Twenty years ago, when there was no danger after dark, Rachel and I took long strolls on summer evenings trying to reach an understanding, and failing. I remembered her musical voice and accent; when she was distressed she spoke rapidly, but always with perfect diction. I looked up, searching for my living-room window. I was light-headed now and stumbling, but I knew I was close. The Hancock was to my left, as big as a mountain and as sheer, looming like some futuristic religious icon over the low, crabbed sprawl of the Back Bay. I leaned against a tree, out of breath. There was only a little way now; I could see the light in the window. My right eye was almost closed, and my vision blurred. The wind bit into my face, sending huge tears running down my cheeks. I hunched my shoulders against the wind and struggled on, through the empty streets of the city I hated so.

MRS. SEN'S

ELIOT HAD BEEN GOING to Mrs. Sen's for nearly a month, ever since school started in September. The year before he was looked after by a university student named Abby, a slim, freckled girl who read books without pictures on their covers, and refused to prepare any food for Eliot containing meat. Before that an older woman, Mrs. Linden, greeted him when he came home each afternoon, sipping coffee from a thermos and working on crossword puzzles while Eliot played on his own. Abby received her degree and moved off to another university, while Mrs. Linden was, in the end, fired when Eliot's mother discovered that Mrs. Linden's thermos contained more whiskey than coffee. Mrs. Sen came to them in tidy ballpoint script, posted on an index card outside the supermarket: "Professor's wife, responsible and kind, I will care for your child in my home." On the telephone Eliot's mother told Mrs. Sen that the previous babysitters had come to their house. "Eliot is eleven. He can feed and entertain himself; I just want an adult in the house, in case of emergency." But Mrs. Sen did not know how to drive.

"As you can see, our home is quite clean, quite safe for a child," Mrs. Sen had said at their first meeting. It was a university apartment located on the fringes of the campus. The lobby was tiled in unattractive squares of tan, with a row of mailboxes marked with masking tape or white labels. Inside, intersecting shadows left by a vacuum cleaner were frozen on the surface of a plush pear-colored carpet. Mismatched remnants of other carpets were positioned in front of the sofa and chairs, like individual welcome mats anticipating where a person's feet would contact the floor. White drum-shaped lampshades flanking the sofa were still wrapped in the manufacturer's plastic. The TV and the telephone were covered by pieces of yellow fabric with scalloped edges. There was tea in a tall gray pot, along with mugs, and butter biscuits on a tray. Mr. Sen, a short, stocky man with slightly protuberant eyes and glasses with black rectangular frames, had been there, too. He crossed his legs with some effort, and held his mug with both hands very close to his mouth, even when he wasn't drinking. Neither Mr. nor Mrs. Sen wore shoes; Eliot noticed several pairs lined on the shelves of a small bookcase by the front door. They wore flip-flops. "Mr. Sen teaches mathematics at the university," Mrs. Sen had said by way of introduction, as if they were only distantly acquainted.

She was about thirty. She had a small gap between her teeth and faded pockmarks on her chin, yet her eyes were beautiful, with thick, flaring brows and liquid flourishes that extended beyond the natural width of the lids. She wore a shimmering white sari patterned with orange paisleys, more suitable for an evening affair than for that quiet, faintly drizzling August afternoon. Her lips were coated in a complementary coral gloss, and a bit of the color had strayed beyond the borders.

Yet it was his mother, Eliot had thought, in her cuffed, beige shorts and her rope-soled shoes, who looked odd. Her cropped hair, a shade similar to her shorts, seemed too lank and sensible, and in that room where all things were so carefully covered, her shaved knees and thighs too exposed. She refused a biscuit each time Mrs. Sen extended the plate in her direction, and asked a long series of questions, the answers to which she recorded on a steno pad. Would there be other children in the apartment? Had Mrs. Sen cared for children before? How long had she lived in this country? Most of all she was concerned that Mrs. Sen did not know how to drive.

Eliot's mother worked in an office fifty miles north, and his father, the last she had heard, lived two thousand miles west.

"I have been giving her lessons, actually," Mr. Sen said, setting his mug on the coffee table. It was the first time he had spoken. "By my estimate Mrs. Sen should have her driver's license by December."

"Is that so?" Eliot's mother noted the information on her pad.

"Yes, I am learning," Mrs. Sen said. "But I am a slow student. At home, you know, we have a driver."

"You mean a chauffeur?"

Mrs. Sen glanced at Mr. Sen, who nodded.

Eliot's mother nodded, too, looking around the room. "And that's all . . . in India?"

"Yes," Mrs. Sen replied. The mention of the word seemed to release something in her. She neatened the border of her sari where it rose diagonally across her chest. She, too, looked around the room, as if she noticed in the lampshades, in the teapot, in the shadows frozen on the carpet, something the rest of them could not. "Everything is there."

Eliot didn't mind going to Mrs. Sen's after school. By September the tiny beach house where he and his mother lived year-round was already cold; Eliot and his mother had to bring a portable heater along whenever they moved from one room to another, and to seal the windows with plastic sheets and a hair drier. The beach was barren and dull to play on alone; the only neighbors who stayed on past Labor Day, a young married couple, had no children, and Eliot no longer found it interesting to gather broken mussel shells in his bucket, or to stroke the seaweed, strewn like strips of emerald lasagna on the sand. Mrs. Sen's apartment was warm, sometimes too warm; the radiators continuously hissed like a pressure cooker. Eliot learned to remove his sneakers first thing in Mrs. Sen's doorway, and to place them on the bookcase next to a row of

Mrs. Sen's slippers, each a different color, with soles as flat as cardboard and a ring of leather to hold her big toe.

He especially enjoyed watching Mrs. Sen as she chopped things, seated on newspapers on the living room floor. Instead of a knife she used a blade that curved like the prow of a Viking ship, sailing to battle in distant seas. The blade was hinged at one end to a narrow wooden base. The steel, more black than silver, lacked a uniform polish, and had a serrated crest, she told Eliot, for grating. Each afternoon Mrs. Sen lifted the blade and locked it into place, so that it met the base at an angle. Facing the sharp edge without ever touching it, she took whole vegetables between her hands and hacked them apart: cauliflower, cabbage, butternut squash. She split things in half, then quarters, speedily producing florets, cubes, slices, and shreds. She could peel a potato in seconds. At times she sat cross-legged, at times with legs splayed, surrounded by an array of colanders and shallow bowls of water in which she immersed her chopped ingredients.

While she worked she kept an eye on the television and an eye on Eliot, but she never seemed to keep an eye on the blade. Nevertheless she refused to let Eliot walk around when she was chopping. "Just sit, sit please, it will take just two more minutes," she said, pointing to the sofa, which was draped at all times with a green and black bedcover printed with rows of elephants bearing palanquins on their backs. The daily procedure took about an hour. In order to occupy Eliot she supplied him with the comics section of the newspaper, and crackers spread with peanut butter, and sometimes a Popsicle, or carrot sticks sculpted with her blade. She would have roped off the area if she could. Once, though, she broke her own rule; in need of additional supplies, and reluctant to rise from the catastrophic mess that barricaded her, she asked Eliot to fetch something from the kitchen. "If you don't mind, there is a plastic bowl, large enough to hold this spinach, in the cabinet next to the fridge. Careful, oh dear, be careful," she cautioned, as he approached. "Just leave it, thank you, on the coffee table, I can reach."

She had brought the blade from India, where apparently there was at least one in every household. "Whenever there is a wedding in the family," she told Eliot one day, "or a large celebration of any kind, my mother sends out word in the evening for all the neighborhood women to bring blades just like this one, and then they sit in an enormous circle on the roof of our building, laughing and gossiping and slicing fifty kilos of vegetables through the night." Her profile hovered protectively over her work, a confetti of cucumber, eggplant, and onion skins heaped around her. "It is impossible to fall asleep those nights, listening to their chatter." She paused to look at a pine tree framed by the living room window. "Here, in this place where Mr. Sen has brought me, I cannot sometimes sleep in so much silence."

Another day she sat prying the pimpled yellow fat off chicken parts, then dividing them between thigh and leg. As the bones cracked apart over the blade her golden bangles jostled, her forearms glowed, and she exhaled audibly through her nose. At one point she paused, gripping the chicken with both hands, and stared out the window. Fat and sinew clung to her fingers.

"Eliot, if I began to scream right now at the top of my lungs, would someone come?"

"Mrs. Sen, what's wrong?"

"Nothing. I am only asking if someone would come."

Eliot shrugged. "Maybe."

"At home that is all you have to do. Not everybody has a telephone. But just raise your voice a bit, or express grief or joy of any kind, and one whole neighborhood and half of another has come to share the news, to help with arrangements."

By then Eliot understood that when Mrs. Sen said home, she meant India, not the apartment where she sat chopping vegetables. He thought of his own home, just five miles away, and the young married couple who waved from time to time as they jogged at sunset along the shore. On Labor Day they'd had a party. People were piled on the deck, eating, drinking, the sound of their laughter rising above the weary sigh of the waves. Eliot and his mother weren't invited. It was one of the rare days his mother had off, but they didn't go anywhere. She did the laundry, balanced the checkbook, and, with Eliot's help, vacuumed the inside of the car. Eliot had suggested that they go through the car wash a few miles down the road as they did every now and then, so that they could sit inside, safe and dry, as soap and water and a circle of giant canvas ribbons slapped the windshield, but his mother said she was too tired, and sprayed the car with a hose. When, by evening, the crowd on the neighbors' deck began dancing, she looked up their number in the phone book and asked them to keep it down.

"They might call you," Eliot said eventually to Mrs. Sen. "But they might complain that you were making too much noise."

From where Eliot sat on the sofa he could detect her curious scent of mothballs and cumin, and he could see the perfectly centered part in her braided hair, which was shaded with crushed vermilion and therefore appeared to be blushing. At first Eliot had wondered if she had cut her scalp, or if something had bitten her there. But then one day he saw her standing before the bathroom mirror, solemnly applying, with the head of a thumbtack, a fresh stroke of scarlet powder, which she stored in a small jam jar. A few grains of the powder fell onto the bridge of her nose as she used the thumbtack to stamp a dot above her eyebrows. "I must wear the powder every day," she explained when Eliot asked her what it was for, "for the rest of the days that I am married."

"Like a wedding ring, you mean?"

"Exactly, Eliot, exactly like a wedding ring. Only with no fear of losing it in the dishwater."

By the time Eliot's mother arrived at twenty past six, Mrs. Sen always made sure all evidence of her chopping was disposed of.

The blade was scrubbed, rinsed, dried, folded, and stowed away in a cupboard with the aid of a stepladder. With Eliot's help the newspapers were crushed with all the peels and seeds and skins inside them. Brimming bowls and colanders lined the countertop, spices and pastes were measured and blended, and eventually a collection of broths simmered over periwinkle flames on the stove. It was never a special occasion, nor was she ever expecting company. It was merely dinner for herself and Mr. Sen, as indicated by the two plates and two glasses she set, without napkins or silverware, on the square formica table at one end of the living room.

As he pressed the newspapers deeper into the garbage pail, Eliot felt that he and Mrs. Sen were disobeying some unspoken rule. Perhaps it was because of the urgency with which Mrs. Sen accomplished everything, pinching salt and sugar between her fingernails, running water through lentils, sponging all imaginable surfaces, shutting cupboard doors with a series of successive clicks. It gave him a little shock to see his mother all of a sudden, in the transparent stockings and shoulder-padded suit she wore to her job, peering into the corners of Mrs. Sen's apartment. She tended to hover on the far side of the door frame, calling to Eliot to put on his sneakers and gather his things, but Mrs. Sen would not allow it. Each evening she insisted that his mother sit on the sofa, where she was served something to eat: a glass of bright pink yogurt with rose syrup, breaded mincemeat with raisins, a bowl of semolina halvah.

"Really, Mrs. Sen. I take a late lunch. You shouldn't go to so much trouble."

"It is no trouble. Just like Eliot. No trouble at all."

His mother nibbled Mrs. Sen's concoctions with eyes cast upward, in search of an opinion. She kept her knees pressed together, the high heels she never removed pressed into the pear-colored carpet. "It's delicious," she would conclude, setting down the plate after a bite or two. Eliot knew she didn't like the tastes; she'd told him so once in the car. He also knew she didn't eat lunch at work, because the first thing she did when they were back at the beach house was pour herself a glass of wine and eat bread and cheese, sometimes so much of it that she wasn't hungry for the pizza they normally ordered for dinner. She sat at the table as he ate, drinking more wine and asking how his day was, but eventually she went to the deck to smoke a cigarette, leaving Eliot to wrap up the leftovers.

Each afternoon Mrs. Sen stood in a grove of pine trees by the main road where the school bus dropped off Eliot along with two or three other children who lived nearby. Eliot always sensed that Mrs. Sen had been waiting for some time, as if eager to greet a person she hadn't seen in years. The hair at her temples blew about in the breeze, the column of vermilion fresh in her part. She wore navy blue sunglasses a little too big for her face. Her sari, a different pattern each day, fluttered below the hem of a checkered all-weather coat. Acorns and caterpillars dotted the asphalt loop that framed the complex of about a dozen brick buildings, all identical, embedded in a communal expanse of log chips. As they walked back from the bus stop she produced a sandwich bag from her pocket, and offered Eliot the peeled wedges of an orange, or lightly salted peanuts, which she had already shelled.

They proceeded directly to the car, and for twenty minutes Mrs. Sen practiced driving. It was a toffee-colored sedan with vinyl seats. There was an AM radio with chrome buttons, and on the ledge over the back seat, a box of Kleenex and an ice scraper. Mrs. Sen told Eliot she didn't feel right leaving him alone in the apartment, but Eliot knew she wanted him sitting beside her because she was afraid. She dreaded the roar of the ignition, and placed her hands over her ears to block out the sound as she pressed her slippered feet to the gas, revving the engine.

"Mr. Sen says that once I receive my license, everything will improve. What do you think, Eliot? Will things improve?"

"You could go places," Eliot suggested. "You could go anywhere."

"Could I drive all the way to Calcutta? How long would that take, Eliot? Ten thousand miles, at fifty miles per hour?"

Eliot could not do the math in his head. He watched Mrs. Sen adjust the driver's seat, the rearview mirror, the sunglasses on top of her head. She turned the radio to a station that played symphonies. "Is it Beethoven?" she asked once, pronouncing the first part of the composer's name not "bay," but "bee," like the insect. She rolled down the window on her side, and asked Eliot to do the same. Eventually she pressed her foot to the brake pedal, manipulated the automatic gear shift as if it were an enormous, leaky pen, and backed inch by inch out of the parking space. She circled the apartment complex once, then once again.

"How am I doing, Eliot? Am I going to pass?"

She was continuously distracted. She stopped the car without warning to listen to something on the radio, or to stare at something, anything, in the road. If she passed a person, she waved. If she saw a bird twenty feet in front of her, she beeped the horn with her index finger and waited for it to fly away. In India, she said, the driver sat on the right side, not the left. Slowly they crept past the swing set, the laundry building, the dark green trash bins, the rows of parked cars. Each time they approached the grove of pine trees where the asphalt loop met the main road, she leaned forward, pinning all her weight against the brake as cars hurtled past. It was a narrow road painted with a solid yellow stripe, with one lane of traffic in either direction.

"Impossible, Eliot. How can I go there?"

"You need to wait until no one's coming."

"Why will not anybody slow down?"

"No one's coming now."

"But what about the car from the right, do you see? And look, a truck is behind it. Anyway, I am not allowed on the main road without Mr. Sen."

"You have to turn and speed up fast," Eliot said. That was the way his mother did it, as if without thinking. It seemed so simple when he sat beside his mother, gliding in the evenings back to the beach house. Then the road was just a road, the other cars merely part of the scenery. But when he sat with Mrs. Sen, under an autumn sun that glowed without warmth through the trees, he saw how that same stream of cars made her knuckles pale, her wrists tremble, her English falter.

"Everyone, this people, too much in their world."

Two things, Eliot learned, made Mrs. Sen happy. One was the arrival of a letter from her family. It was her custom to check the mailbox after driving practice. She would unlock the box, but she would ask Eliot to reach inside, telling him what to look for, and then she would shut her eyes and shield them with her hands while he shuffled through the bills and magazines that came in Mr. Sen's name. At first Eliot found Mrs. Sen's anxiety incomprehensible; his mother had a p.o. box in town, and she collected mail so infrequently that once their electricity was cut off for three days. Weeks passed at Mrs. Sen's before he found a blue aerogram, grainy to the touch, crammed with stamps showing a bald man at a spinning wheel, and blackened by postmarks.

"Is this it, Mrs. Sen?"

For the first time she embraced him, clasping his face to her sari, surrounding him with her odor of mothballs and cumin. She seized the letter from his hands.

As soon as they were inside the apartment she kicked off her slippers this way and that, drew a wire pin from her hair, and slit the top and sides of the aerogram in three strokes. Her eyes darted back and forth as she read. As soon as she was finished, she cast aside the embroidery that covered the telephone, dialed, and asked, "Yes, is Mr. Sen there, please? It is Mrs. Sen and it is very important."

Subsequently she spoke in her own language, rapid and riotous to Eliot's ears; it was clear that she was reading the contents of the letter, word by word. As she read her voice was louder and seemed to shift in key. Though she stood plainly before him, Eliot had the sensation that Mrs. Sen was no longer present in the room with the pear-colored carpet.

Afterward the apartment was suddenly too small to contain her. They crossed the main road and walked a short distance to the university quadrangle, where bells in a stone tower chimed on the hour. They wandered through the student union, and dragged a tray together along the cafeteria ledge, and ate french fries heaped in a cardboard boat among students chattering at circular tables. Eliot drank soda from a paper cup, Mrs. Sen steeped a tea bag with sugar and cream. After eating they explored the art building, looking at sculptures and silk screens in cool corridors thick with the fragrance of wet paint and clay. They walked past the mathematics building, where Mr. Sen taught his classes.

They ended up in the noisy, chlorine-scented wing of the athletic building where, through a wide window on the fourth floor, they watched swimmers crossing from end to end in glaring turquoise pools. Mrs. Sen took the aerogram from India out of her purse and studied the front and back. She unfolded it and reread it to herself, sighing every now and then. When she had finished she gazed for some time at the swimmers.

"My sister has had a baby girl. By the time I see her, depending if Mr. Sen gets his tenure, she will be three years old. Her own aunt will be a stranger. If we sit side by side on a train she will not know my face." She put away the letter, then placed a hand on Eliot's head. "Do you miss your mother, Eliot, these afternoons with me?"

The thought had never occurred to him.

"You must miss her. When I think of you, only a boy, separated from your mother for so much of the day, I am ashamed."

"I see her at night."

"When I was your age I was without knowing that one day

I would be so far. You are wiser than that, Eliot. You already taste the way things must be."

The other thing that made Mrs. Sen happy was fish from the seaside. It was always a whole fish she desired, not shellfish, or the fillets Eliot's mother had broiled one night a few months ago when she'd invited a man from her office to dinner—a man who'd spent the night in his mother's bedroom, but whom Eliot never saw again. One evening when Eliot's mother came to pick him up, Mrs. Sen served her a tuna croquette, explaining that it was really supposed to be made with a fish called bhetki. "It is very frustrating," Mrs. Sen apologized, with an emphasis on the second syllable of the word. "To live so close to the ocean and not to have so much fish." In the summer, she said, she liked to go to a market by the beach. She added that while the fish there tasted nothing like the fish in India, at least it was fresh. Now that it was getting colder, the boats were no longer going out regularly, and sometimes there was no whole fish available for weeks at a time.

"Try the supermarket," his mother suggested.

Mrs. Sen shook her head. "In the supermarket I can feed a cat thirty-two dinners from one of thirty-two tins, but I can never find a single fish I like, never a single." Mrs. Sen said she had grown up eating fish twice a day. She added that in Calcutta people ate fish first thing in the morning, last thing before bed, as a snack after school if they were lucky. They ate the tail, the eggs, even the head. It was available in any market, at any hour, from dawn until midnight. "All you have to do is leave the house and walk a bit, and there you are."

Every few days Mrs. Sen would open up the yellow pages, dial a number that she had ticked in the margin, and ask if there was any whole fish available. If so, she would ask the market to hold it. "Under Sen, yes, S as in Sam, N as in New York. Mr. Sen will be there to pick it up." Then she would call Mr. Sen at the university. A few minutes later Mr. Sen would arrive, patting Eliot on the head but not kissing Mrs. Sen. He read his mail at the Formica table and drank a cup of tea before heading out; half an hour later he would return, carrying a paper bag with a smiling lobster drawn on the front of it, and hand it to Mrs. Sen, and head back to the university to teach his evening class. One day, when he handed Mrs. Sen the paper bag, he said, "No more fish for a while. Cook the chicken in the freezer. I need to start holding office hours."

For the next few days, instead of calling the fish market, Mrs. Sen thawed chicken legs in the kitchen sink and chopped them with her blade. One day she made a stew with green beans and tinned sardines. But the following week the man who ran the fish market called Mrs. Sen; he assumed she wanted the fish, and said he would hold it until the end of the day under her name. "Isn't that nice of him, Eliot? The man said he looked up my name in the telephone book. He said there is only one Sen. Do you know how many Sens are in the Calcutta telephone book?"

She told Eliot to put on his shoes and his jacket, and then she called Mr. Sen at the university. Eliot tied his sneakers by the bookcase and waited for her to join him, to choose from her row of slippers. After a few minutes he called out her name. When Mrs. Sen did not reply, he untied his sneakers and returned to the living room, where he found her on the sofa, weeping. Her face was in her hands and tears dripped through her fingers. Through them she murmured something about a meeting Mr. Sen was required to attend. Slowly she stood up and rearranged the cloth over the telephone. Eliot followed her, walking for the first time in his sneakers across the pear-colored carpet. She stared at him. Her lower eyelids were swollen into thin pink crests. "Tell me, Eliot. Is it too much to ask?"

Before he could answer, she took him by the hand and led him to the bedroom, whose door was normally kept shut. Apart from the bed, which lacked a headboard, the only other things in the room were a side table with a telephone on it, an ironing board, and a bureau. She flung open the drawers of the bureau and the door of the closet, filled with saris of every imaginable texture and shade, brocaded with gold and silver threads. Some were transparent, tissue thin, others as thick as drapes, with tassels knotted along the edges. In the closet they were on hangers; in the drawers they were folded flat, or wound tightly like thick scrolls. She sifted through the drawers, letting saris spill over the edges. "When have I ever worn this one? And this? And this?" She tossed the saris one by one from the drawers, then pried several from their hangers. They landed like a pile of tangled sheets on the bed. The room was filled with an intense smell of mothballs.

"'Send pictures,' they write. 'Send pictures of your new life.' What picture can I send?" She sat, exhausted, on the edge of the bed, where there was barely room for her. "They think I live the life of a queen, Eliot." She looked around the blank walls of the room. "They think I press buttons and the house is clean. They think I live in a palace."

The phone rang. Mrs. Sen let it ring several times before picking up the extension by the bed. During the conversation she seemed only to be replying to things, and wiping her face with the ends of one of the saris. When she got off the phone she stuffed the saris without folding them back into the drawers, and then she and Eliot put on their shoes and went to the car, where they waited for Mr. Sen to meet them.

"Why don't you drive today?" Mr. Sen asked when he appeared, rapping on the hood of the car with his knuckles. They always spoke to each other in English when Eliot was present.

"Not today. Another day."

"How do you expect to pass the test if you refuse to drive on a road with other cars?"

"Eliot is here today."

"He is here every day. It's for your own good. Eliot, tell Mrs. Sen it's for her own good."

She refused.

They drove in silence, along the same roads that Eliot and his mother took back to the beach house each evening. But in the back seat of Mr. and Mrs. Sen's car the ride seemed unfamiliar, and took longer than usual. The gulls whose tedious cries woke him each morning now thrilled him as they dipped and flapped across the sky. They passed one beach after another, and the shacks, now locked up, that sold frozen lemonade and quahogs in summer. Only one of the shacks was open. It was the fish market.

Mrs. Sen unlocked her door and turned toward Mr. Sen, who had not yet unfastened his seat belt. "Are you coming?"

Mr. Sen handed her some bills from his wallet. "I have a meeting in twenty minutes," he said, staring at the dashboard as he spoke. "Please don't waste time."

Eliot accompanied her into the dank little shop, whose walls were festooned with nets and starfish and buoys. A group of tourists with cameras around their necks huddled by the counter, some sampling stuffed clams, others pointing to a large chart illustrating fifty different varieties of North Atlantic fish. Mrs. Sen took a ticket from the machine at the counter and waited in line. Eliot stood by the lobsters, which stirred one on top of another in their murky tank, their claws bound by yellow rubber bands. He watched as Mrs. Sen laughed and chatted, when it was her turn in line, with a man with a bright red face and yellow teeth, dressed in a black rubber apron. In either hand he held a mackerel by the tail.

"You are sure what you sell me is very fresh?"

"Any fresher and they'd answer that question themselves."

The dial shivered toward its verdict on the scale.

"You want this cleaned, Mrs. Sen?"

She nodded. "Leave the heads on, please."

"You got cats at home?"

"No cats. Only a husband."

Later, in the apartment, she pulled the blade out of the cupboard, spread newspapers across the carpet, and inspected her treasures. One by one she drew them from the paper wrapping, wrinkled and tinged with blood. She stroked the tails, prodded the bellies, pried apart the gutted flesh. With a pair of scissors she clipped the fins. She tucked a finger under the gills, a red so bright they made her vermilion seem pale. She grasped the body, lined with inky streaks, at either end, and notched it at intervals against the blade.

"Why do you do that?" Eliot asked.

"To see how many pieces. If I cut properly, from this fish I will get three meals." She sawed off the head and set it on a pie plate.

In November came a series of days when Mrs. Sen refused to practice driving. The blade never emerged from the cupboard, newspapers were not spread on the floor. She did not call the fish store, nor did she thaw chicken. In silence she prepared crackers with peanut butter for Eliot, then sat reading old aerograms from a shoebox. When it was time for Eliot to leave she gathered together his things without inviting his mother to sit on the sofa and eat something first. When, eventually, his mother asked him in the car if he'd noticed a change in Mrs. Sen's behavior, he said he hadn't. He didn't tell her that Mrs. Sen paced the apartment, staring at the plastic-covered lampshades as if noticing them for the first time. He didn't tell her she switched on the television but never watched it, or that she made herself tea but let it grow cold on the coffee table. One day she played a tape of something she called a raga; it sounded a little bit like someone plucking very slowly and then very quickly on a violin, and Mrs. Sen said it was supposed to be heard only in the late afternoon, as the sun was setting. As the music played, for nearly an hour, she sat on the sofa with her eyes closed. Afterward she said, "It is more sad even than your Beethoven, isn't it?" Another day she played a cassette of people talking in her language—a farewell present, she told Eliot, that her family had made for her. As the succession of voices laughed and said their bit, Mrs. Sen identified each speaker. "My third uncle, my cousin, my father, my grandfather." One speaker sang a song. Another recited a poem. The final voice on the tape belonged to Mrs. Sen's mother. It was quieter and sounded more serious than the others. There was a pause between each sentence, and during this pause Mrs. Sen translated for Eliot: "The price of goat rose two rupees. The mangoes at the market are not very sweet. College Street is flooded." She turned off the tape. "These are things that happened the day I left India." The next day she played the same cassette all over again. This time, when her grandfather was speaking, she stopped the tape. She told Eliot she'd received a letter over the weekend. Her grandfather was dead.

A week later Mrs. Sen began cooking again. One day as she sat slicing cabbage on the living room floor, Mr. Sen called. He wanted to take Eliot and Mrs. Sen to the seaside. For the occasion Mrs. Sen put on a red sari and red lipstick; she freshened the vermilion in her part and rebraided her hair. She knotted a scarf under her chin, arranged her sunglasses on top of her head, and put a pocket camera in her purse. As Mr. Sen backed out of the parking lot, he put his arm across the top of the front seat, so that it looked as if he had his arm around Mrs. Sen. "It's getting too cold for that top coat," he said to her at one point. "We should get you something warmer." At the shop they bought mackerel, and butterfish, and sea bass. This time Mr. Sen came into the shop with them. It was Mr. Sen who asked whether the fish was fresh and to cut it this way or that way. They bought so much fish that Eliot had to hold one of the bags. After they put the bags in the trunk, Mr. Sen announced that he was hungry, and Mrs. Sen agreed, so they crossed the street to a restaurant where the take-out window was still open. They sat at a picnic table and ate two baskets of clam cakes. Mrs. Sen put a good deal of Tabasco sauce and black pepper on hers. "Like pakoras, no?" Her face was flushed, her lipstick faded, and she laughed at everything Mr. Sen said.

Behind the restaurant was a small beach, and when they were done eating they walked for a while along the shore, into a wind so strong that they had to walk backward. Mrs. Sen pointed to the water, and said that at a certain moment, each wave resembled a sari drying on a clothesline. "Impossible!" she shouted eventually, laughing as she turned back, her eyes teary. "I cannot move." Instead she took a picture of Eliot and Mr. Sen on the sand. "Now one of us," she said, pressing Eliot against her checkered coat and giving the camera to Mr. Sen. Finally the camera was given to Eliot. "Hold it steady," said Mr. Sen. Eliot looked through the tiny window in the camera and waited for Mr. and Mrs. Sen to move closer together, but they didn't. They didn't hold hands or put their arms around each other's waists. Both smiled with their mouths closed, squinting into the wind, Mrs. Sen's red sari leaping like flames under her coat.

In the car, warm at last and exhausted from the wind and the clam cakes, they admired the dunes, the ships they could see in the distance, the view of the lighthouse, the peach and purple sky. After a while Mr. Sen slowed down and stopped by the side of the road.

"What's wrong?" Mrs. Sen asked.

"You are going to drive home today."

"Not today."

"Yes, today." Mr. Sen stepped out of the car and opened the door on Mrs. Sen's side. A fierce wind blew into the car, accompanied by the sound of waves crashing on the shore. Finally she slid over to the driver's side, but spent a long time adjusting her sari and her sunglasses. Eliot turned and looked through the black window. The road was empty. Mrs. Sen turned on the radio, filling up the car with violin music.

"There's no need," Mr. Sen said, clicking it off.

"It helps me concentrate," Mrs. Sen said, and turned the radio on again.

"Put on your signal," Mr. Sen directed.

"I know what to do."

For about a mile she was fine, though far slower than the other cars that passed her. But when the town approached, and traffic lights loomed on wires in the distance, she went even slower.

"Switch lanes," Mr. Sen said. "You will have to bear left at the rotary."

Mrs. Sen did not.

"Switch lanes, I tell you." He shut off the radio. "Are you listening to me?"

A car beeped its horn, then another. She beeped defiantly in response, stopped, then pulled without signaling to the side of the road. "No more," she said, her forehead resting against the top of the steering wheel. "I hate it. I hate driving. I won't go on."

She stopped driving after that. The next time the fish store called she did not call Mr. Sen at his office. She had decided to try something new. There was a town bus that ran on an hourly schedule between the university and the seaside. After the university it made two stops, first at a nursing home, then at a shopping plaza without a name, which consisted of a bookstore, a shoe store, a drugstore, a pet store, and a record store. On benches under the portico, elderly women from the nursing home sat in pairs, in knee-length overcoats with oversized buttons, eating lozenges.

"Eliot," Mrs. Sen asked him while they were sitting on the bus, "will you put your mother in a nursing home when she is old?"

"Maybe," he said. "But I would visit every day."

"You say that now, but you will see, when you are a man your life will be in places you cannot know now." She counted on her fingers: "You will have a wife, and children of your own, and they will want to be driven to different places at the same time. No matter how kind they are, one day they will complain about visiting your mother, and you will get tired of it too, Eliot. You will miss one day, and another, and then she will have to drag herself onto a bus just to get herself a bag of lozenges."

At the fish shop the ice beds were nearly empty, as were the lobster tanks, where rust-colored stains were visible through the water. A sign said the shop would be closing for winter at the end of the month. There was only one person working behind the counter, a young boy who did not recognize Mrs. Sen as he handed her a bag reserved under her name.

"Has it been cleaned and scaled?" Mrs. Sen asked.

The boy shrugged. "My boss left early. He just said to give you this bag."

In the parking lot Mrs. Sen consulted the bus schedule. They would have to wait forty-five minutes for the next one, and so they crossed the street and bought clam cakes at the take-out window they had been to before. There was no place to sit. The picnic tables were no longer in use, their benches chained upside down on top of them.

On the way home an old woman on the bus kept watching them, her eyes shifting from Mrs. Sen to Eliot to the blood-lined bag between their feet. She wore a black overcoat, and in her lap she held, with gnarled, colorless hands, a crisp white bag from the drugstore. The only other passengers were two college students, boyfriend and girlfriend, wearing matching sweatshirts, their fingers linked, slouched in the back seat. In silence Eliot and Mrs. Sen ate the last few clam cakes in the bag. Mrs. Sen had forgotten napkins, and traces of fried batter dotted the corners of her mouth. When they reached the nursing home the woman in the overcoat stood up, said something to the driver, then stepped off the bus. The driver turned his head and glanced back at Mrs. Sen. "What's in the bag?"

Mrs. Sen looked up, startled.

"Speak English?" The bus began to move again, causing the driver to look at Mrs. Sen and Eliot in his enormous rearview mirror.

"Yes, I can speak."

"Then what's in the bag?"

"A fish," Mrs. Sen replied.

"The smell seems to bothering the other passengers. Kid, maybe you should open her window or something."

One afternoon a few days later the phone rang. Some very tasty halibut had arrived on the boats. Would Mrs. Sen like to pick one up? She called Mr. Sen, but he was not at his desk. A second time she tried calling, then a third. Eventually she went to the kitchen and returned to the living room with the blade, an eggplant, and some newspapers. Without having to be told Eliot took his place on the sofa and watched as she sliced the stems off the eggplant. She divided it into long, slender strips, then into small squares, smaller and smaller, as small as sugar cubes.

"I am going to put these in a very tasty stew with fish and green bananas," she announced. "Only I will have to do without the green bananas."

"Are we going to get the fish?"

"We are going to get the fish."

"Is Mr. Sen going to take us?"

"Put on your shoes."

They left the apartment without cleaning up. Outside it was so cold that Eliot could feel the chill on his teeth. They got in the car, and Mrs. Sen drove around the asphalt loop several times. Each time she paused by the grove of pine trees to observe the traffic on the main road. Eliot thought she was just practicing while they waited for Mr. Sen. But then she gave a signal and turned.

The accident occurred quickly. After about a mile Mrs. Sen took a left before she should have, and though the oncoming car managed to swerve out of her way, she was so startled by the horn that she lost control of the wheel and hit a telephone pole on the opposite corner. A policeman arrived and asked to see her license, but she did not have one to show him. "Mr. Sen teaches mathematics at the university" was all she said by way of explanation.

The damage was slight. Mrs. Sen cut her lip, Eliot complained briefly of a pain in his ribs, and the car's fender would have to be straightened. The policeman thought Mrs. Sen had also cut her scalp, but it was only the vermilion. When Mr. Sen arrived, driven by one of his colleagues, he spoke at length with the policeman as he filled out some forms, but he said nothing to Mrs. Sen as he drove them back to the apartment. When they got out of the car, Mr. Sen patted Eliot's head. "The policeman said you were lucky. Very lucky to come out without a scratch."

After taking off her slippers and putting them on the bookcase, Mrs. Sen put away the blade that was still on the living room floor and threw the eggplant pieces and the newspapers into the garbage pail. She prepared a plate of crackers with peanut butter, placed them on the coffee table, and turned on the television for Eliot's benefit. "If he is still hungry give him a Popsicle from the box in the freezer," she said to Mr. Sen, who sat at the Formica table sorting through the mail. Then she went into her bedroom and shut the door. When Eliot's mother arrived at a quarter to six, Mr. Sen told her the details of the accident and offered a check reimbursing November's payment. As he wrote out the check he apologized on behalf of Mrs. Sen. He said she was resting, though when Eliot had gone to the bathroom he'd heard her crying. His mother was satisfied with the arrangement, and in a sense, she confessed to Eliot as they drove home, she was relieved. It was the last afternoon Eliot spent with Mrs. Sen, or with any baby-sitter. From then on his mother gave him a key, which he wore on a string around his neck. He was to call the neighbors in case of an emergency, and to let himself into the beach house after school. The first day, just as he was taking off his coat, the phone rang. It was his mother calling from her office. "You're a big boy now, Eliot," she told him. "You okay?" Eliot looked out the kitchen window, at gray waves receding from the shore, and said that he was fine.

THE SECRET LIFE OF WALTER MITTY

E'RE GOING THROUGH!" The Commander's voice was like thin ice breaking. He wore his full-dress uniform, with the heavily braided white cap pulled down rakishly over one cold gray eye. "We can't make it, sir. It's spoiling for a hurricane, if you ask me." "I'm not asking you, Lieutenant Berg," said the Commander. "Throw on the power lights! Rev her up to 8,500! We're going through!" The pounding of the cylinders increased: ta-pocketa-pocketa-pocketa-*pocketa-pocketa*. The Commander stared at the ice forming on the pilot window. He walked over and twisted a row of complicated dials. "Switch on No. 8 auxiliary!" he shouted. "Switch on No. 8 auxiliary!" repeated Lieutenant Berg. "Full strength in No. 3 turret!" shouted the Commander. "Full strength in No. 3 turret!" The crew, bending to their various tasks in the huge, hurtling eight-engined Navy hydroplane, looked at each other and grinned. "The Old Man'll get us through," they said to one another. "The Old Man ain't afraid of Hell!". . .

"Not so fast! You're driving too fast!" said Mrs. Mitty. "What are you driving so fast for?"

"Hmm?" said Walter Mitty. He looked at his wife, in the seat beside him, with shocked astonishment. She seemed grossly unfamiliar, like a strange woman who had yelled at him in a crowd. "You were up to fifty-five," she said. "You know I don't like to go more than forty. You were up to fifty-five." Walter Mitty drove on toward Waterbury in silence, the roaring of the SN202 through the worst storm in twenty years of Navy flying fading in the remote, intimate airways of his mind. "You're tensed up again," said Mrs. Mitty. "It's one of your days. I wish you'd let Dr. Renshaw look you over."

Walter Mitty stopped the car in front of the building where his wife went to have her hair done. "Remember to get those overshoes while I'm having my hair done," she said. "I don't need overshoes," said Mitty. She put her mirror back into her bag. "We've been through all that," she said, getting out of the car. "You're not a young man any longer." He raced the engine a little. "Why don't you wear your gloves? Have you lost your gloves?" Walter Mitty reached in a pocket and brought out the gloves. He put them on, but after she had turned and gone into the building and he had driven on to a red light, he took them off again. "Pick it up, brother!" snapped a cop as the light changed, and Mitty hastily pulled on his gloves and lurched ahead. He drove around the streets aimlessly for a time, and then he drove past the hospital on his way to the parking lot.

. . . "It's the millionaire banker, Wellington McMillan," said the pretty nurse. "Yes?" said Walter Mitty, removing his gloves slowly. "Who has the case?" "Dr. Renshaw and Dr. Benbow, but there are two specialists here, Dr. Remington from New York and Mr. Pritchard-Mitford from London. He flew over." A door opened down a long, cool corridor and Dr. Renshaw came out. He looked distraught and haggard. "Hello, Mitty," he said. "We're having the devil's own time with McMillan, the millionaire banker and close personal friend of Roosevelt. Obstreosis of the ductal tract. Tertiary. Wish you'd take a look at him." "Glad to," said Mitty.

In the operating room there were whispered introductions: "Dr. Remington, Dr. Mitty. Mr. Pritchard-Mitford, Dr. Mitty." "I've read your book on streptothricosis," said Pritchard-Mitford, shaking hands. "A brilliant performance, sir." "Thank you," said Walter Mitty. "Didn't know you were in the States, Mitty," grumbled Remington. "Coals to Newcastle, bringing Mitford and me up here for a tertiary." "You are very kind," said Mitty. A huge, complicated machine, connected to the operating table, with many tubes and wires, began at this moment to go pocketa-pocketa-pocketa. "The new anesthetizer is giving way!" shouted an interne. "There is no one in the East who knows how to fix it!" "Quiet, man!" said Mitty, in a low, cool voice. He sprang to the machine, which was now going pocketa-pocketa-queep-pocketa-queep. He began fingering delicately a row of glistening dials. "Give me a fountain pen!" he snapped. Someone handed him a fountain pen. He pulled a faulty piston out of the machine and inserted the pen in its place. "That will hold for ten minutes," he said. "Get on with the operation." A nurse hurried over and whispered to Renshaw, and Mitty saw the man turn pale. "Coreopsis has set in," said Renshaw nervously. "If you would take over, Mitty?" Mitty looked at him and at the craven figure of Benbow, who drank, and at the grave, uncertain faces of the two great specialists. "If you wish," he said. They slipped a white gown on him; he adjusted a mask and drew on thin gloves; nurses handed him shining . . .

"Back it up, Mac! Look out for that Buick!" Walter Mitty jammed on the brakes. "Wrong lane, Mac," said the parking-lot attendant, looking at Mitty closely. "Gee. Yeh," muttered Mitty. He began cautiously to back out of the lane marked "Exit Only." "Leave her sit there," said the attendant. "I'll put her away." Mitty got out of the car. "Hey, better leave the key." "Oh," said Mitty, handing the man the ignition key. The attendant vaulted into the car, backed it up with insolent skill, and put it where it belonged.

They're so damn cocky, thought Walter Mitty, walking along Main Street; they think they know everything. Once he had tried to take his chains off, outside New Milford, and he had got them wound around the axles. A man had had to come out in a wrecking car and unwind them, a young, grinning garageman. Since then Mrs. Mitty always made him drive to a garage to have the chains taken off. The next time, he thought,

I'll wear my right arm in a sling; they won't grin at me then. I'll have my right arm in a sling and they'll see I couldn't possibly take the chains off myself. He kicked at the slush on the sidewalk. "Overshoes," he said to himself, and he began looking for a shoe store.

When he came out into the street again, with the overshoes in a box under his arm, Walter Mitty began to wonder what the other thing was his wife had told him to get. She had told him twice, before they set out from their house for Waterbury. In a way he hated these weekly trips to town—he was always getting something wrong. Kleenex, he thought, Squibb's, razor blades? No. Toothpaste, toothbrush, bicarbonate, carborundum, initiative and referendum? He gave it up. But she would remember it. "Where's the what's-its-name?" she would ask. "Don't tell me you forgot the what's-its-name." A newsboy went by shouting something about the Waterbury trial.

. . . "Perhaps this will refresh your memory." The District Attorney suddenly thrust a heavy automatic at the quiet figure on the witness stand. "Have you ever seen this before?" Walter Mitty took the gun and examined it expertly. "This is my Webley-Vickers 50.80," he said calmly. An excited buzz ran around the courtroom. The judge rapped for order. "You are a crack shot with any sort of firearms, I believe?" said the District Attorney, insinuatingly. "Objection!" shouted Mitty's attorney. "We have shown that the defendant could not have fired the shot. We have shown that he wore his right arm in a sling on the night of the fourteenth of July." Walter Mitty raised his hand briefly and the bickering attorneys were stilled. "With any known make of gun," he said evenly, "I could have killed Gregory Fitzhurst at three hundred feet *with my left hand.*" Pandemonium broke loose in the courtroom. A woman's scream rose above the bedlam and suddenly a lovely, dark-haired girl was in Walter Mitty's arms. The District Attorney struck at her savagely. Without rising from his chair, Mitty let the man have it on the point of his chin. "You miserable cur!" . . .

"Puppy biscuit," said Walter Mitty. He stopped walking and the buildings of Waterbury rose up out of the misty courtroom and surrounded him again. A woman who was passing laughed. "He said 'Puppy biscuit,'" she said to her companion. "That man said 'Puppy biscuit' to himself." Walter Mitty hurried on. He went into an A. & P., not the first one he came to but a smaller one farther up the street. "I want some biscuit for small, young dogs," he said to the clerk. "Any special brand, sir?" The greatest pistol shot in the world thought a moment. "It says 'Puppies Bark for It' on the box," said Walter Mitty.

His wife would be through at the hairdresser's in fifteen minutes, Mitty saw in looking at his watch, unless they had trouble drying it; sometimes they had trouble drying it. She didn't like to get to the hotel first; she would want him to be there waiting for her as usual. He found a big leather chair in the lobby, facing a window, and he put the overshoes and the puppy biscuit on the floor beside it. He picked up an old copy of *Liberty* and sank down into the chair. "Can Germany Conquer the World Through the Air?" Walter Mitty looked at the pictures of bombing planes and of ruined streets.

... "The cannonading has got the wind up in young Raleigh, sir," said the sergeant. Captain Mitty looked up at him through tousled hair. "Get him to bed," he said wearily. "With the others. I'll fly alone." "But you can't, sir," said the sergeant anxiously. "It takes two men to handle that bomber and the Archies are pounding the hell out of the air. Von Richtman's circus is between here and Saulier." "Somebody's got to get that ammunition dump," said Mitty. "I'm going over. Spot of brandy?" He poured a drink for the sergeant and one for himself. War thundered and whined around the dugout and battered at the door. There was a rending of wood and splinters flew through the room. "A bit of a near thing," said Captain Mitty carelessly. "The box barrage is closing in," said the sergeant. "We only live once, Sergeant," said Mitty, with his faint, fleeting smile. "Or do we?" He poured another brandy and tossed it off. "I never see a man could hold his brandy like you, sir," said the sergeant. "Begging your pardon, sir." Captain Mitty stood up and strapped on his huge Webley-Vickers automatic. "It's forty kilometers through hell, sir," said the sergeant. Mitty finished one last brandy. "After all," he said softly, "what isn't?" The pounding of the cannon increased; there was the rat-tat-tatting of machine guns, and from somewhere came the menacing pocketa-pocketa-pocketa of the new flame-throwers. Walter Mitty walked to the door of the dugout humming "Auprès de Ma Blonde." He turned and waved to the sergeant. "Cheerio!" he said. . . .

Something struck his shoulder. "I've been looking all over this hotel for you," said Mrs. Mitty. "Why do you have to hide in this old chair? How did you expect me to find you?" "Things close in," said Walter Mitty vaguely. "What?" Mrs. Mitty said. "Did you get the what's-its-name? The puppy biscuit? What's in that box?" "Overshoes," said Mitty. "Couldn't you have put them on in the store?" "I was thinking," said Walter Mitty. "Does it ever occur to you that I am sometimes thinking?" She looked at him. "I'm going to take your temperature when I get you home," she said.

They went through the revolving doors that made a faintly derisive whistling sound when you pushed them. It was two blocks to the parking lot. At the drugstore on the corner she said, "Wait here for me. I forgot something. I won't be a minute." She was more than a minute. Walter Mitty lighted a cigarette. It began to rain, rain with sleet in it. He stood up against the wall of the drugstore, smoking. . . . He put his shoulders back and his heels together. "To hell with the handkerchief," said Walter Mitty scornfully. He took one last drag on his cigarette and snapped it away. Then, with a faint, fleeting smile playing about his lips, he faced the firing squad; erect and motionless, proud and disdainful, Walter Mitty the Undefeated, inscrutable to the last.

VI.

The Story

AS REPORTED EXPERIENCE

Stories taking the form of reportage recount their main characters' experience of a pivotal event. The object is to convey the quality of that experience and the impact of the event, transmitting to the reader the immediacy and texture of both.

Denis Johnson

CAR CRASH WHILE HITCHHIKING

A SALESMAN WHO SHARED his liquor and steered while sleeping . . . A Cherokee filled with bourbon . . . A VW no more than a bubble of hashish fumes, captained by a college student . . .

And a family from Marshalltown who head-onned and killed forever a man driving west out of Bethany, Missouri . . .

. . . I rose up sopping wet from sleeping under the pouring rain, and something less than conscious, thanks to the first three of the people I've already named—the salesman and the Indian and the student—all of whom had given me drugs. At the head of the entrance ramp I waited without hope of a ride. What was the point, even, of rolling up my sleeping bag when I was too wet to be let into anybody's car? I draped it around me like a cape. The downpour raked the asphalt and gurgled in the ruts. My thoughts zoomed pitifully. The traveling salesman had fed me pills that made the linings of my veins feel scraped out. My jaw ached. I knew every raindrop by its name. I sensed everything before it happened. I knew a certain Oldsmobile would stop for me even before it slowed, and by the sweet voices of the family inside it I knew we'd have an accident in the storm.

I didn't care. They said they'd take me all the way.

The man and the wife put the little girl up front with them and left the baby in back with me and my dripping bedroll. "I'm not taking you anywhere very fast," the man said. "I've got my wife and babies here, that's why."

You are the ones, I thought. And I piled my sleeping bag

against the left-hand door and slept across it, not caring whether I lived or died. The baby slept free on the seat beside me. He was about nine months old.

. . . But before any of this, that afternoon, the salesman and I had swept down into Kansas City in his luxury car. We'd developed a dangerous cynical camaraderie beginning in Texas, where he'd taken me on. We ate up his bottle of amphetamines, and every so often we pulled off the Interstate and bought another pint of Canadian Club and a sack of ice. His car had cylindrical glass holders attached to either door and a white, leathery interior. He said he'd take me home to stay overnight with his family, but first he wanted to stop and see a woman he knew.

Under Midwestern clouds like great gray brains we left the superhighway with a drifting sensation and entered Kansas City's rush hour with a sensation of running aground. As soon as we slowed down, all the magic of traveling together burned away. He went on and on about his girlfriend. "I like this girl, I think I love this girl—but I've got two kids and a wife, and there's certain obligations there. And on top of everything else, I love my wife. I'm gifted with love. I love my kids. I love all my relatives." As he kept on, I felt jilted and sad: "I have a boat, a little sixteen-footer. I have two cars. There's room in the back yard for a swimming pool." He found his girlfriend at work. She ran a furniture store, and I lost him there.

The clouds stayed the same until night. Then, in the dark, I didn't see the storm gathering. The driver of the Volkswagen, a college man, the one who stoked my head with all the hashish, let me out beyond the city limits just as it began to rain. Never mind the speed I'd been taking, I was too overcome to stand up. I lay out in the grass off the exit ramp and woke in the middle of a puddle that had filled up around me.

And later, as I've said, I slept in the back seat while the Oldsmobile—the family from Marshalltown—splashed along through the rain. And yet I dreamed I was looking right through my eyelids, and my pulse marked off the seconds of time. The Interstate through western Missouri was, in that era, nothing more than a two-way road, most of it. When a semi truck came toward us and passed going the other way, we were lost in a blinding spray and a warfare of noises such as you get being towed through an automatic car wash. The wipers stood up and lay down across the windshield without much effect. I was exhausted, and after an hour I slept more deeply.

I'd known all along exactly what was going to happen. But the man and his wife woke me up later, denying it viciously.

"Oh—*no!*"

"NO!"

I was thrown against the back of their seat so hard that it broke. I commenced bouncing back and forth. A liquid which I knew right away was human blood flew around the car and rained down on my head. When it was over I was in the back seat again, just as I had been. I rose up and looked around. Our headlights had gone out. The radiator was hissing steadily. Beyond that, I didn't hear a thing. As far as I could tell, I was the only one conscious. As my eyes adjusted I saw that the baby was lying on its back beside me as if nothing had happened. Its eyes were open and it was feeling its cheeks with its little hands.

In a minute the driver, who'd been slumped over the wheel, sat up and peered at us. His face was smashed and dark with blood. It made my teeth hurt to look at him—but when he spoke, it didn't sound as if any of his teeth were broken.

"What happened?"

"We had a wreck," he said.

"The baby's okay," I said, although I had no idea how the baby was.

He turned to his wife.

"Janice," he said. "Janice, Janice!"

"Is she okay?"

"She's dead!" he said, shaking her angrily.

"No, she's not." I was ready to deny everything myself now.

Their little girl was alive, but knocked out. She whimpered in her sleep. But the man went on shaking his wife.

"Janice!" he hollered.

His wife moaned.

"She's not dead," I said, clambering from the car and running away.

"She won't wake up," I heard him say.

I was standing out here in the night, with the baby, for some reason, in my arms. It must have still been raining, but I remember nothing about the weather. We'd collided with another car on what I now perceived was a two-lane bridge. The water beneath us was invisible in the dark.

Moving toward the other car I began to hear rasping, metallic snores. Somebody was flung halfway out the passenger door, which was open, in the posture of one hanging from a trapeze by his ankles. The car had been broadsided, smashed so flat that no room was left inside it even for this person's legs, to say nothing of a driver or any other passengers. I just walked right on past.

Headlights were coming from far off. I made for the head of the bridge, waving them to a stop with one arm and clutching the baby to my shoulder with the other.

It was a big semi, grinding its gears as it decelerated. The driver rolled down his window and I shouted up at him, "There's a wreck. Go for help."

"I can't turn around here," he said.

He let me and the baby up on the passenger side, and we just sat there in the cab, looking at the wreckage in his headlights.

"Is everybody dead?" he asked.

"I can't tell who is and who isn't," I admitted.

He poured himself a cup of coffee from a thermos and switched off all but his parking lights.

"What time is it?"

"Oh, it's around quarter after three," he said.

By his manner he seemed to endorse the idea of not doing anything about this. I was relieved and tearful. I'd thought something was required of me, but I hadn't wanted to find out what it was.

When another car showed coming in the opposite direction, I thought I should talk to them. "Can you keep the baby?" I asked the truck driver.

"You'd better hang on to him," the driver said. "It's a boy, isn't it?"

"Well, I think so," I said.

The man hanging out of the wrecked car was still alive as I passed, and I stopped grown a little more used to the idea now of how really badly broken he was, and made sure there was nothing I could do. He was snoring loudly and rudely. His blood bubbled out of his mouth with every breath. He wouldn't be taking many more. I knew that, but he didn't, and therefore I looked down into the great pity of a person's life on this earth. I don't mean that we all end up dead, that's not the great pity. I mean that he couldn't tell me what he was dreaming, and I couldn't tell him what was real.

Before too long there were cars backed up for a ways at either end of the bridge, and headlights giving a night-game atmosphere to the steaming rubble, and ambulances and cop cars nudging through so that the air pulsed with color. I didn't talk to anyone. My secret was that in this short while I had gone from being the president of this tragedy to being a face-less onlooker at a gory wreck. At some point an officer learned that I was one of the passengers, and took my statement. I don't remember any of this, except that he told me, "Put out your cigarette." We paused in our conversation to watch the dying man being loaded into the ambulance. He was still alive, still dreaming obscenely. The blood ran off him in strings. His knees jerked and his head rattled.

There was nothing wrong with me, and I hadn't seen anything, but the policeman had to question me and take me to the hospital anyway. The word came over his car radio that the man was now dead, just as we came under the awning of the emergency-room entrance.

I stood in a tiled corridor with my wet sleeping bag bunched against the wall beside me, talking to a man from the local funeral home.

The doctor stopped to tell me I'd better have an X-ray.

"No."

"Now would be the time. If something turns up later . . . "

"There's nothing wrong with me."

Down the hall came the wife. She was glorious, burning. She didn't know yet that her husband was dead. We knew. That's what gave her such power over us. The doctor took her into a room with a desk at the end of the hall, and from under the closed door a slab of brilliance radiated as if, by some stupendous process, diamonds were being incinerated in there. What a pair of lungs! She shrieked as I imagined an eagle would shriek. It felt wonderful to be alive to hear it! I've gone looking for that feeling everywhere.

"There's nothing wrong with me"—I'm surprised I let those words out. But it's always been my tendency to lie to doctors, as if good health consisted only of the ability to fool them.

Some years later, one time when I was admitted to the Detox at Seattle General Hospital, I took the same tack.

"Are you hearing unusual sounds or voices?" the doctor asked.

"Help us, oh God, it hurts," the boxes of cotton screamed.

"Not exactly," I said.

"Not exactly," he said. "Now, what does that mean."

"I'm not ready to go into all that," I said. A yellow bird fluttered close to my face, and my muscles grabbed. Now I was flopping like a fish. When I squeezed shut my eyes, hot tears exploded from the sockets. When I opened them, I was on my stomach.

"How did the room get so white?" I asked.

A beautiful nurse was touching my skin. "These are vitamins," she said, and drove the needle in.

It was raining. Gigantic ferns leaned over us. The forest drifted down a hill. I could hear a creek rushing down among rocks. And you, you ridiculous people, you expect me to help you.

BROWNIES

BY OUR SECOND DAY at Camp Crescendo, the girls in my Brownie troop had decided to kick the asses of each and every girl in Brownie Troop 909. Troop 909 was doomed from the first day of camp; they were white girls, their complexions a blend of ice cream: strawberry, vanilla. They turtled out from their bus in pairs, their rolled-up sleeping bags chromatized with Disney characters: Sleeping Beauty, Snow White, Mickey Mouse; or the generic ones cheap parents bought: washed-out rainbows, unicorns, curly-eyelashed frogs. Some clutched Igloo coolers and still others held on to stuffed toys like pacifiers, looking all around them like tourists determined to be dazzled.

Our troop was wending its way past their bus, past the ranger station, past the colorful trail guide drawn like a treasure map, locked behind glass.

"Man, did you smell them?" Arnetta said, giving the girls a slow once-over, "They smell like Chihuahuas. *Wet* Chihuahuas." Their troop was still at the entrance, and though we had passed them by yards, Arnetta raised her nose in the air and grimaced.

Arnetta said this from the very rear of the line, far away from Mrs. Margolin, who always strung our troop behind her like a brood of obedient ducklings. Mrs. Margolin even looked like a mother duck—she had hair cropped close to a small ball of a head, almost no neck, and huge, miraculous breasts. She wore enormous belts that looked like the kind that weightlifters wear, except hers would be cheap metallic gold or rabbit fur or covered with gigantic fake sunflowers, and often these belts would become nature lessons in and of themselves. "See," Mrs. Margolin once said to us, pointing to her belt, "this one's made entirely from the feathers of baby pigeons."

The belt layered with feathers was uncanny enough, but I was more disturbed by the realization that I had never actually *seen* a baby pigeon. I searched weeks for one, in vain—scampering after pigeons whenever I was downtown with my father.

But nature lessons were not Mrs. Margolin's top priority. She saw the position of troop leader as an evangelical post. Back at the A.M.E. church where our Brownie meetings were held, Mrs. Margolin was especially fond of imparting religious aphorisms by means of acrostics—"Satan" was the "Serpent Always Tempting and Noisome"; she'd refer to the "Bible" as "Basic Instructions Before Leaving Earth." Whenever she quizzed us on these, expecting to hear the acrostics parroted back to her, only Arnetta's correct replies soared over our vague mumblings. "Jesus?" Mrs. Margolin might ask expectantly, and Arnetta alone would dutifully answer, "Jehovah's Example, Saving Us Sinners."

Arnetta always made a point of listening to Mrs. Margolin's religious talk and giving her what she wanted to hear. Because of this, Arnetta could have blared through a megaphone that the white girls of Troop 909 were "wet Chihuahuas" without so much as a blink from Mrs. Margolin. Once, Arnetta killed the troop goldfish by feeding it a french fry covered in ketchup, and when Mrs. Margolin demanded that she explain what had happened, claimed the goldfish had been eyeing her meal for *hours,* then the fish—giving in to temptation—had leapt up and snatched a whole golden fry from her fingertips.

"*Serious* Chihuahua," Octavia added, and though neither Arnetta nor Octavia could *spell* "Chihuahua," had ever *seen* a Chihuahua, trisyllabic words had gained a sort of exoticism within our fourth-grade set at Woodrow Wilson Elementary. Arnetta and Octavia would flip through the dictionary, determined to work the vulgar-sounding ones like "Djibouti" and "asinine" into conversation.

"*Caucasian* Chihuahuas," Arnetta said.

That did it. The girls in my troop turned elastic: Drema and Elise doubled up on one another like inextricably entwined kites; Octavia slapped her belly; Janice jumped straight up in the air, then did it again, as if to slam-dunk her own head. They could not stop laughing. No one had laughed so hard since a boy named Martez had stuck a pencil in the electric socket and spent the whole day with a strange grin on his face.

"Girls, girls," said our parent helper, Mrs. Hedy. Mrs. Hedy was Octavia's mother, and she wagged her index finger perfunctorily, like a windshield wiper. "Stop it, now. Be good." She said this loud enough to be heard, but lazily, bereft of any feeling or indication that she meant to be obeyed, as though she could say these words again at the exact same pitch if a button somewhere on her were pressed.

But the rest of the girls didn't stop; they only laughed louder. It was the word "Caucasian" that got them all going. One day at school, about a month before the Brownie camping trip, Arnetta turned to a boy wearing impossibly high-ankled floodwater jeans and said, "What are you? *Caucasian?*" The word took off from there, and soon everything was Caucasian. If you ate too fast you ate like a Caucasian, if you ate too slow you ate like a Caucasian. The biggest feat anyone at Woodrow Wilson could do was to jump off the swing in midair, at the highest point in its arc, and if you fell (as I had, more than once) instead of landing on your feet, knees bent Olympic gymnast-style, Arnetta and Octavia were prepared to comment. They'd look at each other with the silence of passengers who'd narrowly escaped an accident, then nod their heads, whispering with solemn horror, "*Caucasian.*"

Even the only white kid in our school, Dennis, got in on the Caucasian act. That time when Martez stuck a pencil in the socket, Dennis had pointed and yelled, "That was *so* Caucasian!"

/ / / /

When you lived in the south suburbs of Atlanta, it was easy to forget about whites. Whites were like those baby pigeons: real and existing, but rarely seen or thought about. Everyone had been to Rich's to go clothes shopping, everyone had seen white girls and their mothers coo-cooing over dresses; everyone had gone to the downtown library and seen white businessmen swish by importantly, wrists flexed in front of them to check the time as though they would change from Clark Kent into Superman at any second. But those images were as fleeting as cards shuffled in a deck, whereas the ten white girls behind us—*invaders,* Arnetta would later call them—were instantly real and memorable, with their long shampoo-commercial hair, straight as spaghetti from the box. This alone was reason for envy and hatred. The only black girl most of us had ever seen with hair that long was Octavia, whose hair hung past her butt like a Hawaiian hula dancer's. The sight of Octavia's mane prompted other girls to listen to her reverentially, as though whatever she had to say would somehow activate their own follicles. For example, when, on the first day of camp, Octavia made as if to speak, and everyone fell silent. "Nobody," Octavia said, "calls us niggers."

At the end of that first day, when half of our troop made their way back to the cabin after tag-team restroom visits, Arnetta said she'd heard one of the Troop 909 girls call Daphne a nigger. The other half of the girls and I were helping Mrs. Margolin clean up the pots and pans from the campfire ravioli dinner. When we made our way to the restrooms to wash up and brush our teeth, we met up with Arnetta midway.

"Man, I completely heard the girl," Arnetta reported. "Right, Daphne?"

Daphne hardly ever spoke, but when she did, her voice was petite and tinkly, the voice one might expect from a shiny new earring. She'd written a poem once, for Langston Hughes Day, a poem brimming with all the teacher-winning ingredients—

trees and oceans, sunsets and moons—but what cinched the poem for the grown-ups, snatching the win from Octavia's musical ode to Grandmaster Flash and the Furious Five, were Daphne's last lines:

> You are my father, the veteran
> When you cry in the dark
> It rains and rains and rains in my heart

She'd always worn clean, though faded, jumpers and dresses when Chic jeans were the fashion, but when she went up to the dais to receive her prize journal, pages trimmed in gold, she wore a new dress with a velveteen bodice and a taffeta skirt as wide as an umbrella. All the kids clapped, though none of them understood the poem. I'd read encyclopedias the way others read comics, and I didn't get it. But those last lines pricked me, they were so eerie, and as my father and I ate cereal, I'd whisper over my Froot Loops, like a mantra, *"You are my father, the veteran. You are my father, the veteran, the veteran, the veteran,"* until my father, who acted in plays as Caliban and Othello and was not a veteran, marched me up to my teacher one morning and said, "Can you tell me what's wrong with this kid?"

I thought Daphne and I might become friends, but I think she grew spooked by me whispering those lines to her, begging her to tell me what they meant, and I soon understood that two quiet people like us were better off quiet alone.

"Daphne? Didn't you hear them call you a nigger?" Arnetta asked, giving Daphne a nudge.

The sun was setting behind the trees, and their leafy tops formed a canopy of black lace for the flame of the sun to pass through. Daphne shrugged her shoulders at first, then slowly nodded her head when Arnetta gave her a hard look.

Twenty minutes later, when my restroom group returned to the cabin, Arnetta was still talking about Troop 909. My restroom group had passed by some of the 909 girls. For the most part, they deferred to us, waving us into the restrooms, letting us go even though they'd gotten their first.

We'd seen them, but from afar, never within their orbit enough to see whether their faces were the way all white girls appeared on TV—ponytailed and full of energy, bubbling over with love and money. All I could see was that some of them rapidly fanned their faces with their hands, though the heat of the day had long passed. A few seemed to be lolling their heads in slow circles, half purposefully, as if exercising the muscles of their necks, half ecstatically, like Stevie Wonder.

"We can't let them get away with that," Arnetta said, dropping her voice to a laryngitic whisper. "We can't let them get away with calling us niggers. I say we teach them a lesson." She sat down cross-legged on a sleeping bag, an embittered Buddha, eyes glimmering acrylic-black. "We can't go telling Mrs. Margolin, either. Mrs. Margolin'll say something about doing unto others and the path of righteousness and all. Forget that shit." She let her eyes flutter irreverently till they half closed, as though ignoring an insult not worth returning. We could all hear Mrs. Margolin outside, gathering the last of the metal campware.

Nobody said anything for a while. Usually people were quiet after Arnetta spoke. Her tone had an upholstered confidence that was somehow both regal and vulgar at once. It demanded a few moments of silence in its wake, like the ringing of a church bell or the playing of taps. Sometimes Octavia would ditto or dissent to whatever Arnetta had said, and this was the signal that others could speak. But this time Octavia just swirled a long cord of hair into pretzel shapes.

"Well?" Arnetta said. She looked as if she had discerned the hidden severity of the situation and was waiting for the rest of us to catch up. Everyone looked from Arnetta to Daphne. It was, after all, Daphne who had supposedly been called the name, but Daphne sat on the bare cabin floor, flipping through the pages of the Girl Scout handbook, eyebrows arched in mock wonder, as if the handbook were a catalogue full of bright and startling foreign costumes. Janice broke the silence. She clapped her hands to broach her idea of a plan.

"They gone be sleeping," she whispered conspiratorially, "then we gone sneak into they cabin, then we'll put daddy long-legs in they sleeping bags. Then they'll wake up. Then we gone beat 'em up till they're as flat as frying pans!" She jammed her fist into the palm of her hand, then made a sizzling sound.

Janice's country accent was laughable, her looks homely, her jumpy acrobatics embarrassing to behold. Arnetta and Octavia volleyed amused, arrogant smiles whenever Janice opened her mouth, but Janice never caught the hint, spoke whenever she wanted, fluttered around Arnetta and Octavia futilely offering her opinions to their departing backs. Whenever Arnetta and Octavia shooed her away, Janice loitered until the two would finally sigh and ask, "What *is* it, Miss Caucasoid? What do you *want?*"

"Shut up, Janice," Octavia said, letting a fingered loop of hair fall to her waist as though just the sound of Janice's voice had ruined the fun of her hair twisting.

Janice obeyed, her mouth hung open in a loose grin, unflappable, unhurt.

"All right," Arnetta said, standing up. "We're going to have a secret meeting and talk about what we're going to do."

Everyone gravely nodded her head. The word "secret" had a built-in importance, the modifier form of the word carried more clout than the noun. A secret meant nothing; it was like gossip: just a bit of unpleasant knowledge about someone who happened to be someone other than yourself. A secret *meeting,* or a secret *club* was entirely different.

That was when Arnetta turned to me as though she knew that doing so was both a compliment and a charity.

"Snot, you're not going to be a bitch and tell Mrs. Margolin, are you?"

I had been called "Snot" ever since first grade, when I'd

sneezed in class and two long ropes of mucus had splattered a nearby girl.

"Hey," I said. "Maybe you didn't hear them right—I mean—"

"Are you gonna tell on us or not?" was all Arnetta wanted to know, and by the time the question was asked, the rest of our Brownie troop looked at me as though they'd already decided their course of action, me being the only impediment.

Camp Crescendo used to double as a high-school-band and field hockey camp until an arcing field hockey ball landed on the clasp of a girl's metal barrette, knifing a skull nerve and paralyzing the right side of her body. The camp closed down for a few years and the girl's teammates built a memorial, filling the spot on which the girl fell with hockey balls, on which they had painted—all in nail polish—get-well tidings, flowers, and hearts. The balls were still stacked there, like a shrine of ostrich eggs embedded in the ground.

On the second day of camp, Troop 909 was dancing around the mound of hockey balls, their limbs jangling awkwardly, their cries like the constant summer squeal of an amusement park. There was a stream that bordered the field hockey lawn, and the girls from my troop settled next to it, scarfing down the last of lunch: sandwiches made from salami and slices of tomato that had gotten waterlogged from the melting ice in the cooler. From the stream bank, Arnetta eyed the Troop 909 girls, scrutinizing their movements to glean inspiration for battle.

"Man," Arnetta said, "we could bumrush them right now if that damn lady would *leave*."

The 909 troop leader was a white woman with the severe pageboy hairdo of an ancient Egyptian. She lay on a picnic blanket, sphinxlike, eating a banana, sometimes holding it out in front of her like a microphone. Beside her sat a girl slowly flapping one hand like a bird with a broken wing. Occasionally, the leader would call out the names of girls who'd attempted leapfrogs and flips, or of girls who yelled too loudly or strayed far from the circle.

"I'm just glad Big Fat Mama's not following us here," Octavia said. "At least we don't have to worry about her." Mrs. Margolin, Octavia assured us, was having her Afternoon Devotional, shrouded in mosquito netting, in a clearing she'd found. Mrs. Hedy was cleaning mud from her espadrilles in the cabin.

"I handled them." Arnetta sucked on her teeth and proudly grinned. "I told her we was going to gather leaves."

"Gather leaves," Octavia said, nodding respectfully. "That's a good one. Especially since they're so mad-crazy about this camping thing." She looked from ground to sky, sky to ground. Her hair hung down her back in two braids like a squaw's. "I mean, I really don't know why it's even called *camping*—all we ever do with Nature is find some twigs and say something like, 'Wow, this fell from a tree.'" She then studied her sandwich. With two disdainful fingers, she picked out a slice of dripping tomato, the sections congealed with red slime. She pitched it into the stream embrowned with dead leaves and the murky effigies of other dead things, but in the opaque water, a group of small silver-brown fish appeared. They surrounded the tomato and nibbled.

"Look!" Janice cried. "Fishes! Fishes!" As she scrambled to the edge of the stream to watch, a covey of insects threw up tantrums from the wheatgrass and nettle, a throng of tiny electric machines, all going at once. Octavia sneaked up behind Janice as if to push her in. Daphné and I exchanged terrified looks. It seemed as though only we knew that Octavia was close enough—and bold enough—to actually push Janice into the stream. Janice turned around quickly, but Octavia was already staring serenely into the still water as though she was gathering some sort of courage from it. "What's so funny?" Janice said, eyeing them all suspiciously.

Elise began humming the tune to "Karma Chameleon," all the girls joining in, their hums light and facile. Janice also

began to hum, against everyone else, the high-octane opening
chords of "Beat It."

"I love me some Michael Jackson," Janice said when she'd
finished humming, smacking her lips as though Michael
Jackson were a favorite meal. "I *will* marry Michael Jackson."

Before anyone had a chance to impress upon Janice the
impossibility of this, Arnetta suddenly rose, made a sun visor
of her hand, and watched Troop 909 leave the field hockey
lawn.

"Dammit!" she said. "We've got to get them *alone.*"

"They won't ever be alone," I said. All the rest of the girls
looked at me, for I usually kept quiet. If I spoke even a word,
I could count on someone calling me Snot. Everyone seemed
to think that we could beat up these girls; no one entertained
the thought that they might fight *back.* "The only time they'll
be unsupervised is in the bathroom."

"Oh shut up, Snot," Octavia said.

But Arnetta slowly nodded her head. "The bathroom," she said.
"The bathroom," she said, again and again. "The bathroom!
The bathroom!"

According to Octavia's watch, it took us five minutes to
hike to the restrooms, which were midway between our
cabin and Troop 909's. Inside, the mirrors above the sinks
returned only the vaguest of reflections, as though someone
had taken a scouring pad to their surfaces to obscure the
shine. Pine needles, leaves, and dirty, flattened wads of
chewing gum covered the floor like a mosaic. Webs of hair
matted the drain in the middle of the floor. Above the sinks
and below the mirrors, stacks of folded white paper towels
lay on a long metal counter. Shaggy white balls of paper
towels sat on the sinktops in a line like corsages on display.
A thread of floss snaked from a wad of tissues dotted with
the faint red-pink of blood. One of those white girls, I
thought, had just lost a tooth.

Though the restroom looked almost the same as it had the night before, it somehow seemed stranger now. We hadn't noticed the wooden rafters coming together in great V's. We were, it seemed, inside a whale, viewing the ribs of the roof of its mouth.

"Wow. It's a mess," Elise said.

"You can say that again."

Arnetta leaned against the doorjamb of a restroom stall. "This is where they'll be again," she said. Just seeing the place, just having a plan seemed to satisfy her. "We'll go in and talk to them. You know, 'How you doing? How long'll you be here?' That sort of thing. Then Octavia and I are gonna tell them what happens when they call any one of us a nigger."

"I'm going to say something, too," Janice said.

Arnetta considered this. "Sure," she said. "Of course. Whatever you want."

Janice pointed her finger like a gun at Octavia and rehearsed the lines she'd thought up, "'We're gonna teach you a *lesson!*' That's what I'm going to say." She narrowed her eyes like a TV mobster. "'We're gonna teach you little girls a lesson!'"

With the back of her hand, Octavia brushed Janice's finger away. "You couldn't teach me to shit in a toilet."

"But," I said, "what if they say, 'We didn't say that? We didn't call anyone an N-I-G-G-E-R.'"

"Snot," Arnetta said, and then sighed. "Don't think. Just fight. If you even know how."

Everyone laughed except Daphne. Arnetta gently laid her hand on Daphne's shoulder. "Daphne. You don't have to fight. We're doing this for you."

Daphne walked to the counter, took a clean paper towel, and carefully unfolded it like a map. With it, she began to pick up the trash all around. Everyone watched.

"C'mon," Arnetta said to everyone. "Let's beat it." We all ambled toward the doorway, where the sunshine made one large white rectangle of light. We were immediately blinded, and we shielded our eyes with our hands and our forearms.

"Daphne?" Arnetta asked. "Are you coming?"

We all looked back at the bending girl, the thin of her back hunched like the back of a custodian sweeping a stage, caught in limelight. Stray strands of her hair were lit near-transparent, thin fiber-optic threads. She did not nod yes to the question, nor did she shake her head no. She abided, bent. Then she began again, picking up leaves, wads of paper, the cotton fluff innards from a torn stuffed toy. She did it so methodically, so exquisitely, so humbly, she must have been trained. I thought of those dresses she wore, faded and old, yet so pressed and clean. I then saw the poverty in them; I then could imagine her mother, cleaning the houses of others, returning home, weary.

"I guess she's not coming."

We left her and headed back to our cabin, over pine needles and leaves, taking the path full of shade.

"What about our secret meeting?" Elise asked.

Arnetta enunciated her words in a way that defied contradiction: "We just had it."

It was nearing our bedtime, but the sun had not yet set.

"Hey, your mama's coming," Arnetta said to Octavia when she saw Mrs. Hedy walk toward the cabin, sniffling. When Octavia's mother wasn't giving bored, parochial orders, she sniffled continuously, mourning an imminent divorce from her husband. She might begin a sentence, "I don't know what Robert will do when Octavia and I are gone. Who'll buy him cigarettes?" and Octavia would hotly whisper, *"Mama,"* in a way that meant: Please don't talk about our problems in front of everyone. Please shut up.

But when Mrs. Hedy began talking about her husband, thinking about her husband, seeing clouds shaped like the head of her husband, she couldn't be quiet, and no one could dislodge her from the comfort of her own woe. Only one thing could perk her up—Brownie songs. If the girls were quiet, and Mrs. Hedy was in her dopey, sorrowful mood, she would say, "Y'all know I like those songs, girls. Why don't you sing one?" Everyone would groan, except me and Daphne. I, for one, liked some of the songs.

"C'mon, everybody," Octavia said drearily. "She likes the Brownie song best."

We sang, loud enough to reach Mrs. Hedy:

> "I've got something in my pocket;
> It belongs across my face.
> And I keep it very close at hand
>   in a most convenient place.
> I'm sure you couldn't guess it
> If you guessed a long, long, while.
> So I'll take it out and put it on—
> It's a great big Brownie smile!"

The Brownie song was supposed to be sung cheerfully, as though we were elves in a workshop, singing as we merrily cobbled shoes, but everyone except me hated the song so much that they sang it like a maudlin record, played on the most sluggish of rpms.

"That was good," Mrs. Hedy said, closing the cabin door behind her. "Wasn't that nice, Linda?"

"Praise God," Mrs. Margolin answered without raising her head from the chore of counting out Popsicle sticks for the next day's craft session.

"Sing another one," Mrs. Hedy said. She said it with a sort of joyful aggression, like a drunk I'd once seen who'd refused to leave a Korean grocery.

"God, Mama, get over it," Octavia whispered in a voice meant only for Arnetta, but Mrs. Hedy heard it and started to leave the cabin.

"Don't go," Arnetta said. She ran after Mrs. Hedy and held her by the arm. "We haven't finished singing." She nudged us with a single look. "Let's sing the 'Friends Song.' For Mrs. Hedy."

Although I liked some of the songs, I hated this one:

> Make new friends
> But keep the o-old,
> One is silver
> And the other gold.

If most of the girls in the troop could be any type of metal, they'd be bunched-up wads of tinfoil, maybe, or rusty iron nails you had to get tetanus shots for.

"No, no, no," Mrs. Margolin said before anyone could start in on the "Friends Song." "An uplifting song. Something to lift her up and take her mind off all these earthly burdens."

Arnetta and Octavia rolled their eyes. Everyone knew what song Mrs. Margolin was talking about, and no one, no one, wanted to sing it.

"Please, no," a voice called out. "Not 'The Doughnut Song.'"

"Please not 'The Doughnut Song,'" Octavia pleaded.

"I'll brush my teeth two times if I don't have to sing 'The Doughnut—'"

"Sing!" Mrs. Margolin demanded.

We sang:

> "Life without Jesus is like a do-ough-nut!
> Like a do-ooough-nut!
> Like a do-ooough-nut!
> Life without Jesus is like a do-ough-nut!
> There's a hole in the middle of my soul!"

There were other verses, involving other pastries, but we stopped after the first one and cast glances toward Mrs. Margolin to see if we could gain a reprieve. Mrs. Margolin's eyes fluttered blissfully. She was half asleep.

"Awww," Mrs. Hedy said, as though giant Mrs. Margolin were a cute baby, "Mrs. Margolin's had a long day."

"Yes indeed," Mrs. Margolin answered. "If you don't mind, I might just go to the lodge where the beds are. I haven't been the same since the operation."

I had not heard of this operation, or when it had occurred, since Mrs. Margolin had never missed the once-a-week Brownie meetings, but I could see from Daphne's face that she was concerned, and I could see that the other girls had decided that Mrs. Margolin's operation must have happened a long time ago in some remote time unconnected to our own. Nevertheless, they put on sad faces. We had all been taught that adulthood was full of sorrow and pain, taxes and bills, dreaded work and dealings with whites, sickness and death. I tried to do what the others did. I tried to look silent.

"Go right ahead, Linda," Mrs. Hedy said. "I'll watch the girls." Mrs. Hedy seemed to forget about divorce for a moment; she looked at us with dewy eyes, as if we were mysterious, furry creatures. Meanwhile, Mrs. Margolin walked through the maze of sleeping bags until she found her own. She gathered a neat stack of clothes and pajamas slowly, as though doing so was almost painful. She took her toothbrush, her toothpaste, her pillow. "All right!" Mrs. Margolin said, addressing us all from the threshold of the cabin. "Be in bed by nine." She said it with a twinkle in her voice, letting us know she was allowing us to be naughty and stay up till nine-fifteen.

"C'mon everybody," Arnetta said after Mrs. Margolin left. "Time for us to wash up."

Everyone watched Mrs. Hedy closely, wondering whether she would insist on coming with us since it was night, making a fight with Troop 909 nearly impossible. Troop 909 would soon be in the bathroom, washing their faces, brushing their teeth—completely unsuspecting of our ambush.

"We won't be long," Arnetta said. "We're old enough to go to the restrooms by ourselves."

Mrs. Hedy pursed her lips at this dilemma. "Well, I guess you Brownies are almost Girl Scouts, right?"

"Right!"

"Just one more badge," Drema said.

"And about," Octavia droned, "a million more cookies to sell." Octavia looked at all of us, *Now's our chance,* her face seemed to say, but our chance to do *what,* I didn't exactly know.

Finally, Mrs. Hedy walked to the doorway where Octavia stood dutifully waiting to say goodbye but looking bored doing it. Mrs. Hedy held Octavia's chin. "You'll be good?"

"Yes, Mama."

"And remember to pray for me and your father? If I'm asleep when you get back?"

"Yes, Mama."

When the other girls had finished getting their toothbrushes and washcloths and flashlights for the group restroom trip, I was drawing pictures of tiny birds with too many feathers. Daphne was sitting on her sleeping bag, reading.

"You're not going to come?" Octavia asked.

Daphne shook her head.

"I'm gonna stay, too," I said. "I'll go to the restroom when Daphne and Mrs. Hedy go."

Arnetta leaned down toward me and whispered so that Mrs. Hedy, who'd taken over Mrs. Margolin's task of counting Popsicle sticks, couldn't hear. "No, Snot. If we get in trouble, you're going to get in trouble with the rest of us."

We made our way through the darkness by flashlight. The tree branches that had shaded us just hours earlier, along the same path, now looked like arms sprouting menacing heads. The stars sprinkled the sky like spilled salt. They seemed fastened to the darkness, high up and holy, their places fixed and definite as we stirred beneath them.

Some, like me, were quiet because we were afraid of the dark; others were talking like crazy for some reason.

"Wow!" Drema said, looking up. "Why are all the stars out here? I never see stars back on Oneida Street."

"It's a camping trip, that's why," Octavia said. "You're supposed to see stars on camping trips."

Janice said, "This place smells like my mother's air freshener."

"These woods are *pine,*" Elise said. "Your mother probably uses *pine* air freshener."

Janice mouthed an exaggerated "Oh," nodding her head as though she just then understood one of the world's great secrets.

No one talked about fighting. Everyone was afraid enough just walking through the infinite deep of the woods. Even though I didn't fight to fight, was afraid of fighting, I felt I was part of the rest of the troop; like I was defending something. We trudged against the slight incline of the path, Arnetta leading the way.

"You know," I said, "their leader will be there. Or they won't even be there. It's dark already. Last night the sun was still in the sky. I'm sure they're already finished."

Arnetta acted as if she hadn't heard me. I followed her gaze with my flashlight, and that's when I saw the squares of light in the darkness. The bathroom was just ahead.

But the girls were there. We could hear them before we could see them.

"Octavia and I will go in first so they'll think there's just two of us, then wait till I say, 'We're gonna teach you a lesson,'" Arnetta said. "Then, bust in. That'll surprise them."

"That's what I was supposed to say," Janice said.

Arnetta went inside, Octavia next to her. Janice followed, and the rest of us waited outside.

They were in there for what seemed like whole minutes, but something was wrong. Arnetta hadn't given the signal yet. I was with the girls outside when I heard one of the Troop 909 girls say, "NO. That did NOT happen!"

That was to be expected, that they'd deny the whole thing. What I hadn't expected was *the voice* in which the denial was said. The girl sounded as though her tongue were caught in her mouth. "That's a BAD word!" the girl continued. "We don't say BAD words!"

"Let's go in," Elise said.

"No," Drema said, "I don't want to. What if we get beat up?"

"Snot?" Elise turned to me, her flashlight blinding. It was the first time anyone had asked my opinion, though I knew they were just asking because they were afraid.

"I say we go inside, just to see what's going on."

"But Arnetta didn't give us the signal," Drema said. "She's supposed to say, 'We're gonna teach you a lesson,' and I didn't hear her say it."

"C'mon," I said. "Let's just go in."

We went inside. There we found the white girls—about five girls huddled up next to one big girl. I instantly knew she was the owner of the voice we'd heard. Arnetta and Octavia inched toward us as soon as we entered.

"Where's Janice?" Elise asked, then we heard a flush. "Oh."

"I think," Octavia said, whispering to Elise, "they're retarded."

"We ARE NOT retarded!" the big girl said, though it was obvious that she was. That they all were. The girls around her began to whimper.

"They're just pretending." Arnetta said, trying to convince herself. "I know they are."

Octavia turned to Arnetta. "Arnetta. Let's just leave."

Janice came out of a stall, happy and relieved, then she suddenly remembered her line, pointed to the big girl, and said, "We're gonna teach you a lesson."

"Shut up, Janice," Octavia said, but her heart was not in it. Arnetta's face was set in a lost, deep scowl. Octavia turned to the big girl and said loudly, slowly, as if they were all deaf,

"We're going to leave. It was nice meeting you, O.K.? You don't have to tell anyone that we were here. O.K.?"

"Why not?" said the big girl, like a taunt. When she spoke, her lips did not meet, her mouth did not close. Her tongue grazed the roof of her mouth, like a little pink fish. "You'll get in trouble. I know. *I* know."

Arnetta got back her old cunning. "If you said anything, then you'd be a tattletale."

The girl looked sad for a moment, then perked up quickly. A flash of genius crossed her face. "I *like* tattletale."

"It's all right, girls. It's gonna be all right!" the 909 troop leader said. All of Troop 909 burst into tears. It was as though someone had instructed them all to cry at once. The troop leader had girls under her arm, and all the rest of the girls crowded about her. It reminded me of a hog I'd seen on a field trip, where all the little hogs gathered about the mother at feeding time, latching onto her teats. The 909 troop leader had come into the bathroom, shortly after the big girl had threatened to tell. Then the ranger came, then, once the ranger had radioed the station, Mrs. Margolin arrived with Daphne in tow.

The ranger had left the restroom area, but everyone else was huddled just outside, swatting mosquitoes.

"Oh. They *will* apologize," Mrs. Margolin said to the 909 troop leader, but she said this so angrily, I knew she was speaking more to us than to the other troop leader. "When their parents find out, every one a them will be on punishment."

"It's all right, it's all right," the 909 troop leader reassured Mrs. Margolin. Her voice lilted in the same way it had when addressing the girls. She smiled the whole time she talked. She was like on of those TV-cooking-show women who talk and dice onions and smile all at the same time.

"See. It could have happened. I'm not calling your girls fibbers or anything." She shook her head ferociously from side to side, her Egyptian-style pageboy flapping against her cheeks like heavy drapes. "It *could* have happened. See. Our girls are *not* retarded. They are *delayed* learners." She said this in a syrupy instructional voice, as though our troop might be delayed learners as well. "We're from the Decatur Children's Academy. Many of them just have special needs."

"Now we won't be able to walk to the bathroom by ourselves!" the big girl said.

"Yes you will," the troop leader said, "but maybe we'll wait till we get back to Decatur—"

"I don't want to wait!" the girl said. "I want my Independence badge!"

The girls in my troop were entirely speechless. Arnetta looked stoic, as though she were soon to be tortured but was determined not to appear weak. Mrs. Margolin pursed her lips solemnly and said, "Bless them, Lord. Bless them."

In contrast, the Troop 909 leader was full of words and energy. "Some of our girls are echolalic—" She smiled and happily presented one of the girls hanging onto her, but the girl widened her eyes in horror, and violently withdrew herself from the center of attention, sensing she was being sacrificed for the village sins. "Echolalic," the troop leader continued. "That means they will say whatever they hear, like an echo—that's where the word comes from. It comes from 'echo.'" She ducked her head apologetically, "I mean, not all of them have the most *progressive* of parents, so if they heard a bad word, they might have repeated it. But I guarantee it would not have been *intentional.*"

Arnetta spoke. "I saw her say the word. I heard her." She pointed to a small girl, smaller than any of us, wearing an oversized T-shirt that read: "Eat Bertha's Mussels."

The troop leader shook her head and smiled, "That's impossible. She doesn't speak. She can, but she doesn't."

Arnetta furrowed her brow. "No. It wasn't her. That's right. It was *her.*"

The girl Arnetta pointed to grinned as though she'd been paid a compliment. She was the only one from either troop actually wearing a full uniform: the mocha-colored A-line shift, the orange ascot, the sash covered with badges, though all the same one—the Try-It patch. She took a few steps toward Arnetta and made a grand sweeping gesture toward the sash. "See," she said, full of self-importance, "I'm a Brownie." I had a hard time imagining this girl calling anyone a "nigger"; the girl looked perpetually delighted, as though she would have cuddled up with a grizzly if someone had let her.

On the fourth morning, we boarded the bus to go home.

The previous day had been spent building miniature churches from Popsicle sticks. We hardly left the cabin. Mrs. Margolin and Mrs. Hedy guarded us so closely, almost no one talked for the entire day.

Even on the day of departure from Camp Crescendo, all was serious and silent. The bus ride began quietly enough. Arnetta had to sit beside Mrs. Margolin; Octavia had to sit beside her mother. I sat beside Daphne, who gave me her prize journal without a word of explanation.

"You don't want it?"

She shook her head no. It was empty.

Then Mrs. Hedy began to weep. "Octavia," Mrs. Hedy said to her daughter without looking at her, "I'm going to sit with Mrs. Margolin. All right?"

Arnetta exchanged seats with Mrs. Hedy. With the two women up front, Elise felt it safe to speak. "Hey," she said, then she set her face into a placid, vacant stare, trying to imitate that of a Troop 909 girl. Emboldened, Arnetta made a gesture of mock pride toward an imaginary sash, the way the girl in full uniform had done. Then they all made a game of it, trying to do the most exaggerated imitations of the Troop 909 girls, all without speaking, all without laughing loud enough to catch the women's attention.

Daphne looked down at her shoes, white with sneaker polish. I opened the journal she'd given me. I looked out the window, trying to decide what to write, searching for lines, but nothing could compare with what Daphne had written, *"My father, the veteran,"* my favorite line of all time. It replayed itself in my head, and I gave up trying to write.

By then, it seemed that the rest of the troop had given up making fun of the girls in Troop 909. They were now quietly gossiping about who had passed notes to whom in school. For a moment the gossiping fell off, and all I heard was the hum of the bus as we sped down the road and the muffled sounds of Mrs. Hedy and Mrs. Margolin talking about serious things.

"You know," Octavia whispered, "why did *we* have to be stuck at a camp with retarded girls? You know?"

"*You* know why," Arnetta answered. She narrowed her eyes like a cat. "My mama and I were in the mall in Buckhead, and this white lady just kept looking at us. I mean, like we were foreign or something. Like we were from China."

"What did the woman say?" Elise asked.

"Nothing," Arnetta said. "She didn't say nothing."

A few girls quietly nodded their heads.

"There was this time," I said, "when my father and I were in the mall and—"

"Oh shut up, Snot," Octavia said.

I stared at Octavia, then rolled my eyes from her to the window. As I watched the trees blur, I wanted nothing more than to be through with it all: the bus ride, the troop, school—all of it. But we were going home. I'd see the same girls in school the next day. We were on a bus, and there was nowhere else to go.

"Go on, Laurel," Daphne said to me. It seemed like the first time she'd spoken the whole trip, and she'd said my name. I turned to her and smiled weakly so as not to cry, hoping she'd remember when I'd tried to be her friend, thinking maybe that her gift of the journal was an invitation of friendship. But she didn't smile back. All she said was, "What happened?"

I studied the girls, waiting for Octavia to tell me to shut up again before I even had a chance to utter another word, but everyone was amazed that Daphne had spoken. The bus was silent. I gathered my voice. "Well," I said. "My father and I were in this mall, but *I* was the one doing the staring." I stopped and glanced from face to face. I continued. "There were these white people dressed like Puritans or something, but they weren't Puritans. They were Mennonites. They're these people who, if you ask them to do a favor, like paint your porch or something, they have to do it. It's in their rules."

"That sucks," someone said.

"C'mon," Arnetta said. "You're lying."

"I am not."

"How do you know that's not just some story someone made up?" Elise asked, her head cocked full of daring. "I mean, who's gonna do whatever you ask?"

"It's not made up. I know because when I was looking at them, my father said, 'See those people? If you ask them to do something, they'll do it. Anything you want.'"

No one would call anyone's father a liar—then they'd have to fight the person. But Drema parsed her words carefully. "How does your *father* know that's not just some story? Huh?"

"Because,' I said, "he went up to the man and asked him would he paint our porch, and the man said yes. It's their religion."

"Man, I'm glad I'm a Baptist," Elise said, shaking her head in sympathy for the Mennonites.

"So did the guy do it?" Drema asked, scooting closer to hear if the story got juicy.

"Yeah," I said. "His whole family was with him. My dad drove them to our house. They all painted our porch. The woman and the girl were in bonnets and long, long skirts with buttons up to their necks. The guy wore this weird hat and these huge suspenders."

"Why," Arnetta asked archly, as though she didn't believe a

word, "would someone pick a *porch?* If they'll do anything, why not make them paint the whole *house?* Why not ask for a hundred bucks?"

I thought about it, and then remembered the words my father had said about them painting our porch, though I had never seemed to think about his words after he'd said them.

"He said," I began, only then understanding the words as they uncoiled from my mouth, "it was the only time he'd have a white man on his knees doing something for a black man for free."

I now understood what he meant, and why he did it, though I didn't like it. When you've been made to feel bad for so long, you jump at the chance to do it to others. I remembered the Mennonites bending the way Daphne had bent when she was cleaning the restroom. I remembered the dark blue of their bonnets, the black of their shoes. They painted the porch as though scrubbing a floor. I was already trembling before Daphne asked quietly, "Did he thank them?"

I looked out the window. I could not tell which were the thoughts and which were the trees. "No," I said, and suddenly knew there was something mean in the world that I could not stop.

Arnetta laughed. "If I asked them to take off their long skirts and bonnets and put on some jeans, would they do it?"

And Daphne's voice, quiet, steady: "Maybe they would. Just to be nice."

VII.

The Story

AS LETTERS

In the epistolary form, stories unfold in the present tense, like a film or stage play. Viewpoints can be presented in such rapid succession that they seem simultaneous, giving the page the occasional effect of a split screen.

A. A. Milne

THE RISE AND FALL OF
MORTIMER SCRIVENS

Extract from "Readers' Queries" in "The Literary Weekly":
   Q. What is it which determines First Edition values? Is it entirely a question of the author's literary reputation?
   A. Not entirely, but obviously to a great extent. An additional factor is the original size of the first edition, which generally means that an established author's earliest books are more valuable than his later ones. Some authors, moreover, are more fashionable than others with bibliophiles, for reasons not always easy to detect; nor does there seem to be any explanation why an author, whose reputation as a writer has never varied, should be highly sought after by collectors at one time, and then suddenly become completely out of fashion. So perhaps all that we can say with confidence is that prices of First Editions, like those of everything else, are determined by the Laws of Supply and Demand.

Mr. Henry Winters to Mr. Brian Haverhill.
Dear Mr. Haverhill,
   It may be within your memory that on the occasion of an afternoon visit which you and Mrs. Haverhill were good enough to pay us two years ago I was privileged to lend her Chapman's well-known manual on the Viola, which, somewhat surprisingly, she had never come across; I say surprisingly, for undoubtedly he is our greatest authority on the subject. If by any chance she has now read it, I should be very much obliged by its return at your convenience. I would not

trouble you in this matter but for the fact that the book is temporarily out of print, and I have been unable therefore to purchase another copy for myself.

Miss Winters is away for a few days, or she would join me in sending compliments to you and Mrs. Haverhill.

Yours very truly,
Henry Winters.

Mr. Brian Haverhill to Mr. Henry Winters.
Dear Winters,

I was much distressed to get your letter this morning and to discover that Sally and I had been behaving so badly. It is probably as much my fault as hers, but she is away with her people in Somerset just now, and I think must have taken your book with her; so for the moment I can do nothing about it but apologise humbly for both of us. I have of course written to her, and asked her to send it back to you at once, or, if it is here in the house, to let me know where she has hidden it.

Again all my apologies,

Yours sincerely,
Brian Haverhill.

Brian Haverhill to Sally Haverhill.
Darling,

Read the enclosed and tell me how disgraced you feel—and how annoyed you think Winters is. I don't care for that bit about purchasing another copy for himself. He meant it nasty-like, if you ask me. Still, two years is a long time to take over a book, and you ought to have spelt it out to yourself more quickly. I could have helped you with the longer words.

The funny thing is I don't seem to remember anything about this viola book, nor whether it is the sort you play or the sort you grow, but I do seem to remember some other book which he forced on us—essays of some sort, at a guess. Can you help? Because if there were two, we ought to send both back together. I have staved him off for a bit by saying that you were so devoted to Chapman that you had taken the damned book with you. It doesn't sound likely to me, but it may to him. And why haven't we seen Winters and his saintly sister for two years? Not that I mind—on the contrary—but I just wondered. Are we cutting them or are they cutting us? One would like to know the drill in case of an accidental meeting in the village.

My love to everybody, and lots of a very different sort to your darling self. Bless you. Your Brian.

Sally Haverhill to Brian Haverhill.

Darlingest, I did mean to ring you up last night but our line has broken down or the rent hasn't been paid or something, and I couldn't do it in the village, not properly.

How awful about Mr. Winters! It was flowers of course, silly, not musical instruments, because I was talking about violas to him when you were talking about the Litany to Honoria, I remember it perfectly, I was wearing my blue and yellow cotton and one of her stockings was coming down. But you're quite right about the other one, it was called *Country Filth* and *very* disappointing. It must be somewhere. Do send them both back at once, darling—you'll find Chapman among the garden books—and say how sorry I am. And then I'll write myself. Yes, I think he's really angry, he's not a very nice man.

No, I don't think we've quarreled. I did ask them both to our cocktail party a few weeks later, but being strict T.T.'s which I only found out afterwards, Honoria was rather stiff about it. Don't you remember? And then I asked them to tea, and they were away, and then I sort of felt that it was their turn to write. I'll try again if you like when I come home . . .

Brian Haverhill to Sally Haverhill.
Darling Sal,
    1. Don't try again.

2. I have found Chapman nestling among the detective stories. I deduced that it would be there as soon as you said garden books.

3. Books aren't called *Country Filth,* not in Honoria's house anyway, and if they were, what would you be hoping that they were like? Tell your mother that I'm surprised at you.

4. There are a thousand books in the library, not to mention hundreds all over the place, and I can't possibly look through them all for one whose title, size, colour and contents are completely unknown to me. So pull yourself together, there's a dear, and send me a telegram with all that you remember about it.

5. I adore you.

Brian.

Sally Haverhill to Brian Haverhill.

Something about country by somebody like Morgan or Rivers sort of ordinary size and either biscuit color or blue all my love Sal.

Country Tilth: The Prose Ramblings of a Rhymester:
by Mortimer Scrivens (Street and Co.)

1. *A World Washed Clean.*

Long ere His Majesty the Sun had risen in His fiery splendour, and while yet the first faint flush of dawn, rosy herald of His coming, still lingered in the east, I was climbing (but how blithely!) the ribbon of road, pale-hued, which spanned the swelling mother-breasts of the downland. At melodic intervals, with a melancholy which little matched my mood, the lone cry of the whimbrel. . . .

Brian Haverhill to Sally Haverhill.

O lord, Sally, we're sunk! I've found the damned book—*Country Tilth* by Mortimer Scrivens. It's ghastly enough inside, but outside—darling, there's a large beer-ring such as could never have been there originally, and looking more like the ring made by a large beer-mug than any beer-ring ever did. You can almost smell the beer. I swear *I* didn't do it, I don't treat books like that, not even ghastly books, it was probably Bill when he was last here. Whoever it was, we can't possibly send it back like this.

What shall I do?

1. Send back Chapman and hope that he has forgotten about this one; which seems likely as he didn't mention it in his letter.

2. Send both back, and hope that he's a secret beer-drinker and made the mark himself.

3. Apologise for the mark, and say I think it must be milk.

4. Get another copy and pass it off as the one he lent us. I suppose Warbecks would have it.

What do you advise? I must do something about the viola book soon, I feel. I wish you were here . . .

Sally Haverhill to Brian Haverhill.
One and Four darling writing Sal.

Mr. Brian Haverhill to Messrs. Warbecks Ltd.
Dear Sirs,

I shall be glad if you can find me a first-edition of *Country Tilth* by Mortimer Scrivens. It was published by Street in 1923. If it is a second-hand copy, it is important that it should be fairly clean, particularly the cover. I should doubt if it ever went into a second edition.

Yours faithfully,
Brian Haverhill.

Mr. Brian Haverhill to Mr. Henry Winters.
Dear Winters,

I now return your book with our most profound apologies for keeping it so long. I can only hope that you were not greatly inconvenienced by its absence. It is, as you say, undoubtedly the most authoritative work on the subject, and our own violas have profited greatly by your kindness in introducing us to it.

Please give my kindest regards to Miss Winters if she is now with you. I hope you are both enjoying the beautiful weather.

Yours sincerely,
Brian Haverhill.

Mrs. Brian Haverhill to Mr. Henry Winters.
Dear Mr. Winters,

Can you ever forgive me for my unpardonable carelessness in keeping that delightful book so long? I need hardly say that I absorbed every word of it, and then put it carefully away, meaning to return it next morning, but somehow it slipped my memory in the way things do—well, it's no good trying to explain, I must just hope that you will forgive me, and when I come home—I am staying with my people for three weeks—perhaps you will let us show you and Miss Winters how well our violas are doing now—thanks entirely to you!

A very nice message to Miss Winters, please, and try to forgive,

Yours most sincerely,
Sarah Haverhill.

Sally Haverhill to Brian Haverhill.
Darling,

I hope you have sent the book back because I simply grovelled to the man yesterday, and I had to say I hoped they'd come and see our violas when I got back, but of course it doesn't mean anything. What I meant by my telegram was send the book back, which I expect you've done, and try and get a copy of the other just in *case* he remembers later on. If it's such a very bad book it can't cost much. Bill is here for a few days and says that he never makes beer-rings on books, and it must be one of *your* family, probably Tom, and Mother says that there is a way of removing beer-rings from books if only she could remember what it was, which looks as though she must have got the experience from my family not yours, but it doesn't help much. Anyhow I'm *sure* he's forgotten all about the book, and it *was* clever of you to find it, darling, and I do hope my telegram helped . . .

Messrs. Warbecks Ltd. to Mr. Brian Haverhill.
Dear Sir,

We have received your instructions *re Country Tilth,* and shall do our best to obtain a copy of the first edition for you. If it is not in stock, we propose to advertise for it. We note that it must be a fairly clean copy.

Assuring you of our best attention at all times,

Yours faithfully,
H. and E. Warbecks Ltd.
(p.p. J. W. F.)

Mr. Henry Winters to Mr. Brian Haverhill.
Dear Mr. Haverhill,

I am glad to acknowledge receipt of *The Care of the Viola* by Reynolds Chapman which arrived this morning. My impression was that the copy which I had the pleasure of lending Mrs. Haverhill two years ago was a somewhat newer and cleaner edition, but doubtless the passage of so long a period of time would account for the difference. I am not surprised to hear from Mrs. Haverhill that the book has been of continued value to her. It has been so to me, whenever in my possession, for a good many years.

Yours very truly,
Henry Winters.

Brian Haverhill to Sally Haverhill.
Darling Sally,

Just to get your values right before you come back to me: It is the Haverhills who are cutting the Winterses, and make no mistake about it. I enclose his foul letter. From now on no grovelling. Just a delicate raising of the eyebrows when you meet him, expressing surprise that the authorities have done nothing and he is still about.

Warbecks are trying to get another copy of *Country Tilth,* but I doubt if they will, because I can't see anybody keeping such a damn silly book. Well, I don't mind if they don't. Obviously Winters has forgotten all about it, and after his ill-mannered letter I see no reason for reminding him. . . .

Sally Haverhill to Brian Haverhill.

Sweetie Pie,

What a *brute* the man is, he never even acknowledged *my* letter, and I *couldn't* have been nicer. I think you should definitely tell Warbecks that you don't want the book now, and if he does ask for it ever, you either say he never lent it to you or else send back the copy we've got, and say that the beer-mark was always there because you remember wondering at the time, him being *supposed* not to have beer in the house, which was why you hadn't sent it back before, just seeing it from the outside and not thinking it could possibly be *his* copy. Of *course* I shall never speak to him again, horrible man. Mother says there used to be a Dr. Winters in Exeter when she was a girl, and he had to leave the country suddenly, but of course it may not be any relation. . . .

Brian Haverhill to Sally Haverhill.

Sally darling, you're ingenious and sweet and I love you dearly, but you must learn to distinguish between the gentlemanly lies you *can* tell and the other sort. Don't ask your mother to explain this to you, ask your father or Bill. Not that it matters as far as Winters is concerned. We've finished with him, thank God . . .

Mr. Henry Winters to Messrs. Warbecks Ltd.

Dear Sirs,

My attention has been fortuitously called to your advertisement enquiring for a copy of the 1st Edition of Mortimer

Scrivens' *Country Tilth.* I am the fortunate possessor of a 1st Edition of this much-sought-after item, which I shall be willing to sell if we can come to a suitable financial arrangement. I need hardly remind you that 1st editions of Mortimer Scrivens are a considerable rarity in the market, and I shall await your offer with some interest.

Yours faithfully,
Henry Winters.

Mr. Henry Winters to Miss Honoria Winters.

Dear Honoria,

I trust that your health is profiting by what I still consider to be your unnecessary visit to Harrogate. Do you remember a book of essays by Mortimer Scrivens called *Country Tilth,* which used to be, and had been for upwards of twenty-five years, in the middle shelf on the right-hand side of the fireplace? I have looked for it, not only there but in all the other shelves, without result, and I can only conclude that you have taken it up to your bedroom recently, and that it has since been put away in some hiding place of your own. It is of the *utmost importance* that I should have this book at once, and I shall be obliged by your immediate assistance in the matter.

The weather remains fine, but I am gravely inconvenienced by your absence, and shall be relieved by your return.

Your affec. brother,
Henry Winters.

Miss Honoria Winters to Mr. Henry Winters.

Dear Henry,

Thank you for your letter. I am much enjoying my stay here, and Frances and I have been making a number of pleasant little "sorties" to places of interest in the neighbourhood, including one or two charming old churches. Our hotel is very quiet, thanks to the fact that it has no license to provide intoxicating drink, with the result that an extremely nice class of person comes here. Already we are feeling the beneficial effects of the change, and I hope that when I return— on Monday the 24th—I shall be completely restored to health.

Frances sends her kindest remembrances to you, for although you have never met her, she has so often learnt of you in my letters that she feels that she knows you quite well!

Your affectionate sister,
Honoria.

P.S. Don't forget to tell Mrs. Harding in advance if you are *not* going to London next Thursday, as this was the day when we had arranged for the window-cleaner to come. She can then arrange for any other day suitable to you. You lent that book to the Haverhills when they came to tea about two years ago, together with your Viola book. I remember because you told me to fetch it for you. I haven't seen it since, so perhaps you lent it afterwards to somebody else.

Messrs. Warbecks Ltd. to Mr. Brian Haverhill.

Dear Sir,

Country Tilth

We have received notice of a copy of the 1st edition of this book in private possession, but before entering into negotiations with the owner it would be necessary to have some idea of the outside price which you would be prepared to pay. We may say that we have no replies from the trade, and if this copy is not secured, it may be difficult to obtain another. First editions of this author are notoriously scarce, and we should like to feel that, if necessary, we could go as high as £5, while endeavouring, of course, to obtain it for less. Trusting to have your instructions in the matter at your early convenience,

Yours faithfully,
H. & E. Warbecks Ltd.

Mr. Brian Haverhill to Messrs. Warbecks Ltd.
Dear Sirs,

Country Tilth.

I had assumed when I wrote to you that a first edition of this book, being of no literary value, would not have cost more than a few shillings, and in any case £1 would have been my limit, including your own commission. In the circumstances I will ask you to let the matter drop and to send me your account for any expense to which I have put you.

Yours faithfully,
Brian Haverhill.

Mr. Henry Winters to Mr. Brian Haverhill.
Dear Sir,

I now find, as must always have been known to yourself, that at the time of my lending Mrs. Haverhill *The Care of the Viola* by Reynolds Chapman, I also lent her, or you, a 1st edition of *Country Tilth* by Mortimer Scrivens. In returning the first named book to me two years later, you ignored the fact that you had this extremely rare book in your possession, presumably in the hope that I should not notice its absence from my shelves. I must ask you therefore to return it *immediately*, before I take other steps in the matter.

Yours faithfully,
Henry Winters.

Mr. Brian Haverhill to Messrs. Warbecks Ltd.
Dear Sirs,

This is to confirm my telephone message this morning that I am prepared to pay up to £5 for a 1st edition of *Country Tilth,* provided that it is in reasonably good condition. The matter, I must say again, is of the most urgent importance.

Yours faithfully,
Brian Haverhill.

Brian Haverhill to Sally Haverhill.

O hell, darling, all is discovered. I had a snorter from that devil this morning, demanding the instant return of *Country Tilth,* and this just after I had told Warbecks not to bother any more! They had written to say that they only knew of one copy in existence (I told you nobody would keep the damn thing) and that the man might want £5 for it. So naturally I said "£5 my foot." I have now rung them up to withdraw my foot, which I had so rashly put in it, and say "£5." But £5 for a blasted book, which nobody wants to read—and just because of a beer-ring which is its only real contact with life—seems a bit hard. Let this be a lesson to all of us never to borrow books, at least never from T.T.'s. Alternatively, of course, to return them in less than two years—there *is* that . . .

Messrs. Warbecks Ltd. to Mr. Henry Winters.
Dear Sir,

Country Tilth.

If you will forward us your copy of the 1st edn. of this book for our inspection, we shall then be in a position to make what we hope you will consider a very satisfactory offer for it in accordance with its condition. Awaiting a reply at your earliest convenience, as the matter is of some urgency,

Yours faithfully,
H. and E. Warbecks Ltd.

Mr. Henry Winters to Mr. Brian Haverhill.
Sir,

Country Tilth.

Unless I receive my copy of this book within 24 hours I shall be compelled to consult my solicitors.

Yours faithfully,
Henry Winters.

Mr Brian Haverhill to Messrs. Warbecks Ltd.
Dear Sirs,

Country Tilth.

In confirmation of my telephone message this morning I authorise you to make a firm offer of £10 for the 1st edn. of this book for which you are negotiating, provided that it is delivered within the next 24 hours.

Yours faithfully,
Brian Haverhill.

Messrs. Warbecks Ltd. to Mr. Henry Winters.
Sir,

Country Tilth

We are still awaiting a reply to our letter of the 18th asking you to forward your copy of the 1st edn. of this book for our inspection. We are now authorised by our client to say that he is prepared to pay £10 for your copy, provided that its condition is satisfactory to him, and that we receive delivery of it by the 22nd inst. After that date he will not be interested in the matter.

Yours faithfully,
H. & E. Warbecks Ltd.

Mr. Henry Winters to Brian Haverhill.
Sir,

The enclosed copy of a letter from Messrs. Warbecks speaks for itself. You have the alternative of returning my book *immediately* or sending me your cheque for £10. Otherwise I shall take legal action.

H. Winters.

Sally Haverhill to Brian Haverhill.

Darling one, *what* do you think has happened!!! This morning we drove into Taunton just after you rang up, Mother having suddenly remembered it was Jacqueline's birthday

to-morrow, and in a little bookshop down by the river I found
a copy of *Country Tilth* in the 6d box! Quite clean too and no
name inside it, so I sent it off at once to Mr. Winters, with a
little letter just saying how sorry I was to have kept it so long,
and not telling a single "other sort" except for being a little
sarcastic which I'm sure is quite a gentlemanly thing to be. So,
darling, you needn't bother any more, and after I come back
on Monday (HOORAY!) we'll go up to London for a night and
spend the £10 I've saved you. What fun! Only of course you
must ring up Warbecks *at once* . . .

Mrs. Brian Haverhill to Mr. Henry Winters.
Dear Mr. Winters,

I am sending back the other book you so kindly lent me. I
am so sorry I kept it so long, but it had *completely* disappeared,
and poor Brian has been looking everywhere for it, and wor-
rying *terribly,* thinking you would think I was trying to steal
it or something! Wasn't it *crazy* of him? As if you would!—
and as if the book was worth stealing when I saw a copy of it
in the 6d box at Taunton this very morning! I expect you'll
be wondering where I found your copy. Well, it was most
odd. I happened to be looking in my dressing-case just now,
and there is a flap in the lid which I hardly ever use, and I
noticed it was rather bulging—and there was the book! I've
been trying to remember when I last used this particular
dressing-case, because it looks as though I must have taken
the book away with me directly after you so kindly lent it to
me, and of course I remembered that it *was* just before I came
to see my people, which I do every year at this time, that we
came to see *you!*

I must now write and tell Brian the good news, because
after turning the house upside down looking for it, he was
actually *advertising* for a copy to replace it, and offering £10—
ten *pounds,* think of it, when its actual value is *sixpence!*
Wouldn't it have been awful if some horrible mercenary per-

son who happened to have a copy had taken advantage of his ignorance of book prices and swindled him? But, whatever its value, it doesn't make it any less kind of you to have lent it to me, or careless of me to have forgotten about it so quickly.

Yours most sincerely,
Sarah Haverhill.

P.S. Isn't this hot weather delightful? Just perfect for sunbathing. I can see you and Miss Winters simply *revelling* in it.

ADDRESS UNKNOWN

SCHULSE-EISENSTEIN GALLERIES
SAN FRANCISCO, CALIFORNIA, U.S.A

November 12, 1932

Herrn Martin Schulse
Schloss Rantzenburg
Munich, Germany

My Dear Martin:

Back in Germany! How I envy you! Although I have not seen it since my school days, the spell of *Unter den Linden* is still strong upon me—the breadth of intellectual freedom, the discussions, the music, the lighthearted comradeship. And now the old Junker spirit, the Prussian arrogance and militarism are gone. You go to a democratic Germany, a land with a deep culture and the beginnings of a fine political freedom. It will be a good life. Your new address is impressive and I rejoice the crossing was so pleasant for Elsa and the young sprouts.

As for me, I am not so happy. Sunday morning finds me a lonely bachelor without aim. My Sunday home is now transported over the wide seas. The big old house on the hill—your welcome that said the day was not complete until we were together again! And our dear jolly Elsa, coming out beaming, grasping my hand and shouting "Max! Max!" and hurrying indoors to open my favorite *Schnapps*. The fine boys, too, especially your handsome young Heinrich; he will be a grown man before I set eyes upon him again.

And dinner—shall I evermore hope to eat as I have eaten? Now I go to a restaurant and over my lonely roast beef come visions of *gebackner Schinken* steaming in its Burgundy sauce, of *Spatzle,* ah! of *Spatzle* and *Spargel!* No, I shall never again become reconciled to my American diet. And the wines, so carefully slipped ashore from the German boats, and the pledges we made as the glasses brimmed for the fourth and fifth and sixth times.

Of course you are right to go. You have never become American despite your success here, and now that the business is so well established you must take your sturdy German boys back to the homeland to be educated. Elsa too has missed her family through the long years and they will be glad to see you as well. The impecunious young artist has now become the family benefactor, and that too will give you a quiet little triumph.

The business continues to go well. Mrs. Levine has bought the small Picasso at our price, for which I congratulate myself, and I have old Mrs. Fleshman playing with the notion of the hideous Madonna. No one ever bothers to tell her that any particular piece of hers is bad, because they are all so bad. However I lack your fine touch in selling to the old Jewish matrons. I can persuade them of the excellence of the investment, but you alone had the fine spiritual approach to a piece of art that unarmed them. Besides they probably never entirely trust another Jew.

A delightful letter came yesterday from Griselle. She writes that she is about to make me proud of my little sister. She has the lead in a new play in Vienna and the notices are excellent—her discouraging years with the small companies are beginning to bear fruit. Poor child, it has not been easy for her, but she has never complained. She has a fine spirit, as well as beauty, and I hope the talent as well. She asked about you, Martin, in a very friendly way. There is no bitterness left there, for that passes quickly when one is young as she is. A few years and there is only a memory of the hurt, and of course neither of you was to be blamed. Those things are like quick storms, for a moment you are drenched and blasted, and you are so wholly helpless before them. But then the sun comes, and although you have neither quite forgotten, there remains only gentleness and no sorrow. You would not have had it otherwise, nor would I. I have not written Griselle that you are in Europe but perhaps I shall if you think it wise, for she does not make friends easily and I know she would be glad to feel that friends are not far away.

Fourteen years since the war! Did you mark the date? What a long way we have traveled, as peoples, from that bitterness! Again, my dear Martin, let me embrace you in spirit, and with the most affectionate remembrances to Elsa and the boys, believe me,

Your ever most faithful,
Max

SCHLOSS   RANTZENBURG
MUNICH ,   GERMANY

December 10, 1932

Mr. Max Eisenstein
Schulse-Eisenstein Galleries
San Francisco, California, U.S.A.

Max, Dear Old Fellow:

The check and accounts came through promptly, for which my thanks. You need not send me such details of the business. You know how I am in accord with your methods, and here at Munich I am in a rush of new activities. We are established, but what a turmoil! The house, as you know, I had long in mind. And I got it at an amazing bargain. Thirty rooms and about ten acres of park; you would never believe it. But then, you could not appreciate how poor is now this sad land of mine. The servants' quarters, stables and outbuildings are most extensive, and would you believe it, we employ now ten servants for the same wages of our two in the San Francisco home.

The tapestries and pieces we shipped make a rich show and some other fine furnishings I have been able to secure, so that we are much admired, I was almost to say envied. Four full services in the finest china I have bought and much crystal, as well as a full service of silver for which Elsa is in ecstasies.

And for Elsa—such a joke! You will, I know, laugh with me. I have purchased for her a huge bed. Such a size as never was before, twice the bigness of a double bed, and with great posters in carved wood. The sheets I must have made to order, for there are no sheets made that could fit it. And they are of linen, the finest linen sheets. Elsa laughs and laughs, and her old *Grossmutter* stands shaking her head and grumbles, "*Nein,* Martin, *nein.* You have made it so and now you must take care or she will grow to match it."

"*Ja,*" says Elsa, "five more boys and I will fit it just nice and snug." And she will, Max.

For the boys there are three ponies (little Karl and Wolfgang are not big enough to ride yet) and a tutor. Their German is very bad, being too much mixed with English.

Elsa's family do not find things so easy now. The brothers are in the professions and, while much respected, must live together in one house. To the family we seem American millionaires and while we are far from that yet our American income places us among the wealthy here. The better foods are high in price and there is much political unrest even now under the presidency of Hindenburg, a fine liberal whom I much admire.

Already old acquaintances urge me that I interest myself in administrative matters in the town. This I take under consideration. It may be somewhat to our benefit locally if I become an official.

As for you, my good Max, we have left you alone, but you must not become a misanthrope. Get yourself at once a nice fat little wife who will busy herself with all your cares and feed you into a good humor. That is my advice and it is good, although I smile as I write it.

You write of Griselle. So she wins her success, the lovely one! I rejoice with you, although even now I resent it that she must struggle to win her way, a girl alone. She was made, as any man can see, for luxury and for devotion and the charming and beautiful life where ease allows much play of the sensibilities. A gentle, brave soul is in her dark eyes, but there is something strong as iron and very daring too. She is a woman who does nothing and gives nothing lightly. Alas, dear Max, as always, I betray myself. But although you were silent during our stormy affair, you know that the decision was not easy for me. You never reproached me, your friend, while the little sister suffered, and I have always felt you knew that I suffered too, most gravely. What could I do? There was Elsa and my little sons. No other decision was possible to make. Yet for Griselle I keep a tenderness that will last long after she has taken a much younger man for husband or lover. The old wound has healed but the scar throbs at times, my friend.

I wish that you will give her our address. We are such a short distance from Vienna that she can feel there is for her a home close at hand. Elsa, too, knows nothing of the old feeling between us and you know with what warmth she would welcome your sister, as she would welcome you. Yes, you must tell her that we are here and urge her to soon make a contact with us. Give her our most warm congratulations for the fine success that she is making.

Elsa asks that I send to you her love, and Heinrich would also say "hello" to Uncle Max. We do not forget you, Maxel.

My heartiest greetings to you,
Martin

SCHULSE-EISENSTEIN GALLERIES
SAN FRANCISCO, CALIFORNIA, U.S.A

January 21, 1933

Herrn Martin Schulse
Schloss Rantzenburg
Munich, Germany

My Dear Martin:

I was glad to forward your address to Griselle. She should have it shortly, if she has not yet already received it. What jollification there will be when she sees you all! I shall be with you in spirit as heartily as if I also could rejoin you in person.

You speak of the poverty there. Conditions have been bad here this winter, but of course we have known nothing of the privations you see in Germany.

Personally, you and I are lucky that we have such a sound following for the gallery. Of course our own clientele are cutting their purchases but if they buy only half as much as before we shall be comfortable, not extravagantly so, but very comfortable. The oils you sent are excellent, and the prices are amazing. I shall dispose of them at an appalling profit almost at once. And the ugly Madonna is gone! Yes, to old Mrs. Fleshman. How I gasped at her perspicacity in recognizing its worth, hesitating to set a price! She suspected me of having another client, and I named an indecent figure. She pounced on it, grinning shyly as she wrote her check. How I exulted as she bore the horror off with her, you alone will know.

Alas, Martin, I often am ashamed of myself for the delight I take in such meaningless little triumphs. You in Germany, with your country house and your affluence displayed before Elsa's relatives, and I in America, gloating because I have tricked a giddy old woman into buying a monstrosity. What a fine climax for two men of forty! Is it for this we spend our lives, to scheme for money and then to strut it publicly? I am always castigating myself, but I continue to do as before. Alas, we are all caught in the same mill. We are vain and we are dishonest because it is necessary to triumph over other vain and dishonest persons. If I do not sell Mrs. Fleshman our horror, somebody else will sell her a worse one. We must accept these necessities.

But there is another realm where we can always find something true, the fireside of a friend, where we shed our little conceits and find warmth and understanding, where small selfishnesses are impossible and where wine and books and talk give a different meaning to existence. There we have made something that no falseness can touch. We are at home.

Who is this Adolf Hitler who seems rising toward power in Germany? I do not like what I read of him.

Embrace all the young fry and our abundant Elsa for

Your ever affectionate,

Max

SCHLOSS   RANTZENBURG
MUNICH,   GERMANY

March 25, 1933

Mr. Max Eisenstein
Schulse-Eisenstein Galleries
San Francisco, California, U.S.A.

Dear Old Max:

You have heard of course of the new events in Germany, and you will want to know how it appears to us here on the inside. I tell you truly, Max, I think in many ways Hitler is good for Germany, but I am not sure. He is now the active head of the government. I doubt much that even Hindenburg could now remove him from power, as he was truly forced to place him there. The man is like an electric shock, strong as only a great orator and a zealot can be. But I ask myself, is he quite sane? His brown shirt troops are of the rabble. They pillage and have started a bad Jew-baiting. But these may be minor things, the little surface scum when a big movement boils up. For I tell you, my friend, there is a surge—a surge. The people everywhere have had a quickening. You feel it in the streets and shops. The old despair has been thrown aside like a forgotten coat. No longer the people wrap themselves in shame; they hope again. Perhaps there may be found an end to this poverty. Something, I do not know what, will happen. A leader is found! Yet cautiously to myself I ask, a leader to where? Despair overthrown often turns us in mad directions.

Publicly, as is natural, I express no doubt. I am now an official and a worker in the new regime and I exult very loud indeed. All of us officials who cherish whole skins are quick to join the National Socialists. That is the name for Herr Hitler's party. But also it is not only expedient, there is something more, a feeling that we of Germany have found our destiny and that the future sweeps toward us in an overwhelming wave. We too must move. We must go with it. Even now there are being wrongs done. The storm troopers are having their moment of victory, and there are bloody heads and sad hearts to show for it. But these things pass; if the end in view is right they pass and are forgotten. History writes a clean new page.

All I now ask myself, and I can say to you what I cannot say to any here is: Is the end right? Do we make for a better goal? For you know, Max, I have seen these people of my race since I came here, and I have learned what agonies they have suffered, what years of less and less bread, of leaner bodies, of the end of hope. The quicksand of despair held them, it was at their chins. Then just before they died a man came and pulled them out. All they now know is, they will not die. They are in hysteria of deliverance, almost they worship him. But whoever the savior was, they would have done the same. God grant it is a true leader and no black angel they follow so joyously. To you alone, Max, I say I do not know. I do not know. Yet I hope.

So much for politics. Ourselves, we delight in our new home and have done much entertaining. Tonight the mayor is our guest, at a dinner for twenty-eight. We spread ourselves a little, maybe, but that is to be forgiven. Elsa has a new gown of blue velvet, and is in terror for fear it will not be big enough. She is with child again. There is the way to keep a wife contented, Max. Keep her so busy with babies she has no time to fret.

Our Heinrich has made a social conquest. He goes out on his pony and gets himself thrown off, and who picks him up but the Baron Von Freische. They have a long conversation about America, and one day the baron calls and we have coffee. Heinrich will go there to lunch next week. What a boy! It is too bad his German is not better but he delights everyone.

So we go, my friend, perhaps to become part of great events, perhaps only to pursue our simple family way, but never abandoning that trueness of friendship of which you speak so movingly. Our hearts go out to you across the wide sea, and when the glasses are filled we toast "Uncle Max."

Yours in affectionate regard,

Martin

SCHULSE-EISENSTEIN GALLERIES
SAN FRANCISCO, CALIFORNIA, U.S.A

May 18, 1933

Herrn Martin Schulse
Schloss Rantzenburg
Munich, Germany

Dear Martin:
I am in distress at the press reports that come pouring in

to us from the Fatherland. Thus it is natural that I turn to you for light while there are only conflicting stories to be had here. I am sure things cannot be as bad as they are pictured. A terrible pogrom, that is the consensus of our American papers.

I know your liberal mind and warm heart will tolerate no viciousness and that from you I can have the truth. Aaron Silberman's son has just returned from Berlin and had, I hear, a narrow escape. The tales he tells of what he has seen, floggings, the forcing of quarts of castor oil through clenched teeth and the consequent hours of dying through the slow agony of bursting guts, are not pretty ones. These things may be true, and they may, as you have said, be but the brutal surface froth of human revolution. Alas, to us Jews they are a sad story familiar through centuries of repetition, and it is almost unbelievable that the old martyrdom must be endured in a civilized nation today. Write me, my friend, and set my mind at ease.

Griselle's play will come to a close about the end of June after a great success. She writes that she has an offer for another role in Vienna and also for a very fine one in Berlin for the autumn. She is talking most of the latter one, but I have written her to wait until the anti-Jewish feeling has abated. Of course she used another name which is not Jewish (Eisenstein would be impossible for the stage anyway), but it is not her name that would betray her origin. Her features, her gestures, her emotional voice proclaim her a Jewess no matter what she calls herself, and if this feeling has any real strength she had best not venture into Germany just at present.

Forgive me, my friend, for so distrait and brief a letter but I cannot rest until you have reassured me. You will, I know, write in all fairness. Pray do so at once.

With the warmest protestations of faith and friendship for you and yours, I am ever your faithful

Max

Deutsch-Völkische Bank und Handelsgesellschaft,
München

July 9, 1933

Mr. Max Eisenstein
Schulse-Eisenstein Galleries
San Francisco, California, U.S.A.

Dear Max:

You will see that I write upon the stationary of my bank. This is necessary because I have a request to make of you and I wish to avoid the new censorship which is most strict. We must for the present discontinue writing each other. It is impossible for me to be in correspondence with a Jew even if it were not that I have an official position to maintain. If communication becomes necessary you must enclose it with the bank draft and not write to me at my house again.

As for the stern measures that so distress you, I myself did not like them at first, but I have come to see their painful necessity. The Jewish race is a sore spot to any nation that harbors it. I have never hated the individual Jew—yourself I have always cherished as a friend, but you will know that I speak in all honesty when I say I have loved you, not because of your race but in spite of it.

The Jew is the universal scapegoat. This does not happen without reason, and it is not the old superstition about "Christ-killers" that makes them distrusted. But this Jew trouble is only an incident. Something bigger is happening.

If I could show you, if I could make you see—the rebirth of this new Germany under our Gentle Leader! Not for always can the world grind a great people down in subjugation. In defeat for fourteen years we bowed our heads. We ate the bitter bread of shame and drank the thin gruel of poverty. But now we are free men. We rise in our might and hold our heads up before the nations. We purge our bloodstream of its baser elements. We go singing through our valleys with strong muscles tingling for new work—and from the mountains ring the voices of Wodan and Thor, the old, strong gods of the German race.

But no. I am sure as I write, as with the new vision my own enthusiasm burns, that you will not see how necessary is all this for Germany. You will see only that your own people are troubled. You will not see that a few must suffer for the millions to be saved. You will be a Jew first and wail for your people. This I understand. It is the Semitic character. You lament but you are never brave enough to fight back. This is why there are pogroms.

Alas, Max, this will pain you, I know, but you must realize the truth. There are movements far bigger than the men who make them up. As for me, I am a part of the movement. Heinrich is an officer in the boys' corps which is headed by Baron Von Freische whose rank is now shedding a luster upon our house, for he comes often to visit with Heinrich and Elsa, whom he much admires. Myself, I am up to the ears in work. Elsa concerns herself little with politics except to adore our Gentle Leader. She gets tired too easily this last month. Perhaps the babies come too fast. It will be better for her when this one is born.

I regret our correspondence must close this way, Max. Perhaps we can someday meet again on a field of better understanding.

As ever your,
Martin Schulse

SCHULSE-EISENSTEIN GALLERIES
SAN FRANCISCO, CALIFORNIA, U.S.A

August 1, 1933

Herrn Martin Schulse
(kindness of J. Lederer)
Schloss Rantzenburg
Munich, Germany

Martin, My Old Friend:

I am sending this by the hand of Jimmy Lederer, who will shortly pass through Munich on a European vacation. I cannot rest after the letter you last sent me. It is so unlike you I can only attribute its contents to your fear of the censorship. The man I have loved as a brother, whose heart has ever been brimming with sympathy and friendship, cannot possibly partake of even a passive partnership in the butchery of innocent people. I trust and pray that it may be so, that you will write me no exposition, which might be dangerous for you,—only a simple "yes." That will tell me that you play the part of expediency but that your heart has not changed, and that I was not deluded in believing you to be always a man of fine and liberal spirit to whom wrongs are wrongs in whosoever's name they may be committed.

This censorship, this persecution of all men of liberal thought, the burning of libraries and corruption of the universities would arouse your antagonism if there had been no finger laid on one of my race in Germany. You are a liberal, Martin. You have always taken the long view. I know that you cannot be swept away from sanity by a popular movement which has so much that is bad about it, no matter how strong it may be.

I can see why the Germans acclaim Hitler. They react against the very real wrongs which have been laid on them since the disaster of the war. But you, Martin, have been almost an American since the war. I know that it is not my friend who has written to me, that it will prove to have been only the voice of caution and expediency.

Eagerly I await the one word that will set my heart at peace. Write your "yes" quickly.

My love to you all,
Max

Deutsch-Völkische Bank und Handelsgesellschaft,
München

August 18, 1933

Mr. Max Eisenstein
Schulse-Eisenstein Galleries
San Francisco, California, U.S.A.

Dear Max:

I have your letter. The word is "no." You are a sentimentalist. You do not know that all men are not cut to your pattern. You put nice little tags on them, like "liberal" and expect them to act so-and-so. But you are wrong. So, I am an American liberal? No! I am a German patriot.

A liberal is a man who does not believe in doing anything. He is a talker about the rights of man, but just a talker. He likes to make a big noise about freedom of speech, and what is freedom of speech? Just the chance to sit firmly on the backside and say that whatever is being done by the active men is wrong. What is so futile as the liberal? I know him well because I have been one. He condemns the passive government because it makes no change. But let a powerful man arise, let an active man start to make a change, then where is your liberal? He is against it. To the liberal any change is the wrong one.

He calls this the "long view," but it is merely a bad scare that he will have to do something himself. He loves words and high-sounding precepts but he is useless to the men who make the world what it is. These are the only important men, the doers. And here in Germany a doer has risen. A vital man is changing things. The whole tide of a people's life changes in a minute because the man of action has come. And I join him. I am not just swept along by a current. The useless life that was all talk and no accomplishment I drop. I put my back and shoulders behind the great new movement. I am a man because I act. Before that I am just a voice. I do not question the ends of our action. It is not necessary. I know it is good because it is so vital. Men are not drawn into bad things with so much joy and eagerness.

You say we persecute men of liberal thought, we destroy libraries. You should wake from your musty sentimentalizing. Does the surgeon spare the cancer because he must cut it to remove it? We are cruel. Of course we are cruel. As all birth is brutal, so is this new birth of ours. But we rejoice. Germany lifts high her head among the nations of the world. She follows her Glorious Leader to triumph. What can you know of this, you who only sit and dream? You have never known a Hitler. He is a drawn sword. He is a white light, but hot as the sun of a new day.

I must insist that you write no further. We are no longer in sympathy, as now we must both realize.

Martin Schulse

EISENSTEIN GALLERIES
SAN FRANCISCO, CALIFORNIA, U.S.A

September 5, 1933

Herrn Martin Schulse
C/o Deutsch-Voelkische Bank
und Handelgeselschaft
Munich, Germany

Dear Martin:

Enclosed are your draft and the month's accounts. It is of necessity that I send a brief message. Griselle has gone to Berlin. She is too daring. But she has waited so long for success she will not relinquish it, and laughs at my fears. She will be at the Koenig Theater. You are an official. For old friendship's sake, I beg of you to watch over her. Go to Berlin if you can and see whether she is in danger.

It will distress you to observe that I have been obliged to remove your name from the firm's name. You know who our principal clients are, and they will touch nothing now from a firm with a German name.

Your new attitude I cannot discuss. But you must understand me. I did not expect you would take up arms for my people because they are my people, but because you were a man who loved justice.

I commend my rash Griselle to you. The child does not realize what a risk she is taking. I shall not write again.

Goodbye, my friend,

Max

EISENSTEIN GALLERIES
SAN FRANCISCO, CALIFORNIA, U.S.A

November 5, 1933

Herrn Martin Schulse
^c/o Deutsch-Voelkische Bank
und Handelgeselschaft
Munich, Germany

Martin:

I write again because I must. A black foreboding has taken possession of me. I wrote Griselle as soon as I knew she was in Berlin and she answered briefly. Rehearsals were going brilliantly; the play would open shortly. My second letter was more encouragement than warning, and it has been returned to me, the envelope unopened, marked only addressee unknown, *(Adressant Unbekannt)*. What a darkness those words carry! How can she be unknown? It is surely a message that she has come to harm. They know what has happened to her, those stamped letters say, but I am not to know. She has gone into some sort of void and it will be useless to seek her. All this they tell me in two words, *Adressant Unbekannt.*

Martin, need I ask you to find her, to succor her? You have known her graciousness, her beauty and sweetness. You have had her love, which she has given to no other man. Do not attempt to write to me. I know I need not even ask you to aid. It is enough to tell you that something has gone wrong, that she must be in danger.

I leave her in your hands, for I am helpless.

Max

EISENSTEIN GALLERIES
SAN FRANCISCO, CALIFORNIA, U.S.A

November 23, 1933

Herrn Martin Schulse
c/o Deutsch-Voelkische Bank
und Handelgeselschaft
Munich, Germany

Martin:

I turn to you in despair. I could not wait for another month to pass so I am sending some information as to your investments. You may wish to make some changes and I can thus enclose my appeal with a bank letter.

It is Griselle. For two months there has been only silence from her, and now the rumors begin to come in to me. From Jewish mouth to Jewish mouth the tales slowly come back from Germany, tales so full of dread I would close my ears if I dared, but I cannot. I must know what has happened to her. I must be sure.

She appeared in the Berlin play for a week. Then she was jeered from the audience as a Jewess. She is so headstrong, so foolhardy, the splendid child! She threw the word back in their teeth. She told them proudly that she *was* a Jewess.

Some of the audience started after her. She ran backstage. Someone must have helped her for she got away with the whole pack at her heels and took refuge with a Jewish family in a cellar for several days. After that she changed her appearance as much as she could and started south, hoping to walk back to Vienna. She did not dare try the railroads. She told those she left that she would be safe if she could reach friends in Munich. That is my hope, that she has gone to you, for she has never reached Vienna. Send me word, Martin, and if she has not come there make a quiet investigation if you can. My mind cannot rest. I torture myself by day and by night, seeing the brave little thing trudging all those long miles through hostile country, with winter coming on. God grant you can send me a word of relief.

Max

Deutsch-Völkische Bank und Handelsgesellschaft, München

December 8, 1933

Heil Hitler! I much regret that I have bad news for you. Your sister is dead. Unfortunately she was, as you have said, very much a fool. Not quite a week ago she came here, with a bunch of storm troopers right behind her. The house was very active—Elsa has not been well since little Adolf was born last month—the doctor was here, and two nurses, with all the servants and children scurrying around.

By luck I answer the door. At first I think it is an old woman and then I see the face, and then I see the storm troopers have turned in the park gates. Can I hide her? It is one chance in thousands. A servant will be on us at any minute. Can I endure to have my house ransacked with Elsa ill in bed and to risk being arrested for harboring a Jew and to lose all I have built up here? Of course as a German I have one plain duty. She has displayed her Jewish body on the stage before pure young German men. I should hold her and turn her over to the storm troopers. But this I cannot do.

"You will destroy us all, Griselle," I tell her. "You must run back further in the park." She looks at me and smiles (she was always a brave girl) and makes her own choice.

"I would not bring you harm, Martin," she says, and she runs down the steps and out toward the trees. But she must be tired. She does not run very fast and the storm troopers have caught sight of her. I am helpless. I go in the house and in a few minutes she stops screaming, and in the morning I have the body sent down to the village for burial. She was a fool to come to Germany. Poor little Griselle. I grieve with you, but as you see, I was helpless to aid her.

I must now demand you do not write again. Every word that comes to the house is now censored, and I cannot tell how soon they may start to open the mail to the bank. And I will no longer have any dealings with Jews, except for the receipt of money. It is not so good for me that a Jewess came here for refuge, and no further association can be tolerated.

A new Germany is being shaped here. We will soon show the world great things under our Glorious Leader.

Martin

CABLEGRAM

MUNICH JANUARY 2 1934

MARTIN SCHULSE

YOUR TERMS ACCEPTED NOVEMBER TWELVE AUDIT
SHOWS THIRTEEN PERCENT INCREASE FEBRUARY
SECOND FOURFOLD ASSURED PAN EXHIBITION MAY
FIRST PREPARE LEAVE FOR MOSCOW IF MARKET
OPENS UNEXPECTEDLY FINANCIAL INSTRUCTIONS
MAILED NEW ADDRESS

EISENSTEIN

EISENSTEIN GALLERIES
SAN FRANCISCO, CALIFORNIA, U.S.A

January 3, 1934

Herrn Martin Schulse
Schloss Rantzenburg
Munich, Germany

Our Dear Martin:
Don't forget grandma's birthday. She will be 64 on the 8th. American contributors will furnish 1,000 brushes for your German Young Painters' League. Mandelberg has joined in supporting the league. You must send 11 Picasso reproductions, 20 by 90 to branch galleries on the 25th, no sooner. Reds and blues must predominate. We can allow you $8,000 on this transaction at present. Start new accounts book 2.
Our prayers follow you daily, dear brother,

Eisenstein

EISENSTEIN GALLERIES
SAN FRANCISCO, CALIFORNIA, U.S.A

January 17, 1934

Herrn Martin Schulse
Schloss Rantzenburg
Munich, Germany

Martin, Dear Brother:
Good news! Our stock reached 116 five days ago. The Fleishmans have advanced another $10,000. This will fill your Young Painters' League quota for a month but let us know if opportunities increase. Swiss miniatures are having a vogue.

You must watch the market and plan to be in Zurich after May first if any unexpected opportunities develop. Uncle Solomon will be glad to see you and I know you will rely heavily on his judgment.

The weather is clear and there is little danger of storms during the next two months. You will prepare for your students the following reproductions: Van Gogh 15 by 103, red; Poussin 20 by 90, blue and yellow; Vermeer 11 by 33, red and blue.

Our hopes will follow your new efforts.

Eisenstein

EISENSTEIN GALLERIES

SAN FRANCISCO, CALIFORNIA, U.S.A

January 29, 1934

Dear Martin:

Your last letter was delivered by mistake at 457 Geary St., Room 4. Aunt Rheba says tell Martin he must write more briefly and clearly so his friends can understand all that he says. I am sure everyone will be in readiness for your family reunion on the 15th. You will be tired after these festivities and may want to take your family with you on your trip to Zurich.

Before leaving however, procure the following reproductions for branches of German Young Painters' League, looking forward to the joint exhibit in May or earlier: Picasso 17 by 81, red; Van Gogh 5 by 42, white; Rubens 15 by 4, blue and yellow.

Our prayers are with you.

Eisenstein

SCHLOSS RANTZENBURG
MUNICH, GERMANY

February 12, 1934

Mr. Max Eisenstein
Eisenstein Galleries
San Francisco, California, U.S.A.

Max, My Old Friend:

My God, Max, do you know what you do? I shall have to try
to smuggle this letter out with an American I have met here.
I write an appeal from a despair you cannot imagine. This
crazy cable! These letters you have sent. I am called in to
account for them. The letters are not delivered, but they bring
me in and show me letters from you and demand I give them
the code. A code? And how can you, a friend of long years, do
this to me?

Do you realize, have you any idea that you destroy me?
Already the results of your madness are terrible. I am bluntly
told I must resign my office. Heinrich is no longer in the boys'
corps. They tell him it will not be good for his health. God in
heaven, Max, do you see what that means? And Elsa, to whom
I dare not tell anything, comes in bewildered that the officials
refuse her invitations and Baron Von Freische does not speak
to her upon the street.

Yes, yes, I know why you do it—but do you not understand I could do nothing? What could I have done? I did not
dare to try. I beg of you, not for myself, but for Elsa and the
boys—think what it means to them if I am taken away and
they do not know if I live or die. Do you know what it is to
be taken to a concentration camp? Would you stand me
against a wall and level the gun? I beg of you, stop. Stop now,
while everything is not yet destroyed. I am in fear for my life,
for my life, Max.

Is it you who does this? It cannot be you. I have loved you like a brother, my old Maxel. My God, have you no mercy? I beg you, Max, no more, no more! Stop while I can be saved. From a heart filled with old affection I ask it.

Martin

EISENSTEIN GALLERIES
SAN FRANCISCO, CALIFORNIA, U.S.A

February 15, 1934

Herrn Martin Schulse
Schloss Rantzenburg
Munich, Germany

Our Dear Martin:

Seven inches of rainfall here in 18 days. What a season! A shipment of 1,500 brushes should reach the Berlin branch for your painters by this weekend. This will allow time for practice before the big exhibition. American patrons will help with all the artists' supplies that can be provided, but you must make the final arrangements. We are too far out of touch with the European market and you are in a position to gauge the extent of support such a showing would arouse in Germany. Prepare these for distribution by March 24th: Rubens 12 by 77, blue; Giotto 1 by 317, green and white; Poussin 20 by 90, red and white.

Young Blum left last Friday with the Picasso specifications. He will leave oils in Hamburg and Leipzig and will then place himself at your disposal.

Success to you!
Eisenstein

EISENSTEIN GALLERIES
SAN FRANCISCO, CALIFORNIA, U.S.A

March 3, 1934

Martin Our Brother:

Cousin Julius has two nine-pound boys. The family is happy. We regard the success of your coming artists' exhibition as assured. The last shipment of canvases was delayed due to difficulties of international exchange but will reach your Berlin associates in plenty of time. Consider reproduction collection complete. Your best support should come from Picasso enthusiasts but neglect no other lines.

We leave all final plans to your discretion but urge an early date for wholly successful exhibit.

The God of Moses be at your right hand.

Eisenstein

VIII

The Story

AS FANTASY OR FABLE

These stories depart from realism but use seemingly realistic storytelling and rounded characters to draw us into worlds that differ radically from our own. Yet we emerge from these realms with some larger truths about the human situation.

JEALOUS HUSBAND RETURNS IN FORM OF PARROT

I NEVER CAN QUITE SAY as much as I know. I look at other parrots and I wonder if it's the same for them, if somebody is trapped in each of them paying some kind of price for living their life in a certain way. For instance, "Hello," I say, and I'm sitting on a perch in a pet store in Houston and what I'm really thinking is Holy shit. It's you. And what's happened is I'm looking at my wife.

"Hello," she says, and she comes over to me and I can't believe how beautiful she is. Those great brown eyes, almost as dark as the center of mine. And her nose—I don't remember her for her nose but its beauty is clear to me now. Her nose is a little too long, but it's redeemed by the faint hook to it.

She scratches the back of my neck.

Her touch makes my tail flare. I feel the stretch and rustle of me back there. I bend my head to her and she whispers, "Pretty bird."

For a moment I think she knows it's me. But she doesn't, of course. I say "Hello" again and I will eventually pick up "pretty bird." I can tell that as soon as she says it, but for now I can only give her another hello. Her fingertips move through my feathers and she seems to know about birds. She knows that to pet a bird you don't smooth his feathers down, you ruffle them.

But of course she did that in my human life, as well. It's all the same for her. Not that I was complaining, even to myself, at that moment in the pet shop when she found me like I presume she was supposed to. She said it again, "Pretty bird," and this brain that works like it does now could feel that tiny little voice of mine ready to shape itself around these sounds. But before I could get them out of my beak there was this guy at my wife's shoulder and all my feathers went slick flat like to make me small enough not to be seen and I backed away. The pupils of my eyes pinned and dilated and pinned again.

He circled around her. A guy that looked like a meat packer, big in the chest and thick with hair, the kind of guy that I always sensed her eyes moving to when I was alive. I had a bare chest and I'd look for little black hairs on the sheets when I'd come home on a day with the whiff of somebody else in the air. She was still in the same goddamn rut.

A "hello" wouldn't do and I'd recently learned "good night" but it was the wrong suggestion altogether, so I said nothing and the guy circled her and he was looking at me with a smug little smile and I fluffed up all my feathers, made myself about twice as big, so big he'd see he couldn't mess with me. I waited for him to draw close enough for me to take off the tip of his finger.

But she intervened. Those nut-brown eyes were before me and she said, "I want him."

And that's how I ended up in my own house once again. She bought me a large black wrought-iron cage, very large, convinced by some young guy who clerked in the bird department and who took her aside and made his voice go much too soft when he was doing the selling job. The meat packer didn't like it. I didn't either. I'd missed a lot of chances to take a bite out of this clerk in my stay at the shop and I regretted that suddenly.

But I got my giant cage and I guess I'm happy enough about that. I can pace as much as I want. I can hang upside down. It's full of bird toys. That dangling thing over there with knots and strips of rawhide and a bell at the bottom needs a good thrashing a couple of times a day and I'm the bird to do it. I look at the very dangle of it and the thing is rough, the rawhide and the knotted rope, and I get this restlessness back in my tail, a burning thrashing feeling, and it's like all the times when I was sure there was a man naked with my wife. Then I go to this thing that feels so familiar and I bite and bite and it's very good.

I could have used the thing the last day I went out of this house as a man. I'd found the address of the new guy at my wife's office. He'd been there a month in the shipping department and three times she'd mentioned him. She didn't even have to work with him and three times I heard about him, just dropped into the conversation. "Oh," she'd say when a car commercial came on the television, "that car there is like the one the new man in shipping owns. Just like it." Hey, I'm not stupid. She said another thing about him and then another and right after the third one I locked myself in the bathroom because I couldn't rage about this anymore. I felt like a damn fool whenever I actually said anything about this kind of feeling and she looked at me like she could start hating me real easy and so I was working on saying nothing, even if it meant locking myself up. My goal was to hold my tongue about half the time. That would be a good start.

But this guy from shipping. I found out his name and his address and it was one of her typical Saturday afternoons of vague shopping. So I went to his house, and his car that was just like the commercial was outside. Nobody was around in the neighborhood and there was this big tree in the back of the house going up to a second floor window that was making funny little sounds. I went up. The shade was drawn but not quite all the way. I was holding on to a limb with arms and legs wrapped around it like it was her in those times when I could forget the others for a little while. But the crack in the shade was just out of view and I crawled on along till there was no limb left and I fell on my head. Thinking about that now, my wings flap and I feel myself lift up and it all seems so avoidable. Though I know I'm different now. I'm a bird.

Except I'm not. That's what's confusing. It's like those times when she would tell me she loved me and I actually believed her and maybe it was true and we clung to each other in bed and at times like that I was different. I was the man in her life. I was whole with her. Except even at that moment, holding her sweetly, there was this other creature inside me who knew a lot more about it and couldn't quite put all the evidence together to speak.

My cage sits in the den. My pool table is gone and the cage is sitting in that space and if I come all the way down to one end of my perch I can see through the door and down the back hallway to the master bedroom. When she keeps the bedroom door open I can see the space at the foot of the bed but not the bed itself. That I can sense to the left, just out of sight. I watch the men go in and I hear the sounds but I can't quite see. And they drive me crazy.

I flap my wings and I squawk and I fluff up and I slick down and I throw seed and I attack that dangly toy as if it was the guy's balls, but it does no good. It never did any good in the other life either, the thrashing around I did by myself. In that other life I'd have given anything to be standing in this den with her doing this thing with some other guy just down the hall and all I had to do was walk down there and turn the corner and she couldn't deny it anymore.

But now all I can do is try to let it go. I sidestep down to the opposite end of the cage and I look out the big sliding glass doors to the backyard. It's a pretty yard. There are great placid maple trees with good places to roost. There's a blue sky that plucks at the feathers on my chest. There are clouds. Other birds. Fly away. I could just fly away.

I tried once and I learned a lesson. She forgot and left the door to my cage open and I climbed beak and foot, beak and foot, along the bars and curled around to stretch sideways out the door and the vast scene of peace was there at the other end of the room. I flew.

And a pain flared through my head and I fell straight down and the room whirled around and the only good thing was she held me. She put her hands under my wings and lifted me and clutched me to her breast and I wish there hadn't been bees in my head at the time so I could have enjoyed that, but she put me back in the cage and wept awhile. That touched me, her tears. And I looked back to the wall of sky and trees. There was something invisible there between me and that dream of peace. I remembered, eventually, about glass, and I knew I'd been lucky, I knew that for the little fragile-boned skull I was doing all this thinking in, it meant death.

She wept that day but by the night she had another man. A guy with a thick Georgia truck-stop accent and pale white skin and an Adam's apple big as my seed ball. This guy has been around for a few weeks and he makes a whooping sound down the hallway, just out of my sight. At times like that I want to fly against the bars of the cage, but I don't. I have to remember how the world has changed.

She's single now, of course. Her husband, the man that I was, is dead to her. She does not understand all that is behind my "hello." I know many words, for a parrot. I am a yellow-nape Amazon, a handsome bird, I think, green with a splash of yellow at the back of my neck. I talk pretty well, but none of my words are adequate. I can't make her understand.

And what would I say if I could? I was jealous in life. I admit it. I would admit it to her. But it was because of my connection to her. I would explain that. When we held each other, I had no past at all, no present but her body, no future but to lie there and not let her go. I was an egg hatched beneath her crouching body, I entered as a chick into her wet sky of a body, and all that I wished was to sit on her shoulder and fluff my feathers and lay my head against her cheek, my neck exposed to her hand. And so the glances that I could see in her troubled me deeply, the movement of her eyes in pub-lic to other men, the laughs sent across a room, the tracking of her mind behind her blank eyes, pursuing images of others, her distraction even in our bed, the ghosts that were there of men who'd touched her, perhaps even that very day. I was not part of all those other men who were part of her. I didn't want to connect to all that. It was only her that I would fluff for but these others were there also and I couldn't put them aside. I sensed them inside her and so they were inside me. If I had the words, these are the things I would say.

But half an hour ago there was a moment that thrilled me. A word, a word we all knew in the pet shop, was just the right word after all. This guy with his cowboy belt buckle and rattlesnake boots and his pasty face and his twanging words of love trailed after my wife, through the den, past my cage, and I said, "Cracker." He even flipped his head back a little at this in surprise. He'd been called that before to his face, I realized. I said it again, "Cracker." But to him I was a bird and he let it pass. "Cracker," I said. "Hello, cracker." That was even better. They were out of sight through the hall doorway and I hustled along the perch and I caught a glimpse of them before they made the turn to the bed and I said, "Hello, cracker," and he shot me one last glance.

It made me hopeful. I eased away from that end of the cage, moved toward the scene of peace beyond the far wall. The sky is chalky blue today, blue like the brow of the blue-front Amazon who was on the perch next to me for about a week at the store. She was very sweet, but I watched her carefully for a day or two when she first came in. And it wasn't long before she nuzzled up to a cockatoo named Gordo and I knew she'd break my heart. But her color now in the sky is sweet, really. I left all those feelings behind me when my wife showed up. I am a faithful man, for all my suspicions. Too faithful, maybe. I am ready to give too much and maybe that's the problem.

The whooping began down the hall and I focused on a tree out there. A crow flapped down, his mouth open, his throat throbbing, though I could not hear his sound. I was feeling very odd. At least I'd made my point to the guy in the other room. "Pretty bird," I said, referring to myself. She called me "pretty bird" and I believed her and I told myself again, "Pretty bird."

But then something new happened, something very difficult for me. She appeared in the den naked. I have not seen her naked since I fell from the tree and had no wings to fly. She always had a certain tidiness in things. She was naked in the bedroom, clothed in the den. But now she appears from the hallway and I look at her and she is still slim and she is beautiful. I think—at least I clearly remember that as her husband I found her beautiful in this state. Now, though, she seems too naked. Plucked. I find that a sad thing. I am sorry for her and she goes by me and she disappears into the kitchen. I want to pluck some of my own feathers, the feathers from my chest, and give them to her. I love her more in that moment, seeing her terrible nakedness, than I ever have before.

And since I've had success in the last few minutes with words, when she comes back I am moved to speak. "Hello," I say, meaning, You are still connected to me, I still want only you. "Hello," I say again. Please listen to this tiny heart that beats fast at all times for you.

And she does indeed stop and she comes to me and bends to me. "Pretty bird," I say and I am saying, You are beautiful, my wife, and your beauty cries out for protection. "Pretty." I want to cover you with my own nakedness. "Bad bird," I say. If there are others in your life, even in your mind, then there is nothing I can do. "Bad." Your nakedness is touched from inside by the others. "Open," I say. How can we be whole together if you are not empty in the place that I am to fill?

She smiles at this and she opens the door to my cage. "Up," I say, meaning, Is there no place for me in this world where I can be free of this terrible sense of others?

She reaches in now and offers her hand and I climb onto it and I tremble and she says, "Poor baby."

"Poor baby," I say. You have yearned for wholeness too and somehow I failed you. I was not enough. "Bad bird," I say. I'm sorry.

And then the cracker comes around the corner. He wears only his rattlesnake boots. I take one look at his miserable, featherless body and shake my head. We keep our sexual parts hidden, we parrots, and this man is a pitiful sight. "Peanut," I say. I presume that my wife simply has not noticed. But that's foolish, of course. This is, in fact, what she wants. Not me. And she scrapes me off her hand onto the open cage door and she turns her naked back to me and embraces this man and they laugh and stagger in their embrace around the corner.

For a moment I still think I've been eloquent. What I've said only needs repeating for it to have its transforming effect. "Hello," I say. "Hello. Pretty bird. Pretty. Bad bird. Bad. Open. Up. Poor baby. Bad bird." And I am beginning to hear myself as I really sound to her. "Peanut." I can never say what is in my heart to her. Never.

I stand on my cage door now and my wings stir. I look at the corner to the hallway and down at the end the whooping has begun again. I can fly there and think of things to do about all this.

But I do not. I turn instead and I look at the trees moving just beyond the other end of the room. I look at the sky the color of the brow of a blue-front Amazon. A shadow of birds spanks across the lawn. And I spread my wings. I will fly now. Even though I know there is something between me and that place where I can be free of all these feelings, I will fly. I will throw myself there again and again. Pretty bird. Bad bird. Good night.

MIRIAM

F OR SEVERAL YEARS, Mrs. H. T. Miller had lived alone in a pleasant apartment (two rooms with kitchenette) in a remodeled brownstone near the East River. She was a widow: Mr. H. T. Miller had left a reasonable amount of insurance. Her interests were narrow, she had no friends to speak of, and she rarely journeyed farther than the corner grocery. The other people in the house never seemed to notice her: her clothes were matter-of-fact, her hair iron-gray, clipped and casually waved; she did not use cosmetics, her features were plain and inconspicuous, and on her last birthday she was sixty-one. Her activities were seldom spontaneous: she kept the two rooms immaculate, smoked an occasional cigarette, prepared her own meals and tended a canary.

Then she met Miriam. It was snowing that night. Mrs. Miller had finished drying the supper dishes and was thumbing through an afternoon paper when she saw an advertisement of a picture playing at a neighborhood theater. The title sounded good, so she struggled into her beaver coat, laced her galoshes and left the apartment, leaving one light burning in the foyer: she found nothing more disturbing than a sensation of darkness.

The snow was fine, falling gently, not yet making an impression on the pavement. The wind from the river cut only at street crossings. Mrs. Miller hurried, her head bowed, oblivious as a mole burrowing a blind path. She stopped at a drugstore and bought a package of peppermints.

A long line stretched in front of the box office; she took her place at the end. There would be (a tired voice groaned) a short wait for all seats. Mrs. Miller rummaged in her leather hand-bag till she collected exactly the correct change for admission. The line seemed to be taking its own time and, looking around for some distraction, she suddenly became conscious of a little girl standing under the edge of the marquee.

Her hair was the longest and strangest Mrs. Miller had ever seen: absolutely silver-white, like an albino's. It flowed waist-length in smooth, loose lines. She was thin and fragilely con-structed. There was a simple, special elegance in the way she stood with her thumbs in the pockets of a tailored plum-vel-vet coat.

Mrs. Miller felt oddly excited, and when the little girl glanced toward her, she smiled warmly. The little girl walked over and said, "Would you care to do me a favor?"

"I'd be glad to, if I can," said Mrs. Miller.

"Oh, it's quite easy. I merely want you to buy a ticket for me; they won't let me in otherwise. Here, I have the money." And gracefully she handed Mrs. Miller two dimes and a nickel.

They went into the theater together. An usherette directed them to a lounge; in twenty minutes the picture would be over.

"I feel just like a genuine criminal," said Mrs. Miller gaily, as she sat down. "I mean that sort of thing's against the law, isn't it? I do hope I haven't done the wrong thing. Your mother knows where you are, dear? I mean she does, doesn't she?"

The little girl said nothing. She unbuttoned her coat and folded it across her lap. Her dress underneath was prim and dark blue. A gold chain dangled about her neck, and her fin-gers, sensitive and musical-looking, toyed with it. Examining her more attentively, Mrs. Miller decided the truly distinctive feature was not her hair, but her eyes; they were hazel, steady, lacking any childlike quality whatsoever and, because of their size, seemed to consume her small face.

Mrs. Miller offered a peppermint. "What's your name, dear?"

"Miriam," she said, as though, in some curious way, it were information already familiar.

"Why, isn't that funny—my name's Miriam, too. And it's not a terribly common name either. Now, don't tell me your last name's Miller!"

"Just Miriam."

"But isn't that funny?"

"Moderately," said Miriam, and rolled the peppermint on her tongue.

Mrs. Miller flushed and shifted uncomfortably. "You have such a large vocabulary for such a little girl."

"Do I?"

"Well, yes," said Mrs. Miller, hastily changing the topic to: "Do you like the movies?"

"I really wouldn't know," said Miriam. "I've never been before."

Women began filling the lounge; the rumble of the newsreel bombs exploded in the distance. Mrs. Miller rose, tucking her purse under her arm. "I guess I'd better be running now if I want to get a seat," she said. "It was nice to have met you."

Miriam nodded ever so slightly.

It snowed all week. Wheels and footsteps moved soundlessly on the street, as if the business of living continued secretly behind a pale but impenetrable curtain. In the falling quiet there was no sky or earth, only snow lifting in the wind, frosting the window glass, chilling the rooms, deadening and hushing the city. At all hours it was necessary to keep a lamp lighted, and Mrs. Miller lost track of the days: Friday was no different from Saturday and on Sunday she went to the grocery: closed, of course.

That evening she scrambled eggs and fixed a bowl of tomato soup. Then, after putting on a flannel robe and cold-creaming her face, she propped herself up in bed with a hot-water bottle under her feet. She was reading the *Times* when the doorbell rang. At first she thought it must be a mistake and whoever it was would go away. But it rang and rang and settled to a persistent buzz. She looked at the clock: a little after eleven; it did not seem possible, she was always asleep by ten.

Climbing out of bed, she trotted barefoot across the living room. "I'm coming, please be patient." The latch was caught; she turned it this way and that way and the bell never paused an instant. "Stop it," she cried. The bolt gave way and she opened the door an inch. "What in heaven's name?"

"Hello," said Miriam.

"Oh . . . why, hello," said Mrs. Miller, stepping hesitantly into the hall. "You're that little girl."

"I thought you'd never answer, but I kept my finger on the button; I knew you were home. Aren't you glad to see me?"

Mrs. Miller did not know what to say. Miriam, she saw, wore the same plum-velvet coat and now she had also a beret to match; her white hair was braided in two shining plaits and looped at the ends with enormous white ribbons.

"Since I've waited so long, you could at least let me in," she said.

"It's awfully late . . ."

Miriam regarded her blankly. "What difference does that make? Let me in. It's cold out here and I have on a silk dress." Then, with a gentle gesture, she urged Mrs. Miller aside and passed into the apartment.

She dropped her coat and beret on a chair. She was indeed wearing a silk dress. White silk. White silk in February. The skirt was beautifully pleated and the sleeves long; it made a faint rustle as she strolled about the room. "I like your place," she said. "I like the rug, blue's my favorite color." She touched a paper rose in a vase on the coffee table. "Imitation," she commented wanly. "How sad. Aren't imitations sad?" She seated herself on the sofa, daintily spreading her skirt.

"What do you want?" asked Mrs. Miller.

"Sit down," said Miriam. "It makes me nervous to see people stand."

Mrs. Miller sank to a hassock. "What do you want?" she repeated.

"You know, I don't think you're glad I came."

For a second time Mrs. Miller was without an answer; her hand motioned vaguely. Miriam giggled and pressed back on a mound of chintz pillows. Mrs. Miller observed that the girl was less pale than she remembered; her cheeks were flushed.

"How did you know where I lived?"

Miriam frowned. "That's no question at all. What's your name? What's mine?"

"But I'm not listed in the phone book."

"Oh, let's talk about something else."

Mrs. Miller said, "Your mother must be insane to let a child like you wander around at all hours of the night—and in such ridiculous clothes. She must be out of her mind."

Miriam got up and moved to a corner where a covered bird cage hung from a ceiling chain. She peeked beneath the cover. "It's a canary," she said. "Would you mind if I woke him? I'd like to hear him sing."

"Leave Tommy alone," said Mrs. Miller, anxiously. "Don't you dare wake him."

"Certainly," said Miriam. "But I don't see why I can't hear him sing." And then, "Have you anything to eat? I'm starving! Even milk and a jam sandwich would be fine."

"Look," said Mrs. Miller, rising from the hassock, "look—if I make some nice sandwiches will you be a good child and run along home? It's past midnight, I'm sure."

"It's snowing," reproached Miriam. "And cold and dark."

"Well, you shouldn't have come here to begin with," said Mrs. Miller, struggling to control her voice. "I can't help the weather. If you want anything to eat you'll have to promise to leave."

Miriam brushed a braid against her cheek. Her eyes were

thoughtful, as if weighing the proposition. She turned toward the bird cage. "Very well," she said, "I promise."

How old is she? Ten? Eleven? Mrs. Miller, in the kitchen, unsealed a jar of strawberry preserves and cut four slices of bread. She poured a glass of milk and paused to light a cigarette. *And why has she come?* Her hand shook as she held the match, fascinated, till it burned her finger. The canary was singing; singing as he did in the morning and at no other time. "Miriam," she called, "Miriam, I told you not to disturb Tommy." There was no answer. She called again; all she heard was the canary. She inhaled the cigarette and discovered she had lighted the cork-tip end and—oh, really, she mustn't lose her temper.

She carried the food in on a tray and set it on the coffee table. She saw first that the bird cage still wore its night cover. And Tommy was singing. It gave her a queer sensation. And no one was in the room. Mrs. Miller went through an alcove leading to her bedroom; at the door she caught her breath.

"What are you doing?" she asked.

Miriam glanced up and in her eyes there was a look that was not ordinary. She was standing by the bureau, a jewel case opened before her. For a minute she studied Mrs. Miller, forcing their eyes to meet, and she smiled. "There's nothing good here," she said. "But I like this." Her hand held a cameo brooch. "It's charming."

"Suppose—perhaps you'd better put it back," said Mrs. Miller, feeling suddenly the need of some support. She leaned against the door frame; her hand was unbearably heavy; a pressure weighted the rhythm of her heartbeat. The light seemed to flutter defectively. "Please, child—a gift from my husband . . ."

"But it's beautiful and I want it," said Miriam. *"Give it to me."*

As she stood, striving to shape a sentence which would somehow save the brooch, it came to Mrs. Miller there was no one to whom she might turn; she was alone; a fact that had not been among her thoughts for a long time. Its sheer emphasis was stunning. But here in her own room in the hushed snow-city were evidences she could not ignore or, she knew with startling clarity, resist.

Miriam ate ravenously, and when the sandwiches and milk were gone, her fingers made cobweb movements over the plate, gathering crumbs. The cameo gleamed on her blouse, the blonde profile like a trick reflection of its wearer. "That was very nice," she sighed, "though now an almond cake or a cherry would be ideal. Sweets are lovely, don't you think?"

Mrs. Miller was perched precariously on the hassock, smoking a cigarette. Her hair net had slipped lopsided and loose strands straggled down her face. Her eyes were stupidly concentrated on nothing and her cheeks were mottled in red patches, as though a fierce slap had left permanent marks.

"Is there a candy—a cake?"

Mrs. Miller tapped ash on the rug. Her head swayed slightly as she tried to focus her eyes. "You promised to leave if I made the sandwiches," she said.

"Dear me, did I?"

"It was a promise and I'm tired and I don't feel well at all."

"Mustn't fret," said Miriam. "I'm only teasing."

She picked up her coat, slung it over her arm, and arranged her beret in front of a mirror. Presently she bent close to Mrs. Miller and whispered, "Kiss me good night."

"Please—I'd rather not," said Mrs. Miller.

Miriam lifted a shoulder, arched an eyebrow. "As you like," she said, and went directly to the coffee table, seized the vase containing the paper roses, carried it to where the hard surface of the floor lay bare, and hurled it downward. Glass sprayed in all directions and she stamped her foot on the bouquet.

Then slowly she walked to the door, but before closing it she looked back at Mrs. Miller with a slyly innocent curiosity.

/ / / /

Mrs. Miller spent the next day in bed, rising once to feed the canary and drink a cup of tea; she took her temperature and had none, yet her dreams were feverishly agitated; their unbalanced mood lingered even as she lay staring wide-eyed at the ceiling. One dream threaded through the others like an elusively mysterious theme in a complicated symphony, and the scenes it depicted were sharply outlined, as though sketched by a hand of gifted intensity: a small girl, wearing a bridal gown and a wreath of leaves, led a gray procession down a mountain path, and among them there was unusual silence till a woman at the rear asked, "Where is she taking us?" "No one knows," said an old man marching in front. "But isn't she pretty?" volunteered a third voice. "Isn't she like a frost flower . . . so shining and white?"

Tuesday morning she woke up feeling better; harsh slats of sunlight, slanting through Venetian blinds, shed a disrupting light on her unwholesome fancies. She opened the window to discover a thawed, mild-as-spring day; a sweep of clean new clouds crumpled against a vastly blue, out-of-season sky; and across the low line of roof-tops she could see the river and smoke curving from tug-boat stacks in a warm wind. A great silver truck plowed the snow-banked street, its machine sound humming in the air.

After straightening the apartment, she went to the grocer's, cashed a check and continued to Schrafft's where she ate breakfast and chatted happily with the waitress. Oh, it was a wonderful day—more like a holiday—and it would be so foolish to go home.

She boarded a Lexington Avenue bus and rode up to Eighty-sixth Street; it was there that she had decided to do a little shopping.

She had no idea what she wanted or needed, but she idled along, intent only upon the passers-by, brisk and preoccupied, who gave her a disturbing sense of separateness.

It was while waiting at the corner of Third Avenue that she saw the man: an old man, bowlegged and stooped under an armload of bulging packages; he wore a shabby brown coat and a checkered cap. Suddenly she realized they were exchanging a smile: there was nothing friendly about this smile, it was merely two cold flickers of recognition. But she was certain she had never seen him before.

He was standing next to an El pillar, and as she crossed the street he turned and followed. He kept quite close; from the corner of her eye she watched his reflection wavering on the shopwindows.

Then in the middle of the block she stopped and faced him. He stopped also and cocked his head, grinning. But what could she say? Do? Here, in broad daylight, on Eighty-sixth Street? It was useless and, despising her own helplessness, she quickened her steps.

Now Second Avenue is a dismal street, made from scraps and ends; part cobblestone, part asphalt, part cement; and its atmosphere of desertion is permanent. Mrs. Miller walked five blocks without meeting anyone, and all the while the steady crunch of his footfalls in the snow stayed near. And when she came to a florist's shop, the sound was still with her. She hurried inside and watched through the glass door as the old man passed; he kept his eyes straight ahead and didn't slow his pace, but he did one strange, telling thing: he tipped his cap.

"Six white ones, did you say?" asked the florist. "Yes," she told him, "white roses." From there she went to a glassware store and selected a vase, presumably a replacement for the one Miriam had broken, though the price was intolerable and the vase itself (she thought) grotesquely vulgar. But a series of unaccountable purchases had begun, as if by prearranged plan: a plan of which she had not the least knowledge or control.

She bought a bag of glazed cherries, and at a place called the Knickerbocker Bakery she paid forty cents for six almond cakes.

Within the last hour the weather had turned cold again; like blurred lenses, winter clouds cast a shade over the sun, and the skeleton of an early dusk colored the sky; a damp mist mixed with the wind and the voices of a few children who romped high on mountains of gutter snow seemed lonely and cheerless. Soon the first flake fell, and when Mrs. Miller reached the brownstone house, snow was falling in a swift screen and foot tracks vanished as they were printed.

The white roses were arranged decoratively in the vase. The glazed cherries shone on a ceramic plate. The almond cakes, dusted with sugar, awaited a hand. The canary fluttered on its swing and picked at a bar of seed.

At precisely five the doorbell rang. Mrs. Miller *knew* who it was. The hem of her housecoat trailed as she crossed the floor. "Is that you?" she called.

"Naturally," said Miriam, the word resounding shrilly from the hall. "Open the door."

"Go away," said Mrs. Miller.

"Please hurry. . . I have a heavy package."

"Go away," said Mrs. Miller. She returned to the living room, lighted a cigarette, sat down and calmly listened to the buzzer; on and on and on. "You might as well leave. I have no intention of letting you in."

Shortly the bell stopped. For possibly ten minutes Mrs. Miller did not move. Then, hearing no sound, she concluded Miriam had gone. She tiptoed to the door and opened it a sliver; Miriam was half-reclining atop a cardboard box with a beautiful French doll cradled in her arms.

"Really, I thought you were never coming," she said peevishly. "Here, help me get this in, it's awfully heavy."

It was not spell-like compulsion that Mrs. Miller felt, but rather a curious passivity; she brought in the box, Miriam the doll. Miriam curled up on the sofa, not troubling to remove her coat or beret, and watched disinterestedly as Mrs.

Miller dropped the box and stood trembling, trying to catch her breath.

"Thank you," she said. In the daylight she looked pinched and drawn, her hair less luminous. The French doll she was loving wore an exquisite powdered wig and its idiot glass eyes sought solace in Miriam's. "I have a surprise," she continued. "Look into my box."

Kneeling, Mrs. Miller parted the flaps and lifted out another doll; then a blue dress which she recalled as the one Miriam had worn that first night at the theater; and of the remainder she said, "It's all clothes. Why?"

"Because I've come to live with you," said Miriam, twisting a cherry stem. "Wasn't it nice of you to buy me the cherries . . . ?"

"But you can't! For God's sake go away—go away and leave me alone!"

". . . and the roses and the almond cakes? How really wonderfully generous. You know, these cherries are delicious. The last place I lived was with an old man; he was terribly poor and we never had good things to eat. But I think I'll be happy here." She paused to snuggle her doll closer. "Now, if you'll just show me where to put my things . . ."

Mrs. Miller's face dissolved into a mask of ugly red lines; she began to cry, and it was an unnatural, tearless sort of weeping, as though, not having wept for a long time, she had forgotten how. Carefully she edged backward till she touched the door.

She fumbled through the hall and down the stairs to a landing below. She pounded frantically on the door of the first apartment she came to; a short, red-headed man answered and she pushed past him. "Say, what the hell is this?" he said. "Anything wrong, lover?" asked a young woman who appeared from the kitchen, drying her hands. And it was to her that Mrs. Miller turned.

"Listen," she cried, "I'm ashamed behaving this way but—well, I'm Mrs. H. T. Miller and I live upstairs and . . ." She pressed her hands over her face. "It sounds so absurd. . . ."

The woman guided her to a chair, while the man excitedly rattled pocket change. "Yeah?"

"I live upstairs and there's a little girl visiting me, and I suppose that I'm afraid of her. She won't leave and I can't make her and—she's going to do something terrible. She's already stolen my cameo, but she's about to do something worse— something terrible!"

The man asked, "Is she a relative, huh?"

Mrs. Miller shook her head. "I don't know who she is. Her name's Miriam, but I don't know for certain who she is."

"You gotta calm down, honey," said the woman, stroking Mrs. Miller's arm. "Harry here'll tend to this kid. Go on, lover." And Mrs. Miller said, "The door's open—5A."

After the man left, the woman brought a towel and bathed Mrs. Miller's face. "You're very kind," Mrs. Miller said. "I'm sorry to act like such a fool, only this wicked child . . ."

"Sure, honey," consoled the woman. "Now, you better take it easy."

Mrs. Miller rested her head in the crook of her arm; she was quiet enough to be asleep. The woman turned a radio dial; a piano and a husky voice filled the silence and the woman, tapping her foot, kept excellent time. "Maybe we oughta go up too," she said.

"I don't want to see her again. I don't want to be anywhere near her."

"Uh huh, but what you shoulda done, you shoulda called a cop."

Presently they heard the man on the stairs. He strode into the room frowning and scratching the back of his neck. "Nobody there," he said, honestly embarrassed. "She musta beat it."

"Harry, you're a jerk," announced the woman. "We been sitting here the whole time and we woulda seen . . ." she stopped abruptly, for the man's glance was sharp.

"I looked all over," he said. "and there just ain't nobody there. Nobody, understand?"

"Tell me," said Mrs. Miller, rising, "tell me, did you see a large box? Or a doll?"

"No, ma'am, I didn't."

And the woman, as if delivering a verdict, said, "Well, for cryin out loud. . . . "

Mrs. Miller entered her apartment softly; she walked to the center of the room and stood quite still. No, in a sense it had not changed; the roses, the cakes, and the cherries were in place. But this was an empty room, emptier than if the furnishings and familiars were not present, lifeless and petrified as a funeral parlor. The sofa loomed before her with a new strangeness; its vacancy had a meaning that would have been less penetrating and terrible had Miriam been curled on it. She gazed fixedly at the space where she remembered setting the box and, for a moment, the hassock spun desperately. And she looked through the window; surely the river was real, surely snow was falling—but then, one could not be certain witness to anything: Miriam, so vividly *there*—and yet, where was she? Where, where?

As though moving in a dream, she sank to a chair. The room was losing shape; it was dark and getting darker and there was nothing to be done about it; she could not lift her hand to light a lamp.

Suddenly, closing her eyes, she felt an upward surge, like a diver emerging from some deeper, greener depth. In times of terror or immense distress, there are moments when the mind waits, as though for a revelation, while a skein of calm is woven over thought; it is like a sleep, or a supernatural trance; and during this lull one is aware of a force of quiet reasoning: well, what if she had never really known a girl named Miriam, that she had been foolishly frightened on the street? In the end, like everything else, it was of no importance. For the only thing she had lost to Miriam was her identity, but now she knew she had found again the person who lived in this room, who cooked her own meals, who owned a canary, who was someone she could trust and believe in: Mrs. H. T. Miller.

Listening in contentment, she became aware of a double sound: a bureau drawer opening and closing; she seemed to hear it long after completion—opening and closing. Then gradually, the harshness of it was replaced by the murmur of a silk dress and this, delicately faint, was moving nearer and swelling in intensity till the walls trembled with the vibration and the room was caving under a wave of whispers. Mrs. Miller stiffened and opened her eyes to a dull, direct stare.

"Hello," said Miriam.

Louise Erdrich

THE SHAWL

AMONG THE ANISHINAABEG on the road where I live, it is told how a woman loved a man other than her husband and went off into the bush and bore his child. Her name was Aanakwad, which means cloud, and like a cloud she was changeable. She was moody and sullen one moment, her lower lip jutting and her eyes flashing, filled with storms. The next, she would shake her hair over her face and blow it straight out in front of her to make her children scream with laughter. For she also had two children by her husband, one a yearning boy of five years and the other a capable daughter of nine.

When Aanakwad brought the new baby out of the trees that autumn, the older girl was like a second mother, even waking in the night to clean the baby and nudge it to her mother's breast. Aanakwad slept through its cries, hardly woke. It wasn't that she didn't love her baby; no, it was the opposite—she loved it too much, the way she loved its father, and not her husband. This passion ate away at her, and her feelings were unbearable. If she could have thrown off that wronghearted love, she would have, but the thought of the other man, who lived across the lake, was with her always. She became a gray sky, stared monotonously at the walls, sometimes wept into her hands for hours at a time. Soon, she couldn't rise to cook or keep the cabin neat, and it was too much for the girl, who curled up each night exhausted in her red-and-brown plaid shawl, and slept and slept, until the husband had to wake her to awaken her mother, for he was afraid of his wife's bad temper, and it was he who roused

Aanakwad into anger by the sheer fact that he was himself and not the other.

At last, even though he loved Aanakwad, the husband had to admit that their life together was no good anymore. And it was he who sent for the other man's uncle. In those days, our people lived widely scattered, along the shores and in the islands, even out on the plains. There were no roads then, just trails, though we had horses and wagons and, for the winter, sleds. When the uncle came around to fetch Aanakwad in his wagon fitted out with sled runners, it was very hard, for she and her husband had argued right up to the last about the children, argued fiercely until the husband had finally given in. He turned his face to the wall, and did not move to see the daughter, whom he treasured, sit down beside her mother, wrapped in her plaid robe in the wagon bed. They left right away, with their bundles and sacks, not bothering to heat up the stones to warm their feet. The father had stopped his ears, so he did not hear his son cry out when he suddenly understood that he would be left behind.

As the uncle slapped the reins and the horse lurched forward, the boy tried to jump into the wagon, but his mother pried his hands off the boards, crying, *Gego, gego,* and he fell down hard. But there was something in him that would not let her leave. He jumped up and, although he was wearing only light clothing, he ran behind the wagon over the packed drifts. The horses picked up speed. His chest was scorched with pain, and yet he pushed himself on. He'd never run so fast, so hard and furiously, but he was determined, and he refused to believe that the increasing distance between him and the wagon was real. He kept going until his throat closed, he saw red, and in the ice of the air his lungs shut. Then, as he fell onto the board-hard snow, he raised his head. He watched the back of the wagon and the tiny figures of his mother and sister disappear, and something failed in him. Something broke. At that moment he truly did not care if he was alive or dead. So when he saw the gray shapes, the shadows, bounding lightly from the trees to either side of the trail, far ahead, he was not afraid.

The next the boy knew, his father had him wrapped in a blanket and was carrying him home. His father's chest was broad and, although he already spat the tubercular blood that would write the end of his story, he was still a strong man. It would take him many years to die. In those years, the father would tell the boy, who had forgotten this part entirely, that at first when he talked about the shadows the father thought he'd been visited by *manidoog*. But then, as the boy described the shapes, his father had understood that they were not spirits. Uneasy, he had decided to take his gun back along the trail. He had built up the fire in the cabin, and settled his boy near it, and gone back out into the snow. Perhaps the story spread through our settlements because the father had to tell what he saw, again and again, in order to get rid of it. Perhaps as with all frightful dreams, *amaniso,* he had to talk about it to destroy its power—though in this case nothing could stop the dream from being real.

The shadows' tracks were the tracks of wolves, and in those days, when our guns had taken all their food for furs and hides to sell, the wolves were bold and had abandoned the old agreement between them and the first humans. For a time, until we understood and let the game increase, the wolves hunted us. The father bounded forward when he saw the tracks. He could see where the pack, desperate, had tried to slash the tendons of the horses' legs. Next, where they'd leaped for the back of the wagon. He hurried on to where the trail gave out at the broad empty ice of the lake. There, he saw what he saw, scattered, and the ravens, attending to the bitter small leavings of the wolves.

For a time, the boy had no understanding of what had happened. His father kept what he knew to himself, at least that first year, and when his son asked about his sister's torn plaid

shawl, and why it was kept in the house, his father said nothing. But he wept when the boy asked if his sister was cold. It
was only after his father had been weakened by the disease that
he began to tell the story, far too often and always the same
way: he told how when the wolves closed in Aanakwad had
thrown her daughter to them.

When his father said those words, the boy went still. What
had his sister felt? What had thrust through her heart? Had
something broken inside her, too, as it had in him? Even then,
he knew that this broken place inside him would not be
mended, except by some terrible means. For he kept seeing his
mother put the baby down and grip his sister around the
waist. He saw Aanakwad swing the girl lightly out over the
side of the wagon. He saw the brown shawl with its red lines
flying open. He saw the shadows, the wolves, rush together,
quick and avid, as the wagon with sled runners disappeared
into the distance—forever, for neither he nor his father saw
Aanakwad again.

When I was little, my own father terrified us with his drinking. This was after we lost our mother, because before that the
only time I was aware that he touched the *ishkode waaboo* was
on an occasional weekend when they got home late, or sometimes during berry-picking gatherings when we went out to
the bush and camped with others. Not until she died did he
start the heavy sort of drinking, the continuous drinking,
where we were left alone in the house for days. The kind
where, when he came home, we'd jump out the window and
hide in the woods while he barged around, shouting for us.
We'd go back only after he had fallen dead asleep.

There were three of us: me, the oldest at ten, and my little
sister and brother, twins, and only six years old. I was surprisingly good at taking care of them, I think, and because we
learned to survive together during those drinking years we
have always been close. Their names are Doris and Raymond,

and they married a brother and sister. When we get together, which is often, for we live on the same road, there come times in the talking and card-playing, and maybe even in the light beer now and then, when we will bring up those days. Most people understand how it was. Our story isn't uncommon. But for us it helps to compare our points of view.

How else would I know, for instance, that Raymond saw me the first time I hid my father's belt? I pulled it from around his waist while he was passed out, and then I buried it in the woods. I kept doing it after that. Our father couldn't understand why his belt was always stolen when he went to town drinking. He even accused his *shkwebii* buddies of the theft. But I had good reasons. Not only was he embarrassed, afterward, to go out with his pants held up by rope, but he couldn't snake his belt out in anger and snap the hooked buckle end in the air. He couldn't hit us with it. Of course, being resourceful, he used other things. There was a board. A willow wand. And there was himself—his hands and fists and boots—and things he could throw. But eventually it became easy to evade him, and after a while we rarely suffered a bruise or a scratch. We had our own place in the woods, even a little campfire for the cold nights. And we'd take money from him every chance we got, slip it from his shoe, where he thought it well hidden. He became, for us, a thing to be avoided, outsmarted, and exploited. We survived off him as if he were a capricious and dangerous line of work. I suppose we stopped thinking of him as a human being, certainly as a father.

I got my growth earlier than some boys, and, one night when I was thirteen and Doris and Raymond and I were sitting around wishing for something besides the oatmeal and commodity canned milk I'd stashed so he couldn't sell them, I heard him coming down the road. He was shouting and making noise all the way to the house, and Doris and Raymond looked at me and headed for the back window.

When they saw that I wasn't coming, they stopped. C'mon, *ondaas,* get with it—they tried to pull me along. I shook them off and told them to get out quickly—I was staying. I think I can take him now is what I said.

He was big; he hadn't yet wasted away from the alcohol. His nose had been pushed to one side in a fight, then slammed back to the other side, so now it was straight. His teeth were half gone, and he smelled the way he had to smell, being five days drunk. When he came in the door, he paused for a moment, his eyes red and swollen, tiny slits. Then he saw that I was waiting for him, and he smiled in a bad way. My first punch surprised him. I had been practicing on a hay-stuffed bag, then on a padded board, toughening my fists, and I'd got so quick I flickered like fire. I still wasn't as strong as he was, and he had a good twenty pounds on me. Yet I'd do some damage, I was sure of it. I'd teach him not to mess with me. What I didn't foresee was how the fight itself would get right into me.

There is something terrible about fighting your father. It came on suddenly, with the second blow—a frightful kind of joy. A power surged up from the center of me, and I danced at him, light and giddy, full of a heady rightness. Here is the thing: I wanted to waste him, waste him good. I wanted to smack the living shit out of him. Kill him, if I must. A punch for Doris, a kick for Raymond. And all the while I was silent, then screaming, then silent again, in this rage of happiness that filled me with a simultaneous despair so that, I guess you could say, I stood apart from myself.

He came at me, crashed over a chair that was already broken, then threw the pieces. I grabbed one of the legs and whacked him on the ear so that his head spun and turned back to me, bloody. I watched myself striking him again and again. I knew what I was doing, but not really, not in the ordinary sense. It was as if I were standing calm, against the wall with my arms folded, pitying us both. I saw the boy, the chair leg, the man fold and fall, his hands held up in begging fashion.

Then I also saw that, for a while now, the bigger man had not even bothered to fight back.

Suddenly, he was my father again. And when I knelt down next to him, I was his son. I reached for the closest rag, and picked up this piece of blanket that my father always kept with him for some reason. And as I picked it up and wiped the blood off his face, I said to him, Your nose is crooked again. He looked at me, steady and quizzical, as though he had never had a drink in his life, and I wiped his face again with that frayed piece of blanket. Well, it was a shawl, really, a kind of old-fashioned woman's blanket-shawl. Once, maybe, it had been plaid. You could still see lines, some red, the background a faded brown. He watched intently as my hand brought the rag to his face. I was pretty sure, then, that I'd clocked him too hard, that he'd really lost it now. Gently, though, he clasped one hand around my wrist. With the other hand he took the shawl. He crumpled it and held it to the middle of his fore-head. It was as if he were praying, as if he were having thoughts he wanted to collect in that piece of cloth. For a while he lay like that, and I, crouched over, let him be, hardly breathing. Something told me to sit there, still. And then at last he said to me, in the sober new voice I would hear from then on, *Did you know I had a sister once?*

There was a time when the government moved everybody off the farthest reaches of the reservation, onto roads, into towns, into housing. It looked good at first, and then it all went sour. Shortly afterward, it seemed that anyone who was someone was either drunk, killed, near suicide, or had just dusted himself. None of the old sort were left, it seemed—the old kind of peo-ple, the Gete-anishinaabeg, who are kind beyond kindness and would do anything for others. It was during that time that my mother died and my father hurt us, as I have said.

Now, gradually, that term of despair has lifted somewhat and yielded up its survivors. But we still have sorrows that are passed to us from early generations, sorrows to handle in addition to our own, and cruelties lodged where we cannot forget them. We have the need to forget. We are always walking on oblivion's edge.

Some get away, like my brother and sister, married now and living quietly down the road. And me, to some degree, though I prefer to live alone. And even my father, who recently found a woman. Once, when he brought up the old days, and we went over the story again, I told him at last the two things I had been thinking.

First, I told him that keeping his sister's shawl was wrong, because we never keep the clothing of the dead. Now's the time to burn it, I said. Send it off to cloak her spirit. And he agreed.

The other thing I said to him was in the form of a question. Have you ever considered, I asked him, given how tender-hearted your sister was, and how brave, that she looked at the whole situation? She saw that the wolves were only hungry. She knew that their need was only need. She knew that you were back there, alone in the snow. She understood that the baby she loved would not live without a mother, and that only the uncle knew the way. She saw clearly that one person on the wagon had to be offered up, or they all would die. And in that moment of knowledge, don't you think, being who she was, of the old sort of Anishinaabeg, who thinks of the good of the people first, she jumped, my father, *n'dede,* brother to that little girl? Don't you think she lifted her shawl and flew?

SPUNK

I

A GIANT OF A BROWN-SKINNED MAN sauntered up the one street of the Village and out into the palmetto thickets with a small pretty woman clinging lovingly to his arm.

"Looka theah, folkses!" cried Elijah Mosley, slapping his leg gleefully. "Theah they go, big as life an' brassy as tacks."

All the loungers in the store tried to walk to the door with an air of nonchalance but with small success.

"Now pee-eople!" Walter Thomas gasped. "Will you look at 'em!"

"'But that's one thing Ah likes about Spunk Banks—he ain't skeered of nothin' on God's green footstool—*nothin'!* He rides that log down at saw-mill jus' like he struts 'round wid another man's wife—jus' don't give a kitty. When Tes' Miller got cut to giblets on that circle-saw, Spunk steps right up and starts ridin'. The rest of us was skeered to go near it."

A round-shouldered figure in overalls much too large, came nervously in the door and the talking ceased. The men looked at each other and winked.

"Gimme some soda-water. Sass'prilla Ah reckon," the new-comer ordered, and stood far down the counter near the open pickled pig-feet tub to drink it.

Elijah nudged Walter and turned with mock gravity to the new-comer.

"Say, Joe, how's everything up yo' way? How's yo' wife?"

Joe started and all but dropped the bottle he held in his hands. He swallowed several times painfully and his lips trembled.

"Aw 'Lige, you oughtn't to do nothin' like that," Walter grumbled. Elijah ignored him.

"She jus' passed heah a few minutes ago goin' thata way," with a wave of his hand in the direction of the woods.

Now Joe knew his wife had passed that way. He knew that the men lounging in the general store had seen her, moreover, he knew that the men knew *he* knew. He stood there silent for a long moment staring blankly, with his Adam's apple twitching nervously up and down his throat. One could actually *see* the pain he was suffering, his eyes, his face, his hands and even the dejected slump of his shoulders. He set the bottle down upon the counter. He didn't bang it, just eased it out of his hand silently and fiddled with his suspender buckle.

"Well, Ah'm goin' after her to-day. Ah'm goin' an' fetch her back. Spunk's done gone too fur."

He reached deep down into his trouser pocket and drew out a hollow ground razor, large and shiny, and passed his moistened thumb back and forth over the edge.

"Talkin' like a man, Joe. Course that's *yo'* fambly affairs, but Ah like to see grit in anybody."

Joe Kanty laid down a nickel and stumbled out into the street.

Dusk crept in from the woods. Ike Clarke lit the swinging oil lamp that was almost immediately surrounded by candle flies. The men laughed boisterously behind Joe's back as they watched him shamble woodward.

"You oughtn't to said whut you did to him, 'Lige—look how it worked him up," Walter chided.

"And Ah hope it did work him up. 'Tain't even decent for a man to take and take like he do."

"Spunk will sho' kill him."

"Aw, Ah doan't know. You never kin tell. He might turn up an' spank him fur gettin' in the way, but Spunk wouldn't shoot no unarmed man. Dat razor he carried outa heah ain't gonna run Spunk down an' cut him, an' Joe ain't got the nerve to go up to Spunk with it knowing he totes that Army .45. He makes that

break outa heah to bluff us. He's gonna hide that razor behind
the first likely palmetto root an' sneak back home to bed. Don't
tell me nothin' 'bout that rabbit-foot colored man. Didn't he
meet Spunk an' Lena face to face one day las' week an' mumble
sumthin' to Spunk 'bout lettin' his wife alone?"

"What did Spunk say?" Walter broke in—"Ah like him
fine but 'tain't right the way he carries on wid Lena Kanty, jus'
cause Joe's timid 'bout fightin'.'"

"You wrong theah, Walter. 'Tain't cause Joe's timid at all,
it's cause Spunk wants Lena. If Joe was a passle of wile cats
Spunk would tackle the job just the same. He'd go after *anything* he wanted the same way. As Ah wuz sayin' a minute ago,
he tole Joe right to his face that Lena was his. 'Call her,' he says
to Joe. 'Call her and see if she'll come. A woman knows her
boss an' she answers when he calls.' 'Lena, ain't I yo' husband?'
Joe sorter whines out. Lena looked at him real disgusted but
she don't answer and she don't move outa her tracks. Then
Spunk reaches out an' takes hold of her arm an' says: 'Lena,
youse mine. From now on Ah works for you an' fights for you
an' Ah never wants you to look to nobody for a crumb of
bread, a stitch of close or a shingle to go over yo' head, but *me*
long as Ah live. Ah'll git the lumber foh owah house to-morrow. Go home an' git yo' things together!'

"'Thass mah house,' Lena speaks up. 'Papa gimme that.'

"'Well,' says Spunk, 'doan give up whut's yours, but when
youse inside don't forgit youse mine, an' let no other man git
outa his place wid you!'

"Lena looked up at him with her eyes so full of love that they
wuz runnin' over, an' Spunk seen it an' Joe seen it too, and his
lip started to tremblin' and his Adam's apple was galloping up
and down his neck like a race horse. Ah bet he's wore out half
a dozen Adam's apples since Spunk's been on the job with Lena.
That's all he'll do. He'll be back heah after while swallowin' an'
workin' his lips like he wants to say somethin' an' can't."

"But didn't he do *nothin'* to stop 'em?"

"Nope, not a frazzlin' thing—jus' stood there. Spunk took Lena's arm and walked off jus' like nothin' ain't happened and he stood there gazin' after them till they was outa sight. Now you know a woman don't want no man like that. I'm jus' waitin' to see whut he's goin' to say when he gits back."

II

But Joe Kanty never came back, never. The men in the store heard the sharp report of a pistol somewhere distant in the palmetto thicket and soon Spunk came walking leisurely, with his big black Stetson set at the same rakish angle and Lena clinging to his arm, came walking right into the general store. Lena wept in a frightened manner.

"Well," Spunk announced calmly, "Joe come out there wid a meatax an' made me kill him."

He sent Lena home and led the men back to Joe—Joe crumpled and limp with his right hand still clutching his razor.

"See mah back? Mah cloes cut clear through. He sneaked up an' tried to kill me from the back, but Ah got him, an' got him good, first shot," Spunk said.

The men glared at Elijah, accusingly.

"Take him up an' plant him in 'Stoney lonesome,'" Spunk said in a careless voice. "Ah didn't wanna shoot him but he made me do it. He's a dirty coward, jumpin' on a man from behind."

Spunk turned on his heel and sauntered away to where he knew his love wept in fear for him and no man stopped him. At the general store later on, they all talked of locking him up until the sheriff should come from Orlando, but no one did anything but talk.

A clear case of self-defense, the trial was a short one, and Spunk walked out of the court house to freedom again. He could work again, ride the dangerous log-carriage that fed the singing, snarling, biting, circle-saw; he could stroll the soft dark lanes with his guitar. He was free to roam the woods again; he was free to return to Lena. He did all of these things.

III

"Whut you reckon, Walt?" Elijah asked one night later. "Spunk's gittin' ready to marry Lena!"

"Naw! Why, Joe ain't had time to git cold yit. Nohow Ah didn't figger Spunk was the marryin' kind."

"Well, he is," rejoined Elijah. "He done moved most of Lena's things—and her along wid 'em—over to the Bradley house. He's buying it. Jus' like Ah told yo' all right in heah the night Joe wuz kilt. Spunk's crazy 'bout Lena. He don't want folks to keep on talkin' 'bout her—thass reason he's rushin' so. Funny thing 'bout that bob-cat, wan't it?"

"Whut bob-cat, 'Lige? Ah ain't heered 'bout none."

"Ain't cher? Well, night befo' las' was the fust night Spunk an' Lena moved together an' jus' as they was goin' to bed, a big black bob-cat, black all over, you hear me, *black,* walked round and round that house and howled like forty, an' when Spunk got his gun an' went to the winder to shoot it, he says it stood right still an' looked him in the eye, an' howled right at him. The thing got Spunk so nervoused up he couldn't shoot. But Spunk says twan't no bob-cat nohow. He says it was Joe done sneaked back from Hell!"

"Humph!" sniffed Walter, "he oughter be nervous after what he done. Ah reckon Joe came back to dare him to marry Lena, or to come out an' fight. Ah bet he'll be back time and again, too. Know what Ah think? Joe wuz a braver man than Spunk."

There was a general shout of derision from the group.

"Thass a fact," went on Walter. "Lookit whut he done; took a razor an' went out to fight a man he knowed toted a gun an' wuz a crack shot, too; 'nother thing Joe wuz skeered of Spunk, skeered plumb stiff! But he went jes' the same. It took him a long time to get his nerve up. 'Tain't nothin' for Spunk to fight when he ain't skeered of nothin'. Now, Joe's done come back to have it out wid the man that's got all he ever had. Y'll know Joe ain't never had nothin' nor wanted nothin' besides Lena. It musta been a h'ant cause ain' nobody never seen no black bob-cat."

"'Nother thing," cut in one of the men, "Spunk wuz cussin' a blue streak to-day 'cause he 'lowed dat saw wuz wobblin'— almos' got 'im once. The machinist come, looked it over an' said it wuz alright. Spunk musta been leanin' t'wards it some. Den he claimed somebody pushed 'im but 'twant nobody close to 'im. Ah wuz glad when knockin' off time come. I'm skeered of dat man when he gits hot. He'd beat you full of button holes as quick as he's look atcher."

IV

The men gathered the next evening in a different mood, no laughter. No badinage this time.

"Look, 'Lige, you goin' to set up wid Spunk?"

"Naw, Ah reckon not, Walter. Tell yuh the truth, Ah'm a lil bit skittish. Spunk died too wicket—died cussin' he did. You know he thought he wuz done outa life."

"Good Lawd, who'd he think done it?"

"Joe."

"Joe Kanty? How come?"

"Walter, Ah b'leeve Ah will walk up thata way an' set. Lena would like it Ah reckon."

"But whut did he say 'Lige?"

Elijah did not answer until they had left the lighted store and were strolling down the dark street.

"Ah wuz loadin' a wagon wid scantlin' right near the saw when Spunk fell on the carriage but 'fore Ah could git to him the saw got him in the body—awful sight. Me an' Skint Miller got him off but it was too late. Anybody could see that. The fust thing he said wuz: 'He pushed me, 'Lige—the dirty hound pushed me in the back!'—He was spittin' blood at ev'ry breath. We laid him on the sawdust pile with his face to the East so's he could die easy. He helt mah han' till the last, Walter, and said: 'It was Joe, 'Lige—the dirty sneak shoved me . . . he didn't dare come to mah face . . . but Ah'll git the son-of-a-wood louse soon's Ah get there an' make hell too hot for him. . . . Ah felt him shove me . . . !' Thass how he died.

"If spirits kin fight, there's a powerful tussle goin' on some where ovah Jordan 'cause Ah b'leeve Joe's ready for Spunk an' ain't skeered any more—yas, Ah b'leeve Joe pushed 'im mahself."

They had arrived at the house. Lena's lamentations were deep and loud. She had filled the room with magnolia blossoms that gave off a heavy sweet odor. The keepers of the wake tipped about whispering in frightened tones. Everyone in the village was there, even old Jeff Kanty, Joe's father, who a few hours before would have been afraid to come within ten feet of him, stood leering triumphantly down upon the fallen giant as if his fingers had been the teeth of steel that laid him low.

The cooling board consisted of three sixteen-inch boards on saw horses; a dingy sheet was his shroud.

The women ate heartily of the funeral baked meats and wondered who would be Lena's next. The men whispered coarse conjectures between guzzles of whiskey.

BIOGRAPHICAL NOTES ON THE AUTHORS

TONI CADE BAMBARA (1939–1995) was born in New York City. A writer, editor, and teacher, she was active in the civil rights movement. Her awards include an American Book Award for her novel *The Salt Eaters* (1980). She was the author of the novels *Those Bones Are Not My Child*, (1987) and *If Blessing Comes* (1987), and two short story collections, *Gorilla, My Love* (1972) and *The Sea Birds Are Still Alive* (1977). She was an essayist and screenwriter as well.

ANN BEATTIE was born in Washington, D.C., in 1947. Among her many awards are the 1980 award in literature from the American Academy and Institute of Arts and Letters and a Guggenheim Fellowship in 1978. Among her short story collections are *Secrets and Surprises* (1979), *The Burning House* (1982), *What Was Mine* (1991), and *Park City: New and Selected Stories* (1998). Her novels include *Chilly Scenes of Winter* (1976), *Love Always* (1985), *Picturing Will* (1990), and *The Doctor's House* (2002).

ROBERT OLEN BUTLER was born in Illinois in 1945. He served in Vietnam from 1969 to 1972. *A Good Scent from a Strange Mountain* (1992), a short story collection drawn from his Vietnam experience, was awarded the 1993 Pulitzer Prize for Fiction and the Richard and Hilda Rosenthal Foundation Award from the American Academy of Arts and Letters. His books include the novels *The Alleys of Eden* (1981), *On Distant Ground (1985), The Deep Green Sea* (1998), and *Fair Warning* (2002). The short story collection *Tabloid Dreams* was published in 1996.

TRUMAN CAPOTE (1924–1984) was born in New Orleans. His first novel, *Other Voices, Other Rooms,* was published in 1948 when he was twenty-three. His other works of fiction are *A Tree of Night and Other Stories* (1949), the novel *The Grass Harp* (1951), and *Breakfast at Tiffany's: A Short Novel and Three Stories* (1958). *In Cold Blood: A True Account of a Multiple Murder and Its Consequences* (1965), a landmark book, inaugurated the genre of the nonfiction novel. He was the recipient of many awards, including one from the National Institute of Arts and Letters.

JUNOT DÍAZ was born in 1968 in Santo Domingo, Dominican Republic. He is the author of the short story collection *Drown* (1996) and editor of *Beacon Best of 2001: Great Writing by Women and Men of All Cultures and Colors.* His stories have been published in *The New Yorker, The Paris Review,* and *Best American Short Stories* (1996). His awards include a Guggenheim Fellowship.

LOUISE ERDRICH was born in 1954 in Minnesota and grew up in North Dakota. She is a novelist, short story writer, essayist, and poet. Among her awards are a National Book Critics Circle award for her first novel, *Love Medicine* (1983), the Sue Kaufman Prize from the American Academy and Institute of Arts and Letters, and a Guggenheim Fellowship. Her fiction includes *The Beet Queen* (1986), *Tracks* (1988), *Tales of Burning Love* (1996), *The Antelope Wife* (1998), and *The Master Butchers Singing Club* (2003). She is also the author of two volumes of poetry, *Jacklight* (1984) and *Baptism of Desire* (1989). Her work has been published in many periodicals, including *The New Yorker, Chicago, American Indian Quarterly*, and *The Atlantic*.

IAN FRAZIER was born in Ohio in 1951. For more than twenty years, he has been a staff writer for *The New Yorker*, and he has also published in *The Atlantic, Harper's*, and *The New Republic*. His books include *Dating Your Mom* (1986), *Great Plains* (1989), *On the Rez* (2000), and *The Fish's Eye: Essays about Angling and the Outdoors* (2002). He is the recipient of the Thurber Prize for Humor.

ZORA NEALE HURSTON (1891–1960) grew up in Eatonville, Florida. She received an associate's degree from Howard University in Washington, D.C., in 1920. From 1925 to 1927 she attended Barnard College, where she studied anthropology with Franz Boas and did field work for him in Harlem. In New York City, she actively participated in the Harlem cultural renaissance. Between 1921 and 1951 she published nineteen short stories that—along with seven previously unpublished—were collected in *The Complete Stories* (1994). She published two novels, *Mules and Men* (1935) and *Their Eyes Were Watching God* (1937), and her essays and articles appeared in many publications. In the ten years or so before her death, her work fell into an obscurity matched by the hardships of her life. She was buried in an unmarked grave. In 1973, Alice Walker placed a marker inscribed in her memory in the cemetery. Walker's 1975 essay in *Ms.* magazine, "In Search of Zora Neale Hurston," spurred a revival of her work and reputation.

GISH JEN was born in 1956 and grew up in Scarsdale, New York. She is the recipient of fellowships from the Guggenheim and Lannan foundations and the National Endowment for the Arts. She is the author of the novels *Typical American* (1991) and *Mona in the Promised Land* (1996) and the short story collection, *"Who's Irish?"* (1999). Her work has appeared in *The New Yorker, The Atlantic*, and *The New Republic*.

DENIS JOHNSON was born in 1949 in Munich, Germany, and grew up in Tokyo, Manila, and Washington, D.C. For his first novel, *Angels*

(1983), he received the Sue Kaufman Prize from the American Institute of Arts and Letters. Other awards include fellowships from the Guggenheim and Whiting foundations and the National Endowment for the Arts. He is the author of several novels, including *Fiskadoro* (1985) and *The Name of the World* (2000), and the short story collection *Jesus' Son* (1992). His work has appeared in *Esquire, Rolling Stone, The New Yorker, Paris Review,* and *The Atlantic.*

WARD JUST was born in 1935 in Indiana. He is the author of short story collections, novels, and works of nonfiction, among them *Twenty-One Selected Stories* (1990), *The Translator* (1991), *Ambition and Love* (1994), *Echo House* (1997), and *The Weather in Berlin* (2002). He was the recipient of the Chicago Tribune Heartland Award for his 1989 novel, *Jack Gance.* His stories have been selected for the *Best American Short Stories* and *O. Henry Prize* collections.

KATHRINE KRESSMAN TAYLOR (1903–1996) was born in Portland, Oregon. "Address Unknown," which appeared first in the September 1938 issue of *Story,* was Kressmann Taylor's morally impassioned response to the looming threat of Nazism. The magazine's printing was sold out, and in 1939, when Simon and Schuster published "Address Unknown" as a book, it sold an extraordinary fifty thousand copies. It was published to similar acclaim in Britain, but plans for further European publications were derailed by the Second World War. The story, however, has had a long life. In 1995, when Kressmann Taylor was ninety-one, Story Press reissued it in the fiftieth-year commemoration of the liberation of the concentration camps. Kressmann Taylor taught writing, journalism, and humanities at Gettysburg College in Pennsylvania.

JHUMPA LAHIRI was born in London in 1967 and grew up in Rhode Island. Her short story collection *Interpreter of Maladies* (1999) received the 2000 Pulitzer Prize for fiction and the PEN/Hemingway Award. Her stories have appeared in *The New Yorker* and have been selected for the *Best American Short Stories* and *O. Henry Prize* collections. Her first novel, *The Namesake,* was published in 2003.

A. A. MILNE (1882–1956) was born Alan Alexander Milne in London. A novelist, essayist, and playwright, he is best known for his children's books, *When We Were Very Young* (1924) and *Winnie the Pooh* (1926). His novel *The Red House Mystery* (1922) has been considered a mystery genre classic. He is the author of the collection *A Table Near the Band* (1950), from which "The Rise and Fall of Mortimer Scrivens" is taken.

RICK MOODY was born in 1961 in New York City. His short story collections include *The Ring of Brightest Angels Around Heaven* (1995) and *Demonology* (2000). He is the author of the novels *Garden State* (1992), *The Ice Storm* (1994), *Purple America* (1997), *Joyful Noise* (1997), and the memoir *The Black Veil: A Memoir with Digressions* (2002). His awards include a Guggenheim Fellowship. He has published in *The New Yorker, Harper's, Esquire,* and *The Paris Review.*

LORRIE MOORE was born in 1957 in Glens Falls, New York. Among the awards she has won are National Endowment for the Arts, Rockefeller, and Guggenheim fellowships. She has published in *The New Yorker, The Paris Review, Fiction International,* and *Ms.* She is the author of short story collections, including *Self Help* (1985), *Like Life* (1991), and *Birds of America* (1998), and the novels *Anagrams* (1986) and *Who Will Run the Frog Hospital?* (1994).

TIM O'BRIEN was born in 1946 in Minnesota. From 1968 to 1970 he served in Vietnam and has drawn on the experience in his writing. Among his books are the memoir *If I Die in a Combat Zone* (1973), his National Book Award-winning novel *Going After Cacciato* (1978), and his collection of linked stories *The Things They Carried* (1990). He is also the author of the novels *In the Lake of the Woods* (1994), *Tomcat in Love* (1998), and *July July* (2002).

ZZ PACKER was born in 1973 in Illinois. Her first book, the short story collection *Drinking Coffee Elsewhere*, was published in 2003. Her work has appeared in *The New Yorker, Harper's* and *Story,* and in the annual anthology *Best American Short Stories* (2000). She has received a Whiting Writers' Award and the Rona Jaffe Foundation Writers' Award.

KATHERINE ANNE PORTER (1890–1980) was born in Texas and educated in Texas convent schools. Her career as a writer of fiction spanned five decades, from the twenties to the sixties. Her awards included two Guggenheim Fellowships, the National Book Award, the Pulitzer Prize for fiction, and the Gold Medal for fiction from the National Academy and National Institute of Arts and Letters. Her *Collected Stories* (1965), drawn from her four previously published collections, won both the Pulitzer Prize for fiction and National Book Award. The novel *Ship of Fools,* her only long work, appeared in 1962.

JAMES THURBER (1894–1961) was born and grew up in Columbus, Ohio. During the First World War he was employed as a code clerk at the State

Department in Washington and then at the American Embassy in Paris. In 1927 he went to work at *The New Yorker*, an association that lasted until 1961. He was acclaimed for both his writing and drawings, and they appeared in the magazine's pages regularly over the years. His first book, *Is Sex Necessary?*, written in collaboration with E. B. White, was published in 1929. His more than twenty books include *The Seal in the Bedroom and Other Predicaments* (1932), *My Life and Hard Times* (1933), and *My World and Welcome to It* (1942).

JOHN UPDIKE was born in 1932 in Pennsylvania. A novelist, short story writer, essayist, and poet, he has won most of the major literary awards, including the Pulitzer Prize, the National Book Critics Circle Award, and the National Book Award. His more than fifty books include the novels *Rabbit, Run* (1960) and its sequels *Rabbit Redux* (1971), *Rabbit Is Rich* (1981), and *Rabbit at Rest* (1990); as well as *The Poorhouse Fair* (1959), *The Centaur* (1963), *Couples* (1968), *The Coup* (1978), and *The Witches of Eastwick* (1984); the short story collections *Pigeon Feathers* (1962), *Problems and Other Stories* (1979), and *Licks of Love: Short Stories and a Sequel, Rabbit Remembered* (2000). His work steadily appears in *The New Yorker*.

JOY WILLIAMS was born in Massachusetts in 1944. Her awards include the Academy and Institute Award in Literature from the American Academy of Arts and Letters, and fellowships from the National Endowment for the Arts and the Guggenheim Foundation. Her short story collections include *Taking Care* (1982) and *Escapes* (1990). Among her novels are *State of Grace* (1973), *The Changeling* (1978), *Breaking and Entering* (1988), and *The Quick and the Dead* (2000). She has written for *The New Yorker, The Paris Review, Esquire, Tri-Quarterly, Grand Street,* and *Ms.*

LEX WILLIFORD was born in 1954 in El Paso, Texas. His story collection, *Macauley's Thumb*, was a co-winner of the Iowa Short Fiction Award. He is a recipient of, among other awards, a National Endowment for the Arts Fellowship. He has written for *American Literary Review, Southern Review, Shenandoah, Story Quarterly, Laurel Review,* and *Virginia Quarterly Review.*

ACKNOWLEDGMENTS